Praise for
Kathryn Bihr's
Phantom Moon

Bihr spins a breathing, shifting American epic tale of two families tossed together by fate whose lives are permanently affected by an enduring love denied. As powerful and fearless as the history of the West and all those who lived it, her telling is as intimate and heartbreakingly familiar in detail as the stories of our own lives.

— Ellen Lutter, Costume Designer

Katie Bihr entrapped me in her romantic and tangled tale, floating effortlessly between time, sitting on the edge of my seat then curled up under a blanket…a book I shall cherish and read again and again…will truly stand the test of time itself.

— Kim Collea, Film Producer

Bihr writes from a wellspring of deep humanity, as if drawing buckets of insight and shared experiences upwards toward the illuminating light. The story is skillfully woven and paced with a restrained necessity, leaving the impression that one has revisited a vital memory rather than experience a work of fiction. There is an engagingly unapologetic truth to her characters, who dance across years and reveal themselves as wholly formed yet imperfect reflections of the world built around them. Bihr's writing entices the reader to follow her down the chosen path, and demands that we peek eagerly around each bend.

— Wolfe Coleman, writer, *Shades of Blue* (2016), *Los Alamos* (2016) and *Undrafted* (2016)

Kathryn Bihr is a true storyteller of our time. *Phantom Moon* takes us through generations of love and loss as a reflection of the American Dream. This is not only an absorbing love story, but a classic study of human behavior when placed under societal pressures. She takes us on a journey through time from the 1800s in Spain to the 1960s in California, following the Rivera and Delgado families. She fluently weaves stories of history with the present, with such an overall romantic yet heartbreaking presence. Each character and their story is unique yet undoubtedly relatable. Bihr's powerful voice and usage of such lush detail to describe each family and their struggles over different generations, reminds us of the one universal truth we can all relate to—*love*.

—Alexandra Brown, TV Producer

PHANTOM MOON

Phantom Moon

A Novel

Kathryn Bihr

HANSEN PUBLISHING GROUP, LLC

Phantom Moon
Copyright © 2018 by Kathryn Bihr

22 21 20 19 18   10 9 8 7 6 5 4 3 2 1

ISBN: (PAPER) 978-1-60182-338-0
ISBN: (EBOOK) 978-1-60182-339-7

Cover design by Cheryl Lickona
Book interior design by Jon Hansen

Hansen Publishing Group, LLC
302 Ryders Lane
East Brunswick, NJ 08816
hansenpublishing.com

Author site: http://www.kathrynbihr.com/

To my parents, who inspired me, encouraged me, and let me be who I am.

Rivera

Family Tree

José Rivera ——————————— Angelina Montego
1805–1843 | *1810–1843*

Catherina Garrastozu —— Doctor Dante Rivera —— Fiona O'Donnell
1832–1855 | *1830–1907* | *1831–1915*

Angeles Rivera —— Milhouse Forester
1853–1950 | *1850–1943*

Raul Cristoval Rivera ——————— Simone Vasquez
1851–1935 | *1852–1875*

Gabriel Rivera ——————— Estelle Magritte Smith
1873–1953 | *1874–1918*

Dante René Rivera
1894–1967

Raul Paul Rivera ——————— Rachel Sullivan
1896–1976 | *1899–1980*

Robert Rivera ——————— Cynthia Hutson
1921–1991 | *1922–1986*

Dante Gregory Rivera
1944–

Delgado

Family Tree

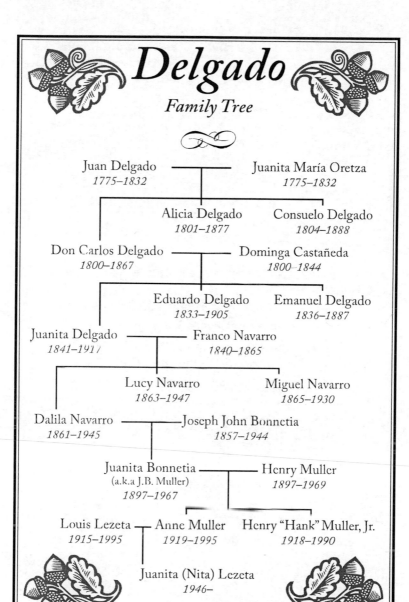

Juan Delgado
1775–1832
—
Juanita María Oretza
1775–1832

Alicia Delgado
1801–1877

Consuelo Delgado
1804–1888

Don Carlos Delgado
1800–1867
—
Dominga Castañeda
1800–1844

Eduardo Delgado
1833–1905

Emanuel Delgado
1836–1887

Juanita Delgado
1841–1917
—
Franco Navarro
1840–1865

Lucy Navarro
1863–1947

Miguel Navarro
1865–1930

Dalila Navarro
1861–1945
—
Joseph John Bonnetia
1857–1944

Juanita Bonnetia
(a.k.a J.B. Muller)
1897–1967
—
Henry Muller
1897–1969

Louis Lezeta
1915–1995
—
Anne Muller
1919–1995

Henry "Hank" Muller, Jr.
1918–1990

Juanita (Nita) Lezeta
1946–

A dark, haloed globe took its proper place in the indigo night, surrounded by thousands of sparkling jewel-like stars. The faint white halo that encircled it seemed to be evaporating but was still visible enough to distinguish it from the night sky. In days to come this globe, which we call our moon, would shine brightly, but for now it was the time of a phantom moon.

PHANTOM MOON

CHAPTER ONE

The Tattered Box

Napa, August 1967

A rattling knock came from the back screen door of J.B. Muller's art studio, startling her, momentarily taking her away from the chalk drawing she was working on. Several pieces of 8 x 10 mimeographed photographic images, smaller versions of the originals, were on the floor in front of her. Earlier she'd moved them around in a purposeful juxtaposition, each jogging different memories in her mind. In a few months, the large original photographs would appear in a one-person retrospective at the Museum of Modern Art in New York, a representation of her life's work in photography to honor her seventieth birthday. The chalk drawing in front of her was a guilty diversion from her main daunting task of the day.

A knock came again. Chalk dust covered her hands. She pushed the drawing to the side and yelled out.

"Nita, is that you?" Her granddaughter and namesake had promised to help with the layout of the photographs. Her granddaughter would have big news for her. Nita was in love with a young man she'd met at Berkeley.

No one answered.

"Come in," J.B. called out, this time her voice a little louder and a bit annoyed there was still no answer. The door opened, making its unique creaking sound. It could be her husband who, since retiring from the family business, sometimes out of boredom and sometimes out of the puppy love he still held for her, would come by unannounced.

"Henry?" she called out. Still no answer.

"Must not be human," she thought to herself. "Must be the hot, dry Napa Valley wind pushing and pulling at that old warped screen door I should have fixed."

She never had the heart to change what was sacred to her. Her father built the screen door and put it up some sixty years earlier, and sometimes when she looked through the rusty screen, earlier times spent with her family or with her lover in the backyard became real again: Lita Nannie snapping green beans, her mother and father at the picnic table near the twin oak trees laughing at some silly thing they'd done or seen during the day, and if she allowed herself, she would see her lover languishing in the old hammock between the oaks watching her draw.

Her lover had climbed one of the oaks to reach her bedroom window the night he proposed to her, the trunk now thicker from the multitude of years. The other oak had been cut down, victim of a storm.

This house, her childhood home, was now her place of work and was more of her life than most could ever understand.

J.B. drifted back to reality, forgetting the past and the knocking at the screen door. She went back to the chalk drawing until her name was called out.

"Juanita."

A feeble man's voice reached her ears. She turned, not recognizing the voice or the old man standing in the doorway.

"Is that you, Raul?"

"Yes," he replied.

She knew that someday this time would come. The day she'd promised to her lover years before. Whoever was to die first, the other would be in their arms.

Raul's voice cracked and his eyes began to water. Instinctively J.B. got up and took his hands in hers, knowing that he was suffering. His beloved brother was leaving him. They'd been companions all their lives except for their time spent apart at school in the East, or Dante René's time spent in Europe during WWI.

"I think I know why you're here," J.B. said, relieving Raul from the verbal declaration, the reason for his visit. He nodded his head yes.

"Give me a minute to prepare. I'll be there."

Raul left.

Water rushed over J.B.'s hands, rinsing the chalk dust off. She watched the colors swirl in the water and wash down the sink's drain. The rainbow of colors reminded her of the day she'd met her lover. "If only things had worked out differently" she thought, but it was too painful to go there. She quickly changed her thoughts to the good life she had despite it not being with the man she loved.

J.B. pushed a small step ladder over to a bookcase in her studio, reaching as far as she could to retrieve the small, tattered cardboard box from the top shelf along with a scrapbook. She placed them on her desk, brushing off the layer of dust that had accumulated on top. The tape holding the box together was curled and dry. She took off her wedding ring, placing it in the back of her desk drawer and opened the lid of the box. Among the memorabilia was a smaller box with a red ribbon tied around it; in it was a small soft tin souvenir ring too fragile to wear and an onyx and diamond ring that she placed on her left ring finger. She left a pink diamond ring and a pin that matched the onyx ring in the box. Next to a lock of dark hair and under a stack of letters tied together with a cream-colored ribbon were the remains of an old flower that had turned to dust. In the scrapbook were some old yellowed ticket stubs, edges frayed from age; a deteriorating telegram, the pasted on words falling off, so delicate it made her afraid to pick it up; a pressed oak leaf that had been waxed to help preserve it; some valentines; a photograph framed in velvet of a young man dressed in a tuxedo and a young woman in a pale pink silk dress. There was another photograph with the couple sticking their heads through a cardboard cutout of cartoon bears. With the box and scrapbook under her arm she headed out the back door.

Outside, a baby blue sky was filled with white fluffy clouds that moved along like a caravan of wandering gypsies exposing the faint white outline of a phantom moon hanging solitary in the day sky, looking lonely without its accompanying stars and darkness. "How ironic," she thought. Her eyes rested on the back of the house and on the old oak tree. Memories guided her momentarily over to the tree trunk. She looked up toward what used to be her bedroom window and stroked the gold band of the onyx and diamond ring before walking with haste and purpose toward her car, thinking about the first time she and her lover made love under a phantom moon.

CHAPTER TWO

The Victorian Cottage

Napa, May 1915

Gnarly, arthritic hands shadowed once long, slender fingers as they snapped the ends off freshly picked green beans. The discarded ends landed on the yellowed newspaper next to the corn husks on the floor. The trimmed green bean was purposely placed in the sorrel brown, red stripped rim bowl sitting on the old woman's lap. She closed her eyes to savor a breeze that mysteriously arrived, caressing her bare arms, face, and hands. She laid her head back against the old wicker rocker and listened to the sounds of singing birds and the rustling leaves. Soon she was back in the great room of her father's formidable hacienda on the same property that this little humble, white Victorian cottage with periwinkle-blue trim was built. She had been born a child of privilege to the wealthiest family in the valley who once owned a ten-thousand-acre cattle ranch. Now her life was modest but filled with love.

In her dream state, she found herself standing in front of her dead mother's portrait, staring at it. Disturbed, her eyes popped open in a start, not knowing how long she'd drifted off. Two men stood on the sidewalk in front of the gated white picket fence leading up to the front porch of the cottage. Lita Nannie, a nickname given to her by her granddaughter when she was little, was alone. Her daughter Dalila and son-in-law Joe Bonnetia, were still at work at the high school where they taught. Her granddaughter and name sake, Juanita, was off sketching. A certain fear and confusion by the presence of visitors filled the old woman whose mind was becoming more fragile with passing years. The older man removed his hat exposing a shock of snowy white hair and sported a salt and pepper mustache and goatee. His tall, lean figure bent forward in a slight bow before he spoke.

"Juanita Delgado Navarro, do you remember me? I'll give you a hint, you gave my sister and me the best gift we ever had, a dog named Buttons."

He flashed a heartwarming smile and opened the gate to walk up the pathway with a stronger stride than was usual for a man in his sixties. The younger man followed.

Without reserve, the old woman stood up from her rocker. The earthen bowl fell onto the porch floor, spilling her afternoon's work of snapped green beans.

"Raul…Raul," rolled off her tongue in an almost sing-song way.

She extended her arms out in an inviting gesture that would soon be filled with Raul Cristoval Rivera's slender sixty-plus year-old body. This old man was once the little boy she'd loved, taught, and cared for. It had been years since the two had seen one another. She tightened her grip around him to let him know how much she'd missed him. The little boy she once cared for was now an important man.

It wasn't until the long, encompassing hug was over that the old woman noticed the younger man. Raul gushed as he introduced his grandson.

"This is my eldest grandson, Dante René Rivera, named after my father. I've told him so much about you; he wanted to come and meet you himself."

The old woman moved closer to study the young man's remarkable face. Her body swayed and she moved backwards, gently landing onto the soft seat of the wicker rocker. The striking looks of the young man with intense dark blue eyes and a swarthy nut-colored skin was a picture image of his grandfather, Dr. Dante Rivera when he was young. The young man reached out taking both her hands in his. She felt the silky-smooth texture of his well-manicured hands, a contrast to her own rough, paper-thin, age-spotted ones.

The two elders talked for over an hour while the young man sat quietly listening to the stories of their past and about important events in each of their lives the other had missed. As they talked a young woman, still in her teens, walked up the sidewalk toward the house carrying an art box. She wore a large brimmed straw hat that partially covered her blue-black hair and was secured only with a large crescent moon hair pin. A fine layer of chalk dust and dirt covered her hands and face. Most prominent, and unbeknownst to her, was a large smudge of red chalk on her cheek. Her thoughts were preoccupied until she glanced up to the front porch and noticed the two men sitting with her grandmother. Her large, brown doe eyes darted back and forth. She hesitated for a moment until her grandmother gestured for her to come over.

"And this is my pride, my nicta, named after me. Juanita, this is Raul Cristoval Rivera, a very important man and his grandson, Dante René Rivera."

Juanita took off her hat and leaned down to place the customary kiss on her grandmother's cheek. Then she extended a hand toward Raul, "Nice to meet you, sir."

The dapper man was about to take her hand when she pulled it back and clasped both hands behind her back.

"I'm so sorry; I forgot about the chalk dust on my hands."

The old man chuckled and touched her shoulder. Her dark eyes sparkled; a slight glow came to her high-boned cheeks at his kind response and her nervousness subsided. Juanita perched herself on the arm of her grandmother's rocker and wrapped an arm around Lita Nannie's neck before turning toward Dante to acknowledge him. Her confident expression turned serious and shy when their eyes met. She lowered her face and diverted her eyes to avoid embarrassment. In that sheer moment of a glance it was as if she could see deep into his soul. Her reaction was not because of his good looks or magnetic appearance, but from something else, something outside of this world. The sound of her grandmother's voice came to her from a foggy distance and traveled toward her until it was right next to her.

"My goodness, mi querido, I've been so rude not offering you anything to drink."

"I'll get it, Lita Nannie," rolled off the young woman's lips making her wonder at first where the voice came from. Juanita needed time for her emotions to catch up with her. She sprung from her seat and moved swiftly toward the front door.

"My grandson can help you. Go with her, Dante," said Raul.

So much for relief, thought Juanita.

She held the door open for Dante to enter, purposefully avoiding eye contact. The interior of the Victorian cottage was modest. A few of Lita Nannie's possessions from her past life of grandeur still belonged to the family, but most had been sold off to provide food for her children when they were young. The furniture was functional and well cared for at best, but Juanita could only imagine the interior of the famous mansion Dante lived in.

What he must be thinking of this typical family house—typical except for Juanita's art that hung on the living room walls.

What was this debonair young man thinking she wondered as she watched Dante scrutinizing her art.

"Just say what you think!" shot out of her mouth like a dagger, making her wish she could take back the stinging inflection in her voice almost immediately.

"I like it very much. I minored in art history at Harvard. I admire this work. Is it yours?"

Feeling a bit foolish, Juanita nodded yes and continued to the kitchen, her face now beet red from embarrassment. She stuck her head deep into the ice box to let the cool air soften the blush in her cheek and then retrieved the pitcher of fresh squeezed lemonade. She turned on the water. The kitchen sink pipes clanked. Water washed over her hands mixing the chalk dust colors together in a rainbow stream swirling down the drain. As she studied the colors Dante stood in the doorway watching. Juanita, feeling his presence, quickly splashed water on her face and grabbed a tray. She took four glasses from a shelf and placed them on the tray. Dante moved closer to Juanita until he stood right next to her. He looked at her face for a moment saying nothing. Her body shuddered when he reached up and wiped the red smudge off her cheek.

"Can we take another glass out?" asked Dante.

She was breathless but managed to say, "Of course."

On the porch Raul had moved closer to Lita Nannie, taking her hand in his. He reached in his pocket for an envelope, handing it to her.

"No, Raul. That is not necessary anymore."

"Please take it. My father would never forgive me if you didn't. I've wanted to come and see you myself so many times. I have another reason for this visit today besides missing you. My father always said, listen to the valley and it will tell you when the grapes are ready. I listened to my heart. I knew my visit was overdue, but I waited until my stepmother's death. She was a good woman, kind to a fault to Angeles and myself, but my father never loved her. With his dying breath he said he saw a golden angel above his head. He said his mother had sent it for him. Then he called out your name and said he loved you."

Tears swelled in the old woman's eyes. Raul pulled an initialed linen handkerchief from his vest pocket and handed it to her. She gently pushed his hand away, grabbing a hanky from her apron pocket.

"We buried my father with the leather-bound book you gave him. He wrote in it daily. They were personal thoughts meant only for his eyes."

The old woman's mind closed off. She was back in Dr. Rivera's study. He was dabbing tears from her eyes and asking her to marry him while he placed an antique ring on her left ring finger.

Hearing the spring on the front door, Lita Nannie discreetly wiped her tears away. The two walked out: Dante carrying a tray with five glasses of lemonade, and Juanita the ice-cold pitcher of the remaining lemonade. Dante handed a glass first to Lita Nannie, then to his grandfather, and one to Juanita. He carried the last two down the walkway and across the street for the chauffeur and himself. They talked for a moment and drank the lemonade before Dante returned to the porch with the empty glasses.

This had to be an act, Juanita thought. He couldn't possibly be that nice.

Dante and Juanita listened to their grandparents talk for a bit before Dante started a conversation with Juanita about art. Dante was impressed by her knowledge and how she could converse about many different subjects unlike the young women in his social group who now seemed shallow. This young woman seemed to know who she was and had a talent beyond her years. She wasn't pulled together with every hair in place but was unpredictably pretty. She even had a slight tan from the sun, something none of the females he knew would ever do.

The more they talked the more they realized what they had in common. She'd heard of contemporary European artists like Marc Chagall and Edvard Munch. They liked the same music: classical to Tin Pan Alley and Irving Berlin. They'd both confessed they'd read Jack London's new book *The Star Rover*. How could this little girl from this small town know so much? He'd gone to the best private schools in the country and traveled to Europe. His mother had seen to that. He was knowledgeable in the arts, business, spoke several languages, and was one of the best equestrians in California. She'd never left the valley and yet he had more in common with her than anyone else he'd ever met.

Time seemed irrelevant. What was to be a short visit turned into a long one tinged with melancholy at times for Raul and Lita Nannie, but enlightening for Dante and Juanita. Finally, Raul pulled out his gold pocket watch.

"My, we've talked hours longer than I imagined."

When Lita Nannie got up to say goodbye, a ring and locket on a faded black ribbon she wore around her neck swung out from the top of her dress. Raul took the ring in his hand.

"You still have it. I remember my father showing it to me on the ship when we came from Spain. I was very little. It was my grandmother's. He told me he had given it to you. I'm so glad you still have it."

He took her hand in his and kissed the back of it. With her other hand, she fingered the locket that bore inside a few strands of Dr. Rivera's long black hair. Dante and Juanita, still deep in conversation, didn't notice. They were talking about the young poet E.E. Cummings, who Dante had gone to Harvard with. Thoughts of the war in Europe filled the back of their minds and were working toward the surface of their conversation when Raul called to Dante twice before the young man responded. He acknowledged his grandfather and took Juanita's hand in his to say goodbye. He was looking down at her long fingers and short unmanicured nails when he noticed a bit of dirt and colored chalk still embedded under each nail. A tingling warmth shot from her hand into his.

***

After the visit, Lita Nannie began to grow more wistful. Long, purposefully forgotten memories flooded her mind. She tried to erase the bad memories and imagine a magical, timeless place to spend with her lover. For days at a time she relived the last evening they spent together in San Francisco, years after they first met and years after she was governess to his children. Her eyes closed and he would be there, young again. His smooth, deep, easy voice with the Castilian accent would resonate throughout her body. The spicy sweet smell of his cologne was still as fresh as the first time she saw him in her father's office. The visions grew so real that she would reach out calling his name and wonder why he wasn't there when she opened her eyes.

Juanita was stuck in Dante's mind. He'd think about something funny she said or how the sun shined on her golden skin.

Dante's platonic date noticed. He picked up Cassandra Gillette for the twenty-first birthday party of one of their peers. They were members of a small elite group of wealthy Napa Valley youth, the sons and daughters of mine owners, bankers, wealthy San Francisco weekenders and others who financially qualified. Dante, who was usually reserved around Cassandra, today seemed carefree, even frivolous. She pressed him on the ride over, questioning him on his giddiness, hoping she might have something to do with it. He casually tossed her questioning off and changed the subject, but her curiosity got the best of her. He laughed, saying she was crazy.

Dante played tennis with his brother Raul while Cassandra sat courtside under an umbrella sipping champagne with some of the other young women, who commented on how this usually serious young man seemed happy today.

The next morning Cassandra called Dante's mother, Magritte, with whom she had developed a close relationship. She hoped Dante would someday see Cassandra as more than a friend.

"I noticed he seemed, well happier than I've ever seen him and wondered if it had anything to do with me," said Cassandra.

"How could he not be happy with your company? I will encourage him to call you when I see him." Magritte continued, "Your family is coming for dinner at the end of the week. I am sure it will be good news. Good day for now."

Dante's thoughts of Juanita became obsessive and constant. He craved to be close to her. His carefree attitude dissolved, replaced with a painful heart fluttering inside his chest. Once he thought he saw her, his breath stopped, and his heart jumped like it was leaving his body. He couldn't sleep and he couldn't eat. He kept his feelings to himself until one day without meaning to he found himself driving past her house, far out of the way from where he was going. He slowed down but had a flight of shyness and didn't stop. Maybe he'd run into her in town, maybe he was going crazy. He had to tell someone; it would have to be his brother Raul who he trusted.

Dante parked his Stutz Bearcat sports car across from the white cottage with the periwinkle blue trim that was surrounded by spring flowers making it look like a hand-painted postcard. He sat in his car nervously wondering if she would be glad to see him. A shot of adrenaline hit him, and before his mind caught up with his body, he was on the porch knocking at the open front door. He looked through the house to the back screen door and saw a figure working in the backyard. Peering through the screen, he could see the working figure in the backyard stop. Juanita turned and looked toward the front door. Dante's heart wanted to tear through his skin.

They sat at a picnic table in the backyard between the twin oaks. Juanita couldn't stop laughing.

"Look at me, I'm a sight."

"A beautiful sight," responded Dante.

She was dressed in men's overalls and wore a painter's cap. Plaster dust covered her from head to toe.

"You must think I'm always a mess. I only look like this when I'm working."

Several plaster casts sat on the table. It was hard for Dante to take his eyes off of Juanita, but he managed to turn his attention momentarily to the plaster casts.

"These are great."

"Will you come to a picture show with me tonight?" The words just leapt out of his mouth.

She seemed a little confused at first. "What? Well, sure I will."

Juanita walked Dante to the front door to say good-bye. He glanced into the front room. Lita Nannie sat in her chair napping.

"I'll pick you up at six."

Dante strolled across the street to his car smiling so wide his face hurt. He drove a few blocks and stopped. His insides had to calm down before he could drive away. She had said yes.

CHAPTER THREE

Magritte Smith Rivera

1890–1915

She was born Estelle Magritte Smith. Magritte was her mother's maiden name and that was what she preferred to be called. She was a slender, statuesque woman with a long line of aristocratic lineage etched on her face. Physically her back was so straight that she looked like she had a book balanced on her head, and she had indeed practiced that for hours when she was young. She always turned out in the best and latest of fashions and sometimes spent on one outfit what some people lived on for a year. She took meticulous care of her skin by staying out of the sun, which accounted for her porcelain colored skin with no freckles. She washed her skin daily with fresh milk and used face cream. Always pampered, on the rare occasions during an argument with her husband when she didn't get her way, a fainting spell in front of him usually got her what she wanted. She met her husband, Gabriel Rivera, in Boston, Massachusetts. Her father, famous Boston lawyer David Barthum Smith, gave a lecture at Harvard. He was so impressed by Gabriel Rivera's questions he invited the young law student to his home for Sunday dinner. Gabriel fell in love with Magritte the first time he saw her.

Her face had an uncanny resemblance to a Byzantine statue of a woman he'd become infatuated with at the Museum of Fine Arts in Copley Square. At that time, he couldn't understand why the statue so engrossed him. Now, he knew it was a precursor to his future.

Long after Magritte's beauty faded and despite their volatile marriage, Gabriel would conjure up the memory of the haunting statue to fall in love with her again.

It took months after they met before Gabriel and Magritte began dating. It was at the encouragement of her father that she agreed to see him. They courted a few months before announcing their engagement. Their wedding was in the Boston social calendar of 1894. Moving to Napa was her only concession in life. Gabriel had responsibilities, and they would have to live in Napa. Gabriel's father, Raul Cristoval, was running the lucrative family wine business, so his father, Dr. Dante Rivera, could devote all his time to running the Rushing River Hospital that he'd founded in the Napa Valley. As Raul's only child, Gabriel would manage the winery business and eventually become chairman of the board of the hospital. Gabriel's position in Napa and the vast wealth he would inherit gave Magritte enough reason to satisfy her ego to live in the rural Napa Valley and not Boston.

Gabriel wanted a large family but Magritte considered that primitive.

After the birth of their second son Raul Paul, named after his grandfather, Magritte rarely slept with Gabriel again, preferring to turn a blind eye to his affairs in exchange for leaving her alone. In her way, she loved Gabriel. She ruled over the family with an ironfisted arrogance that never left them, even after her death.

Raul Paul was physically like his mother with auburn hair, fair skin, and slighter of build than his older brother. When he contracted scarlet fever, he lost fifty percent of his hearing in his right ear and twenty percent in the other. The illness reached a point that all seemed lost. A priest was called in to administer last rights. The next day he began a miraculous recovery. Great grandfather Dr. Rivera said that his mother sent her angels to heal him. Young Dante swore it was his prayers and his promise to care for Raul for the rest of his life.

Dante René was Magritte's favorite. This didn't bother Raul Paul who was glad to receive less of his mother's attention with her white iron glove approach to life, but Dante knew how to charm his mother even as a child. Magritte saw Dante's handsomeness as something she deserved and secretly wished she could have had him as a lover.

Magritte had big plans for her firstborn. He would become an important man. With wealth, a good education, his charming good looks, and breeding, it would be easy. He would become the best, marry the best, and produce the best in the family line.

CHAPTER FOUR

The Snub

Napa, May 1915

Magritte sat at her writing desk addressing invitations to the yearly spring gala at the mansion. Her secretary, Louise, was hunkered down at a small side table. She stuffed and sealed the stack of addressed envelopes and placed them in a neat pile of finished invitations when Dante breezed into the room and over to his mother. He came up behind her and kissed her cheek.

"Mother, I want to invite someone to our party. Someone I want you to meet."

Magritte was about to say no, but the ever charming Dante knew how to convince her and get his way. He reached under her arms and began to tickle her.

"Stop, stop," she laughed.

"Not until you say yes," said Dante.

Magritte screamed in laughter, "Alright!"

Dante stopped tickling his mother and grabbed an invitation off the top.

"Love you, Mother," he said as he scooted out the door.

"Cassandra will be there," she called out.

Juanita told Dante she could find her way to the estate, so that he could help his mother finish the final details the day of the gala. She'd taken the bus as far as she could to the mouth of the winding hillside road that led up to the Rivera estate. Several cars passed her as she walked up the steep road to the mansion.

It had been a warm day filled with the smell of spring flowers. A cool night followed. Juanita needed to catch her breath. The climb was steeper than it appeared, and when she reached the fork in the road and saw the mighty oak tree in the distance, she decided to visit it. The remarkable old tree had become the recognized symbol on every bottle of wine sold at the Rivera family's Mighty Oak Winery. Standing under the old, tree she admired its full branches jutting out from the thick trunk. Its branches created an umbrella-like presence and gave it a majestic dignity, a comforting, protective feeling. Juanita stood under the branches to absorb the tree's energy. She stayed there for a while before walking back down the hill to the fork. She turned to take one last look at the grand tree with her back to the forked road. A car came roaring up the hill and around the bend. Ooga! Ooga! came from the horn as the car narrowly missed her. Juanita jumped off the road. What's wrong with people, she thought. They would rather run me over than be late for the party. She had to laugh. What was she doing going to a party with people she didn't belong with? What did she have in common with them? Nothing. She walked back up to the tree.

She wanted to go home. Why was she here? Because of Dante, sweet Dante, who she'd been spending time with in the weeks since they'd met and who she cared about more than she wanted to admit. He seemed so excited when he asked her to come to the party. She couldn't disappoint him.

The sun had gone down and a chill in the air gave her goose bumps. The thin coat, her best, was inadequate against the oncoming cool evening. She wrapped the coat tightly around her body and walked down to the fork in the road. At the fork she continued up the hill to the mansion looking up at the night sky for inspiration.

The road opened up to a crescent-shaped driveway in front of the mansion. This structure had become an urban legend in the valley. The three stories became progressively smaller. The top two floors with sloping roofs had outside verandas. A light glowed from every window looking like a birthday cake with too many candles, and something inside of her wanted to blow them out.

She only walked a few more steps before her nerves began to get the best of her. She closed her eyes to calm down and let pleasant thoughts into her head. The house was a fantasy castle with pumpkin carriages sitting in the front, and Cinderella came on foot, just like the Mary Pickford movie she'd seen last year. She laughed at herself until a car whizzed by kicking up small stones at her. By the time Juanita reached the front door the passengers of the fancy automobile were spilling out onto the front steps of the mansion. The Gillette family—father Dale, young Howard, mother Willa, and strawberry blond Cassandra—glanced matter-of-factly at Juanita in a dismissive way. Had it not been for the front door opening at that very moment Juanita might have changed her mind and taken off back down the hill. James the butler greeted the Gillette family in a familiar way and smiled at Juanita.

Inside the vestibule was a seventeenth century Italian marble and wormwood side table. A large arrangement of roses, peonies, dahlias, poppies, and grapevines intertwined with yellow ribbons cascaded onto the marble top and partially obscured the view in the massive gold framed mirror above it. Juanita looked at herself in the mirror to see how she'd held up. In the reflection she could see Cassandra's eyes move unforgivingly up and down her body, resting finally on her shoes before giving a curt nose-in-the-air look away. Juanita looked down at her own shoes. What was wrong with them? James finished taking the Gillettes' coats and moved over to Juanita. In a well-meaning manner he said, "The servants entrance is on the side."

Young Howard, who was standing nearby, heard the remark and began to snicker. His demeanor was reminiscent of a hyena with his orange hair and brown-freckled face. He took in air when he laughed and snorted when he exhaled.

Devastated and burning with embarrassment, Juanita backed away toward the door just as Dante appeared at the far end of the hallway. When he noticed Juanita from a distance, he smiled broadly and waved, bounding down the hallway toward the vestibule. Cassandra, though surprised, happily thought he was waving to her. Cassandra waved back and wistfully stepped in front of Juanita as Dante approached. It wasn't until then that Dante noticed Cassandra and the Gillette family. He politely greeted them and moved around Cassandra, giving Juanita a kiss on the cheek. He took her coat, handed it to James, wrapped one arm around her, and guided her down the hallway to the ballroom.

"I'm glad you're finally here. I was getting worried you wouldn't make it."

The Gillette family and James stood in silence.

The elegant Dante with his tall, lean body in a slender black tuxedo and stiff white shirt with black tie, and slicked-back hair looked like he'd stepped out of a Charles Dana Gibson illustration. Juanita looped her hand onto his arm and felt the soft cashmere of his suit under her fingers. She glanced down at her dress and shoes and the slight red tinge returned to her cheeks. She understood the mistake in the hallway; she was terribly underdressed. Dante didn't seem to care. They walked toward the sound of music and people's voices mixing together with the occasional bit of laughter.

They entered the brightly lit ballroom. Five chandeliers dangled from the ceiling in a room entirely surrounded with mirrors. The hundred or so dressed-to-kill guests multiplied many times over in the mirrors. Juanita's body stiffened; she felt caught in a trap. Dante wrapped his arm tightly around her. He smiled as if she was the only one in the room and danced her across the floor to where Magritte stood surrounded by her entourage of friends.

"Mother, this is the girl I wanted you to meet. This is Juanita."

Magritte stared stone-faced at Juanita. Still caught up in Dante's impression, Juanita warmly extended her hand toward Magritte who gazed down at the young girl's open hand and back up to her face. Juanita's empty hand began to shake and her body swayed toward Dante. Both the Gillette family and Grandfather Raul came into the circle at that moment. Grandfather Raul grabbed onto Juanita's hand and twirled her into his arms, greeting her with a warm hug.

"I believe this is my dance," said Grandfather Raul.

The Gillettes stood back as Grandfather Raul guided Juanita away from Magritte. Dante gave his mother a disparaging look and joined them on the dance floor.

Magritte's eyes followed them while the Gillettes moved within the inner circle of the entourage.

"Fascinating, a juvenile crush at his age. I'll see to it that it doesn't last," said Magritte.

Grandfather Raul had suspected the day of their visit that this sweet young thing had stolen his grandson's heart. When their dance was over, Grandfather Raul took Juanita's hand and walked her over to his son Gabriel who greeted her warmly.

Dante and his brother cajoled as Grandfather Raul introduced Juanita to several partygoers.

"She's lovely, Dante," said Raul.

The Rivera men surrounded Juanita all evening in a protective pocket, keeping her away from Magritte and her friends.

Juanita enjoyed herself, much to her surprise.

Most of the guests had left by midnight, including the Gillettes. Magritte excused herself early with one of her headaches. Dante and Juanita laughed and danced until two and were the last ones there except for Raul, who usually left as

early as he could, but this time was enjoying himself, enchant-
ed with his brother's infatuation, Juanita.

The sleek open-air Stutz Bearcat motored down the long
road toward town. Chilly from the night air, Juanita wrapped
her thin coat around herself. Dante, using that as an excuse,
reached over and pulled her closer.

"I can keep you warm."

He looped his arm around her body, holding her tight.

"You're the reason my brother and I enjoyed ourselves
tonight. We usually hate these parties. Did you have fun?"

"Yes, very much. Thank you for inviting me."

Dante pulled his car onto a deserted part of the road and
stopped.

"I've enjoyed every minute I've spent with you, Juanita.
More than I've ever enjoyed spending time with anyone else."

He wrapped his arms around her and kissed her.

"I want you to be my girl. Will you?"

Was she dreaming? A part of her couldn't believe this
spectacularly handsome young man wanted her. The hours
they'd spent together had been magical. She placed her chin
on his shoulder and rocked her head to the side.

"I'm afraid. I like you a lot, but will you get bored with
me? I'm so different from the other girls you know." Dante
kissed Juanita again. This time harder and with more passion.

"You're all I need. I hope you feel the same."

"Yes," she whispered. They kissed again.

***

The glass-enclosed arboretum in the back of the mansion near the kitchen was used as the breakfast room. Its dif-
fused light and airiness were incongruous in daylight with the
rest of the dark and stately mansion. In summer when the
valley heated up, gallons of water were pumped over the top of
the arboretum, flowing, and recycling back to a holding tank
to cool the room and making it a favorite for the family, but

not necessarily Magritte. She allowed it to be built for her husband's whimsy. Gabriel's lush tropical plants and prized exotic birds coexisted in the room. The plants soaked up the surrounding sunlight and canopied over four huge gilded cages that housed cockatiels, macaws, lovebirds, and the latest and most expensive bird, a red-breasted male bullfinch. The bullfinch, imported from Germany, had been painstakingly trained to sing a lullaby by its woodsman trainer who had spent hours whistling to it. The bird knew two songs.

On this morning a sullen faced Magritte waited, still in her nightclothes with her hair loosely tied up. She sat alone waiting in the darkest end of the room, at a small round iron table with a glass top. She nervously picked at a weak spot on the arm of the wicker chair she sat in. Round dark glasses covered her crimson-rimmed eyes. The bright light in the room was too much for her, and it was a rare occasion for her to even be in this room, especially at this hour. She was determined to make her point. She'd taken an extra dose of her nerve-calming medication this morning. The euphoria from the drugs she'd taken the night before had dissipated, leaving her with a feeling of despair and empty longing. This last dosage of her medicine gave her a thin veil of contentment to cover a dark, raging anger festering inside.

Not used to seeing her there, Gabriel didn't notice Magritte sitting at the far end of the room. He seemed bright and cheery as he went to his birds. Gabriel always enjoyed his morning hours with his prized birds, free of his controlling wife and their adversarial relationship.

He took out his favorite lovebird, a butter yellow one named Dolly. He held her up to his lips and gave her a morning peck kiss before placing her back into her cage.

"It's disgusting. The way you treat those birds."

Gabriel turned quickly toward the shrill voice.

"Magritte. I didn't see you."

"I couldn't believe the way you acted with that urchin. She will not do for Dante."

"Quiet, the servants will hear. Stay out of Dante's life. She's a very nice girl."

The argument started after the party the night before when Gabriel entered his room in the master suite and the sliding oak panel doors that separated their rooms opened. Magritte was already in her nightly drug-induced stupor. She started in on him about Dante. He dismissed her and closed the doors locking them from his side. She pounded on them until it was clear he wouldn't open them.

The birds chattered as Gabriel and Magritte argued until the arguing turned to shouts so intense that even the birds quieted down. After about a half hour there was a lull in the arguing. Grandfather Raul had been in the hallway waiting for the argument to reach a respite. His stomach was growling. He entered the room with a quick, blithe good morning to the couple as if nothing distressful had just occurred and went over to the breakfast buffet. Ornate sterling silver chafing dishes held eggs, bacon, and breakfast pastries. He poured himself a cup of coffee and filled a gold-rimmed bone china plate. Gabriel joined him. Magritte sat mute, arms crossed, watching the two men discuss their morning business while they ate breakfast. Usually Grandfather Raul's presence was enough to stop an intense quarrel between the couple, at least for a time.

As the two men ate and talked, Dante breezed into the room. He was dressed in his riding clothes—a white shirt, sleeves rolled up to his elbows, tan riding britches and high black boots. He seemed extra happy this morning. Magritte stood up.

Dante walked to her and gave her a hug and kiss on the cheek.

"Thank you for the wonderful party, Mother."

Dante poured himself a cup of coffee and was about to make a breakfast plate.

"Come to the office this morning, Dante. I want to go over some papers with you," said Gabriel.

Magritte stepped toward the breakfast table. Gabriel was in mid-sentence when she pushed her way into the conversation.

"I forbid you to see that girl again. She and her family are beneath us."

"Stop!" yelled Gabriel. "You not only insult them, you insult my father who is a friend of their family."

Magritte's malicious gaze stupefied Gabriel for a moment. Never looking down, she blindly swept her arm across the table, knocking Gabriel's plate and coffee cup through the air. The bone china smashed to bits on the hard brick floor. The food splattered and hot coffee cascaded out, burning Gabriel's arm. Gabriel quickly got to his feet and grabbed Magritte's arm, twisting it behind her back while Dante stood in horror.

"Let me go, you bastard."

Gabriel grimaced. He let go of her arm.

"Dante can see whomever he likes."

"Did you see that?! You see how he treats me. Bastard."

Tears filled Magritte's eyes as she rushed out of the room. Dante began to follow, but his father held him back.

"I'll go to her. You go riding, and I'll see you later at the office. I mean it, Dante, see who you like. Juanita is a sweet, lovely girl."

Gabriel followed his wife up the back stairs.

Dante looked toward his grandfather who sipped his coffee as if oblivious to what just happened. He smiled at Dante.

"Things never change around here. They seem to always be at one another."

Dante poured himself a glass of port from the decanter and drank it down.

***

The Rivera family's stables housed several horses. Starr was Dante's favorite. She was a blue-black beauty with a white star shape on her head between her eyes along with a white streak near her left hind leg that looked like a shooting star in a black sky. She was a thoroughbred from Kentucky lineage, given when she was a filly to Dante by his great-grandfather on his twelfth birthday, just before he died. They'd seldom been separated since. Dante raised her, and once she was old enough, he rode her every day. Her back was his throne. The year after he got her he was sent to an East Coast school. Starr went with him, traveling in her own boxcar next to his. He boarded her at a stable near the school and every morning at six he would be there to ride her. In the winter the stable had an indoor round pen that he used.

Starr could sense when Dante was coming and would do a familiar prance in her stall signaling the stable groom to saddle her. If he wasn't quick enough, she would whinny until the scent of the saddle was in her nostrils.

Dante rode Starr hard that day. He needed time to think about his life, his future. Riding always gave him the alone time he needed. It was just the two of them. Starr loved it; she would do anything for Dante.

They returned to the stable a little before noon. Dante seemed more relaxed; he'd made up his mind. He nuzzled his head next to Starr's and stroked her, smelling her horse lather. It was like a perfume to him. The groomsman removed her saddle and began her cooldown. Dante removed the bridle and grabbed a brush to help.

Dante showered and changed at the winery that day, not wanting to go back to the mansion. When his meeting with his father was over, he drove into town and spent the rest of the day and early evening with Juanita. That night when he arrived back home, he went straight to his room to avoid a confrontation with his mother who would spoil his wonderful day.

CHAPTER FIVE

Under the Mighty Oak

Napa, late May 1915

In the cool of the early morning Juanita Bonnetia sat on a blanket drawing her favorite subject, Dante René Rivera. They were in the grove next to the mighty oak tree on the road leading up to Dante's great-grandfather's stone ranch house. Dante's Stutz Bearcat sports car was parked on the road further down at the fork where the road led to the Rivera mansion.

Dante changed his stance to a Sandow the strongman pose.

"You don't take this seriously."

"I do," responded Dante. "But I'd rather be over there near you. Let's take a walk before the day heats up. I want to show you my grandfather's ranch house."

Dante fell onto the blanket next to Juanita and playfully pulled her down to lay beside him. He brushed his mouth against her neck and shoulder. She closed her eyes and swayed her body toward him and he gently kissed her. Ever since his unannounced visit and the party when he asked her to be his girlfriend, they'd become inseparable.

"Okay, I feel restless. Let's go," said Juanita.

They strolled up the road for a bit coming to a two-story gabled stone ranch house. All of the windows had been shuttered since the recent death of Dante's step-great-grand-mother Fiona. Lush blooming rosebushes lined the front of the ranch house and hedged the walkway.

"There's talk of using it as an office for the family and bosses during the early spring when the workers are preparing the vines for the growing season and in the fall for the harvest. I want to restore it and live here," said Dante.

"It's beautiful, like a painting," said Juanita.

"Come on, I want to show you the view of the vines surrounding the back of the house. They stretch down the hillside as far as the eye can see. All these grapes are for the Rivera Mighty Oak wines."

Dante took Juanita's hand and unlatched the gate. They walked through a rose-vine-covered trellis and started down the walkway. Juanita looked up at the house and stopped. The slight girl stood strong as Dante tried to pull her toward the house.

"Stop, I want to look at the outside. It's so beautiful."

"Wait until you see the inside."

Dante pushed open the wide-planked oak door of the two-story stone structure and turned to look at the expression on Juanita's face. She hesitated at the front door with a feeling that this was an invasion into the past. Yet she wanted to see the place where her beloved Lita Nannie had once been a governess and to see the rooms from all the stories her grandmother had told so many times.

Dante grabbed her hand and pulled her inside the dark front hall, drawing her close and wrapping his arms around her. He leaned his face close to hers, and placing his hand under her chin, he gently lifted her face into his, giving her a passionate kiss. Juanita pulled away to catch her breath. Only scant daylight filtered through the closed shuttered windows. She looked at Dante in the dim light. His handsome, masculine face looked like it had been chiseled out of stone, and his physique, almost too beautiful to comprehend, overwhelmed her for a moment. She reached up and touched his face with the back of her hand, rubbing from his smooth cheek to his rough beard. Then she took her index finger and outlined his full lips. They paused, looking into each other's eyes.

"Come upstairs with me to see the view of the vineyards and valley below."

"First, I want to look at the great room and the playroom that I've heard so much about from my grandmother's stories."

Through the streams of sunlight tiny bits of dust seemed suspended. Dante threw open the shutters and light poured into the two-story cathedral ceiling great room. The room had hand-hewn oak beams and the most massive stone fireplace Juanita had ever seen. The wide plank floors were still in excellent condition, and a double-wide staircase with wrought iron balusters and a hand carved mahogany banister wound around to the second floor. The furniture that still remained in the house was covered in white sheets and gave the room a ghostly, austere quality. A hallway on one side of the fireplace led down to the children's playroom. Juanita looked into the open door of the room recognizing it from her grandmother's description. Although now it was empty with only a few toys remaining on the low shelves under a bank of French windows.

"Raul and I used to play in here," said Dante.

On the other side of the great room was the dining room. It had a low ceiling and full-length glass doors leading out onto a stone patio. The doors were locked. Juanita looked through the glass. A six-foot stone wall surrounded the patio making it a private outdoor room. She walked into the small breakfast nook next to it and peeked into the kitchen.

"My grandmother talked about Rosa. Did you ever know her?"

"I've heard about her. She died long before I was born. Come on upstairs with me," said Dante.

Again, Juanita hesitated. Something was giving her an uneasy feeling.

"What's the matter?"

"I…don't know."

They walked down the upstairs hallway and Dante swung the master suite bedroom door open.

"I always loved my grandfather's four poster bed, so when my grandmother died, I had the furniture moved into my room at the mansion."

Dark markings on the floor of the master suite were surrounded by faded, sun-bleached wood and indicated where the bed and other pieces of furniture used to be in the now empty room. Dante walked over to the bank of French windows overlooking the vineyards and valley. He threw the windows wide open and unleashed the shutters. His sensitive blue eyes squinted as the morning sun hit his face. A dispirited feeling settled in Juanita.

Acres of grapevines as far as the eye could see grew down the hills into the valley. The vines were covered with maturing grapes, months away from the final harvest. Wind rustled through the trees outside the bedroom window knocking leaves around in the air. Some loose leaves blew inside, landed on the floor, and moved about in a sweeping circular motion.

"Come and look at this."

Juanita moved over to Dante. He stood behind her and wrapped his arms around her waist.

"In a few weeks, we'll harvest some of the grapes. They will taste bitter right now, but the juice from these grapes will be mixed with the ripe fall grapes to give our wine its distinctive Mighty Oak taste. When I was a child, I'd come up here and play with my grandfather's things. He had a table here loaded with books, a telescope, and maps."

Dante kissed the side of Juanita's neck and moved his hand from her waist, slightly cupping her breasts. It made Juanita pull away and walk to the far side of the room.

"You're so beautiful, and I like you very much," said Dante.

"I like you too, but we can't. It might go too far."

"Maybe. To me it feels like it's supposed to be. It seems so natural to touch you."

A golden oak leaf floated through the French windows landing on the floor in front of Dante's feet as if some ancient valley spirit had sent it. He picked it up and gave a gallant sweeping bow. He knelt on one knee and presented Juanita with the leaf.

"For you, my lady."

Juanita laughed and grabbed the leaf from Dante's hand. She touched both his shoulders with it.

"I dub thee Sir Oak Leaf."

Dante continued kneeling and looked up at her. He leaned into her legs and wrapped his arms around them.

"I do love you, you know," he said.

He took Juanita's hand in his and kissed the oak leaf and the inside of her wrist. She slapped his cheek with the leaf and knelt down, falling into his arms.

"Oh God, I can't breathe. Why do you have to be so sweet and…"

Dante kissed Juanita in mid-sentence.

"Let me hold you. I promise to be good."

He laid her down on the floor.

"I'll never hurt you Juanita, I promise. Just let me hold you for a little while. Let me be with you."

"I do love you too, Dante," she whispered.

Dante looked closely at Juanita's face.

"What are you looking at?" she said.

"I'm studying your face. I hope our daughters are as beautiful as you."

CHAPTER SIX

Captain's Journal

1855

One hundred and sixty days from home port of Boston. Left before the first of this year. Liverpool, England in twenty-four days with cargo of tobacco, spars, and lumber. Had to dock in Port Bilbao, Spain for repairs. Took on five passengers. Was off Cape Horn fifteen days with heavy gales. Ship sustained split sail and broken chain plate. Arrived San Francisco May 20.

Cargo: 20 rolls carpet, nails, 24 wagon wheels, 1 case pistols, one case lead, 204 tons of coal, quantities of gin, wine and brandy, horseshoes, boots, 1 clavichord, 3 crates of personal belongings of Dr. Dante Rivera.

Passengers: Mr. Robert Fieldstone and lady, Mrs. Lillian Miller, Mr. Denton Silversmith, Dr. Dante Rivera and two children, Mr. Ramon Salvatore and lady, Mr. Lars Sinclair, and 70 unidentified steerage. Two dead. Samuel Atkins, died and buried at sea. March 3rd, Mr. Miles Mudgen fell overboard and was lost at sea.

— Captain Robert Trunbow, The Silver Cloud

D r. Rivera and the children arrived in Port Bilbao, Spain the day before the *Silver Cloud* was set to continue its journey. Word had come to him about the ship's unexpected docking. It had been fortunate timing for them. Dr. Rivera booked passage along with two other

Spaniards, all needing to leave Spain in haste. The rest of the passengers were British, with a handful of French and Germans who had made their way to England. All were traveling to San Francisco to see the streets paved in gold and to find their riches. Dante's goal was not to find wealth but to find freedom.

The *Silver Cloud* set sail from Spain and immediately hit rough weather that lasted several days. When it finally stopped, the sounds of stomping feet and a lively fiddle rumbled through the ceiling boards of the first-class cabin from the deck above. The young boy watched the ceiling boards bounce. He pressed his father to go up on deck to see the entertainment. The waters were calm enough at last for the passengers to get fresh air. Who knew how long this would last. At times the sea's waters swelled from bad weather becoming so rough the children had to be lashed into their bunks.

On deck an old Irish fiddler sat on a three-legged stool playing his fiddle hard and fast as twenty or so passengers stood around stamping their feet in time watching two sailors dance a jig. The merriment was meant to take advantage of the good weather and to help forget the day before when they buried likable Samuel Atkins at sea. Dr. Dante Rivera carried his small daughter, Angeles, as his son, Raul Cristoval, scampered ahead of him climbing the steep ladder-stairs to the deck. Without wind the ship only moved slightly in the calm waters. The fresh and warm air was a pleasure and helped to take the chill out of their bones.

Raul rushed ahead of his father moving toward the front of the crowd so he could get a better view of the entertainment. Weeks of the swaying ship made Angeles, who was just learning to walk, unsteady. Across the way sultry Anita Salvatore stood, with one hand on her hip, nervously tapping her foot and twirling a long strand of her raven hair. The old fiddler pushed on for nearly an hour playing one tune after another. When he did put his fiddle down to rest, Ramon Salvatore, in a surly mood from waiting, picked up his guitar and strutted in front of the fiddler peering down at him through black condemning eyes. The fiddler, slightly delirious from playing, looked up at him like a child looking at a disciplinarian.

Ramon plucked the strings of his guitar as a cue to Anita who pranced into the center of the circle. She tapped her heels on the ship's deck and raised her long elegant arms high in the air clapping her hands above her crown of thick, black, curly hair. Her taut arm muscles flexed with each clap as she moved like liquid, her feet flying faster and faster until they seemed a blur to Raul. She flicked her lush hair back, swirling her body and clicked a rhythmic sound with her tongue. She grabbed onto her layers of petticoats and raised them up provocatively high exposing a bright red petticoat closest to her shapely tawny-skinned legs. The warm sun made her skin glisten; her full breasts heaved up toward the top of her corset exposing the slightest bit of brown nipple. The few women present reeled and turned around in disgust. Most of the men stayed. Dr. Rivera unceremoniously guided the intrigued Raul away.

CHAPTER SEVEN

San Francisco Harbor

May 20, 1855

Dark harbor waters went from glass to a gentle sway with the tide. The first morning light crossed over the Sierra Mountains in the east seemingly chasing away the night to start a new day and for some a new beginning.

Later, the vivid May sun reflected on the bay's rhythmically swaying waters casting a momentarily blinding and illuminating light into the eyes of the leather-skinned, ancient-faced Chinese workers unloading cargo from the bow of the newly arrived extreme clipper ship, the *Silver Cloud*. The ship slipped into the harbor in the middle of the night on a puff of wind gliding quietly from the Pacific Ocean through the Golden Gate into the San Francisco Bay to end her long voyage. Five thousand yards of sun-bleached canvas were stowed effortlessly to their spares on the three masts.

The dock workers' eyes watered as they struggled to unload the clipper ship in the harbor's fog and unpredictable light, a light that went from murky to piercing. A slippery, heavy dew on the dock made the workers fearful of falling over the edge and into the water to be crushed by the massive weight of the towering clipper ship that lumbered with the rise and fall of the waves. A week earlier a dock worker had been crushed. They slowed for safety only to be forced to a faster pace when the white boss yelled out in broken Chinese that any slackers would have their meager pay docked if they stopped for even a second.

In the fog a faint outline of disembarking passengers appeared on the ship's deck. The passengers moved toward the exit: first as a trickle, but within minutes a swarm congregated at the ship's exit ramp anxious to leave behind their troubled lives in Europe for hopefully a better life in the city of gold.

A silhouette of the young doctor's thin body appeared on top of the deck. It had been an arduous journey fraught with bad weather and other problems that made the trip longer than anticipated. This revolutionary clipper ship, the *Silver Cloud*, had set speed records in the past. Still, Dr. Rivera was thankful, only a bit of luck found the ship in Bilbao when he needed it. Two severe storms took their toll on everyone aboard the ship. Extreme fatigue from this odyssey and recent events in Spain were etched on Dr. Rivera's face as he tried to remain stoic for the children, but inside he was falling apart. Raul seemed brave and trusting in his father's decision, but inside the little boy was confused and often silently cried himself to sleep at night, more from missing his recently dead mother than anything else.

Dr. Rivera carried his daughter, Angeles, on his hip as she clung to her porcelain-head doll her grandparents had given her when they said a heartrending goodbye in Spain knowing they would never see their grandchildren again. The little girl closely resembled her dead mother. Three-year-old Raul held tightly onto his father's coattail with one hand. The other hand gripped a small velvet bag mimicking his father, who with his free hand clutched a black leather doctor's bag with faded gold embossed letters D.R.R.

Ritualistically the new emigrants moved down the ship's long ramp to the wharf below seeking salvation as thousands had done before. The wide-eyed gazes and hopeful anticipation for a better life would soon meet a more austere reality.

Hundreds of times the significance of this moment had filled Dr. Rivera's head. Each step had been meticulously planned in his orderly brain to push down resentful memories of the events that led up to his hasty retreat from his homeland and to preserve his sanity on the long journey from Spain.

Angeles' head tilted. She buried her face in her father's chest rubbing it back and forth. He looked down at his child's face. Sepia-colored circles surrounded her dilated hazel eyes, exaggerated by her alabaster skin. They reflected her mood. She sucked in the moist air and let out a deep hard exhaled sigh. She held her breath and again buried her face into her father's chest.

"Breathe Angeles, the worst is over," Dr. Rivera whispered to his daughter as he kissed her forehead.

In his head Raul was silently singing a familiar tune his mother had taught him. He hit a different note with each step and one had slipped out unconsciously. The mound of curly chestnut locks on top of his head bounced. Somehow his cherub face had retained a healthy glow despite the long journey.

The intense sporadic light reflected into Dr. Rivera's fine-featured weary-thin face making his eyes water. His sad, dark blue eyes scanned around hawk-like trying to take in everything they could. His normally swarthy skin had a yellow cast, his chiseled features were more pronounced from weight loss. Some coarse, gray hairs had appeared overnight in his jet-black hair. His square jaw clenched down tightly causing him to bite his inner bottom lip. He tasted a small bit of blood inside his mouth. His normally six-foot frame stooped over making him look slightly deformed.

At the bottom of the ramp Dr. Rivera stopped. He placed his black valise between his legs so no one could steal it. Passengers passed by them. Dr. Rivera took out a handkerchief to wipe his eyes, not wanting to appear vulnerable. San Francisco was a rough town. He'd been warned it was essential that he appeared to be strong. Too much was at stake. Raul peeked around his father's body and looked up into his face. There was a bit of breakfast stuck on Raul's face. Dr. Rivera knelt down, balancing Angeles on his knee, to wipe Raul's face with the handkerchief.

"You must look clean, Raul. I wish you had washed your hands and face before we left the ship."

Raul's bottom lip quivered from shame. The boy did his best to be good on the long journey and listen to his father. His little sister had been seasick most of the way, and his father's heart was heavy with grief. Raul worked hard to stay happy for them. His father's comment hit his vulnerability hard. He'd washed the night before, but in this morning's excitement he'd forgotten.

Sensing his young son's pain, Dr. Rivera reached out, gently ruffling his curly locks. "Not to worry, Raul. You are a handsome young man. Now hold your head up high so everyone can admire you."

A short distance away Dr. Rivera saw a crudely painted sign above the stables that read O'Grady's Blacksmith, Freight and Livestock.

Some color was returning to Angeles' cheeks after months of sea sickness. Her body still swayed from the rolling motion of the ship even though she was now on land. She wanted to go and be with her brother Raul, who out of impatience as he waited for his father to do his business, walked up and down the rows of stalls looking at the horses and oxen in them. Dr. Rivera held on tightly to Angeles and called for Raul to come back.

A gravelly thick voice with an Irish brogue called out, "Cum into me office."

The office, a converted stall with a rough-hewn piece of pine sitting on two saw horses for a desk, was next to the other stalls and smelled no different. On the far side of the stall sat a cot covered with a horse blanket and a dirty pillow. Bits of straw stuck out from all four sides of the calico printed pillow which had an oil stained head print in the middle. Behind the desk sat Mr. O'Grady. His Wellington top hat was precariously propped on his head of coarse strawberry blonde hair. He was writing something in a ledger, and it took a moment for him to look up. Angeles jerked and hung on to her father tightly when he finally did. His brick-red face had a bulbous nose bigger than anything she'd ever seen, and large pores filled with blackheads dotted his oily skin. A bright red beard covered the lower half of his face. Tufts of red hair jetted out between the buttons and around the neck of his stretched-out, filthy long underwear. When he stood up, the tall Wellington top hat made this six foot five man seem like a giant. His pot belly rolled over the top of his too small, urine-stained striped pants. He hadn't bothered to properly fasten the buttons on his fly the last time he'd taken a leak. He smelled of horse, oxen, alcohol, and his own intense body odor. When he smiled, his stale breath reeked of beer. What few teeth he had left were stained a dark yellow-brown from years of chewing tobacco. A snort ripped from his big nose making his body rumble from top to bottom. He wiped his nose on the sleeve of his food-dribbled plaid shirt.

"What can I do for you?" bellowed O'Grady with a heavy brogue that made the children quake.

"I need to hire some wagons to take my possessions to my new home in the Napa Valley and to buy a horse and buggy for myself."

"Long trip, it'll cost ya. Cash up front. Can't leave until tomorrow."

Dante walked down the long corridor of the lodging looking for the door to their rented room for the night. He and the children would have to be up early the next morning for the last part of their long and tedious journey. A door at the far end of the hall opened. A familiar rhythmic laughter rang out echoing throughout the hall. Dr. Rivera turned to see Anita Salvatore.

Tall, slender Ramon Salvatore, a decade older than his beautiful young wife Anita, walked out behind her followed by two cooperating police officers. The metal taps on Anita's high-heeled shoes clicked on the wooden floor. Two men and a woman walked up the stairs and waited for Anita to pass. She shook her long, thick hair like a prized peacock. Her many petticoats fluffed and swished as she walked. Anita pushed her heaving breasts around inside the lace-cinched top to tantalize the men. She held her head high and placed her clinched hands on her hips and pranced away. The woman stood humiliated next to her husband who threw Anita a lustful stare.

During the voyage from Spain, Anita had made money by pleasuring some of the male passengers who could afford her. Others lost in card games to Ramon, who now reached up to stroke his hair removing some grease from it to smooth his pencil thin mustache and small goatee. Sneers and gossip had followed the couple on the voyage.

Ramon discreetly tilted his head to acknowledge Dr. Rivera, who had not partaken in the whispers and biases of the passengers because the Salvatores were gypsies. The whispers became more prevalent after Anita performed her provocative flamenco dance on the ship's deck. For discretion the Salvatores conversed in Caló to one another, the language of the gypsies. Dante Rivera was one of the few who treated them fairly on the trip, even though he only spoke to them occasionally. As a fair and tolerant man, Dr. Rivera never believed in the stories about the gypsies and abhorred the unfair treatment he'd witnessed firsthand in Spain. He also knew they both had to leave Spain, although for different reasons.

There were three classes of passengers on the ship. Third class consisted of a hammock with a straw-filled mattress and a diet of horse meat, mush, and molasses. Second class, a berth with more wholesome food. First class, a private room and decent food. Like Dr. Rivera when they boarded the ship at Bilbao, the Salvatores had purchased a room instead of steerage or a berth. Dante did so to protect his children; the Salvatores so Anita could entertain men. Dr. Rivera looked the other way and minded his business.

Early the next morning the Riveras returned to the docks. The two wagons were blanketed in a heavy early morning fog as it rolled over the docks. Dr. Rivera watched the last of his possessions being loaded into the wagons. The chimes from an antique family heirloom clock gave off a melodious ring echoing in the fog. It was the only thing Dr. Rivera had left from his mother, Angelina. She inherited the clock from her mother and it was a reminder of the wealth her family once had.

Her death when Dante was thirteen convinced him to become a doctor. He vowed to her on her deathbed that he would work to find a cure for the ugly disease that she was stricken with. Few came near her once the cancer was diagnosed, including her husband José. Fearing he would catch her disease, he left to live in the North leaving their son alone to care for his mother. She died in Dante's arms a few months later. With her last breath, she promised she would send angels down to watch over her beloved son.

Irony struck when his father died soon after from a massive heart attack.

The dock workers moved a hand-carved wooden chest from the dock into a wagon invoking more melancholy memories. In it were a few things he'd saved from his dead wife for their children.

The children grew impatient. Raul skipped around to divert his nervous energy while a weepy Angeles clung to her father. Dr. Rivera stroked the largest crate which held his dead wife Catherina's clavichord.

CHAPTER EIGHT

Pamplona, Spain

Newly orphaned thirteen-year-old Dante Rivera met his future wife, Catherina, the day he arrived at his uncle's home in Pamplona in northern Spain. She was two years younger than him, but looked and acted older than her age. He was being taunted by some young boys, one who was her brother. She told the boys to leave him alone and threatened to turn them in to their parents if they didn't stop. The boys ran leaving the two of them alone. Dante and Catherina were inseparable from that day on.

They married when Catherina turned sixteen. Her dowry put him through medical school in Madrid, and when he finished, they returned to Pamplona to a home in the Carlist held territory to be close to Catherina's mother. Civil war permeated the country with bloody and savage skirmishes that took place all over Spain. The Carlist and Isabellian factions vied for power and territory leaving innocent people caught in the middle, unjustly suffering grisly fates.

His wife Catherina had contracted the flu while doing charity work in the poor part of town the week before. Six days later she died. Her body was buried unceremoniously at dusk immediately after her death for fear of spreading the disease. In the rush, she was buried in a plain pine box. The mahogany coffin her parents purchased arrived hours after her burial and sat in the drawing room waiting to be returned. That was the day a knock came to the back door. Dr. Rivera answered it. A wounded soldier lay crumpled on the ground. Bushes in the distance rustled as someone ran away.

Dr. Rivera took no sides. When the wounded Isabellian soldier was brought to his door, the good doctor remained true to his sworn Hippocratic oath and did not refuse to help the soldier. The doctor dug out a bullet and sewed the young unconscious soldier up. By evening news came of a door to door search by rapidly approaching Carlist soldiers.

A skull hung on the front door, a warning of the illness; still the Carlist soldiers entered. They began searching the house. They looked into the shrouded drawing room at the candlelit coffin. One brave soldier entered and walked up to the coffin that had a death certificate attached to the top of the lid. He hesitated but would have opened it had his captain not stopped him.

"That is not necessary. He is not here."

They left the house, but this moment sealed Dr. Rivera and his children's fate. They would not be safe. In the past Carlist soldiers had burned down homes of suspected Isabellian loyalists with children inside. The wounded soldier who lay inside the coffin regained consciousness right after the soldiers left.

A timely request had come from Salvador Vallejo to the clinic where Dante worked asking for a doctor to come to live in the Napa Valley. This request seemed like a godsend to Dr. Rivera, sent by his mother's angels.

CHAPTER NINE

The Journey to a New Home

May 21, 1855

The morning light revealed the bay's narrow strait named after Istanbul's Golden Horn harbor. The two wagons Dr. Rivera rented from Mr. O'Grady were finished being loaded. He looked out toward the San Francisco harbor where hundreds of ships littered the bay waters having been abandoned by crews who left their ships to mine for gold. Some of the ships had been turned into warehouses, saloons, or lodgings for the influx of forty-niners. Other ships had been plundered to build wooden shanties, even their canvas was used for tents. Still others had sunk to the bottom of the bay.

Gold had changed San Francisco from a sleepy port to a prosperous city in a few years. Brick and wooden mansions sprang up overnight and graced the five hillsides. Crime-laden shanty towns and tent cities were filled with the poor and struggling where corruption ruled. Merchants flocked to the city of gold to make their fortune. The indigent came to find a new and better life. With no immigration rules in place, all who could endure the uncertain life were accepted.

Gruff Mr. O'Grady yelled out that both wagons were full and ready to go. He cursed his men in Gaelic and English with a thick brogue few understood. The timbre in his voice rendered them fearful. Two teams of oxen were harnessed up with heavy yokes and attached to the wagons. The oxen were the only things on earth O'Grady cared about, and he believed they loved him back. He valued them like they were his children—children that he would sell to the stockyards with a tear in his eye when they grew too old to work. He called them by name and affectionately patted them while inspecting their rigs. His workers knew if anything happened to the oxen, O'Grady would hunt them down and do whatever harm came to the oxen to them.

Dr. Rivera placed Angeles into the small buggy he'd purchased from O'Grady. Raul tagged along holding tight the small velvet bag he never let out of his sight. As Dr. Rivera attended to the children, O'Grady approached the buggy. He raised a manure-covered boot up onto the wheel of the buggy and dragged his foot downward to scrape off the dung. He spit out a wad of chewing tobacco the size of a walnut. As it splattered on the ground, O'Grady looked directly at Angeles—terrifying her. Angeles' reaction gave O'Grady a good belly laugh. His stomach shook hard and a button popped off his shirt exposing a tuft of red hair. Dr. Rivera swung Raul's little body up onto the horsehair-filled seat of the buggy next to Angeles. The little boy methodically opened the velvet bag he held so dearly, pulled out one of the tin soldiers inside and began to play while his father finished his business with O'Grady.

"These here men'll take you where you're goin', got to get a draft boat to San Rafael. Got to hurry, tide's comin' in soon, 'bout eleven. You get the trail from there. Be a full two-day trip or more goin' ya know, and they got to come back too. Ain't got no cargo comin' back, ya know. You got a lot of stuff, ya know."

Dr. Rivera paid O'Grady the remainder of the money, climbed into the buggy, and took the reins. He looked toward the seaport as the two wagons filled with his possessions pulled away. He flicked the reins for the horse to move, and his buggy followed behind the two wagons. It rolled away from the dock and down the dirt and wooden streets through the industrial area. With the harbor in the background, they moved into the city through the shanty towns toward the mansions on Russian Hill, and back toward the water to a part of town called the Barbary Coast. By now it was mid-morning and still a long way to Sonoma where he would meet up with Captain Mariano Vallejo. They would have to spend the night there before continuing on to their final destination in the Napa Valley.

Trepidation filled Dr. Rivera over his decision to leave Spain. In these few blocks of the city, he would witness un-savory behavior with cruelty to both human and animal. His anxiety level reached a peak due to lack of sleep, worry, and a weakened physical condition. His head began to spin, his heart palpitated, and it was difficult to swallow. He pulled on the reins to stop the horse so he could collect himself.

The fatigued, hollow look on Dr. Rivera's face quickly changed to alarm when a rag wearing streetwalker ran toward the carriage calling out the name "Mimi." She reached in and grabbed Angeles' curly hair. She had a glazed, crazy look on her face. Dr. Rivera fought to regain his senses but this only made his head spin faster. The woman latched onto Angeles' arm and tried to pull her out of the buggy. Angeles screamed holding onto her father while the woman tugged hard to drag her out. Dr. Rivera held onto Angeles the best he could. He tried to stand, but the spinning in his head made him fall back. A man from the streets ran up to the woman and tried to pull the streetwalker away, but she continued to cling to Angeles. Dr. Rivera regained enough of his senses to push at the wom-an, and she let go of Angeles. He snapped the horse's reins to make them move. The woman fell to the ground. The man from the streets held her down until the buggy was far enough away for him to let her go. The man got up, brushed his tat-tered clothes, and walked away. The rag wearing streetwalker lay on the ground crying with a pathetic vacant look, watch-ing the buggy that carried the memory of her dead daughter as it disappeared down the road. Again she called out, "Mimi, Mimi." Two drunken men who'd been watching by the side of the road picked her up and carried her off, groping her as they did.

Dr. Dante Rivera snapped the reins to catch up with the wagons. His head throbbed, but the spinning was finally clearing up.

His possessions had been hastily gathered during their quick retreat from Spain. Perhaps it had been foolish to bring anything all the way from Spain to America. The price of shipping and this last transportation cost him dearly. Between that and the price of a cabin on the ship, Dr. Rivera had spent a great deal of his money. These possessions were meant for his children to remember their mother and their Spanish heritage. He would have to start work immediately and maybe take a second job, if he could find one, at least until his practice thrived. He was anxious to see his new home. The frightened Angeles had crawled down into the well of the buggy and wrapped her arms tightly around her father's leg. Raul sat on the edge of the seat grasping the iron grip.

"Everything will be alright when we reach our destination and new home," said Dr. Rivera, trying to reassure the children and himself. They pressed on to the draft boat. He looked back at the view of the San Francisco Bay and an affinity with Angel Island grew in the doctor's heart as it seemed to reflect his sense of loneliness.

Warm afternoon sun beat down on the buggy. The wooden wheels of the two wagons kicked up a gray-brown dust from the road that covered the family with a fine layer of California earth. Exhaustion overwhelmed Angeles. After months of torturous travel on the clipper ship and her terrorizing experience leaving San Francisco, the fresh air and the warmth of the day was a catalyst. She fell into a deep sleep, the first since her mother's death. Dr. Rivera let her stay in the buggy's well where she felt safe and placed his coat on top of her. Not long after, Raul's eyes grew heavy. His head nodded up and down as he tried to fight off sleep. Dr. Rivera gently prodded Raul to lay his head on his lap and use it as a pillow. Within seconds Raul fell asleep.

The sun and air had the opposite effect on Dr. Rivera. His fatigue disappeared. Momentary enthusiasm filled his head with hopeful visions and made his heart euphoric. He looked down onto the faces of his sleeping children. Fortune had given them to him. He gave them life; in return they made his life worth living. He looked up toward the clear sky.

They passed a part of the California countryside ravaged by clearcut logging that wreaked havoc with the primeval forest. Once virgin giant oaks had been replaced with muddy rain-soaked tree stump hillsides that looked to him like they were crying out in pain.

A seed had been planted in Dr. Rivera when his mother died, and had turned into a goliath, impatient yearning that had become profound with his wife's death. He'd suppressed this dark obsession in the mad rush to leave Spain and in the daily care of the children on the ship. It resurfaced when his eyes witnessed this barren countryside. His adrenaline fueled euphoria evaporated and was replaced with a haunting despair. It lay hidden deep inside the crevasses of his brain; when it came out, it felt like a dull knife was stuck in his heart making it bleed until it was empty. He wondered how long this darkness would last.

Further up the trail the majestic beauty of the countryside became more prevalent. Golden grasses waved in an almost constant breeze, with amber to emerald green leaved trees in the distance. Dr. Rivera's moment of euphoria returned, only this time tainted with an equal amount of sorrow. Time passed by slowly, giving Dr. Rivera too much time to think.

By the time they reached Sonoma a clear, dark sky sparkled with thousands of stars.

***

Dr. Rivera noticed a small section of crumbling adobe wall, not knowing it was left from the mission San Francisco Solano. A vestige of Spain and the Catholic Church's mission system to further their empire, it had been physically built by the natives in brutal servitude. General Mariano Vallejo claimed the land as his own, adding to his already formidable property, and founded the pueblo Sonoma. His brother Salvador Vallejo received a large piece of the Napa Valley, and their friend Don Carlos Delgado increased the property he had inherited from his uncle. When the United States became victorious in the Mexican-American War, Vallejo was temporarily jailed and his estate pillaged. As a ploy, he invited Belgian-born Reverend John L. Ver Mehr to come and use his home, La Casa Grande, as a girls' preparatory school.

One of Vallejo's requests was that his friend Don Carlos Delgado's sister Consuelo Delgado become a charge for the girls. This request would pay the debt of thanks he owed Delgado for helping him persuade the Californios to accept the change in government.

A half mile out of town, Dr. Rivera reached up and pulled on the heavy iron bell next to the wooden entrance door of General Mariano Vallejo's Gothic Revival home. A deafening tone rang from the bell, a relic of the Russian traders, and Dr. Rivera stepped back to cover his ears. The sound woke the children in a start. Angeles began to cry and call out for her father. A small window in the wooden door opened and a man's chubby face appeared. Cautiously the face peered out into the darkness trying to make out who was ringing the bell.

"State your business," was defensively growled at Dr. Rivera.

"I apologize for the late hour. I am Dr. Dante Rivera, come in response to Salvador Mariano's advertised request for a doctor. It was stated that I contact General Mariano in Sonoma when I arrived. We have come a long way from Spain and my children are very tired."

"I see you are not alone. Come 'round to the back, so I can let you in. Come quickly. The general and his family are asleep."

The small window slammed shut.

The caravan moved around to the side where a barn stood. As they reached the back, the small man struggled to open one of the massive barn doors. One man got off his wagon and shoved the door letting momentum take over. The nervous little man leaped onto the door as it swung free and rode it with one leg out until it came to a quiet rest on a large rock placed next to the wall.

"Señor Vallejo requires quiet at night," said the little man.

The buggy and two wagons pulled up into the barn.

Chubby little Rickie called Dr. Rivera to follow him up a set of stairs that led to the barn's loft. The little man strained with each step of the steep staircase. Holding his candle high to give off enough light, he waddled ahead of the Rivera family. With his free hand, Dr. Rivera pulled Angeles up onto each new stair like it was a game. Raul, ahead of them, was guided by his father as he climbed the stairs slowly on his hands and knees.

The interior passageway was long, dark, and austere. Angeles held her doll and father's hand tightly while Raul grabbed his father's coattail. Dr. Rivera carried two leather satchels, one that contained his doctor's equipment, the other, which was strapped around his shoulder, contained various sundries for the night.

The door hinge screeched as it opened. The loft room, occasionally used by travelers, hadn't been occupied in months.

The candle Rickie held lit the room creating strange elongated shadows on the unadorned walls. A rudimentary cross with a crucified Jesus hung over a crudely made wooden bed with a hard straw mattress. A pine table, chair, and one small cot occupied the rest of the room leaving little area to walk around in. On top of the table sat an oil lamp, an aged white pitcher, and a washbowl with fine spiderweb cracks running through it. On the floor next to the bed was a tin chamber pot. Above the bed was one high-placed window with no curtain. The faint smell of barn animals crept up from below. Rickie took off the glass chimney of the kerosene lamp and lit it with his candle filling the room with a yellow illumination.

"I will bring you water to wash with for tonight. Tomorrow morning we will come get you for breakfast." He grabbed hold of the pitcher and backed out of the room. Raul sat on the cot, his eyes closing, his body swaying back and forth. Before Dr. Rivera could get to him, he fell onto the cot sound asleep. Dr. Rivera covered him with a blanket and attended to Angeles.

"You will sleep with me tonight, Angeles." He pushed the bed against the wall and placed Angeles with her porcelain-head doll on the bed. When he turned around, the door was closing.

"Sleep well," whispered Rickie.

A pitcher filled with rainwater sat on the table. Dr. Rivera poured some water into the bowl and splashed his face. The smell of the rainwater made him feel refreshed. He sat on the bed next to Angeles as she whispered baby talk to her doll. He took off his boots and loosened his belt. He wrapped his left hand around his right wrist and stroked the now prominent bone, visible from weight loss. His stomach growled. Overwhelmed with fatigue and emotion, his eyes watered, and his mind raced. A dizzy spell surfaced.

I have to be strong, I have to persevere, he thought to himself.

"Papa," called out Angeles.

"Go to sleep my darling."

He blew out the light and laid down. Angeles snuggled into her father's back and yawned. Dante's mind raced from one thought to the next. Wide-eyed with anticipation, he knew he would not sleep that night.

A soft hand touched the side of his cheek.

"Are you awake?" she asked

"Yes, where are you?"

"I'm right here with you."

"What was that?" slurred Dr. Rivera.

He shot up in the bed. His wife Catherina stood near the door. A stream of early morning light from the high window settled on the floor in a thin path, and Catherina was walking on it toward him. He lay back down, not knowing if he was awake or asleep. He wondered if his disoriented mind would ever again function normally. Where was he? Slowly his awareness returned. He was in America, in California at Pueblo Sonoma. It was morning, and his children were with him. He opened his eyes again; Catherina was gone.

A firm knock came at the door. Dr. Rivera was sitting on the edge of the bed still fatigued and recovering from his stupor. He forced himself to his feet. His body and head ached. He staggered toward the door, but midway he straightened his body, determined to be presentable by the time he reached it.

Pedro stood at the door with a fresh pitcher of warm water. He was tall, skinny with close-set eyes, and a small nose. His face brightened and his gaze fixed on Dr. Rivera's handsome face. Several of his teeth were missing when he smiled.

"Greetings, I am Pedro. General Vallejo instructed me to tell you breakfast will be ready in half an hour." Pedro bent slightly forward to show his respect. "Here is warm water for you. I will return when you are finished with your grooming and take you to breakfast."

The children never stirred. Dr. Rivera poured warm water into the bowl. A deep, dark depression filled him. He leaned into the bowl and splashed the warm water on his face. His eyes glanced over to his leather satchel. He reached into it and pulled out his shaving kit. His eyes darted around the room. There was no mirror. He unwrapped the kit and pulled out the boar's hair shaving brush. He dipped it into the water and tapped it on the side of the bowl to release excess water.

The bristles moved in a circular motion along the bar of soap creating a frothy lather. He stroked his stubble and covered his face with lather. His hand drifted toward the straight razor strapped into the leather kit. The tip of his finger touched the smooth, sharp steel blade and the deepest of his dark yearnings returned. The doctor closed his eyes and listened to the quiet. His sleeping children's breathing resonated in the room. He concentrated on the sound until it intensified. Raul stirred and rolled over. Angeles baby talked in her sleep. The sound of a flock of singing birds came into his consciousness. Dr. Rivera took a deep breath and exhaled. He picked up the razor and carefully moved the blade along his stubble.

CHAPTER TEN

The Agreement

May 22, 1855

Vallejo took off his wire-rimmed reading glasses and held them up in the air to study the crack on the upper right lens. He leaned his body forward resting his forearms on his desk. Dr. Rivera glanced around the room. Even in the soft light of the room, he noticed things were frayed around the edges.

"My brother only received your letter saying you would accept the post a few days ago. He is still a large land owner in Napa at this time. Who knows what the future holds. Things are in question. We welcome you wholeheartedly, but you must understand this is a remote post. I am familiar with the area where you lived in Spain and want to make you aware your life will be much different here. The house we are providing is not near town but in the district where a doctor is needed, and I have been told it is small and primitive. There is a rudimentary clinic in town, but it is inadequate and too far away in emergencies. If you stay for five years, the property on which the house sits will become yours. It is in the hills with a good amount of acreage. It was donated when the rancher that owned it died. We will provide you with some food until you can set up a proper garden, and there is plenty of game out there. You may charge an appropriate amount for your services, but know most of your patients have little or no money and cannot pay. The town of Napa is substantially growing every year. You've come a long way; I hope it will be worth your while."

General Vallejo pushed the promissory note on his desk toward Dr. Rivera and waited.

"I will make it work," said Dr. Rivera.

"Good."

Vallejo dipped a quill pen in an inkwell and leaned forward over his desk holding the pen out to Dr. Rivera who then signed the note.

"Congratulations, and thank you for accepting the post. My brother, Salvador, will greet you in a few days. In the meantime, I will send Rickie with you to show you the way. He will notify my brother that you are here."

By mid-morning the caravan moved methodically up the old bull trail toward Napa. The lush grapevines on the hillside impressed Dr. Rivera. In the daylight he could marvel at this land. Sun, dry air, and rich volcanic soil hosted the grapes vines, olive and fruit trees. The caravan rambled further up the trail to a valley view that opened up to them as they passed over a ridge. The lush, green land dotted with ranches and cattle grazing between two rivers lifted his spirit.

The sun was well past midday when they came upon a signpost on the trail with a large D painted on it marking the direction toward the Delgado Ranch and town. At a crossing where three paths converged, Rickie pointed to the overgrown path. Their wagon wheels kicked up dust. Impeded by the slow oxen, the horse whinnied in frustration as it tried to pull the buggy up the steep and rutted incline. Halfway up the path in a flat area they passed one of the few remaining mighty oak trees in the area, untouched by the loggers of the 1840s. Dr. Rivera pulled on the reins to stop the horse and studied the grand tree that reminded him of the large oaks of northern Spain. It would become a lasting landmark, a friend for Dr.

Rivera, reminding him of his homeland and how far he had come.

Their excitement faded when the caravan wound to the end of the primitive path and reached a small ramshackle structure cocooned in a small dry ravine behind brambles and overgrown rosebushes. Patches on the roof and large cracks in the walls were visible. Workers had removed the large varmints and traces of their prior residence, but nothing more had been done to the house that was far smaller than Dr. Rivera could have ever imagined.

The three men on the wagons began to unload their possessions. Dr. Rivera stared motionless at the primitive structure while Raul tugged at his father's sleeve.

"Explore around, but don't go too far."

Raul skipped off. Feeling brave, Angeles followed mimicking her big brother's every move the best she could. A disillusioned Dr. Rivera entered the house.

He immediately saw a tar-black, ash-coated potbelly stove with a dilapidated pipe hooked up to a crude defunct chimney of an even more antiquated fireplace. It reminded him of some strange animal, like an albatross with a long neck and squat body. Infested with termites, the mantle above the fireplace was turning to sawdust. A cobweb covered pile of stones and bricks sat in the middle of the hearth, and vines from the outside had worked their way into the firebox through the missing chunks of mortar and stone. Dr. Rivera looked up at the water stained ceiling and then down at the uneven floor where holes were poorly plugged up with paper and covered with squares of scrap wood. The home's three windows had broken or missing panes of glass.

A tiny alcove off to the side, so small only one person could fit, served as a kitchen pantry with a rusted pail for a sink and a rough-hewn wooden shelf holding some chipped fissured bowls and dimpled tin plates. He pushed open the plank door leading out back. Raul and Angeles waved to him as they headed toward a falling down lean-to and a corral of long wooden poles woven into tall uneven posts.

Dr. Rivera called out, "Not too far," and Raul changed his course and headed back up a slight incline toward his father. Angeles followed.

The doctor stood on the remains of the stone patio. A crude outdoor stone oven and fire pit for cooking would be sufficient for the time being. Weeds grew in the cracks between the boards of a wooden table. The well's pump had been jerry-rigged to work. Dr. Rivera primed the pump with a bucket of water left next to it for that purpose and pumped the handle vigorously several times until a thick sepia colored liquid flushed from the pipes followed seconds later by a clear stream of fresh water that flowed free. The doctor cupped his hands, filled them with the clear water, and sampled the cool and pleasant taste. He pumped more water into the bucket and poured it over his head to revive himself. It washed the layer of dust and grime away. The water cooled him and his mood until he looked up at the back façade of the structure. Work would have to start immediately to make it sound enough to live in.

Rickie was sitting in the back of one of the two empty wagons and waved goodbye. The wheels of the two empty wagons made a distinctive crackling, dragging sound as they rolled over the rocks and stones traveling down the dirt path. Blinding memories flooded Dr. Rivera's troubled mind. Their sounds reminded him of the wheels the draft wagon made in the early morning when they carried his wife Catherina to her grave. The cold ripple of death ran down his spine; his body went into a spasm, and his mind once again grew heavy and dark. This last leg of his journey to this small and inhospitable house seemed unbearable—a cruel, odious joke. The infectious laughter of his children brought him back from his emotional stupor. They playfully ran after one another. Having been confined for so long on the ship and travels, they were joyfully expressing their freedom in the open space. Angeles screeched with laughter as she ran after Raul, and then they reversed and Raul chased her until she fell and began to cry. Dr. Rivera scooped her up in his arms and hugged her a little too long. She squirmed to get loose.

That day Dr. Rivera made a solemn promise to the children that with God as his witness, as soon as he could he would build them a suitable house and make their lives better. The children were too young to understand the conviction in their father's voice and too wound up to settle down.

CHAPTER ELEVEN

The Rivera Mansion

Napa, May 1967

Seventy-one-year old Raul Paul Rivera walked up the elegant staircase of the mansion he'd known as home for most of his life. J.B. Muller followed. She grabbed hold of the mahogany hand railing for balance and looked up at the dome ceiling painted as an indigo sky. Reaching the top of the stairs, she thought of the hands that had touched the railing over the years. Her emotions mingled back and forth between excitement and sorrow. The long hallway was lined with several identical hand-carved rosewood doors that led to six bedrooms. She was looking at the long handwoven oriental runner gracing the hall floor when Raul stopped abruptly in front of one of the rosewood doors.

"This is my brother's room. Let me dismiss the nurse before you go in." Raul disappeared behind the door.

Double doors at the end of the hall led to the drama-laden two-bedroom master suite. Both Dante René and Raul Paul were born in the master suite and their mother, Magritte, had died in it. Since their father Gabriel's death, it had not been used. The room where Dante now lay was his childhood room. When he moved back for good during the depression years, he wanted the same room, and it had remained his bedroom all these years since.

She'd only been in the mansion twice many years ago when she was a young woman. Curiosity cajoled her. She'd always wondered and fantasized about what the upstairs was like and couldn't resist walking along the corridor thinking about the past. The large hand-carved doors, identical down to the most minute detail, stood sequentially up and down the corridor seemingly guarding the content of the rooms from harm or invasion like dutiful soldiers. Her eyes traced a long crack in one of the master suite doors. It was the only imperfection on any of them, and she wondered how it had happened.

Halfway down the hall on either side were matching, carved antique Italian side tables with hand blown Venetian glass wall sconces above them. A gigantic stained glass window of grapevines and flowers illuminated the end of the hallway throwing colorful patterns onto the floor and walls. Long celadon colored velvet curtains draped on either side of the window. Next to the double doored master suite was a large glass breakfront filled with several pieces of antique Venetian glass collected by Gabriel Rivera when he visited Europe after his wife's death.

The door to Dante's bedroom opened and Raul waved to J.B. to come in. J.B. walked toward the room, her heart jumping in her chest. She hadn't physically seen her lover in many years. Occasionally she saw his picture in the newspaper when he'd done something remarkable like being honored for one of his many achievements in winemaking or charity works with the hospital. J.B. stood in the doorway looking inside the room. A female nurse gathered up her things and left. J.B. could see the form of a human under a brocade spread in a large mahogany four poster bed. Raul's back was to her and blocked her view of the face in the bed. He leaned down and kissed his brother Dante on the forehead.

"Someone is here to see you."

Raul moved away and Dante's face was revealed. His head turned to watch his brother leave the room and shut the door. Once outside, Raul's face went from a smile to despair knowing he would never see his brother alive again. J.B. moved into Dante's sight and took his hand in hers. His aged, hollow face began to glow, and he seemed suddenly revived. His once intense cobalt blue eyes were dull with a soapy-gray coating, yet with J.B.'s touch the blue became more vibrant. A slight pink flushed his sallow-colored cheeks. J.B. sat on the chair next to his bed. She tried to take her hand away from Dante to adjust the chair. He refused to let go.

"All my life I've had to give you up, Juanita. I never will again as long as I'm on this earth. I will not let you go."

His voice was weak, barely audible. J.B leaned into his face and tenderly kissed his lips.

"I love you, my darling Dante. I've always loved you and I always will. I love you today as much as I loved you that summer night when we made love. I will never stop loving you."

She pulled the blanket back to lie down next to his frail body. His once vigorous physique was only a memory. She stroked his salt and pepper hair and nestled her head into his neck. They kissed again and she whispered.

"There's a phantom moon in the sky today just like that summer day."

CHAPTER TWELVE

Under a Phantom Moon

June 4, 1917

Mr. Bonnetia's Model T sputtered down the road in town. A confused Dante sat stoically in the saddle on his horse Starr trying to make sense of what had just happened. The usually placid man had come at him like a hot, stray bullet out of nowhere, piercing his heart and mangling his euphoria.

Dante happened upon him during his customary early morning ride on Starr. He'd stopped Juanita's father who had always been pleasant to him.

"You run after my daughter whose heart you already have broken once and intend to do again. Your intentions are not honorable!"

Mr. Bonnetia vigorously yelled at Dante, shaking his index finger.

"But I love your daughter and want to marry her."

"She's gone, so you can't ruin her life."

Joe Bonnetia drove off.

Starr reared when the tires from Mr. Bonnetia's Model T spun throwing street cinders toward her legs. Dante stroked Starr's neck to calm her down and to clear his confused brain. Mr. Bonnetia had come from the direction of the train station. Dante knew instinctively to race in that direction. He pushed Starr as fast as she would go toward the San Francisco, Napa, and Calistoga Railway train station. The 6:57 a.m. electric railway train headed down the tracks and was picking up speed. It had to be Juanita's. Dante looked at the schedule board. It arrived in Vallejo at 7:26, too far a distance to make, but the train would have to slow up ahead when it reached a steep pass not far from town. Dante pushed Starr toward a treacherous shortcut hoping to make it to the pass at the same time as the train.

When they reached the pass, the train was there. It had slowed down but was picking up speed as it climbed the incline. Dante raced Starr alongside the train looking in each car window for Juanita.

Juanita sat in the third car from the front, her eyes closed, her insides restless. Dante's image filled her every thought. What possessed her to listen to her father? She would get off the train at Vallejo and go back, talk to Dante, and get to the bottom of what was going on. Filled with fanatic energy, Juanita grabbed her bag and headed toward the back of the train. The train made a sudden jerk and Juanita fell forward. She grabbed the back of a seat for balance and glanced out of the window. In the early morning sky, a phantom new moon was visible. Her eyes also caught sight of something moving outside. Dante galloped Starr looking in every window for her. She screamed out his name and drew the attention of the other passengers, but he couldn't hear her. She waved to him, dropped her bag, and ran toward the back looking out of every window watching him until he noticed her. Dante waved back. He pulled on Starr's reins to lag until the train had almost passed and paced the horse alongside the back car. Juanita reached the rear of the train and struggled to open the back door. Starr was even with the platform when Juanita stepped out onto it. Dante dropped the reins and jumped onto the platform. Juanita grabbed him when he almost lost his balance, and they fell onto the platform holding each other in a tight embrace.

"I love you, Juanita. I love you."

Juanita stroked Dante's hair and held his face in her hands.

"Let's never be apart again," said Juanita.

Juanita helped Dante up and they walked inside. His heart raced out of control beating so fast that he collapsed onto the train car floor. Juanita cradled him, holding him close until he caught his breath. The train picked up speed when it reached the crest of the incline. Juanita helped Dante to his feet, and they held each other in their arms as they walked to a seat nearby. Not long after, the train came to a dead stop. The motion of the train prevented them from feeling the minor earthquake. The earthquake caused a large tree to fall on the tracks in front of the train and also damaged the tracks behind the train. The tracks would need to be repaired before the train could move, and there was no telling how long that would take.

Juanita and Dante found a secluded spot at the edge of a meadow just past a group of pines within shouting distance of the passenger car. The train line had provided them with a blanket. They laid it down under an old sheltering tree and talked for hours. Dante assumed his mother was behind what had transpired. Only a day earlier, Mr. Bonnetia had greeted Dante in a welcoming way. This morning his hostility seemed to come out of nowhere.

They decided they would live in New York away from both families. When the tracks were clear, Juanita would continue on to New York and Dante would get off at Vallejo and return to Napa to get his finances together. He would meet Juanita in New York as soon as possible. By nightfall it became clear the train wouldn't be moving until the morning. They decided to stay outside. Dante looked up at the dark sky and counted stars. Juanita rolled toward him and cradled herself into his body. They began to kiss and didn't stop. They would be married soon. They made love for the first time that night, and in the morning under the final phase of the phantom moon, they made love again until the sound of the train's whistle let them know it was ready to move.

Dante got off at Vallejo to take the train back to Napa.

Juanita looked out of her train window at Dante as it moved out of the station. He looked so vulnerable and alone in his crumpled riding clothes, disheveled hair, and day-old beard. She rolled down the window and leaned out, throwing Dante a kiss.

"I'll see you soon my darling in New York," Dante yelled to her. "I love you." He walked beside her passenger car until the train picked up speed, finally sprinting as far as he could go to the end of the platform, watching the train fade into the distance.

The morning before, Starr had stood for a moment watching the train move away with her master on it after he'd leaped off her back. She limped away retracing the path she'd taken with Dante. It took her hours of physical struggle until she reached the Rivera barn at noon. The groom called up to the house with the news of the limping, riderless horse's return and assumed Dante was hurt or dead.

A search party returned to the mansion. The men had been out all night searching for Dante but turned up nothing. Magritte was so distraught she took to her bed with an extra dose of her nerve medication to calm herself. The men took a few hours rest and went out again searching until midday. Gabriel, Grandfather Raul, and the servants returned in the afternoon losing confidence that Dante was alive.

At three Dante arrived at the mansion in a cab and walked through the front door. He had stayed in town to make arrangements before he returned home. The search party was preparing to leave again. Grandfather Raul and Dante commiserated in the vestibule with a lingering hug. Magritte appeared at the top of the stairs. When Dante saw her, he bolted up the stairs. She pretended to faint and had James help her back to her room. She sniffled into her hankie and told Dante how grateful she was that he was alive. They were so worried, and she had been on her knees praying for him. Dante told James to leave, and he locked Magritte's bedroom door. She got into her bed and pulled the covers up to her chin.

"What did you do, Mother?"

Magritte pretended not to know what he was talking about. Dante's wrath grew until she confessed. He told her he loved Juanita and they would be married soon. They were moving to New York to be together. She would attend the wedding and be happy for them, or he would never see her again. She retreated under the covers sobbing. Dante left the room slamming the door shut with such force it put a crack in the rosewood.

Dante was a new person, mature, relaxed, and confident. His world would be a happy one, and his life would be complete with Juanita. He began to put his life in order, to pack his bags while he waited for Juanita's telegram telling him she had arrived safely in New York.

CHAPTER THIRTEEN

Entering Town

Napa, May 28, 1855

D r. Rivera clicked the whip high over the horse's head. The buggy moved smoothly along the trail that lead into town past ranches with orchards of plums, olives, and fields of grain. He moved past the massive iron gate crowned with a decorative letter D denoting the Delgado Ranch's front border that stretched for over a mile from undisturbed grassland to where the river was dammed.

Between the Delgado Ranch and town was a mill. River water poured over the top of a large wheel making it rotate. The steamboat ferry and a small railroad station were upstream, built to provide fresh produce to the forty-niners in the gold fields and to the people of San Francisco. Napa was bustling and still growing from its 1848 founding.

Eight years later the town was made up of forty transitory buildings. The dirt main street was lined with a dry goods store, bank, saloon, hotel, theater, a few homes, and minstrels. A number of horses were tied up to hitching posts as Dr. Rivera rode to the far end of town where a white wooden building with a crude drawing of a caduceus housed the clinic.

He tied his horse to the hitching post in front of the clinic. The horse leaned down lapping up the cool water from the trough as Raul jumped from the buggy and Dr. Rivera lifted Angeles off. The clinic, though remote, needed to be where it was to serve all the ranchers and the gold fields to the north. Good Samaritan George Hern ran the clinic with the help of a handful of native workers. It was an overwhelming task caring for the patients who suffered from head colds to gunshot wounds. The more severe cases were more than George could handle, and these patients usually died. Hern was in the middle of sewing up a cowboy who'd been gored by a bull when Dr. Rivera and the children came in.

Rosa, a full-figured Native American woman who had a severe limp and used a crutch, greeted them. As a child she and her sister were taken in by the last of the Wappo tribe when their parents died from smallpox. Rosa had gotten smallpox which left large scars on her face and body. Though still very young, these scars made her look older. After the tribe died out and to avoid the Indian enslavement of the time, she traveled north to work as a cook at the many gold fields. Rosa stayed in the fields for seven years until one night a drunk white miner broke into her room, raped her, and beat her to near death. Her unconscious and broken body was brought to the clinic in the back of a buckboard wagon. Little could be done. A medicine man brought in by the native workers chanted around her body. Hern deemed it a miracle when she regained consciousness and recovered. Since the incident she walked with a severe limp and required a crutch to lean on. Rosa, never wanting to return to the gold fields, went to live with her sister and brother-in-law in the hills not far from the land Dr. Rivera had just moved onto. When that didn't work out, she went back to the clinic to live and work there. Despite her overwhelming disfigurements the children took to Rosa.

On the days Dr. Rivera was at the clinic, Rosa watched Raul and Angeles. In time she felt comfortable enough to show Dr. Rivera her leg. The skin had a bad ulceration where the bone had protruded and it had never been properly set. Dr. Rivera told Rosa he could heal it by resetting the bone.

Rosa laid on the table, strapped down so she wouldn't move. Dr. Rivera poured a small amount of chloroform on a rag and placed it on Rosa's face, barely phasing her. He cut open the skin, removed the ulcerated flesh, and cut the poorly healed leg bone in two so it could knit back together. With one swift motion, Dr. Rivera snapped the two pieces of bone into place and sewed the two flaps of skin back together. Rosa barely winced from the excruciating pain. He cleaned the wound and made a cast for the leg by placing splints on either side and wrapped it mummy style with clean cotton rags. When she healed, she walked with only a slight limp.

Word spread of the doctor's talent, and people, even skeptics, came from miles around to be healed by the miracle doctor. With Dr. Rivera's role as a doctor growing, it was becoming difficult to take the children with him when he did his rounds outside of the clinic. The grateful Rosa offered to take care of the children for him full-time. She moved back in with her sister and traveled to Dr. Rivera's every day by mule.

CHAPTER FOURTEEN

At First Sight

The Delgado Ranch, November 1857

Dr. Dante Rivera adjusted himself in the saddle. It was an unusually warm day, and the fine riding clothes he'd decided to wear for his business visit with rancher Don Carlos Delgado made him uncomfortable. In the distance he spotted the iron arched gate with a large D at the top and the long dirt path that led to the hacienda. The ornate, iconic D was now a familiar landmark for the doctor. He had seen it many times but had never been further into the ranch than the gate. He pulled on the reins of his roan horse to direct her through the iron archway and down the dusty path. To take his mind off his discomfort, the doctor mulled over in his head what he was going to say to Don Carlos Delgado. He'd only met the man on a few occasions.

Dr. Rivera had sent Don Carlos a note a week earlier congratulating him on his prestigious congressional appointment and asked if he could talk to him about some business before he left for Washington. Dr. Rivera wanted to buy a few head of cattle, a way to offset some of his expenses. He received a welcoming response in return. For Don Carlos, who possessed one of the largest herds in Northern California, selling a few head of cattle to the young doctor would be an act of goodwill. Don Carlos Delgado would soon leave for

Washington, D.C. as the newly appointed congressman from the eight-year-old state of California after the untimely death of his predecessor, and he appreciated all that Dr. Rivera had done for the Napa Valley in the year and a half he'd been there.

Dr. Rivera wrapped his long muscular legs tightly around his horse and stood up in the saddle's stirrups to see how far away he was to the hacienda. It still wasn't in sight. It was set far back from the road on its huge ten thousand acres of ranch. He sat back down and nervously pulled his wide-brimmed straw hat off to smooth back his long blue-black ponytail with his hand. He took a handkerchief from his white linen vest pocket to wipe the glistening sweat from his forehead before placing his hat back on his head. It seemed an eternity until his blue eyes set on a vision of the beautiful white adobe ranch house in the distance. Wisteria and bougainvillea mingled together covering the top of a pergola that straddled the path. Large California holly bushes graced both sides. Dr. Rivera surreptitiously plucked a piece of red berry-laden holly and placed it in a buttonhole of his vest. He rolled down the sleeves of his shirt and buttoned up the front, one shy of his neck. Noticing some dust on his boots, he reached down and brushed them off. The high riding boots were a payment for services rendered to an actor in a traveling play. He pulled out his watch from the designated pocket of his linen vest to check the time when a thought occurred to him. It was almost four o'clock. If Don Carlos Delgado partook in a siesta, it would be over.

Dr. Rivera had made his good mark both as a doctor and leader in the community since he'd been in the Napa Valley which left a sweet residual taste of freedom in his mouth. He missed his country and still mourned his dead wife Catherina, but his two children were safe and that's what was most important. This new country had welcomed him, and he had expanded the value of the property Vallejo assigned to him to a modest degree. Being a doctor was a noble profession but not very lucrative. He would have to find other means to financially secure his children's future. Raising a few head of cattle each year would be a start.

Don Carlos Delgado awoke from his siesta and drew open the heavy dark drapes and window to let in the cooler afternoon air. The grandfather clock's pendulum swung back and forth and had only moments earlier struck four. Near the far wall was the fainting couch he used for his midday nap. He stretched his arms up and his shoulders back and gave out a big yawn while walking over to his desk to light the two matching brass kerosene lamps. They spilled out a warm amber light onto the smooth walls and low-beamed ceiling in his den and private sanctuary. He placed thin wire-rimmed reading glasses on his face. His hand reached out, playfully spinning the world globe next to his desk while he consulted his daily planner to see what he'd planned for the afternoon. Oh, yes, he thought, the young doctor is coming. Two oversized chamois-colored suede high-backed wing chairs sat in front of his desk.

Don Carlos closed the book he'd been reading on politics that he considered a private affair and placed it in a drawer of the desk. He walked past the bookcases filled with volume after volume of books he'd read and unconsciously ran his hand over the smooth white adobe wall, looking through the open curtained window to see a rider approaching.

Juanita, Don Carlos' fifteen-year-old daughter, held her little dog Buttons, a present from her Aunt Alicia and Uncle Ferdinand for her quinceañera. The dog playfully pulled at the clover green hair ribbon that hung down from Juanita's hair until it loosened enough for the jet-black ringlets to fall around her shoulders. As she fussed with her hair, Buttons reached up and grabbed hold of a shell button on the front of her emerald green satin blouse and yanked it hard enough to pull it off. Juanita reached into the little dog's mouth to retrieve the button before he swallowed it.

"Perrito malo!"

Juanita held on tightly to the squirming dog pretending to scold him and placed him on the bed with a toy to distract him while she changed her top.

She closed the door of her closet filled with beautiful clothing. The clothes were a way for her father to spoil his only daughter and to make up for the loss of her mother when she was very young. She placed the damaged blouse on a chair with the button for her servant Huan to sew it back on. Holding the cherry red blouse up to her body, she looked in the mirror to see if it went with her green plaid skirt. A strange visceral feeling came over her, drawing her to the bedroom window that had a clear view of the front entrance to the adobe hacienda and the path leading up to it. She pushed the French lace curtain aside and looked down toward the walkway. A stranger approached on horseback. Juanita knew the regular visitors by sight; this one she'd never seen before. Don Carlos stepped down off the stone steps and welcomed him. They spoke for a moment before the man swung his leg over his horse and slid down. When he removed his straw hat that covered his face, Juanita gasped.

He was perhaps the most handsome and eloquent man she'd ever seen. His tall, slender, well-formed physique moved with a graceful gait. His fine riding clothes were different from those of the cowboys she knew. He looked up toward her window causing her to jump back when she realized she was standing in the window in her camisole.

Juanita quickly put on her red blouse. She checked her face in her hand mirror and pinched her cheeks for color before walking out onto the hallway's upper landing. Buttons followed. She was about to come down the stairs to make a grand entrance when the front door opened and her father and the man entered. Juanita grabbed Buttons and made herself small by sitting on the step close to the railing. The deep vibration of a man's voice echoed through the hall and up the staircase.

"Please Dr. Rivera, come into my den," said her father.

Juanita managed to gain enough courage to stand and was about to walk down the stairs when the two men went into Don Carlos' den and shut the door. She walked down a few more steps before sitting down and hanging onto the banister. Her eyes closed and her imagination took over. She would wait until the door opened again, so she could float down the stairs and meet this handsome man. His touch would make her swoon, and he would sweep her up in his arms and carry her upstairs to her room, falling madly in love with her on the way.

Some time went by before the door opened again. Juanita tried to get up but fear got the best of her and prevented her from moving. As the two men walked toward the front door, they exchanged a few words before going outside. Juanita rushed down the stairs and into her father's den.

She touched the back of the suede high-backed chair to feel the warmth left by Dr. Rivera's body. Sitting down in the chair, she absorbed as much of his energy as she could. The slight smell of his bay rum fragrance and his horse lingered. She ran her hands over the soft suede arms of the chair and down its sides into the chair's crevasse finding the black ribbon the doctor used to tie back his hair along with a few long black hairs. It was more than she could have hoped for. The chair seemed to engulf her in fantasy. This was the handsome doctor the women of the valley chattered about. A widower with two children who moved to the valley and had made his mark as a doctor and humanitarian. A man who managed to take a rundown property and turn it into a showcase. When he first arrived in the Napa Valley, it was rumored that he was scrawny, but he had grown more handsome and vigorous since then.

Juanita closed her eyes and sighed. Her juvenile imagination became more fertile with thoughts of the doctor. In the quiet of Don Carlos' den, she heard their voices outside. The doctor was still talking to her father. She tiptoed to the open window and hid behind the heavy drape. The handsome doctor stood inches away. She wanted to reach out and touch him. When his chestnut roan nuzzled its head into the doctor's chest, a pang of jealousy ran through Juanita. The two men were discussing politics and Don Carlos' imminent departure for Washington when Dr. Rivera pushed his long hair to the side and noticed that his hair ribbon had fallen off. He turned to the side looking directly at the window. Juanita held her breath. The bushes camouflaged her enough for him not to see her. Don Carlos asked if he'd like to return to his study to search for the hair ribbon. Juanita stood frozen expecting to get caught.

"No need," said the doctor, "it was only a ribbon."

He shook hands with Don Carlos and put on his straw hat. With one elegant leap, he mounted his horse wrapping his long legs around her and nodded to Don Carlos as he rode away. Don Carlos walked a few steps out into the yard before heading back to the hacienda.

Juanita skirted out of the den and left the door ajar, so her father wouldn't hear it shut. Buttons was waiting faithfully on the other side. Juanita scooped him up and bounded up the stairs breathless and light-headed to her room.

Buttons wiggled out of her arms and landed softly on the floor running to his toys. Juanita sat down at her dressing table and looked into her hand mirror. With trembling hands she pressed the black ribbon to her cheek. She removed the gold locket she wore around her neck and placed the few strands of black hair that belonged to Dr. Rivera inside and slipped off the gold chain replacing it with the black ribbon. She put it around her neck. Her heart fluttered and her hands still trembled. She looked into her hand mirror again. This time to study the locket and black ribbon around her neck. Her cheeks flushed. She looked at the long sausage curls in her hair, a style she'd worn since childhood. It was time for a change. She picked up her hair brush and ran the soft bristles of the brush through her hair for one hundred strokes changing her little girl hairstyle to one with more mature waves.

CHAPTER FIFTEEN

Chance Meeting

Napa, November 1857

The Bear Flag Revolt of 1846 stripped General Mariano Vallejo of a great deal of wealth and power, so in November of 1857 he found a small victory. His suggestion was accepted to appoint Don Carlos Delgado as representative for the people of Northern California in Washington after the untimely death of his predecessor. Don Carlos was considered to be a proper man with an impeccable reputation. He would represent them with their best interests at heart. For far too long the West had been thought of as filled with savages, degenerates, and gold hunters. Don Carlos Delgado was a well-read, soft spoken, refined, wealthy entrepreneur of Latino background—a rarity in Washington. His convincing arguments and smooth tongue had, in the past, calmed the nerves and squelched disputes between fellow ranchers, both Latinos and gringos. In his absence, his eldest son Eduardo would take over running the business of the ranch. His son Emanuel would take care of the hands-on day to day animal husbandry. His young daughter Juanita would be sent to live at the girls' preparatory school in Sonoma where her Aunt Consuelo was a charge and could watch over her to keep her safe and pure for her future husband.

Don Carlos would leave for Washington in two days. To get there, he would first have to go to San Francisco. From there he would board a steamer to Panama, take a train across Panama to catch another steamer to Annapolis, and in Maryland a coach to Washington. The newly finished train across Panama cut the amount of time required to travel coast to coast by close to two-thirds making the trip from west to east coast take between two to three weeks.

Juanita helped Huan close the overly full round-top trunk they'd finished packing. Reverend Wilson, who now ran the school, had agreed to let her bring her dog Buttons with her. Buttons ran ahead down the hacienda's staircase; Juanita lagged behind. She looked around the room that had been her life since birth. She'd never been away from the ranch except once when, as a child, she tried to stay a few days with her Aunt Alicia and Uncle Ferdinand. That experience proved a disaster; she cried until she returned home the next day. She was a young woman now, and with her father leaving for Washington, there was no choice. Two of the ranch hands carried the heavy trunk down the stairs. Juanita took one last look before shutting the door on her childhood. Huan carried the carpetbag filled with Juanita's personal things, her jewelry, a small portrait of her dead mother, and her diary. They walked down the staircase.

"I'll miss your wedding, Huan," said Juanita.

Huan, Juanita's Chinese servant and friend since childhood, sniffled. Don Carlos hired Huan's mother, Mai, to be his housekeeper when Juanita was five. Huan played with the lonely master's daughter until Juanita was ten when Huan became Juanita's maid.

Fourteen-year-old Huan stroked her swollen baby belly under her full shift dress.

"Yes, Señorita Juanita, you will be gone."

"Did I see your future husband here the other day?"

Huan lowered her head, her body began to sway.

"Huan, what's wrong?" Juanita grabbed Huan's arm and sat her on the steps. When she placed her arm around Huan, a wall of tears fell from Huan's eyes.

"Tell me Huan, what is it?"

"I do not love that old ugly man they have chosen for me to marry. He is not the father, he is…"

Huan's mother came out of the kitchen at that moment and looked up at her daughter. Huan clenched her jaw so tightly Juanita could hear it click shut.

"I can talk to my father on your behalf," said Juanita.

"No!" protested Huan as she looked down toward her mother. "I will tolerate my marriage and have my baby. I will be here no more."

Huan wiped away her tears with the sleeve of her dress. Mai was about to walk up to them when the front door opened. Don Carlos, Emanuel, and Eduardo came in. Mai silently returned to the kitchen.

"Say nothing, please missy Juanita. I be fine. I do not want to get anyone in trouble," Huan whispered as she grabbed hold of the handle of the carpetbag and maneuvered down the stairs past the men and out the door.

"Mi niña querida," said Don Carlos. "The carriage is ready. Your aunt is waiting anxiously to get back to the school."

Outside Juanita called to Buttons. When he finished his business, he ran into her arms A wave of nostalgia rippled through her.

"I will miss you and pray for you, papá."

"Come, come child. You must get used to being away from me. Two years will fly by. Come niña, no time to waste, you have a long journey. If you hurry, you can make it before dark."

Juanita hugged and kissed her father. She gave each brother a kiss on the cheek, and Don Carlos helped her into the carriage. Aunt Consuelo waved goodbye when the carriage pulled away from the house. The carriage passed the bougainvillea and wisteria-covered pergola and along the rosebush-lined borders down the long dirt path to the massive iron gate crowned with a D. Juanita never looked back or waved good-bye. Her eyes were swimming with tears. At this tender age, she had the body of a woman and the heart of a child.

The trail ran along the back side of Napa with the Napa River in the distance. Juanita had regained her composure but still had red eyes and a runny nose as she took out a lace-trimmed handkerchief. The trail meandered by the pass where a sign for Dr. Rivera pointed to one of the paths. It had been a week since she first saw the handsome doctor.

She turned her head to look up the path hoping that maybe he might be traveling down it. As the carriage moved ahead her position became uncomfortable. She continued to look in the path's direction until it was so physically strain-ing she couldn't stand it anymore. She turned around to look forward. There before her on horseback sat Dr. Rivera waiting for the carriage to move past. He'd removed his hat. Dr. Rivera was now inches away from her and virtually face to face. He gave a slight bow, leaning forward and resting his forearms on the horn of his saddle. She raised a gloved hand to her face covering her mouth as if to stop herself from speaking.

"Good day. Is this not the carriage of Don Carlos Del-gado?" inquired Dr. Rivera.

Juanita tried to talk, but nothing came out. Buttons barked and wagged his tail.

"Such a cute dog, my lady."

Juanita tried to respond again. Nothing came out. Aunt Consuelo responded.

"Thank you, yes, this is the carriage of my brother Don Carlos Delgado."

"Yes, I noticed this handsome carriage when it was re-cently delivered in town. Please extend my regards to Don Carlos and congratulations again on the appointment. Have a safe journey."

Dr. Rivera tipped his hat in his hand before placing it back on his head and riding away. Juanita turned to watch him ride up the path to his ranch.

When they reached Sonoma, the sun was setting. A rosy-violet colored haze haloed the town. Juanita had been silent most of the trip. Since the encounter with Dr. Rivera, her mind danced from one adolescent fantasy to another. It was in the middle of one of her fantasies that the reality of her future life at the school hit her. At the ranch she was protected and sheltered but free to be herself. Here under her aunt's charge, the austere conditions at the preparatory school would be restrictive. She would have to survive this for the next two years.

CHAPTER SIXTEEN

Consuelo

Sonoma, March 1858

Aunt Consuelo Delgado looked at her reflected image in the waters of the town plaza fountain. She reached her hand to her cheek and felt the wrinkles on her face. She thought about her faded youth. She'd been away from her family in Mexico City for over twenty years—years that eventually took away the pain she'd experienced in her earlier life and most of the joy. As a young woman of Juanita's age, she'd been flighty, high-strung, and vivaciously charming. In the year since Juanita came to live at the school, memories from Consuelo's youth resurfaced in her mind and her resentments grew.

She grew up in Mexico City as the youngest child in the Delgado family. She could barely remember when her big brother Don Carlos left or when he lived there. She had many suitors vying for her attention when she came of age, unlike Juanita who'd lived in a sheltered rustic environment.

Her family survived the war with Spain and the cholera epidemic. They would not have survived the shame she would have brought upon them, unlike the situation her brother had been in.

Her brother Don Carlos' problem was solved by leaving Mexico and beginning a new life in California on land left to him by a dead uncle. Don Carlos had killed a man. It was a stupid mistake; Don Carlos thought the man was threatening his life. They'd quarreled over a mundane thing during the day. When the man arrived that night in front of the Delgado villa and reached in his pocket, Don Carlos shot his pistol first, right into the man's heart. When he examined the body, he expected to find a gun in the dead man's hand—instead there was a letter of apology. Don Carlos' father insisted they tell no one. They wrapped the body up in cloth and took it out to a swamp, weighing it down with rocks. The body sank to the bottom. No one ever found it, but to be safe Don Carlos left town.

The story for Consuelo was quite different. She had many suitors, but the one she fell in love with was a young soldier. Her father had arranged a marriage for her with an older, established man. She ran off with the soldier to the hills around Mexico City the night before her arranged marriage was to take place. They rode into the high chaparrals and that night they made love. In the morning when Consuelo awoke, her lover was gone along with all of her money and jewelry. She wandered around in the hills for days before stumbling upon a tribe of natives who took her in and fed and cared for her until she was well enough to return to her family.

The arranged marriage was over, and no other appropriate suitor came around. Soon it was obvious she was pregnant. She was shipped off to a nunnery where she had a miscarriage. She suffered from a deep depression and tried to kill herself twice. She stayed at the nunnery having no other place to go. Years passed—Consuelo survived in a life of fantasy and hope, but she was being pushed to give herself to God and become a nun. The situation became more problematic every day until she felt she no longer had any other choice. Her heart told her no. She wrote to her brother Don Carlos who arranged for her to have a position at the private girl's school in Sonoma where she would be safe. As it turned out, life at the girls' school was no better than the convent. She was trapped.

At the girls school, she met Sarah Frank who came from Germany to teach language at the school when Reverend Ver Mehr and his wife could no longer tolerate being in Sonoma after losing four of their children to diphtheria. At first she met with Consuelo in private to help her with her English. Some of the English-speaking girls had complained they couldn't communicate with her. The two women bonded, enjoying each other's company. After years of depression, pain, and prayer, Consuelo gave herself to Sarah, and they became secret lovers.

Consuelo took a deep breath while looking in the waters of the fountain at her aging face and came out of her moment of vanity when she heard Sarah calling her. Sarah had finished shopping and it was time to return to the school.

In the first months, Aunt Consuelo could hear through the thin walls as Juanita cried herself to sleep. The other girls who attended the school hovered together in their own groups. None accepted Juanita, perhaps because none liked her aunt. They whispered to one another about the two women's close relationship. They were jealous of Juanita's wealth, beautiful clothes, and her blossoming beauty. The older woman showed no compassion for her niece and turned a deaf ear toward the wall. Unlike Consuelo, Juanita had a future ahead of her, one with a husband, a family, and possible happiness. Aunt Consuelo was resentful of her responsibility to keep her niece safe and pure and would not coddle her. No one knew better the consequences of a physical impropriety than the older, egotistical aunt. Having her niece so close destroyed her private time spent with Sarah which angered Consuelo.

Juanita adjusted to her life at the school by reading, making lace, and drawing. Her aunt insisted she pray in a chapel each day, a form of punishment she learned at the nunnery. Juanita did it with an occasional protest when she was deep into a book or drawing. This would not be her life forever. She waited for something to change.

CHAPTER SEVENTEEN

Trip to Sonoma

Napa, 1858

D r. Rivera drew in a long, deep breath. This was the first time using his lightweight buggy. He was enjoying a newfound prosperity in his adopted country. The cattle he'd purchased from Don Carlos Delgado had fattened up and would go to market soon giving him a handsome profit. The breeders that remained would do their job and produce several offspring. His practice was flourishing. One frequent patient owned the feed mill and paid in grain, and others paid in eggs, hens, or with their labor. The completed house that Dr. Rivera had promised his children now allowed him to have an office there as well in addition to the town clinic. Rosa had worked out. The children loved her, and she proved to be a great cook and housekeeper. Dr. Rivera had a room built off the kitchen for Rosa so she could live there. The children were growing and in need of better schooling. The doctor was too busy for that, and since Rosa was not educated and the school in town was too great a distance for his young children, the solution was to find a governess.

Memories of Spain and their mother faded into dreamlike images for Angeles and Raul Cristoval. Raul's image of his mother came freely to him, an angelic interpretation based on the portrait of her that hung over the mantel in the great room of their home and his father's description. For Angeles her mother was an angel with beautiful golden wings and a white silky robe. Her hair was long and flowing, and sometimes at night when Angeles was sleeping, her mother would come into her room and tuck her in.

Dr. Rivera cracked the whip high over the head of his Morgan horse, Patty. Raul and Angeles squealed with delight at Patty's fast pace. Their excitement was enhanced by their father's promise that the trip would end at Albert's Dry Goods Store where each one could pick out a present, but first Dr. Rivera had business in Sonoma with the Vallejo Brothers. It would be a full two-day adventure for Raul and Angeles who'd been cooped up too long at the newly named Mighty Oak Ranch.

At almost four years old, Angeles insisted that Rosa set her hair in rags for her big outing, giving her hair fashionable long sausage curls like she'd recently seen in a catalog. Her dress was a frilly one. Her long dark lashes curled over her green eyes, and her cheeks were filled with a warm pink hue. Raul teased his sister by pulling at her long curls that tossed about with the bounce of the buggy. Raul was a full head taller from the past year. The arms of his jacket that last year hung over his hands now fit him perfectly. All his chestnut curls were gone. Instead he sported new short-cropped hair. His blue eyes sparkled as he flicked at Angeles' curls until her strong protests brought their father into the game. One firm *no* from Dr. Rivera was enough to make Raul stop.

At noon the horse slowed to a ramble. Dr. Rivera guided his buggy through Sonoma. He tied Patty to the rail in front of General Vallejo's office. Raul and Angeles jumped down from the buggy, exhilarated, chasing one another and skipping around.

"Stay here and play, but don't go far," Dr. Rivera called out to the children as he went into the office to take care of business.

With quill pen in hand General Vallejo scrawled his signature on the well-aged parchment paper deed and handed it to Dr. Rivera.

"I know we originally said you could have the land in five years, but you've proved to be such a valuable person to the community and have improved your property above and beyond anyone's expectations that my brother and I agree the property should be yours. Here is the deed."

An unaccustomed modesty came over Dr. Rivera that brought a small smile to his mute lips and nod to his head.

"How can I thank you for giving me a new life? I could never repay you."

"You already have. I have something else for you. They are said to be originally brought from Spain by Cortez in 1522 and were at the mission. They have yielded both my brother and myself many abundant and exceptional harvests. This is a small gift for someone who has done so much."

He handed Dr. Rivera several grapevine cuttings.

"Thank you so much. You are too generous. I came to Sonoma for another reason, as well. I need a governess for my children. They are so young, and I am too busy to teach them. Perhaps someone from Spain."

"Reverend Wilson at the school may help. He may have a suggestion."

Dr. Rivera had only met Reverend Wilson once before when the minister passed through Napa on his way to St. Helena. Dr. Rivera walked over to the bank of windows in Reverend Wilson's office that faced the courtyard and looked out. He had heard the laughter of his children moments earlier. His eyes scanned the yard. They were not in sight.

"Please excuse me, Reverend, I do not see my children. They are rambunctious today from the trip and this adventure. They seem to have disappeared. No telling where they might have made off to." Dr. Rivera headed for the door.

"I will come with you," said Wilson.

Angeles crouched down behind a mound of hay. She covered her eyes and began to count out her numbers slowly, trying to remember them and not make a mistake. "One, two, five, no, three, five." She peeked between her fingers, watching Raul as she counted.

Raul ran as fast as he could while looking for a place to hide. He spied a wooden gate at the far end of the school courtyard and ran to it. When he tried to open the gate, he found it locked. There was a space at the bottom just large enough for him to crawl under.

She will never find me here, he thought as he shimmied under the wooden gate. His pants got stuck on the bottom of one of the pickets and a piece of fabric ripped off. Raul hesitated for a bit but was too excited to stop and ran down a long walkway and under a vine-covered trellis that led into a small, profusely flowering courtyard with a flowing fountain in the middle. Several statues stood in the garden. As Raul ran, one of the laces on his high boots came undone, and he began to fall. He reached out and grabbed hold of a statue to catch his balance. The statue crashed onto the ground.

Juanita sat on the balcony on the second floor outside of her room reading. Buttons was lying next to her on the bench. Hearing a crash in the courtyard, Buttons ran to the edge of the balcony and began to bark. Angeles followed Raul and shimmied under the gate as he had done and was now standing next to him. She was trying to console Raul who fought back tears over the pain of a skinned knee. Buttons ran down the exterior staircase, into the courtyard, and up to the little boy who sat on the ground and began to lick his face. His tail wagged making the children laugh, and they began petting Buttons. Juanita's view of the events in the courtyard were obscured, but after a few calls to Buttons, he ran back up the stairs followed by Raul and Angeles.

Dr. Rivera and the reverend continued searching for the children. They searched most of the school grounds and were about to go inside when Wilson spotted the small piece of fabric on the bottom of the gate leading to the courtyard.

"Over here, Dr. Rivera. Does this look familiar?"

Reverend Wilson rang the heavy bell outside of the gate and after a few minutes an old hunch-backed native woman opened a small window. When she saw who it was, she opened the gate. They didn't walk very far into the courtyard before hearing the children's laughter. The men stood in the garden looking up toward the sounds of the children.

"Are there two children up there?" The reverend's call up summoned Juanita to the balcony railing.

Her first sight was of Dr. Rivera. In the months since Juanita had been at the school, she'd blossomed into a beautiful, young woman.

"Yes, reverend. They followed Buttons up here."

The two started up the stairs. Juanita smoothed out her gray taffeta skirt and brushed back any loose hair into the tight chignon she wore. She was concerned about being seen so informally without a hat and gloves. She'd recognized the doctor, and her heart fluttered wildly in her chest.

"Señorita Delgado, I see you're entertaining the children we've been looking for," the reverend said, looking down at the guilty Raul.

Angeles ran to her father's arms. "Look, papá, at the little dog. Can we have one?"

"Dr. Dante Rivera, may I introduce Señorita Juanita Delgado."

As was the custom, Dr. Rivera gently took Juanita's hand in his and kissed the back of it.

"A pleasure to meet you."

A shiver ran down Juanita's spine and a blush came to her cheeks. Dr. Rivera hadn't remembered the meeting in the carriage. He held Juanita's hand and looked into her eyes. To her it was a moment of bliss as if the world had stopped.

"Excuse me, but your hand is cool and yet you look flushed. Are you feeling well?"

He put his hand on her chin and moved in closer. She gazed into his cobalt blue eyes. His deep, soothing Castilian-accented voice echoed in her head, and his touch reached every pore in her body. She finally gathered enough composure to respond. "Only a slight cold."

The doctor smiled. "Thank you for caring for my children who should not have wandered off like they did." He patted the children lovingly on their heads and hurried them along.

"Come children, we can explore until dinner. We have to be up early in the morning to finish our journey. You do want a present, don't you?"

"Yes, papá!

Reverend Wilson hesitated while closing the gate. He stopped and looked back toward Juanita.

"Perhaps I can recommend someone to be governess, someone nearby."

"Oh," replied Dr. Rivera.

"First I must write a letter. I hope you can stay for dinner."

Wilson invited Juanita, Aunt Consuelo, and Sarah Frank to have dinner with Dr. Rivera and the children. Juanita was elated. They dined in Wilson's private quarters. At one end of the table, Juanita sat with the children and talked to the doctor while at the other end Reverend and Mrs. Wilson sat with Aunt Consuelo and Sarah Frank, who bent the ear of a very patient minister, mostly with complaints. The evening, for Juanita, flew by. Dr. Rivera and the children enjoyed Juanita's company, and later the children played with Buttons as Juanita and the doctor strolled around the courtyard followed by Aunt Consuelo and Sarah Frank.

The Riveras stayed in the guest quarters at the school that evening, far different from the room over the barn at General Vallejo's when they first arrived from Spain. Dr. Rivera had changed. The gloom he'd felt when they first arrived was gone, replaced with a feeling of prosperity and happiness.

Albert's General Store in Napa served as the post office and pharmacy as well as an emporium with shelves lined
top to bottom with supplies from mining equipment to Chinese silks embroidered with intricate flowers. To the left of
the counter were the toys: wooden and tin soldiers, porcelain
head dolls, leather covered balls with crude bats for a game
called rounders, and other toys. In the center of the store sat a
potbellied stove along with a table and four chairs where a few
of the locals congregated.

Mr. Albert welcomed Dr. Rivera with a gleaming face.
Mr. Albert would discuss with Dr. Rivera his aches and pains,
the ones his wife was tired of hearing about. The Rivera children meanwhile went about their important business of finding the right toy. They were allowed only one. After much
looking through Mr. Albert's entire stock, they found what
they wanted. Angeles chose a new bed for her favorite porcelain head doll, and the conservative Raul decided to add United States Army tin soldiers to his collection, so they could be
victorious over his Spanish soldiers on rainy days.

When Dr. Rivera tired of listening to Mr. Albert's ail-
ments, he turned the conversation to ordering supplies, knowing the only thing Mr. Albert liked more than complaining
was making money.

Later, Dr. Rivera and the children dined at the respect-
able Hotel Marie before returning home. It was more upscale
than the other two hotels in town that still catered to the miners and prostitutes.

At dusk they reached the pass and the trail to the ranch.
Raul looked back toward Sonoma and called out followed by
his sister Angeles, "Good bye little doggy and pretty lady we
met."

Angeles repeated it and asked if they could have a little
doggy like Buttons and could go see the pretty lady sometime
soon. When they reached the mighty oak, Dr. Rivera stopped.

"Ask the oak if you can have your wishes." The children
closed their eyes and whispered to the oak.

Dr. Rivera made a clicking sound, and Patty continued up the hill.

Dr. Rivera had the sloping hillside cleared. There he planted the grapevines General Vallejo had given him, so he could watch them grow from his bedroom window. As his passion for the grapes grew, he would purchase more vines from France until the entire hillside was filled with the vines.

Reverend Wilson wrote to Don Carlos Delgado that perhaps Señorita Delgado could become the governess for Dr. Rivera's children. After all, his ranch was close to the doctor's property and Señorita Delgado had been homesick during her time at the school. If he approved, arrangements could be made for her to return to the Delgado Ranch under the guardianship of her Aunt Consuelo. A letter came two months later from Don Carlos. If she was properly chaperoned by her aunt, it would be fine. It would be beneficial for her at her age and with her sheltered life to get a taste of the world before she married.

Juanita walked slowly across the courtyard to the reverend's office. Her aunt followed behind, not moving as fast as her young niece. Juanita slowed down so her aunt could walk beside her. Not having been to the reverend's quarters since her dinner with Dr. Rivera months earlier, she wondered what this was about. Raindrops from an earlier downpour lingered, dripping methodically from the overhang around the courtyard. A euphoric sadness filled her when she thought about her meeting and dinner with Dr. Rivera.

The reverend's lips were moving but Juanita was so stunned that it took a moment for what he was saying to register. Her father had agreed to let her become the governess to Dr. Rivera's children if she wished. She would return to the Delgado Ranch with her aunt as her guardian. It seemed too perfect, almost serendipitous. Aunt Consuelo was in shock.

The difference in her demeanor was dramatic. The thought of being away from her companion consumed her.

A week later Juanita anxiously waited on the front veranda of the Delgado Ranch for Dr. Rivera's buggy. She couldn't remember the last time she had a full night's sleep, and last night she hadn't slept at all, though she had drifted off a few times. Aunt Consuelo whose age was creeping up on her wasn't sleeping either. With each passing day, her resentment toward her niece grew stronger.

It seemed like an eternity until a cloud of dust appeared in the distance on the path to the hacienda. Juanita's heart raced. She picked up Buttons who sat faithfully next to her and hugged him tightly. She would take him with her, at least for the first day, to help win the children's attention.

"Calm down, child," said Aunt Consuelo, "or your day will be fraught with trouble."

Glee turned to disappointment when Simon, a worker for Dr. Rivera, pulled the open buggy next to the stepping stone and got out. Of course, thought Juanita, Dr. Rivera would be too busy to come himself. She said nothing but Aunt Consuelo noticed the difference in Juanita and couldn't help but gloat a little. She'd suspected the night they had dinner with Dr. Rivera that her niece had a strong liking for the doctor.

The moisture of Juanita's hands soaked through her gloves leaving stains on the palms, and she sat so erect that every bounce of the buggy sent a shock up her spine. Buttons wiggled to get down from her firm grip so she placed him on the floor between her feet and held tightly to his lead. Aunt Consuelo's nimble fingers moved rapidly knitting while she whispered her morning prayers.

CHAPTER EIGHTEEN

The Rivera Ranch

Napa, June 1858

When they approached the vine-covered stone ranch house, Button's tail began to wag like a wind-up toy. Some men were building a low stone wall around the yard with a white trellised wooden gate. The house, though not as imposing as the Delgado Ranch house, had a simple elegance. The children, playing in the yard, ran to greet Juanita. Buttons, unable to contain himself, leaped from the moving carriage and ran to Raul and Angeles who screamed with delight when Buttons jumped into their arms.

Rosa held the door open for Juanita whose arms were full with the first day's lessons for the children. Aunt Consuelo trailed behind. The door to the left led to Dr. Rivera's study where he often saw patients. Rosa directed Juanita to the main living quarters that had a substantial two-story great room where a bank of windows faced west. An ornate, iron-railed staircase sloped up in a semicircle at the far end of the room to the second story. A large chandelier hung down from the middle of the room with a swag tied rope, so it could be lowered to light the candles. A passage way with a rough-hewn log header to the left led to the dining area, breakfast nook, and kitchen. Directly in front was a massive stone fireplace with a two-story chimney. Rosa led Juanita to a playroom filled with toys. The children ran ahead of Juanita as Aunt Consuelo shadowed behind.

"I will come get you when lunch is ready," Rosa said. Her accent was thick and barely understandable. The children danced and played with Buttons and made too much noise for Aunt Consuelo who moments later said, "I will go help the house-keeper." The morning went by quickly. Juanita worked through numbers and the alphabet with the children. In the back of her mind she was waiting for Dr. Rivera who never came. When the door opened again, it was Rosa—lunch was ready.

The children held on to Juanita's hands and pulled her toward the dining room. The narrow, low-ceilinged dining room had a long plank table with twelve cane back chairs and a floor-to-ceiling bank of windows at the far end leading out to a garden veranda. They went through to the breakfast nook which had a round table, four chairs, and one wall of windows making it bright. A discontented Aunt Consuelo was already at the table. Buttons ran to the outside veranda where a bowl of fresh cooked meats awaited him. Aunt Consuelo bowed out of the rest of the day with a bad headache. Simon would take her back to the Delgado Ranch.

After lunch Juanita was led upstairs for siesta. Rosa shooed the children to their rooms and went into the master suite to prepare it for the doctor. Juanita closed the door to her room and listened for the swishing of Rosa's skirt and uneven thump of her feet going down the hall. She peeked out to see Rosa walking down the stairs before quietly sneaking out of her room and crossing the hall to look into the master suite. A four-poster mahogany bed with a canopy showcased the room. A cream-colored crocheted bedspread was pulled back for the afternoon siesta. A matching mahogany highboy dresser and armoire sat on the north wall. The table next to the bed had several books and a kerosene lamp. At the far end of the room were French windows flanked by two upholstered club chairs and a round table covered with several more books. A lamp, a globe of the world, and a telescope on a tripod were next to it.

A temptation too great to resist made Juanita enter the room. She walked over to the bank of windows that had a view down the sloping hillside all the way to the valley. A silk robe hung on a hook behind the door. She pushed her nose into the soft threads of the robe to smell Dr. Rivera. His masculine scent mixed in with the spicy cologne he wore sent her into a fantasy until she heard voices echoing up the staircase and his unmistakable Castilian accent. She could only make out a few words, one was her name. Juanita peeked around the door. She could now hear footsteps coming up the winding staircase. She dashed to her room and quickly shut the door just as Dr. Rivera reached the top of the stairs. He looked in on his sleeping children before going to his room. Juanita pressed her ear up against the door. He was so close she could hear him breathing; then his door closed quietly.

Her heart raced, fueled with adrenaline from almost being caught. She fell back onto the daybed and touched her warm cheeks, closing her eyes to daydream. A knocking sound came into her dream.

"Señorita Delgado?"

Rosa's voice filled Juanita's head.

"Yes, yes, Rosa, what is it?"

"You sleep long time!"

It seemed like minutes ago she'd closed her eyes. She stood up and looked in the small crescent moon-shaped mirror hanging on the wall. Her cheeks were fire red and her hair a mess. She quickly splashed water on her face and pulled out the tortoise hair pins, letting down her long jet-black hair, and twisted it up to redo it, securing the pins back in.

She opened the door with a smile, half expecting to see Dr. Rivera. Rosa was in the master suite straightening the covers of the doctor's bed. Rosa glanced over to Juanita when she heard the door open.

"The doctor, he miss you, wanting to talk to you."

Devastated, her head still swimming in a fog, Juanita walked down the staircase to the playroom. The children were waiting with Buttons and greeted her with a hug. Their little inquisitive faces looked up at her.

At the end of the day, Juanita and the children sang a traditional Spanish folk song. The whistling sound in the middle of the song got Button's attention, and he began to howl whenever he heard it. The children laughed and soon even Juanita was doubled over in laughter that resonated throughout the house.

The playroom door opened and Dr. Rivera walked in. Juanita and the children were sitting on the floor laughing so hard tears rolled down their faces. Dr. Rivera chuckled at the sight of the howling dog. Raul and Angeles ran to their father and hugged him. Juanita covered her face to get control of herself. He reached out his hand to help her up. When she got to her feet, he held on to her hand and kissed the back of it which turned her to melting flesh and rendered her speechless.

"Thank you, Señorita Delgado. I cannot tell you how happy it made me to come home and be greeted with my children's laughter."

The sporadic moments with Dr. Rivera when their paths crossed grew more frequent but remained casual and fleeting. Juanita tried to suppress her feelings for Dr. Rivera. She was only the governess, yet every day she felt more attached to his children.

Aunt Consuelo could not tolerate being away from her companion Sarah Frank and became so ill Eduardo feared for her life and decided it would be best for her to recover back in Sonoma. She would return to the ranch when she felt better.

CHAPTER NINETEEN

Blindfolded Innocence

Napa, June 1915

Dante had been teasing Juanita about a surprise. Now she found herself blindfolded and being led up a hillside by Dante. At the top of the hill they stopped. Juanita heard a slight whooshing sound and inhaled a strange smell. She reached up to pull off the blindfold, but Dante held her hands.

"Not yet my sweet," he whispered.

He picked her up into his arms and placed her in something that rocked. She could hear some whispering; then Dante jumped in and held her tight as they lifted off the ground. Juanita's stomach fluttered and her breath left her for a moment. Dante pulled off the blindfold and when Juanita's eyes focused, they were leaving the earth.

She looked up to see fire shoot through the hole at the bottom of a brightly colored hot air balloon.

"Do you like my hobby, baby," said Dante. Juanita gave out a nervous, laughing scream, "It's wonderful!"

The valley was getting smaller.

"Now look out into the distance as far as you can see. We're free as a bird flying high above the world with no cares, no concerns except to be together," said Dante.

When the basket listed, Juanita grabbed him. He twisted her body around and held on to her tightly. Wind rustled through Juanita's hair, and a few long strands came loose. Dante reached up and pulled the tortoise pins out letting her hair fall loose.

"You're a beautiful, free raven soaring high above it all," said Dante.

Juanita bravely stretched, extending her arms out and up. She felt like a bird with the wind rushing over her. He pulled on a lever, and they moved higher and higher. She could see the entire valley as if it was in miniature: the towns and fields, the lake, the vineyards and orchards, the rivers, their tributaries, and the mountains. She felt like the whole world was opening up to her, as if Dante had given it to her. Warm welcoming winds pushed the balloon high over the land.

The unsettling stillness in the valley caused an unspoken dread about what lie ahead. The rest of the world was at war and much of the country was restless.

The valley protected the lovers allowing them to spend lingering hours together undisturbed. As the summer advanced toward fall, Juanita became increasingly concerned about making a decision. Should she leave Napa to study at the Art Student League in New York, her ambition for as long as she could remember? But now there was Dante, and if she left, she would be leaving the man she loved.

***

The first thing out on the streets of Napa every morning, heralding in a new day, was an old swaybacked dappled work horse with blinders pulling a covered wooden milk wagon with the red and white sign of the company's name, Rose Dairy, painted on the side. A painted rose dotted the *i* in dairy. The horse instinctively knew the house of every paying customer on the route and would stop when he reached each destination.

The first thing Sawyer, the milkman, did when he got on the wagon in the morning was to loosely tie the horse's reins on a side post. He would then rest his head against the post so he could sleep sitting up. His six-year-old son Ned traveled with him and would jump off the wagon and run a bottle of milk up to each milk box on every front porch where the horse stopped. If there was a note inside the milk box for cheese or cream, the boy would run back to the wagon and fetch it. When they reached the center of town, he would run a bottle of milk into the saloon and carry out a bucket of beer filled up to the top with suds running over the side. The boy loved to run his index finger over the top of the bucket to catch the bubbly foam and suck it off his finger before delivering the bucket to his father. When they finished the route, it was time for Ned to go to school.

Next down the streets came the bakery wagon steaming with fresh baked rolls and bread. A line of stray dogs followed the wagon in hopes of an occasional baked good falling out of the back.

Not much later the first ferry from San Francisco docked at the terminal. It carried the morning San Francisco newspapers, letters from the East and various parts of the world, and some sundries the locals had ordered from mail-order catalogs. Seven days a week, inclement weather or shine, a young courier greeted the ferry to pick up and deliver the morning San Francisco newspapers door to door, making his nickel a day.

Lita Nannie was always the first person up in the morning at the Bonnetia household. She was washed and dressed before going down to the kitchen to start breakfast. Her son-in-law was next. Like clockwork Joe Bonnetia walked downstairs at six each morning hungry for breakfast and his mind ravenous for the news. His first stop was the front porch where the early morning *San Francisco Chronicle* had been tossed by the news boy. It was his one luxury in life. He rationalized it as a necessity to teach his high school history students. Having the morning newspaper was a more important priority than having a telephone.

"A telephone is for the rich and foolish," he would say.

Joe grabbed the paper, bread, and milk from the porch on his way to the kitchen. The aroma of frying eggs and bacon led him there. Lita Nannie had finished squeezing the last of the spring season oranges into juice and was placing a pitcher on the table next to a pot of hot, steaming coffee. With a "Good morning, Mother," he handed the milk to her, so she could skim the cream off the top of the bottle for his coffee. Day-old bread was toast for the morning, and the fresh bread was used for lunch sandwiches and for dinner in the evening.

Next Dalila came down the stairs fresh-faced, happy, and ready to greet the day. Her perky morning attitude, though never brought up, annoyed Joe and made him wonder how anyone could be so cheerful first thing in the morning.

Dalila woke Juanita and told her it was time to get ready. Dante was taking her to the Panama-Pacific International Exposition in San Francisco. Juanita had wanted to go to the expo, but the trip was more than she or her family could afford. Her parents agreed to let her go if Lita Nannie would go along as a chaperon. They would spend two days and one night in San Francisco.

Dante drove his father's brand new Locomobile Sportif Model 38 to Juanita's house and parked. He had a silent chuckle thinking about his father driving his Stutz Bearcat for the next few days. It would be their secret. He told his mother he was going to the expo with some friends and did not elaborate on who they were.

By now Lita Nannie sat on her chair in the living room waiting. She was meticulously dressed with her hat and gloves in hand and her valise next to her. She squelched the secret excitement she had about going to the expo, not wanting at her age to appear foolish to the children. With Dante's familiar knock at the front door, Juanita bounded from the kitchen eating toast.

"Who is it?" she mocked through the door.

"The big bad wolf," said Dante.

Juanita opened the door excited and looked around to make sure no one was looking before she gave Dante a sweet morning kiss.

CHAPTER TWENTY

Panama-Pacific International Exposition

San Francisco, June 1915

To celebrate the completion of the Panama Canal, the World's Expo committee selected San Francisco to hold the 1915 World's Fair in its honor. The city's fathers had campaigned vigorously wanting to show the world how San Francisco had rebuilt itself from the 1906 earthquake that had devastated it.

Years of planning gave way to the rise of cool gray ephemeral buildings with brightly colored archways built on the former site of a homeless camp for the victims of the earthquake. The 635 acres on the north shore of the marina area were flanked by the Presidio of San Francisco to its west, the gray waters of the bay to the north and east, and the city to its south.

The morning sun caught the cut-glass facets of the Tower of Jewels that made sparkling light dance on the water. Lita Nannie's big brown eyes showed her joy. She found the fountain at the entrance of the expo spectacular, thinking that the image of it was as phenomenal as any feat of mankind.

They spent the morning in the half-moon shaped Palace of Fine Arts building looking at art until hunger took over. They lunched at the nearby French exhibit and walked through the Japanese garden next to it before returning to the Palace of Fine Arts for the afternoon. Lita Nannie walked slower now, her mind set. She would stay outside near the reflecting lake while the youngsters looked at the art. Finding a spot in a shaded area, she watched women in the latest fashions and remembered as a young girl her closet full of beautiful clothes. She looked down at her ten-year-old dress purchased from a catalog. She'd repaired it several times and only wore it on special occasions. It was the very popular shirtwaist style dress of that season. She had to wait over a month for the dress to arrive, and it was one of the last things she ever bought.

The smell of the sea filled her nostrils, and salt clung to her skin producing a slight stinging memory. It had been a long time since she'd seen her old friend, the bay, and surely these two welcoming signs meant the water wasn't far away.

CHAPTER TWENTY-ONE

Memories

During the years of her troubled life in San Francisco, it had been a comfort for Lita Nannie to come down to the water's edge and look out at the bay. Her ears filled with the soothing sounds of the water lapping against the shore. She sat on a bench and looked out toward Alcatraz Island and in the distance Angel Island. Years ago she and her lover had an unplanned meeting on this very spot, and he told her what little Angel Island meant to him.

Lita Nannie closed her eyes and drifted off. She was young again, and it was 1875. She'd returned to San Francisco to care for her mother-in-law who, after several weeks of illness, had died. Weary and in somewhat fragile health herself, Lita Nannie decided to get some fresh air and walked to the harbor. She walked down the hill toward the waterfront, narrowly dodging one of the new cable cars. She'd heard the clanging bell, but it was an unfamiliar sound and her mind was on other things. She looked out at the bay to contemplate her future. Since she became a widow nine years ago, she'd been living in Napa Valley on a ranch with her three young children. The livelihood of the Delgado Ranch where she, her children, her brother Emanuel, and his wife Esmeralda lived was in jeopardy. First the drought of the 1860s had killed off most of the cattle. When the cattle started to flourish again, there was an outbreak of hoof and mouth disease, and the herd had to be destroyed. They'd barely recovered financially when the 1873 depression hit. Eastern demand for beef was waning. The cost of running the ranch was greater than its profits. Juanita's tormented life with her husband left her with some money that she'd managed to squirrel away, but it was dwindling. She watched the fog roll in over the water and listened to the silence. The cries of a flock of seagulls swelled overhead. A figure of a tall man with a familiar walk came toward her disappearing in and out of the rolling fog. They were almost next to one another when their eyes locked. It had been nine years since their last meeting. Over these years their only connection had been memories and a scant few old love letters they had exchanged years earlier that each would take out periodically in private and reread.

Dr. Dante Rivera—handsomely dressed, now in his late forties, his black hair scattered with shades of gray and all gray at the temples, his thin muscular body sun-kissed tawny from time spent in his maturing vineyards—stood next to her. His intense blue eyes penetrated her. He was in town to raise money for his hospital. His name was known by everyone in the Napa Valley for his good deeds and hard-earned prosperity.

In the valley they lived a few miles apart, yet their paths never crossed. The reversal of their fortune was profound. Dr. Rivera sat down next to Juanita. He took her hand in his and kissed the back. Then he held her hand to his cheek and told her why he'd walked down to the waterfront and of his first sighting of Angel Island as he crossed over the bay from San Francisco heading to Napa when he arrived from Spain.

"Look at you now," she said. "A successful doctor with your own hospital, owner of the Mighty Oak Vineyards. And here am I. The once patrician daughter of the most successful rancher in the valley with callouses on my hands from hard physical work. I don't mind; I love my family."

He kissed the back of her hand again before cradling it between both of his. They sat not speaking, looking out at the harbor like no time had passed and they'd always been together. At their chance meeting nine years earlier, Juanita was married. He'd come to observe the state-of-the-art nursery in San Francisco where she happened to work. Now things had changed. She was a widow, he was in a loveless marriage, and both were adults no longer under the scrutiny of the world.

Dr. Rivera was staying at the newly opened Palace Hotel. In the morning each would return to the valley and resume their normal lives. For tonight their lives were their own and they belonged to one another.

They dined in his hotel suite and agreed to speak only of that day, not the past or the future. For the first time they made love. Both experienced what physical love could be—a passionate, ethereal joining of two people's flesh into a timeless moment. They made love all night long until the unwelcomed first morning light came into their world and made them aware that this coupling would soon end.

Dr. Rivera held Juanita in his arms running his hand over her long neck and kissing her.

He said, "I will love you forever. Through this life and the next and every life after."

Tears formed in Juanita's eyes. She remembered when he asked her to marry him. How cruel life can be.

Juanita boarded the ferry to Napa with an ache in her heart so strong she thought she wouldn't survive it. She waved good-bye to Dr. Rivera who stood on the deck of the ferry terminal. They would see each other only a few more times. Once when they passed one another on the streets of Napa and another time at a political rally. They could only acknowledge each other with a nod and a smile. Juanita Delgado Navarro's children never figured out how or why things got better, but they did. An envelope would arrive for their mother four times a year, at the beginning of each season.

CHAPTER TWENTY-TWO

The Exposition

June 1915

After Juanita and Dante René walked out of the Palace of Fine Arts, Lita Nannie was nowhere to be seen. Panic set in.

Dante walked around one side of the lake, Juanita the other. When he looked back in the distance at Juanita, his heart filled with joy. How lucky he was to have met her, to be with her, to love her, and to have her in his life. Not paying attention, Dante bumped into a woman walking with her children. She nodded to Dante as he apologized not knowing the woman was General Black Jack Pershing's wife and that in a few years General Pershing would change Dante's life forever.

Dante walked over to Juanita who was talking to a woman.

"She said she saw Lita Nannie go toward the water."

A voice in the distance called out her name. She could hear the familiar voice, but she was happy with her lover and didn't want to leave him. The calls came closer, then a hand touched her. She opened her eyes and gasped. Dante stood before her, a mirror image of her lover, his great grandfather. She smiled. Her granddaughter's hand rested on her shoulder.

"We were so worried when we didn't find you. What's the matter, aren't you feeling well?"

"Yes," said Lita Nannie, as she looked up into Dante's deep blue eyes. "Only a slight cold," she said.

The seagulls flocked overhead.

"Come on," said Dante. "My friend has some hot air balloons here, and said I could take both of you up in one. We can be like those gulls and fly."

The three walked away. Lita Nannie looked back toward the water. Her ghost lover stood in the fog smiling at her. "I'll see you soon," she thought.

The balloon floated high above the expo. Lita Nannie held her hands over her eyes sneaking peeks at the land below until she felt comfortable. She looked down toward the fairgrounds and saw what looked like tiny people. The massiveness of the expo and the city of San Francisco lay at their feet. Lita Nannie did not recognize the newly restored city, only the water, Alcatraz Island, and Angel Island, the holder of private memories.

That night they stayed in adjoining rooms at the new Palace Hotel, built to replace the original destroyed in the 1906 earthquake. When Lita Nanny was safely asleep, Juanita slipped out to meet Dante in the dining room for dinner. The two lovers were engrossed in each other's conversation and didn't see Cassandra and her mother come in, but the two women saw them and assumed the worst. Cassandra's mother Willa turned to her, "What a shame that Dante is smitten with such a loose woman who would spend the night at a hotel with him without being married."

***

The next morning Lita Nannie decided to stay in the hotel until the afternoon to rest. The true reason was for her to relive the memories of the evening she spent with her lover. The youngsters could go to the expo on their own.

The amusement section called the Zone was like nothing ever seen before. A seven city-block area at the southeast end of the expo near the Fillmore Street entrance had two fifty-foot replica wooden soldiers standing sentry, flanking either side of the entrance. The Aeroscope, designed and built by Joseph Strauss who later designed the Golden Gate Bridge, was a small two-story structure mounted on the end of a 285-foot swingarm giving the riders an aerial view of the expo and San Francisco.

Hamburgers and hot dogs sizzled on grills, and popcorn and cotton candy on a stick were sold from small push carts—things Juanita and most of the expo visitors had never seen. There was a working model of the Panama Canal, a ride on five acres of land where people sat in chairs on an elevated track that circled a model of the canal and through earphones could hear a description of the canal from a phonograph, a miraculous development in its day. There were also models of the Grand Canyon, Yellowstone Park, Toyland and a submarine ride. Expo goers could see real babies in incubators, freak shows, air shows, demonstrations on art and different crafts, and concerts.

Dante purchased a souvenir display of cut crystal jewels from the Tower of Jewels as a keepsake for Lita Nannie who had so marveled at the tower when she first saw it entering the expo. When he saw a souvenir ring of the expo's seal made of a mostly tin metal, he got it for Juanita. In a mocking but serious way Dante turned to Juanita, fell on one knee, and placed the souvenir ring on her finger, asking her to marry him. Juanita laughed and playfully pulled at his hand to make him get up.

"Come on, Romeo, I want to see the Grand Canyon." She pulled on his hand. He pulled back pretending to struggle with her until he let her pull him up so she could drag him to the ride. They stuck their heads into cutout holes of a mama and papa bear with little bears around them and had their picture taken. They toured the Grand Canyon and the Panama Canal. The last ride was Yellowstone.

In the afternoon they picked up Lita Nannie who loved her gift. They walked around the expo the rest of the day and had dinner at Delmonico's that night. Lita Nannie would talk about the dinner for the rest of her life, sometimes confusing the young Dante with her lover when she retold the story.

They watched the fireworks display at the day's close of the expo before driving back to Napa. When they arrive at the Bonnetia house, Juanita kissed Dante and woke up her grand-mother who was asleep in the back.

"Thank you, Dante. I can't remember having a better time."

In her room that night, Juanita scavenged around in her closet until she found a relatively new cardboard box. She placed the tin ring, some ticket stubs, photographs and pamphlets from the expo in it. She opened the top drawer of her dresser and took out other things. Ticket stubs from the movies, a Valentine from Dante, some love letters. He'd written to her nearly every day since they became a couple. She saved a pink ribbon from a gift Dante gave her to mark their first month anniversary and placed all the things from Dante in the box.

CHAPTER TWENTY-THREE

The Mighty Oak Ranch

Napa, May 30, 1859

Juanita had been governess for almost a year. She gathered up her things in her siesta room to wait for Simon to take her home. She walked back down stairs to say goodbye to the children in the playroom. There was a note with her name on it attached to the playroom door. She studied the hand writing before she opened it.

> *Dear Señorita Delgado,*
>   *It would be our pleasure if you would attend a dinner and party to celebrate Angeles' fifth birthday.*
>   *Yours very truly,*
>   *Dr. Dante Rivera*

She looked closely at the writing and imagined his fingers clutching the fountain pen that wrote it.

The next morning when Simon picked her up a thin, veil of fog covered the low valley. It followed them onto the roads and up into the hills toward the Mighty Oak Ranch. Once they were up the path and at the ranch, the air cleared.

Juanita carried a small, fabric-wrapped present for Angeles in her hands. She purposely wore one of her more elegant dresses, not casual enough for the day but appropriate for the party later. The day flew by for Juanita, and she was too excited to sleep at siesta time. In the afternoon the children practiced a song and dance they'd been working on to be performed after dinner as a surprise for their father. Rosa made tea for Juanita and the children to tide them over until dinner. After tea Juanita took Buttons for a walk. Buttons ran down the side of the hill and disappeared into the fog. There was an uncanny stillness. After a few calls Buttons ran back toward the house shaking off his dewy fur and running to his cushion in the playroom.

Dr. Rivera had taken the buckboard in the morning instead of his horse, so he could pick up a dollhouse for Angeles a carpenter in town had made. Passing the orchards in the valley, he could only see sporadically through the patchy fog. Young leaves, maturing blossoms, and virgin fruit setting covered the trees and vines. The scarlet red blossoms of the pomegranate trees were showy beauty queens through a fine veil of fog.

He'd had a difficult day. An old man had died in his arms. He stayed to console his widow until her daughter arrived. A small boy around Raul's age had fallen out of a tree and banged his head. The father carried the unconscious child into the clinic and asked Dr. Rivera to revive him, something the doctor could not do. The boy was in the care of the native workers at the clinic who prayed and chanted for him. Dr. Rivera hoped he would survive. The warm day was giving way to a cooler night. With the prevailing fog and clouds covering the stars in the sky, it made for an exceptionally dark night.

The children waited and watched for their father by the window, looking at the darkness outside. When they heard the clip clop of the horse and creaking of the wheels on the stones, they ran outside to greet him. Dr. Rivera pulled the buckboard into the barn and made sure the tarp securely covered the dollhouse as the children made their way to the barn.

For dinner they had a freshly killed quail with tender young vegetables from the lower garden roasted in the oven along with a wild rice and nut dressing. There was a sweet cake for dessert.

After dinner in the great room, Dr. Rivera threw a dry log on the fire and methodically stoked it. He watched the flames leap higher. Sparks crackled and spit upward into the chimney, leaving long trails of dark gray streaks when they burned out. He had calmed down now from his sad-filled, weary day. Rosa lit the candles on the cake and carried it into the great room where Angeles eagerly waited to open her gifts. She jumped up and down and clapped as they sang a birthday song to her. Warm amber light from the chandelier danced around with the movement in the room.

Juanita silently motioned for the children to come, and she and the children moved to the clavichord. No one had played it since their mother had died. Juanita lifted the keyboard lid and began to play. Dr. Rivera hearing the keys on the clavichord turned abruptly toward the sound, alarmed at first until the children began to sing. With the second chorus the children danced, and the doctor beamed a smile ear to ear. He asked them to do it again. They did it three times before Angeles begged to open her presents. Dr. Rivera grabbed both his children in his arms and smothered them with kisses. Raul screeched in protest while Angeles loved it and hugged her father back, hanging from around his neck as he carried her over to her gifts.

With each gift Angeles squealed with delight. She received a frilly dress from her father, a hand-drawn picture from Raul, a hand-knitted pair of socks from Rosa, and a book of songs from Juanita. Dr. Rivera excused himself and went outside to the buckboard. He stumbled in the pitch-black night on his way back carrying the dollhouse that made Angeles beside herself with joy.

They sang from Angeles' new songbook until ten when Rosa stuck her head into the great room to tell Dr. Rivera she wanted to go to bed. Adrenaline kept the children awake until sheer exhaustion overtook them, and their eyes began to close. Dr. Rivera threw Raul over his shoulder and carried him upstairs. Juanita carried Angeles in her arms.

Juanita sat on the edge of Angeles' bed looking into the face of the sleeping child when Dr. Rivera came into his daughter's room to kiss her good night. He leaned down over his daughter to kiss her forehead. His body brushed against Juanita.

"We haven't enjoyed ourselves as we have tonight in a long time," whispered Dr. Rivera.

He stood up and reached out his hands to help Juanita up. Her body swung up close to his. They looked into each other's eyes. The doctor leaned into Juanita when a loud knock came from the front door, breaking the moment.

The stableman stood at the front door. "A ranch hand just got back from town and told me the weather in the valley was changing for the worse. If you want to get Miss Delgado home this evening, she should leave immediately." A storm was heading in from the south, probably from over the Pacific, which usually meant heavy rain.

Juanita gathered up Buttons and waited in the semi-dark vestibule with Dr. Rivera for Simon to pull the buggy around. Dr. Rivera helped Juanita wrap her shawl around her shoulders and took her hand in his and kissed the back. He looked intensely at her face. Her heart palpitated. Simon called out that the buggy was ready with Patty, their fastest horse.

Fog from the valley to the pass had been creeping up all day to the Rivera property. At times it was so thick it was impossible to see beyond even a few feet. Dr. Rivera thought of asking Juanita if she would prefer to spend the night but hesitated. His unspoken desire for her could be considered scandalous. Her close proximity was already too much of a temptation. He helped her into the carriage and held onto her hand.

"Be careful, Simon, take your time."

Simon snapped the whip high over Patty's head to encourage her to go faster. Dr. Rivera let go of Juanita's hand as the buggy took off heading down the path and bolted into the night. The light from a small oil lamp attached to the side of the buggy was the last thing Dr. Rivera saw. He stayed outside in the darkness waiting until there was no light and no sound, engrossed in the last few minutes he'd had with Juanita. The winds picked up and began to howl.

The buggy traveled down the path in total darkness. When they reached the pass and headed onto the trail toward town, the fog engulfed them. Juanita could hear Simon make his low clicking sounds, but the fog was so thick the light from the lamp only illuminated his profile enough for her to faintly see him sitting next to her. Juanita's body quaked as thrilling thoughts about her first intimate moments with Dr. Rivera engrossed her. Perhaps he did feel the same toward her as she felt for him. She held Buttons close to her body and wrapped her shawl tightly around them both. Romance filled her mind until the storm replaced it with fear.

Simon pulled on the reins when they reached a steep part in the trail. The thick layer of fog thinned the farther down the trail they traveled until it disappeared, replaced by a fine misty rain that quickly changed into a hard, heavy downpour. Simon clicked for Patty to move faster. Winds moved the rain in a sideways pattern, pelting them with water and spooking Patty. Howling gusts made it difficult for Simon to keep a steady hand on the buggy that swayed at the mercy of the tropical wind. Juanita held Buttons even tighter. The little dog whined and pushed his way deeper under her shawl as the buggy swayed from side to side. Patty picked up speed on the bumpy trail when they reached the flats. Simon clicked his voice to calm Patty as the hard rain continued.

A magnified cracking sound filled the air when a swooping gust of wind sent a large tree branch airborne, landing in front of the horse and spooking her beyond Simon's control. Patty bolted erratically, going one way and then the other. She reared up, thrashing in her harness and took off. Simon yelled to the horse to calm her, but she could hear nothing in her state of fright. She galloped blindly into the pitch-black night, running out of control. Simon stood up cursing her and pulling with all his might on the reins. The horse ignored him, moving faster and veering off the trail onto rough rocky ground heading back toward the ranch. The buggy bounced when it hit a big rock and flew into the air.

Time stopped for Juanita. She held on tightly to Buttons with one hand and to the wet buggy rail with the other until her hand slipped off. Her body soared through the air and landed hard on the ground, her head hitting a rock. Blood mingled with the earth in a stream of rainwater washing down the side of the hill.

Patty's harness broke away from the buggy, but Simon held tightly onto her reins, his body crashing to the rocky ground. His arm was broken with bones protruding through his skin and twigs were impaled in his flesh. Finally he had to let go. Patty galloped back up the hill toward the ranch with the reins and harness dragging behind her.

It was close to midnight when the stableman knocked hard on the ranch house door. He had been asleep when he heard the horse dragging something behind her into the barn.

The stableman and Dr. Rivera saddled up their horses and rode out into the wall of weather. An hour passed as they methodically searched up and down the path to the pass and down toward the trail. The storm was beginning to wane but not the ink-black night. A stooped-over figure walking aimlessly, stumbling on the side of the path caught the stableman's eye. He blew a whistle so the doctor would know. Simon's broken body swayed; he seemed to be searching for something. Dr. Rivera reached them. Simon was disoriented but managed to tell them what happened. He was looking for Juanita and Patty. They wrapped Simon in a blanket and put him on the stableman's horse.

"Take him back, wake up Rosa, and warm him up with whiskey and dry clothes. Have Rosa dress his wounds the best she can until I get back."

The stableman mounted his horse behind Simon who was going in and out of consciousness, his arm so broken it hung limp like a marionette. They took off into the night while Dr. Rivera continued his search for Juanita down to the trail.

He called out Juanita's name. The night echoed it back. His horse stumbled on a piece of broken buggy. Dr. Rivera called out Juanita's name again. Still nothing. He called louder and more often until his voice began to crack, his throat was going numb. He persevered, going off the trail. He called out Juanita's name one more time. This time a sound came back to him. He galloped toward it. The first thing he saw was the outline of a little dog sitting on the ground barking nonstop. He called to Buttons and the dog's tail began to wag. As Dr. Rivera moved closer, he saw Juanita's unconscious body.

He jumped off his horse and knelt down next to her rain-soaked, limp body. There was a large gash on her head and blood puddled on the brown earth. Dr. Rivera felt for a pulse. It was weak but there. When he picked her up to carry her to his horse, it became apparent how frail she had become. He wrapped her in a blanket, placed Buttons in a saddlebag, and cradled Juanita in his arms. With the wind pushing at his back, he rode as fast as humanly possible back to the ranch. Her skin had taken on a pale hue, like fine porcelain. He held her tightly trying to will his body warmth into her and fighting back his strong emotions. Rain and wind persisted. When he reached the confines of the ranch, he yelled out to the stableman who ran out. He helped Dr. Rivera take Juanita off the horse. Buttons ran toward the house, and Dr. Rivera followed carrying Juanita's limp body.

Rosa was pouring the last of the hot water she had heated on the stove into the freestanding iron tub in the kitchen. She pulled the curtain around it and helped Dr. Rivera undress Juanita. Her clothes were soaked, her lips blue. Rosa removed her shoes and stockings while Dr. Rivera attended to the cut on her head. He cleaned it with soap and water several times until all the dirt was removed. When he touched her head, her body cringed from pain. They removed her outer clothes down to her underwear and Dr. Rivera lowered her body into the warm water. Her body shivered and a low moan came from her lips.

Slowly the color returned to her skin, her lips pinked up. Dr. Rivera instructed Rosa to stay with Juanita while he tended to Simon. Rosa had done what she could in cleaning and dressing his wounds, but his arm was broken and hanging out of his skin. Dr. Rivera examined Simon's shoulder and broken arm. He dabbed a bit of chloroform on a rag and placed it for a second on Simon's nose. The semiconscious man passed out totally. Dr. Rivera quickly snapped the arm bone back into place. He felt around Simon's shoulder. The ball socket attaching his arm to his shoulder was out of place. He snapped it back. He revived Simon with smelling salts and placed a makeshift cast on Simon's arm, telling him in the morning he would make a better one. Simon would need rest to heal.

When Dr. Rivera returned to the ranch house, Juanita's face had a rosy glow. He lifted her out of the water. Her wet thin undergarments were transparent. They wrapped her in a blanket, and Dr. Rivera carried her up to the guest room. He told Rosa to bring up a bottle of whiskey. He laid her on the bed and unwrapped her from the blanket. He untied and removed her wet camisole and pantaloons. A creamy color returned to her skin and had replaced the ghost white from before, but despite the warmth an underlying coolness remained. He placed his ear to her bare chest to hear her heart beat. It quickened with the touch of his warm hand. She moved slightly. Dr. Rivera studied her beautiful, still face. He glanced down at her breasts and at her perfectly formed rosebud pink-brown nipples. He longed to kiss them. He heard Rosa's footsteps in the hall and quickly covered Juanita with a blanket and cradled her head in his arms. She poured whiskey into a glass and handed it to Dr. Rivera. He poured a tablespoonful into Juanita's mouth.

"Go to sleep now, Rosa, you've been a great help, but you need your rest."

She hesitated before backing out of the door. Dr. Rivera was alone again with Juanita. He waited until he heard Rosa going down the stairs and her door shut. He poured a bit more whiskey into Juanita's mouth. A slight cough helped it to go down. He laid her back down on the bed. She was magnificent, flawless in face, body, and soul. When he thought he saw her open her eyes, he pulled a chair up next to her bed. He was in love. He knew that now. He was hopelessly and desperately in love. Since the night they had dinner in Sonoma, he'd thought about her. What a fluke when Wilson suggested her to be the governess. The doctor had purposely stayed away, searching his mind for answers. She was so very young, so naive, so sweet, so beautiful. He touched her shoulder to see if she was awake. Her breathing didn't change. He leaned into her face until he could feel the breath coming out of her mouth. He gently kissed her soft pink lips. He couldn't help himself. He prayed for her recovery. There was a part of him that enjoyed a feeling of possessing her at least for this moment.

He stayed with her throughout the night. When the first morning light filtered into the window, Juanita briefly regained consciousness. Dr. Rivera was asleep in the chair next to her bed. Seeing him, she thought she must be dreaming. She didn't remember what happened. Her eyes closed and she fell back asleep.

Dr. Rivera tried to send word to the Delgado Ranch in the morning that there had been an accident, that Juanita had been hurt, and she would have to convalesce at Mighty Oak until she could be moved. The ranch hand, Tony, returned with the note. The river had swollen and flooded the trail into town. It wasn't until the following day that he was able to get word to the Delgado Ranch.

Rosa stayed with Juanita most of the day as she went in and out of consciousness. Her brother Eduardo arrived two days later to see her. It was clear she couldn't be moved and was in the best care possible with Dr. Rivera.

After the third day, Juanita awoke but was weak. Rosa brought Buttons up to her room for a visit and the children were allowed a short stay a few times during the day to see her. When Juanita slept, she dreamed Dr. Rivera would come to her, gently kissing her lips and stroking her face. If he was there when she was awake, she glowed. Her body ached, but she was happier than she could ever remember in the warmth and confines of Dr. Rivera and the Rivera children.

CHAPTER TWENTY-FOUR

The Delgado Ranch

Late 1859

She stayed a week before returning to the Delgado Ranch. Much to Aunt Consuelo's chagrin Eduardo insisted she return from the school to care for Juanita. Mai was too busy, and with Huan gone, there would be no female to help her. Dr. Rivera came several times to see Juanita that first week she was home, even staying for lunch one day. Aunt Consuelo noticed the doctor's new affection for her niece but said nothing. Instead she moped and complained about being away from her duties at the school. A few days later Juanita, tired of hearing Consuelo's complaints, said she was well enough to take care of herself so Aunt Consuelo could return to her companion. Eduardo asked Mai to find someone to be Juanita's maid and Ju was hired.

Time passed. When the winter season's starkness began, a melancholy came over Juanita. It had been several weeks since she'd seen Dr. Rivera. She'd recovered and returned to tutor the children in July; since then their time spent together was spotty at best. With the affectionate moments spent with the doctor the night of the accident and his care, she'd assumed their feelings were mutual. Now he seemed to avoid her. His absence in her life was disturbing. Maybe she was mistaken, and the doctor was just taking care of her. Maybe the moments spent together the night of the party were a figment of her fertile imagination, or she had misconstrued his intentions.

She grew more anxious with each passing day. The anniversary of when she first saw him made her desires fester. She would find out what went wrong. She jotted off a note to him opening up her heart and attached it to his office door.

It had been two weeks since she left the note, and there was still no reply from Dr. Rivera. She was feeling foolish. She'd made a mistake. Her love felt real, and she loved his children, but he was older and sophisticated. At such a young age, perhaps she wasn't woman enough for him.

Dr. Rivera read the note Juanita left again. He mulled it over and his feelings for her many times. He'd suppressed his carnal desires to hold her, to touch her. He kept his distance, hoping it would go away. He genuinely loved her. She was used to luxury, and he did not have the kind of money her family had. She was so very young. Their age difference would grow in time and would be profound. His decision to restrain himself had been difficult.

***

Mai rambled up the stairs and knocked on Juanita's door. "Letter come for you, Señorita Delgado."

Juanita took the letter and shut the door. She studied the decorative way the doctor had scrolled her name on the outside of the parchment paper and his uniquely designed wax seal. She sat down at her dressing table, not taking her eyes off the letter. She smelled his distinct cologne that lingered on the paper. She held the unopened letter up to her chest and closed her eyes. Unable to wait any longer, her fingers fumbled when she picked up the letter opener.

December 14, 1859

Señorita Delgado,

The children and I would like to invite you to a pre-Christmas dinner on Friday, the 16th. Please let us know if you can attend.

Our fondest regards,

Dr. Dante Rivera

Friday morning Juanita woke early. She would find out tonight how he felt about her. The rest of the day dragged on until five when she began to dress. She tried on several dresses, settling on a simple sepia brown taffeta skirt, a lace collar silk blouse with a brocade jacket, and matching hat.

Tony, the young Rivera ranch hand, arrived at six to pick up Juanita. After months Simon was still recuperating but improving with each day.

Rosa had prepared the meal earlier, so she could spend the evening with her sister and return later. Dinner was at seven, and by eight they sat near the fire in the great room to exchange gifts. Juanita was anxious, and she wondered if she would have any time alone with the doctor or if he would send her off without an explanation. She admired the beautiful old nativity scene that sat on top of the mantel. He told her he had brought it with him from Spain when he arrived in 1855. A large pine tree decorated with handmade ornaments and garlands of popcorn sat in the great room. The tree was given to Dr. Rivera by Otto Muller and Son Butcher shop along with a fat goose because he recently saved young Fredrick Muller's wife and baby boy during a complicated birth.

The children wanted Juanita to open the gifts from them first. Six tiny wrapped presents sat in a basket. The children quarreled over who would carry the basket to Juanita until Dr. Rivera suggested they both carry it. With the help of Rosa, they had made bread doll ornaments for Juanita in the Mexican tradition. The first one she opened was of Buttons and the next was of her. The rest were of Rosa, their father, and themselves.

"So you won't forget us when you are not here," Angeles said.

Juanita's eyes moistened as she thanked them each with a hug. The children ripped open their presents from Juanita. She'd wrapped them in red silk fabric from an old dress and tied them in green ribbon. The gifts were matching hats and scarves she'd knitted. They immediately put them on and danced around the room. Juanita handed Dr. Rivera her present. He was surprised, not expecting anything from her. It was a fine burgundy leather-bound journal with the initials D.R. in gold. After opening their gifts, they sang from Angeles' songbook while Juanita played the clavichord. At nine the children reluctantly went up to bed.

Dr. Rivera carried a small oil lamp with him as he opened the door to his dark study and held the door open for Juanita to enter. He lit the oil lamp on his desk and opened his desk drawer. He took out an envelope and handed it to Juanita. There was a sizable sum of money in it. Juanita's head dropped. This was not what she was hoping for.

"Thank you, but you don't need to do this. I enjoy my time with the children, that is pay enough."

"Please take it. You deserve much more than that. My children love you, and you have brought back a joy into our lives that had been missing."

Disappointed, Juanita turned to leave.

"Please," stammered out of Dr. Rivera's mouth. "I have something else."

He reached in the drawer again, this time pulling out a black velvet-covered box.

"Please, this is from me."

Juanita opened it. Inside was a red ruby ring surrounded with small opalescent stones. Dr. Rivera moved closer to her.

"The ring belonged to my mother. I hope you will accept it and consider becoming my wife."

His words registered in Juanita's head. He brought her hand up to his mouth and kissed the inside of her wrist. He did this without taking his eyes off Juanita's face. Faint chills ran up and down her spine, and she fell into his arms.

"Is this real or a fantasy. Yes, yes."

"When I received your letter that you had feelings for me and how you loved my children, I finally had hope that perhaps you cared for me as I cared for you."

He kissed her softly on the lips. The kiss became more passionate working to a full embrace. Uncontrollable tears of joy streamed down Juanita's cheeks. Dr. Rivera held her tightly and wiped away the tears with his handkerchief. He kissed her cheeks, then her lips again.

"I will keep this handkerchief always, and when I look at it, I will remember this wonderful moment when we acknowledged our love for one another," he said softly.

A moment later Rosa called out she was back.

The trotting horse pulled the buggy down the path toward the Delgado Ranch. Juanita unwrapped her arm from Dr. Rivera's and studied the ruby ring on her finger he had just given her. "It would be best if I talk to your father first, before you say anything to anyone, my darling. When your father returns in a few days, I will come. After that we will start our courtship and spend time together."

He kissed her hand again.

He pulled on the horse's reins shy of the circular path in front of the Delgado Ranch hacienda, shielding them from the ranch's view behind a grove of olive trees. They waited silently, listening to the quiet. He placed his arm around her waist and pulled her close. He touched the skin of her cheek and softly kissed her neck and lips. He looked into her brown eyes.

"We must stop now, before I go too far. I should not take such liberties with you before I talk to your father. My flesh has gotten the better of me."

He flicked the reins and the horse took off. When they reached the stepping stone, Dr. Rivera got out and helped

Juanita down, walking her to the front door. They moved into the shadows and were about to kiss again when the front door swung open. Her brother Eduardo stepped out from the hacienda.

Dr. Rivera stepped forward from the shadows.

"Good evening, Eduardo," said Dr. Rivera.

"Good evening, Dr. Rivera. Come Juanita, it is late."

Juanita walked into the hacienda. She turned and smiled at Dr. Rivera as Eduardo closed the front door.

CHAPTER TWENTY-FIVE

The Roundup

November 1859

Blood pulsed into Emanuel's biceps as his palomino Wanton, mouth foaming, ran at top speed out of a wooded area and into an open field. High over his head Emanuel's arm twisted around throwing a lasso out and high as possible. The hemp rope soared through the air, successfully landing around the calf's neck. In one continual motion man and horse worked together. Emanuel pulled on Wanton's reins, and the horse dropped his head and came to a quicksilver stop. Emanuel leapt off and onto the calf to tether its legs before it could get away. The calf wiggled under Emanuel's body, but Emanuel laid his lithesome, muscular body on the calf. Soon enough, the calf would be free again. He stroked the calf's head to calm him down and checked to make sure nothing was broken. He tightened the rope around the calf's neck and loosened its tethered legs.

"Okay little poke, it's your time to get branded."

The other cowboys were back at the camp when Emanuel arrived riding Wanton and guiding the escaped calf by the rope around its neck. Emanuel swung his body around and slid off Wanton. He held the calf's head, so it would be blind to the hot iron that seared the D brand into the flesh on the its backside. The calf pulled as Emanuel slid off the rope releasing him back onto the open range to find the herd and his mother. Sweat poured off Emanuel. Wall-eyed Cookie handed him a cup of coffee.

"Breakfast's ready, if you're hungry," said Cookie.

Emanuel took a few sips and walked back to Wanton.

"Good work, boy." Emanuel removed the saddle and brushed him down. The November roundup was over, and in the morning they would return to the ranch for a cattle drive. Part of the cattle would go directly to slaughter for local meat and their skins to a tannery. The treated hides were sent to San Francisco harbor for auction to eastern traders. Others were sent east on cattle drives to slaughterhouses in the Midwest.

He was the fairest of Don Carlos Delgado's children, a throwback on his mother's side to her northern Spanish relatives with dirty blond hair and green eyes. He inherited two things from his father—his small, tight, muscular frame and his temper. There was a stubbornness in Emanuel since the day he was born that sometimes turned into a streak of blue anger. It was only a matter of time before it would surface again. He loved the outdoors, unlike his brother Eduardo who preferred books and the business duties of the ranch. Emanuel cherished his callused hands and fair skin weather-beaten from the sun.

Emanuel returned with a sizable profit from selling the cattle. With the final roundup and drive over, traditionally, the cowboys headed into town for a week of debauchery, including Emanuel. There was always a feast on the ranch beforehand when the cowhands' bonuses were handed out. Wall-eyed Cookie roasted a pig. The festivities included horse racing, bronco riding, and a game to catch a greased pig. It ended with fireworks.

After the fireworks were over, the men who'd been up in the hills all summer took their bonuses into Napa, which was already teeming with silver and gold miners who were settling in for the winter. They got drunk, gambled, and got laid by the local prostitutes. Any decent woman would not be seen on the streets of town that week. Fist fights and an occasional killing were common. When word came back to the ranches that the cowboys were spent, the ranch owners went into town to the jail, gambling halls, and brothels to collect their ranch hands.

Emanuel celebrated for two days before he headed north to St. Helena with a supply of whiskey to sleep with the woman he loved.

CHAPTER TWENTY-SIX

Returning Home

December 20, 1859

Smoke curled out from the kitchen chimney of the ranch hacienda. Gardenias lined the stone steps leading up to the open front door draped with garlands of hibiscus and holly. Rich and inviting aromas from the kitchen found their way outside and greeted Don Carlos. These smells signaled he was home, away from the basic, somewhat bland Eastern diet he'd gotten used to. He'd been yearning for the rich Mexican-Spanish food he loved, and Mai would not disappoint him.

Juanita flung herself into her father's arms and into a deep embrace. He'd missed his family, and the thought of leaving them again left a nauseating feeling in the pit of his stomach. He would have to forget about his return to Washington and think only of the present.

Emanuel carried his father's bags into the house and up the stairs to the master suite. The house was alive with workers placing Christmas decorations around the great room in anticipation of the holiday and the annual party thrown at the Delgado Ranch. Prominent families of the valley looked forward to this occasion and talked about it for the rest of the year. A large tree stood in the great room with a few gifts underneath that were to be opened January 6, Three Kings Day. A fire flickered in the fireplace warming the room. For

Don Carlos Delgado it was wonderful to be home. He'd spent a few days in San Francisco taking care of necessary business and had been anxious to get home. He would have to finish his business before he returned to Washington but that was a month away. For now, he would savor his time spent home with his children. Today they would catch up on events; tomorrow he would discuss ranch business with his sons.

Dinner was filled with laughter and small talk; only Emanuel was quiet. Don Carlos was upset hearing how long his sister Consuelo had been away from the ranch. He dismissed any concern about his daughter. She seemed fine from her accident and more mature from her time spent with the Rivera children. Don Carlos, exhausted from politics in Washington and his long journey home, did his best to stay awake but fatigue got the better of him and before nine he excused himself and went up to his room.

***

It was very early the next morning. Suffering from insomnia and still in her nightclothes, Juanita let Buttons out the front door to do his business. Buttons sniffed around his usual bushes before becoming distracted by a black-tailed jackrabbit. He barked and rushed off, running to one of the far horse barns. He ran to the far end of the barn past the silhouette of a woman who stood in the doorway holding a baby. Juanita headed toward the back door after Buttons. She came to a dead stop when she was close enough to recognize her servant Huan.

"Huan! Huan, you're back!"

Juanita approached Huan, who stood stoically saying nothing.

"Huan, you have a baby."

Huan pulled the blanket around the baby to shield it from Juanita's eyes. A tuft of fair hair from the little girl poked out from between Huan's fingers.

Juanita moved next to Huan.

"No see my baby."

Juanita wondered why her friend and servant was doing this. Emanuel and a little boy, not yet two, walked up behind Juanita.

"Go ahead. Show her," he said.

Huan scowled, but she obeyed him and pulled the blanket away from the baby's face. Beautiful green eyes looked toward Juanita. A fair-skinned, fair-haired, weeks-old baby smiled and cooed at her.

"Congratulations, you're the first one in the family to meet my children," said Emanuel.

Muddled thoughts ran around Juanita's head. She looked again at the baby and the little boy who clung to his father's leg. They were Emanuel's. The similarity was unmistakable.

"Eduardo knows, but he won't acknowledge my relationship with Huan. Father sent her away thinking I would stop loving her, but I found her. We're going to be together no matter what. No one knows they're here."

"I promise I won't say anything."

Juanita smiled and took another peek at the baby.

"May I?"

Huan handed the baby to Juanita who looked up into Juanita's face, smiling and cooing.

"Her name is Lotus."

The words that formed in Emanuel's mind came out as a stutter. He stopped to take a breath, finally able to blurt out the words.

"We're leaving, going east to Montana. I bought a small spread there, so we can live our lives without interference or threats. I don't care about anything except Huan and my children."

"Does Mai know you're here?" asked Juanita.

"No."

As planned for that day, Don Carlos, Eduardo and Emanuel mounted their horses and rode the range to assess the progress the ranch had made during Don Carlos' absence. It took the better part of the day with a ride that was long and rough. Don Carlos, still exhausted from his trip and the day's excursion, excused himself early to rest.

For Juanita thoughts of Dante seemed to fill every pore. She could barely eat all day. When she tried to lay down for siesta, her body would not let her rest. She'd received a note at noon from Dante saying he would be at the party the next day and talk to her father that evening.

CHAPTER TWENTY-SEVEN

The Christmas Party

December 22, 1859

Ju brushed Juanita's hair and rolled up the sides, pinning it in place with tortoise hair combs encrusted with semiprecious stones that Juanita had inherited from her mother. Soft curl ringlets of jet-black hair fell around her face, framing it. Juanita held tightly to one of her bedposts as Ju pulled at the waist cinch until it began to torture her.

On her bed lay a gift from her father that he'd brought from Washington to symbolize her womanhood, a Parisian haute couture ensemble designed by Charles Frederick Worth. The gown had a low-cut neckline trimmed in ivory colored lace with tiny silk tassels. The skintight, moss green satin bodice had tiny white flowers and bees embroidered on it and a slight puffed cap sleeve. At the waist was a long pink velvet ribbon that tied in the back. The pale pink satin skirt, layered waist to hem in matching pink tulle ruffles and big coral silk roses, covered a full crinoline and several layers of petticoats. Her satin-heeled slippers matched the moss green bodice and had bees and flowers embroidered on them as well. On her legs she wore pale-toned silk stockings.

Juanita dabbed an appropriate amount of rouge on her cheeks and lips and powdered her winter pale skin before putting on a necklace and matching earrings that she also inherited from her mother. She splashed a vanilla scented perfume inside her cleavage and on her wrists and twisted Dante's ring around to show off the stone. Then she slipped on her lacy fingerless gloves. Looking at herself in the freestanding mirror, she adjusted her skirt and looked to Ju for approval.

"You look beautiful, Senorita Delgado."

"Thank you, Ju."

Her father knocked. Don Carlos stood on the other side of the door with sounds of a Mariachi band playing from the party below.

"Our guests are arriving, Juanita."

Juanita made her entrance down the staircase to the grand room, already full with guests enjoying themselves. Several clay and papier-mâché Christmas piñatas, filled with coins and hard candy, hung along with garlands from the large beams in the great room and on the veranda. The long table in the dining room was abundant with food—a goose, stuffed turkey, ham, bacalao, tamales, ensalada nochebuena, buñuelos, potatoes, corn, plum pudding, churros, ponche, cakes, and a cornucopia of fruit.

Don Carlos seemed revived. He looked younger and more vigorous than the day before. Eduardo was already mingling with the crowd and looked handsome in his black evening suit. Of the family only Emanuel was nowhere to be seen. Juanita waited in anticipation for Dr. Rivera to arrive. A slight smugness came over her. After his talk with her father, they would be together. Everyone here would know they were a couple.

The evening pushed on, and Juanita looked toward the door at every arrival. She was becoming fraught with worry, and her charming manners were beginning to wane.

The room overflowed with people. It seemed everyone who had been invited had arrived when Don Carlos worked his way toward the staircase. He stepped up to the third step and called for silence.

"I wish to make a toast and a few announcements. Does everyone have a glass of punch?"

The front door pushed open. A dark and brooding Emanuel, still in his work clothes, stood inside the door frame with a look of sheer anger. There was a quiet rush of voices among the guests closest to the door who noticed Emanuel and fixated on him. Don Carlos called for silence again. Emanuel stared at his father, his green eyes possessed an energy so intense the crowd spontaneously parted when he started to walk toward his father. With their eyes fixed on Emanuel, no one noticed Dr. Rivera arrive, not even Juanita.

Don Carlos discreetly nodded to two of the larger ranch hands who surrounded Emanuel and guided him toward the veranda while Don Carlos kept talking. Don Carlos clicked his silver ring on his punch glass to draw the crowd's attention back to him.

"I have some wonderful news. I am not getting any younger and want to officially announce the engagement of my son Eduardo."

Juanita took a breath before her father's words registered in her head as a shocking surprise. This engagement had never been discussed, and she had never met her brother's intended. Eduardo walked to the staircase and stood smiling next to his father. Someone touched Juanita's arm. Startled, she sounded a gasp. It was Dr. Rivera. She wanted to jump into his arms. She took his hand and guided him to the punch bowl and poured him a cup of the rum-laced liquid.

"My oldest son will marry Palmira Vazquez. They will start their courtship in a few days," said Don Carlos. The guests clapped.

Eduardo was the most amenable of his children, and Don Carlos had discussed the arranged marriage with him when he'd returned from San Francisco.

The crowd rallied around the two men.

"I knew nothing of this, Eduardo never mentioned it to me," Juanita whispered to Dante.

"Quiet please. I have more," called out Don Carlos. "I wish to announce the engagement of my son Emanuel to Esmeralda Sims. Their wedding will be in the spring."

The two ranch hands that had guided Emanuel onto the veranda grabbed him when he tried to push forward back into the room toward his father. The men pulled him off the veranda and out toward the barns. A hush settled over the crowd.

Juanita was stunned. She looked toward Dr. Rivera.

The sound of breaking glass on the veranda startled her. She was still trying to process the announcement her father had just made. It put her nerves on edge.

"And my last announcement, the engagement of my daughter Juanita to Franco Navarro of the San Francisco shipping family."

Cheers and shouts rang from the guests.

All of Juanita's senses shut down. Her pleading eyes looked toward Dr. Rivera as she collapsed toward his body. He stared ahead motionless supporting her body weight. They were both in a time warp trying to register what had just happened. The crowd near them surrounded Juanita sweeping her away from Dr. Rivera. As they congratulated her, they moved her toward her father who was calling her name. Juanita couldn't hear or see anything; she was locked in a vacuum of confusion. She could barely breathe, like a spider had wrapped a web so tightly around her body that she would suffocate. Somehow she was standing next to her father. She twisted her head around trying to find Dr. Rivera in the crowd when her senses returned more acute than normal. Her ears hurt from the crowd's noise, and her skin crawled. Her father tried to cradle her in his arms, but the physical pain she experienced made her push him away. She looked over the crowd straining to find Dr. Rivera until she saw him standing near the door. She was unaware of the tears rolling down her face.

"Enjoy everyone, and Feliz Navidad!" shouted Don Carlos as he drank from his cup, signaling for the crowd to do the same.

"No, Father," slipped from Juanita's lips. Her father swept her by the waist into the congratulatory crowd where he left her. She felt smothered as people embraced her shaking body. She could only think of Dante, and when she finally reached him, he pulled her to a safe corner in the vestibule.

"I should have known a man like your father would believe in arranged marriages."

"No, it can't be. I knew nothing. I want to marry you."

"I will talk to him, I promise. Tonight is not a good time. I will come back tomorrow."

"Please don't go. Stay with me, I couldn't bear it. I want everyone to see us together."

"That is not a good idea, my darling, please understand. If people start to talk about us, things will be much worse. Come outside with me."

They moved into the darkness outside of the front entrance. When he was sure they were alone, he kissed Juanita. She kissed him back.

"The thought of life without you is horrible. I want to spend forever with you.

"I will come and live with you, I don't care what people think, I love you," said Juanita.

They kissed again. Inside loud shouts overtook the sounds of the party and the music stopped. The front door swung open and Emanuel rushed outside past them, heading back toward the barns. Dr. Rivera pulled Juanita deeper into the darkness around the side of the hacienda.

"You must go inside before someone misses you. Go and pretend to enjoy yourself. I will come tomorrow by noon to talk to your father."

He backed away. Juanita watched him until he turned the corner and headed to his horse. The crowd of people outside began to grow around the back entrance. Juanita picked up her skirt and hurried around to the kitchen door. The kitchen was empty. She felt as if she would faint and collapsed onto a chair when Emanuel entered.

"Do you know where she is? And my children, where are they?"

He grabbed Juanita by the arms and pulled her up to her feet, shaking her. Her legs buckled and she landed on the floor. He pulled her partway up by the arm.

"I know nothing, Emanuel. I knew nothing about this evening."

"You told him, you were the only one who knew they were here."

Emanuel raised his hand to Juanita.

"I said nothing, Emanuel. I promise."

Mai was standing on the other side of the kitchen now, under the stairs listening. She pushed the door open.

"Me say they here. Me know. Huan come to me, show me new baby girl. I telly boss."

"What did he do with them?"

"They okay, boss promise."

Emanuel formed a fist so tight his knuckles turned white, accentuating a streak of fresh blood on them. He shot out the back door in a fiery anger.

Juanita's delicate emotions reached a breaking point. All she wanted to do was go to her room. She thought about what Dante had said, insisting she go back to the party. Her name was being called from the great room. She straightened her body and looked at her reflection in the window. She pushed her hair back into place and wiped away her tear streaks in her powdered face. She would do it for Dante.

Moments earlier Emanuel had broken away from his handlers and run into the hacienda pushing his way to his father. When Don Carlos saw his son coming at him, to be discreet he moved to the hallway under the stairs knowing Emanuel would follow.

"Where are they?"

"Lower your voice. They are safe. You will see them soon, but there is no way you are leaving to live in Montana or marrying her. You will marry one of your own, Esmeralda Sims, and be happy. You will have Huan on the side. Be realistic, my son. As it is now, the gringos think of us as beneath them. If you marry a Chinese you will be met with prejudice like you've never seen. As for tonight you will go change into your evening clothes and be pleasant to our guests, for the sake of the family name, your brother, your sister, your children and Huan. Stop being so selfish. You have always been a good son, and I am proud of you. You must understand I have your best interest at heart. Now act like a man."

Emanuel's rage blinded him.

"My family is as good as yours," said Emanuel.

Emanuel formed a fist and with one sucker punch hit his father hard in the face. The old man fell backward into a side dresser and crumpled onto the floor. Emanuel's instinct was to kill him. He looked at the vulnerable old man lying on the tile floor. Remembering this was his father, Emanuel felt enough compassion to turn away. He pushed through the crowd toward the front door, screaming as the music stopped and the crowd quieted.

Don Carlos dabbed blood from the cut in the corner of his mouth with his handkerchief and composed himself. He pulled his body up from the floor, steadying himself. Once composed he walked back to the great room and stood on the third step. He smiled and called out for Juanita and to the remaining party revelers crowded around him.

"It is nothing. My son Emanuel is strongheaded like me, that is all. Please return to your merriment. Where is my daughter? I want to dance with my daughter. Juanita!"

An emotionally hollow Juanita drifted back into the crowd from the kitchen, a shell of herself. Her father smiled at her and held out his hand for her to come to him. She walked toward him thinking she would pray to the angels tonight. They had always come and helped her in the past. She could reason with her father. After all, he was the loving, kind man who had always wanted the best for her. Dante would talk to him. Her loving father would understand what their love was and would see they were meant to be together. Don Carlos wrapped her in a warm embrace. She looked into her father's face and noticed the blood in the corner of his mouth. He smiled and began telling a story about life in Washington. Don Carlos, forever the raconteur, continued his story and dabbed fresh blood from his mouth with his handkerchief as if nothing had happened.

***

Emanuel stroked his horse Wanton's head as he placed the bridle on and saddled him. He slung packed saddlebags over the horse's back. Lastly he placed his bed roll on and mounted Wanton. They moved into the night toward the field between the house and the trail passing the brightly lit hacienda where the party was beginning to break up. Several carriages moved down the path toward the trail. Emanuel looked back one more time thinking of what his father had done; his rage intensified as he spit on the ground. He would go to St. Helena. Huan and the children must be there. Watton passed under the iron arched entrance with the large D and headed north toward St. Helena.

***

Emanuel pounded on the door of the old Chinese man who Huan had married.

"Huan, no here," was all the old man said.

Emanuel's heart turned to stone with thoughts of his father's actions. Maybe he'd hurt them or banished them so far away Emanuel would never find them. No he thought, the only other place they might be was the hunting cabin high in the mountains where their father had taken his sons hunting since they were children.

The aromatic smell of the redwoods brought back childhood memories of better times spent with his father which soothed Emanuel's cluttered, angry mind. Perhaps the old man thought his intentions were for the best, but nothing would stop him from being with Huan. The farther up into the mountains Emanuel went, the worse the weather became, until it was impossible to see. The falling snow became a whiteout. The path narrowed into a sheer cliff on one side and a wall of frozen earth on the other. Wanton stepped cautiously and finally refused to travel farther, forcing Emanuel to walk Wanton back down the path. Like a blind man he used his hand feeling along the wall of the canyon to guide them until he found the opening to a cave he and his brother Eduardo used to play in. It was big enough to hold even a horse until the storm was over.

**

The next morning hired handlers brought Huan and the children back to the ranch. They'd been held overnight at the clinic in town. The day turned bitter cold. Huan wrapped the baby up tightly in swaddling and they rushed into the kitchen to warm up. Don Carlos sat at the kitchen table eating his breakfast.

"Go get Emanuel, Mai, so we can all talk."

Mai knocked on Emanuel's bedroom door as Don Carlos had requested, but there was no answer. She pushed the door open. The room was dark and empty, and the wood stove was cold. Emanuel's good suit for the party was still lying on the bed where she'd placed it the day before. She returned to the kitchen.

"Mr. Emanuel no there," she told Don Carlos.

"Go look in the barn, he must have slept there last night." Mai left.

"Have breakfast," said Don Carlos.

Huan slowly responded to Don Carlos. He looked into the face of his grandchildren. The little boy chewed on a roll and smiled at his grandfather. The little girl's face conjured up a memory of his dead wife. Don Carlos softened and pushed the plate of fresh sweet rolls toward Huan.

"Eat," he said.

She only hesitated for a moment. She grabbed a roll biting into it, her belly growling with hunger.

By the time Juanita worked her way down the back stairs, no one was in the kitchen. She went into the hallway under the stairs. Mai and Huan sat in their rooms off the kitchen with the door open. The boy and baby girl napped on the bed.

"Where is my father, Huan?" asked Juanita.

"Emanuel gone," said Huan. "Father and brother go looky for him."

As promised, Dante came. Juanita seeing him riding up to the hacienda ran down the stairs greeting him at the front door. She guided him into her father's den and shut the door so they could be alone.

"Emanuel has taken off and my father and brother have gone to look for him."

With Don Carlos gone there was nothing Dante could do.

They spent some time together in the den until Ju called out for Juanita.

"I must go. I have to be at the clinic today. I'll check back on my way home and see if your father has returned. I hope Emanuel is found soon. Tonight will be very cold," said Dante.

As the lovers kissed, Juanita heard Ju call out to her. Juanita open the door enough to call out and tell to Ju to meet her upstairs in ten minutes. Once Ju was out of sight, Dante left by the front door.

Juanita stood by her bedroom window and watched Dante ride down the path toward the trail. A renewed sense of hope consumed her.

It wasn't until late evening that the men returned carrying Emanuel's unconscious frozen body into the house and upstairs to his room. His skin was gray, his breath shallow. Parts of his fingers and toes had already turned black. They took off his wet frozen clothes and dressed him in dry ones and layered several blankets on him for warmth. Don Carlos, exhausted well beyond his strength, collapsed onto a chair next to Emanuel's bed. Mai had woken up Huan. She rushed into the room as the door was shutting. Juanita saw her father put his head in his hands and weep.

CHAPTER TWENTY-EIGHT

A Mother's Love

Napa, August 1915

Cassandra Gillette waited to see if Dante René would ask her to the end of summer Pavilion Dance at the country club. She'd made subtle hints whenever they were together, and Magritte had made it blatantly clear that Cassandra was the pick for her son. During the summer Cassandra and Dante had occasionally gone to the movies together at the request of Magritte but always in the company of other friends. They would also see each other at the weekly dinners her family attended at the Rivera mansion; whenever he was there, he was always charming and attentive but nothing more. He would purposely leave early to see Juanita to avoid any possibility of having to take Cassandra home. She'd heard rumors that Dante was still seeing the girl who lived in the valley. Magritte reassured Cassandra that Dante was losing interest in Juanita, saying all young men had urges.

Dante avoided his mother as much as he could that week. The day before the dance Cassandra called Magritte and told her that she hadn't heard from Dante. He'd pushed it for as long as he could. At breakfast Magritte's steel-blue eyes shot a penetrating look at Dante. His mouth went dry. The moment had come. He'd planned what to say but lying was never easy for him, especially to his mother.

"We're going stag this year, Mother—Raul, my buddies, and me."

I'm a coward sat silently in his throat. Thoughts swam through his head. Maybe we should run off and get married. I can't be happy without Juanita. I will have it out with mother soon, and let her know I want to be with Juanita forever.

Juanita wouldn't make the same mistake she'd made at the Rivera gala months earlier. When Dante asked her to the dance, it gave her close to a month to get ready. She found a picture of a dress she liked in a magazine, a pink silk empire waist dress with a scalloped square low-cut neckline, puff sleeves, and a slim skirt with a modern ankle-length hem, only seen on sporting clothes a few years earlier. White stockings and white gloves were a must. Lita Nannie would make the dress.

Lita Nannie struggled and tried to keep her mind busy so it wouldn't slip back into the past. She'd touch a piece of lace and remember the night of the Christmas party when she waited for Dr. Rivera to arrive, so he could ask her father's permission to marry her. Unconsciously she reached up to touch the jewel-encrusted tortoise combs that she wore that night. Her hands fumbled around the top of her head before she remembered that she sold them off when her children needed food. She pulled herself back from the brink when she remembered her granddaughter, her beautiful granddaughter who was dating her lover's grandson. She prayed her granddaughter would not suffer the same fate she had.

Dante had asked Juanita to the Pavilion Dance right after they returned from the Panama-Pacific International Exposition. Juanita didn't understand the significance of the invitation or what it meant until the night of the dance. It would be a confirmation to all his friends and to the world that he and Juanita were a couple. After their relationship was recognized, he would go to his mother and tell her they were to be married. He drove to San Francisco and purchased an onyx and diamond ring along with a diamond brooch shaped in a double knotted flower wreath. He would give it to Juanita when he asked her to marry him at the dance.

Dante knocked on the Bonnetia front door at seven-fifteen with a pink rose corsage and a dance card in hand. He was elated. After tonight the world would know they were in love and were a couple. Juanita answered the door, radiant in her pale pink dress with her hair parted in a soft, loose, roll with white flowers placed around it. Dante gave her the corsage and the dance card which was filled entirely with his name. Mr. Bonnetia took a picture of the couple with his Brownie camera.

The outdoor pavilion at the country club was a fairyland with hundreds of tiny white lights. It was crowded by the time Dante and Juanita arrived. Cassandra was already there as was Raul, who'd promised his brother he'd be there for support when Dante announced to the people at the dance they were engaged.

Dante glided Juanita onto the floor with the other couples. The band played the Columbia Waltz. Cassandra sat silently mortified in the corner with a group of girls that she'd moments earlier been bragging to that Dante René would be meeting her soon. She'd dance with him. He was her unofficial date. The other girls snickered and commented that her boyfriend was there with another girl.

Raul had come early and returned to the pavilion dance floor when he saw Dante. The brothers acknowledged one another. Cassandra caught Raul's eye. She was working her way across the dance floor toward Dante. Uncharacteristically, Raul followed her onto the floor, and when he reached her, he touched her arm. Before she could react, he grabbed her by the waist and with a firm grip began to waltz. She struggled to get away, but he danced her off to the side. She glanced over to the other corner where the wallflowers sat. This seemed to calm down the gossip, so Cassandra stopped her struggling.

A lull in the music indicated that the next number, a fast-paced fox trot, was about to start. Cassandra pushed at Raul's chest, determined this time to get away, but Raul held her tight and danced her around the perimeter of the dance floor. When the band finished, a ukulele's strings began a slow dance. A singer sang.

Oh! you beautiful doll,
you great, big beautiful doll!

Dante held Juanita tightly as they circled around the floor.

Let me put my arms about you,
I could never live without you.

"I love you," whispered Dante into Juanita's ear, first humming then singing quietly to Juanita as they danced.

If you ever leave me how my heart will ache,
I want to hug you but I fear you'd break.

Dante danced Juanita off the dance floor to the outside. They could hear the music in the background. They looked at the sky with thousands of sparkling stars while they walked into the darkness to be alone. They passed some other party-goers and headed toward the lake. Juanita slipped her dance card into Dante's jacket pocket, so she wouldn't lose it.

Starlight reflected on the surface of the water. Dante placed his arm around Juanita's waist and kissed her.

"Let's go for a swim," he said.

"My grandmother worked hard on this dress, I don't want to ruin it."

"Take it off," Dante said.

He kissed her again and began to cup his hand under her breast. She stayed in his arms for a minute but pulled away and walked a few feet from him.

"We can't, you know that."

"I can."

He pulled his tie off first, then his shoes, socks, coat, shirt and pants until he was down to his underwear. He dove into the cool waters of the lake and swam into the darkness. For a moment Juanita lost sight of Dante. She heard hard splashing of the water and then it abruptly stopped. Juanita moved to the edge of the water.

"Dante, come out," she called out. There was no reply. She moved closer

"Dante, where are you? This isn't funny!"

Something grabbed at her ankles. She screamed and jumped back. Dante laughed.

"Come on, take that pretty dress off and come in with me. You know I love you."

Dante yelled out over the lake. "I love Juanita."

His words echoed back over the waters to them.

Juanita crossed her arms and moved back into the darkness. Dante jumped out of the lake.

"Okay, if you come over here, I have something for you. I promise to be good," he said.

"Promise and cross your heart," she said.

He reached down into the pile of his cloths and grabbed a small box from his coat.

"I promise to be good, to love you, and cherish you for the rest of my life, so help me God." He crossed his heart and extended the box to her.

A questioning smile came to her face. She took the box and opened it. The deep onyx stone absorbed the starlight, and the diamonds on the ring and brooch sparkled the light back.

"Will you marry me?" he asked.

Juanita gasped and jumped into Dante's arms, hugging his wet body.

"I will, I will," she replied.

Moments later Juanita moved over to the bushes and took off her shoes and garters rolling off her stockings. She would tell her parents in the morning she would not be going to New York to study at the Arts Student League. She stripped off her dress. Tiny pebbles stuck to her bare feet. She hesitated only for a moment as she stood in her slip, ready to step out.

Dante was deep in thought. He would announce to the crowd they were engaged when they went back to the dance. Maybe they should run off and get married tonight. That way nothing could stop them from being together. His mother would have to accept her or be out of his life. Then he heard Juanita's piercing scream.

A stinging pain ran up Juanita's leg. She looked down and saw a snake slither away. Dante ran over, cradled her in his arms, and carried her back to the pavilion. The panic in Dante lulled a bit when he saw the bright lights of the pavilion. A singer voice belted out "I Ain't Got Nobody." He shouted as loud as he could, but the music drowned out his cries. His bare feet touched the wooden dance floor. His voice grew louder. The music stopped.

Young Dr. Williams attended to Juanita. He heated a pocket knife in a candle flame and cut a crisscross incision to suck the out the venom. The crowd cheered and the revelry began again.

Raul took off his jacket to cover Juanita and Dante went back for their clothes. Cassandra wore a look of vindication.

CHAPTER TWENTY-NINE

A Mother's Lesson

Napa, August 1915

The next morning Magritte sat stoically in bed listening on the telephone to Cassandra. She hung up the phone and with furious purpose flung herself from her bed and down the hall to her son's room. She pushed the door open. Dante was not there. His bed was made. She looked around his room. His desk was open. She rummaged through his papers looking at the correspondence until she found letters and Valentines from Juanita tucked inside a desk drawer. She pulled out one letter and read it before crushing it in her hands and throwing it on the floor. She began to walk out of the room but stopped. She reached down and picked up the crumpled letter and envelope off the floor. She placed them in the pocket of her dressing gown and closed the door as she left.

Concerned about her health, Dante stayed with Juanita at her home all night. He wouldn't leave even after Juanita assured him she felt fine. They spent most of the next day sitting under the twin oaks talking about their future. When Dante returned home later that day, Magritte was waiting. He came through the back door with his tie off and his shirt open at the neck, his wrinkled tuxedo jacket slung over his shoulder. James rang Magritte to let her know Dante had arrived. She caught him when he reached the top of the stairs and called to him, asking him to come to the drawing room. He took a deep breath. Magritte sat serenely medicated in an overstuffed chair, a cut crystal glass filled with sherry in her hand. The decanter on the table next to her had been full in the morning but was now almost empty. Magritte asked Dante how his day was.

"Wonderful," he replied.

He waited for her response. Her calmness unsettled him. He hesitated before giving her the usual kiss on the cheek. She smiled and kissed him back.

"I've had the happiest twenty-four hours of my life and your response makes it even better," said Dante.

"Really?" she said. "Today I found out my son was a liar." She calmly took another sip of sherry. "How dare you tell me you were not taking anyone to the dance and then you show up with that wench. Then you humiliate me acting like a commoner and undressing in front of everyone. And the expo, you were together there too. All the good breeding, the manners I've taught you, and the good schools I sent you to. A short time with that trollop has corrupted you. That urchin!"

Dante backed away—a war of words had begun.

"How dare you call Juanita those names. She's none of that. She comes from a very good family, and everyone likes her but you, Mother. Only you could see someone as sweet and lovely as Juanita in that way. She was hurt. I was worried I was going to lose her, but she's going to be okay. We're going to be married, Mother. I'm going to marry Juanita, and you can't stop me."

"Oh yes I can, you'll see!" said Magritte.

Dante approached her. "No, you can't."

Magritte struggled to her feet and grabbed onto Dante. She swung her hand, backhanding him on the cheek, cutting into his flesh with the heavy ring she wore. He stepped back and blocked her next swing. Magritte fell to the floor hysterically crying.

"Mother!" called out Dante.

Dante helped Magritte to her feet. She wobbled as she walked. Dante tried to help her, but she pushed him as hard as she could, catching him off guard and knocking him into the small side table next to her desk. The table fell on its side and everything on it fell to the floor. Dante reached down to pick up the things off the floor. Behind his back Magritte picked up a vase and came after Dante. She swung around with the vase in her hand to hit him, but in her stupor she missed.

"Stop it, Mother, you're drunk, you're crazy." She grabbed onto Dante and tried to shake him. Her long nails dug into his arm.

"I worked hard to make sure you'd be the best, have the best, and what do you do? I'd rather see you dead than with that thing."

"Let go!" He tried to get away from her. Her long nails dug deeper into his arm. He grabbed onto her hand to pull it loose. Magritte let go and staggered backwards with a cold dead stare in her eyes. Losing her balance, she slammed into the stone fireplace, and her head hit the marble mantle hard. She collapsed onto the floor.

For Dante time stopped; he screamed out for help.

Magritte lay unconscious in her bed. Dante sat asleep in a chair next to her. Grandfather Raul decided it would be better for Magritte to be treated at home where few would know about her mental state and her addictions. As chairman of the board of the Rushing River Hospital, he summoned the head surgeon and a loyal friend to come and care for her. Five stitches and bed rest was ordered. The distraught Dante insisted he stay by his mother's side. Gabriel had not returned home that night or the next morning. Grandfather Raul assumed he was with one of his mistresses.

Daylight broke into the room. Magritte looked over at her sleeping son in the overstuffed chair next to her bed, still in his tuxedo shirt and pants. He never left his mother's side throughout the night and into the morning. She cast her sight toward the pocket doors separating her room from her husband's. They were closed. That meant he hadn't returned home last night. She clutched her chest and let out a deep moan. Dante remained sound asleep. She moaned louder this time and screamed out that she had a severe pain in her chest. Dante woke up. She said she was having a heart attack. The doctor was summoned again, this time out of surgery. Magritte's closed eyes fluttered.

"Mrs. Rivera should be fine. I can't hear any irregularity. Let her sleep today. I gave her some sleeping powders to help. I'll come by later," said the doctor.

Even in her stupor, Magritte could hear the pocket doors slide open, then close back again. Only a small crack of light streamed through the door. Magritte strained to hear the hushed conversation between her husband and son.

"Go be with the one you love, Dante. Your mother will be fine. It wasn't your fault that she fell."

Magritte heard Gabriel's bedroom door shut. She called out to him, but got no response. The glass pharmaceutical bottle of medicine the doctor had left sat on the bedside table. She poured some of the white powder into a glass of water and drank it. The taste was bitter. She began to gag and cough. Most of the white liquid came up; she leaned over the side of the bed and spit it out of her mouth onto the floor. She stifled the sound of her coughing until it subsided. She sat up and filled the glass with water again and poured more white powder in. This time she forced it down and leaned back on her pillow. As time passed, her mind grew fuzzy, her vision blurred, and her head began to spin. She panicked and struggled to get out of bed unsuccessfully. Maybe she'd taken too much. Her head was spinning. With what little strength she had, she rolled over onto her stomach and pushed the lamp on her side table off, making a crashing sound. The pocket door slid open, and she faintly saw her husband entering the room.

Gabriel forced two of his fingers down her throat making her retch the white liquid she'd drunk. The smell of vomit permeated the room.

Her head hung over the side of the bed. Gabriel's hands were covered in vomit. Holding his hands in front of him, he pushed the pocket door open with his hip and went into his bathroom. Water rushed over his hands. He lathered them with a soap bar and called out.

"You better not do that again, Magritte, or the next time I might let you."

He listened for a response, but got none. He rushed back into the room to see her taking the last of some pills and washing them down with whiskey. Gabriel grabbed her by the shoulders and began shaking her as hard as he could.

"What's wrong with you? Why are you doing this?"

Suddenly her body jerked forward and a stream of pills vomited out. Gabriel tried to repeat what he did before and put two fingers down her throat. This time she bit him. He retracted his fingers and stared at her face.

"Enough!" he screamed, slapping her face with the back of his hand. He grabbed her again inserting his fingers down her throat as he pulled her off the bed. She vomited again.

She was on her knees on the floor, her long auburn tresses covering her face. The few remaining pills had come out.

"I should have you committed for this."

"You can't stop me if I want to do it."

"So you can control your son's life? What kind of a mad woman are you? I won't let you do it, to him or Raul or to me."

She sat back on her buttocks and pushed her hair out of her face revealing her blood-red, demonic eyes. Tears streamed down her face and with a victorious smirk she stared at Gabriel.

"I'll do whatever it takes."

"Bitch! I'm staying here with you until you calm down."

Magritte's hysterical laughter forced Gabriel to reach down and pull her to her feet. Holding her by her shoulders, he looked into her face. His emotions seething, he pushed her back onto the bed and pulled the covers over her.

"If I have to, I'll use a strait jacket on you, so calm down and go to sleep."

Magritte rolled on her side away from Gabriel and closed her eyes.

By mid-afternoon Gabriel was slumped over, asleep in the chair next to Magritte's bed. Magritte looked at her sleeping husband. A quiet breath rose from his chest.

"Gabriel," she called out quietly, and then a little louder. She pushed the covers to the side and silently slithered out of her bed. He moved slightly and she stopped. His head fell to the side, still asleep. There was enough space between the partially opened pocket doors to squeeze though.

The covers on his stately four-poster bed were smoothed out. His butler had already fixed the room for the day and placed a fresh suit with a clean shirt on the bed. Magritte purposely left the bathroom door open. She reached down and placed the stopper in the tub's drain and turned the gold-plated faucets. Steamy hot water shot full force into the six-foot white porcelain tub. Her head was spinning a bit. She steadied herself and walked over to the sink and opened the medicine cabinet.

Gabriel's straight-edged razor and shaving cup sat on the bottom shelf. She picked up the razor. Pushing her hair to the side, she looked at her image in the mirror and saw her pink cheeks, creamy-white skin, and bloodshot eyes. The victorious smile resurfaced. She held up her right arm and looked at the inside of her wrist.

She'd read a novel many years before in which the heroine had slashed her wrists not to die but to get her way. She turned on the water in the sink and ran the razor blade over her right wrist. Her mouth quivered, and she winced from the pain. Blood ran down her arm onto her white lace nightdress. She studied the blood on the white silk. The pink color was leaving her cheeks, and her skin was turning a chalky white.

Steamy water pulsed in a constant flow and the tub began to overflow. She dragged the blade over her left wrist. She didn't feel any pain this time. The sink also began to overflow flooding the bathroom floor. Her body weakened, and she began to black out. Surely someone would find her soon, she thought. Her head throbbed and the pain from her wounds was more intense than she could bear. She called out. Losing her balance, she slipped onto the flooded floor. Water red with blood streamed out of the bathroom onto the oak floor and oriental rug. The bloody stream was the last thing she saw as her head sank onto the watery floor.

James knocked on Gabriel's door. There was no answer, so he opened the door and entered. His feet sloshed on the wet rug, and he noticed the water coming from the bathroom.

***

Dante wished the Bonnetia family had a telephone. He had no time. He jotted down a note on his stationery and handed it to James.

"Please make sure Juanita gets this," were his last words to James.

The car was running outside. They had to hurry to make it to the boat before dark. Magritte was in the back of a limousine wrapped in a blanket, her wrists bandaged, her head nodding back and forth, so weak she could barely open her eyes. Gabriel and the doctor sat with her in the back seat as their car drove off. Raul Paul and Grandfather Raul waited for Dante in another car. A boat would take them to the Channel Islands, so they could get away from Napa as quickly as possible until things blew over. Grandfather Raul insisted that the entire family go immediately. They couldn't afford a scandal right now with the big fund-raiser in preparation for the new wing at the hospital. If the family wasn't there, what happened couldn't be confirmed. Dante could return soon, but for now his family needed him. In the Rivera servants' quarters only James knew the truth, and he was loyal to the family, especially to Magritte. He washed up the blood himself and sent the rug off to be dry cleaned.

CHAPTER THIRTY

Since You Went Away

August 7, 1915

> *My Darling Juanita,*
>
> *I must go away for a few days. You know I love you, and when I return, we can discuss our future together.*
>
> *All my love,*
>
> *Dante*

James held the note and watched Dante dash to the car. The limousine circled the crescent-shaped driveway and headed down the inclined road. When the car was out of sight, James placed the note in his pocket. He walked down the back staircase into the kitchen area. The cook was busy making dinner.

"The family will not be here for dinner tonight. They will be gone for some time," James told the cook.

"All of them?" questioned the cook.

James walked past the cook and went over to the stove. He lifted up a burner and looked down. A small fire burned inside. He slipped the note out of his pocket, ripped it in quarters, and threw it into the fire. Flames shot up as the paper ignited, and James replaced the burner.

"Yes, all of them," replied James.

The Rivera family reached their Channel Island compound the next morning. A horse-drawn carriage carried the family to the retreat on a secluded part of the island.

A week went by. An antsy Dante wanted to return to the valley. Magritte begged him to stay. She asked for his forgiveness. She wanted her sons near her during her recovery. She was warming up to the idea that Dante and Juanita were a couple. She wanted to spend time with Juanita when she was better. She was so sorry for what she did. She only wanted her family around her for a few more days. Dante jotted off a letter to Juanita explaining everything and left it on a table in the front hall with the other mail and went for a walk.

The doctor injected Magritte twice a day with morphine to calm her nerves and stop any pain she had. Vacant-eyed, her mind would soar after each injection. When the drug wore off, the period in-between became excruciating. Only her nerve pills could relieve her anxiety until it was time for another injection. As she waited for her injection, she slipped downstairs. She saw Dante's letter on the hallway table. Magritte picked it up and tore it apart placing the pieces in her dressing gown. She opened the table draw and took out an envelope addressed to her servant James. Inside were two letters: one to Juanita that Magritte had carefully written in Dante's handwriting and one to Dante in Juanita's handwriting that she had copied from the letter she took from Dante's room.

One week later the boat arrived with a package from James. The horse-drawn wagon wound its way up the path to the Rivera retreat. The old driver shuffled toward the cottage. With anticipation Dante came to the door and thanked the old man with a tip and took the package. He ripped it open. There was a letter from Juanita. He tore open the envelope.

Dante,

I want to thank you for taking me to the dance. I know you care for me. and I wish I felt the same. I think it would be best if we

stopped seeing one another. I hope you understand. I care for you but not in the way you care for me. Please don't contact me.
>   *Sincerely,*
>   *Juanita Bonnetia*

He read the letter again. Something wasn't right. He was empty, in shock. This couldn't be. She loved him, and he loved her. She told him she loved him and would love him forever. He would go see her despite her not wanting him to. She owed him an explanation, but the weekly boat from the island was gone and it would be another week before he could leave.

Juanita went to the mailbox. There was a letter for her from Dante. She ripped open the envelope.

Dear Juanita,
>   *I hope this letter finds you in good health. I have had second thoughts about our relationship. I think you're a wonderful person, but I realize now we're too young to understand what love is. I think we should stop seeing one another for now and see other people. Please don't try and contact me. It would be better to cut ties now.*
>   *Fondest regards,*
>   *Dante*

CHAPTER THIRTY-ONE

The Arrangement

Don Carlos Delgado's father, Juan, arranged the union between Don Carlos and Dominga Castañeda's family in Spain in 1830. Dominga, a distant cousin of Don Carlos going back many generations, lived in the Spanish town his father's family was originally from.

It took several years of hard work before Don Carlos felt comfortable enough to bring a wife to his remote northern California ranch. He and a cousin traveled to Spain where he married Dominga having never met her until then. The newly married couple, virtual strangers, left Spain for America a week later. They had the two boys early on in their surprisingly happy union. After the two boys were born, Dominga suffered several miscarriages, and her health became compromised. Don Carlos was overwrought about her health. She had become weak and vulnerable to any illness that came around.

His mind was distracted as he tried to concentrate on his duties of running the ranch. One of his cowhands informed him there was a squatter living on the farthest point to the southeast of the ranch tucked in a ravine on a hillside. Don Carlos insisted he would investigate it alone. He needed time to sort out his thoughts, and this was a good opportunity to be alone and do that. Smoke curled up from a makeshift metal pipe chimney in a one-room cabin the squatter had built from trees he cut down in the nearby woods. A few goats were staked outside. Goats and sheep were the cattleman's nightmare. A herd of these animals could strip a grassland bare in little time leaving nothing for the cows. As Don Carlos approached, the man came out of his shack.

"Howdy," the white man said, seemingly friendly.

"I need to inform you that you are on my property," said Don Carlos. The man only laughed.

"No," he said. "I claimed this property and it's mine."

Don Carlos dismounted his horse and approached the man on foot, a man who was a good bit taller than Don Carlos. He seemed scruffy by nature with an unkempt appearance in contrast to Don Carlos' meticulous grooming.

"I have a deed, my friend, to this land and all the land around you. I can take you into town and show you, or you can leave now and go someplace else," said Don Carlos.

"I ain't goin' nowhere. This here was open land, and I claimed it. No half-breed Mexican is gonna tell me what to do, I'm a citizen of this here country, born here, and…."

He never uttered another word. Angered by the slur, Don Carlos pulled out his gun and shot the man in the heart. This was the second time he'd killed. Only this time Don Carlos felt justified in his action. The man's searing words had sealed his fate. Don Carlos dug a shallow grave with a shovel he found in the man's shack and tossed the body in. He marked it with a pile of rocks. He gathered up the goats and took them back to the ranch. The goats' milk revived Dominga, and a year later she became pregnant with Juanita.

When Juanita was born, they looked upon her as a blessing. Dominga never fully recovered from all the miscarriages and her difficult pregnancy with Juanita. In her last years, she was often bedridden. Just before Juanita turned five Dominga died. Juanita's memories of her mother were of her holding her hand while Dominga would pat it and tell her stories. Juanita dwelled upon her sweet smile and kindness when she looked at her portrait that hung over the mantel in the great room.

Don Carlos never told anyone about the killing. When he and the Vallejo Brothers decided it was time for a doctor, Don Carlos offered the land around the shack as an inducement. He went back to the shack and searched for the pile of rocks. He walked the edge of the ridge as his horse grazed ahead of him. The horse moved a clump of grass exposing the pile of rocks about twenty feet on the other side of Don Carlos' property. He had killed an innocent man on his own property, not a squatter.

CHAPTER THIRTY-TWO

The Choice

Napa, December 25, 1859

Juanita fell asleep on the couch in front of her mother's portrait. She prayed throughout the night, asking the angels for help. In the morning she knelt and prayed for her brother's life and that her love for Dr. Rivera would persevere.

The vitality Don Carlos had regained had now gone. When Juanita found him in the kitchen, she asked him how Emanuel was.

"His pulse is stronger," replied Don Carlos.

Mai poured Don Carlos a cup of coffee. He sat at the table, a broken man with his head in hand. Why, he wondered?

"Why has this happened? Where did I go wrong? I only want the best for my children," he said.

"We love you Papa, but maybe Emanuel loves Huan."

Don Carlos said nothing. He straightened his body and slightly turned his head toward Mai in a moment of silence that seemed an eternity. Juanita's emotions turned up fast inside her until they couldn't be contained. She blurted it out.

"I am in love as well. To a wonderful man, and I want to marry him."

Don Carlos focused on Juanita, digesting the words she'd just uttered. He said nothing.

"I want to marry him, to be with him. He is coming to talk to you. Please, Papa, understand. We love one another as Huan and Emanuel love one another."

"You are too young to understand what love is. You simply have a crush on someone and crushes always burn hot and go out fast."

"I do know what love is. I have experienced it."

Don Carlos stood up, towering over his daughter.

"Did you give yourself to him?"

Juanita gave him a confused look. "What? I love him."

Don Carlos grabbed Juanita and began shaking her.

"Did you have relations with him? Who is he and where did you meet him?" The words spit out of Don Carlos' mouth.

Juanita cowered in her chair. She'd never seen her father like this before. He bent forward until his face was inches away from hers. He didn't touch her, but he wanted to. He questioned her with such vicious anger that Juanita's body began to quake, and she had to cover her ears.

"I knew when I heard my sister deserted you, something like this might happen. She was supposed to protect you, keep you pure. I forbid it and will kill this man before I see you with him. You will marry Franco Navarro as agreed, and Emanuel will marry Esmeralda Sims."

Frightened, Juanita pushed away from her father. She had never seen such wrath from him before.

"Don't think about running away like your brother did. You will stay in your room until I decide what to do next. For now, I worry about your brother, not you, and hope he survives. Do your duty and go pray for him."

Hysteria overtook Juanita. She rushed up the stairs to her room, shut the door, and sobbed on her bed. Buttons tried to comfort her. A short time later she heard her father's footsteps on the stairs and in the hallway. There was a key working its way into the lock on her door. Then a click. Juanita rushed over and tried to open her door. It was locked. A note had been slipped under the door. She was locked in for her safe keeping.

CHAPTER THIRTY-THREE

Christmas

December 25, 1859

D r. Rivera saved as much of Emanuel's right foot as he could, but some of his toes and fingers that had turned black from frostbite had to be amputated before more infection set in. It would take time before they knew about the extent of nerve damage.

Emanuel lay unconscious, lashed to his bed with rope to keep him still. Juanita could hear Dr. Rivera's voice downstairs and knew he'd been there. She looked out her window at the ominous winter skies. She worried about her brother's health.

The next day Dr. Rivera sat in the suede, wingback chair in Don Carlos' den. Don Carlos thanked him. Dante's mind turned—there would be no better time to talk to Don Carlos.

"Emanuel will live, but you must be careful about infection—it could still kill him. Things around him must remain very clean, and his bandages must be changed daily."

"Dr. Rivera, you have saved my son's life," said Don Carlos.

"It will be months, if ever, that Emanuel fully recovers. Maybe in the spring we will know the extent of the damage," replied Dr. Rivera.

In the last few days the two men had grown closer together as friends as they dealt with Emanuel's condition. Don

Carlos had broken down in tears several times and the doctor consoled him. He was grateful his son would live and grateful for the doctor's help.

"You, Dr. Rivera, made the difference. I believe without your help the outcome would have been different. I am now even more thankful my friend Salvador Vallejo wrote to you in Spain and had you come live here. The land you have as your own has gone to good use," Don Carlos said tearfully.

"Your son is a good man, and I feel a special bond with your family. Juanita has become part of my family. I have wanted to talk to you for several days, but the time has not been right. I believe today it is and you may be more understanding. I am in love with your daughter and wish to marry her."

Don Carlos looked up from his tears into Dr. Rivera's face.

"It was you? A man I trusted with my daughter's well-being. You were the one who soiled my daughter, you invaded her naive soul and jeopardized her, tarnishing her reputation. You committed a sin in the eyes of God, the church, and myself. My beautiful daughter was pure, and now she is, what? What did you do with her? No one knows about this except the three of us, and it will stay that way. If it was anyone else you would be dead by now, but you just saved my son's life. You will leave my house now and never return. You will never see my daughter again, and if you try, I will ruin you. Think of your own children. They have already lost one parent. Do you want to make them orphans? You have worked hard to make a life for yourself and for them here in the valley. I could change that in a matter of seconds. But I am a generous man. You should say a thank you at this year's end that you are still alive. Go now and never have contact with Juanita again."

"Please, Don Carlos, let me reason with you," replied Dr. Rivera. The answer was swift. Don Carlos pulled out his Smith and Wesson from top desk drawer and pointed it at Dr. Rivera's head. The doctor didn't move until Don Carlos cocked the gun.

"I will say it was an accident, and you know they will believe me. I am the justice here in the valley. Leave now and mind what I said, never see or have contact with my daughter again or I will ruin you. And say not one word of this or your indiscretion with my daughter to anyone."

Dr. Rivera slowly got up and backed up to the door.

Through her bedroom window Juanita watched Dante ride off. A brief glimmer of hope streamed into her consciousness and faded just as quickly. Somehow at that moment she knew the man she loved was leaving her life. The door to her bedroom flung open and her father walked in.

"I know now who it was. You will begin your courtship with Franco Navarro when you arrive in San Francisco and marry him one year later. You will never see Dr. Rivera again, and if you do, I will kill him. Do you understand?"

Don Carlos slammed the bedroom door shut and locked it again. The father Juanita had loved so dearly, the caring, kind man who would do anything for her, was gone.

Before sunrise the next morning, fully dressed Juanita waited in her room, and while holding Buttons, she rang her bell for Ju to come. When Ju opened the locked door, Juanita pushed her out of the way saying she was sorry and locked Ju in. Juanita held onto Buttons' mouth tightly, so he wouldn't bark and listened at the back stairs. No sounds came from the kitchen. She rushed out of the back door and ran to the barns. Wanton was in his stall. She threw on a set of Emanuel's work clothes, tucked her hair up under his cowboy hat and saddled Wanton. Juanita placed Buttons in a saddlebag and rode off. She reached The Mighty Oak Ranch and knocked on the front door. Rosa answered. Buttons squirmed in her arms wanting to go inside. In the great room, she could see a large Christmas tree. The children were not yet up. The gifts for Three Kings Day sat under the tree. Rosa closed the door slightly, a look of pity on her face. With her partially lame foot, she held the door firm.

"No one here, Señorita Juanita, they all go. I don't know when they come back."

Juanita sank. She had her answer. Her love had deserted her. She pushed Buttons through the slightly open door to Rosa.

"Buttons is a gift to the children who love him so very much."

Juanita stroked Buttons one more time and backed away from the house. When Rosa shut the door, the life force floated out of Juanita. Dejected, Juanita rode off on Wanton.

The morning sun was beginning its rise over the eastern slope of the mountains. Juanita galloped down the path toward the pass. The trail was deserted on this early post-Christmas day. She rode toward the river to a secluded spot away from town and away from the ferry landing where no one would see her. She was almost there when she noticed another rider galloping toward her. The rider was a good distance down the trail before veering off toward Juanita. She tried to take Wanton from a gallop to a run toward the high grasses and the steep riverbank, but Wanton's still weak legs began to give out and he began to limp.

Don Carlos kicked his heels into his horse to push him to a gallop when he saw his daughter. Juanita looked back. His face was ominously dark, almost villainous. Within reach of the river, Juanita pulled on the reins, jumped off the lame horse, and ran toward the river's bank. Don Carlos flipped the ends of the long rawhide leather reins from side to side wrapping them into the tender underbelly of his horse making him run faster. As Juanita looked back, she stumbled to the ground and hit her stomach on a log, which knocked the wind out of her. She gasped for air, crawling toward the riverbank on all fours. He was the fox and she the rabbit. Juanita got to her feet and waded into the shallows. She had almost reached the deep water when Don Carlos galloped his horse into the water. He grabbed Juanita by her hair. Juanita's head pulled back; she let out a scream. She reached up to push his hand away.

Don Carlos held tightly without letting go. He jumped off his horse, splashed into the water, and caught her by the waist. The old man was pumped with adrenaline. She tried to fight him but to no avail. Before she realized what was happening, he had tied her hands together and dragged her to the shore. Don Carlos' horse waited. Wanton stood nearby.

"You can either get on my horse or walk back to the ranch. It's up to you."

Juanita tugged at the rope. She almost pulled it away, but Don Carlos was quicker. He forced her up on his horse's back and tethered her to the saddle. He grabbed Wanton's reins and mounted his horse while holding on to Juanita.

"Foolish child of mine. Life is a precious gift, and you would throw it away for this man. I will not let you do it if I have to keep you tied up for the rest of it. Soon you will see how silly you almost were. This man did not fight for you when he confronted me. No. He caved like a cowardly dog and rode off with his tail between his legs, and you would die for that."

The next morning Aunt Alicia and Uncle Ferdinand arrived. In the afternoon they left with Juanita for San Francisco. Don Carlos unleashed a condemning rage at Consuelo for leaving Juanita alone at the ranch when it was her duty to watch the young woman. No one knew the circumstances better than she did of what might happen if Juanita was not chaste. It had been selfish for her to leave. Consuelo's shame consumed her. Her brother had taken her in and made sure she was taken care of. She failed him. Aunt Alicia and Uncle Ferdinand would keep a watchful eye on Juanita.

CHAPTER THIRTY-FOUR

August's End

August 1915

August 22, 1915

My dearest Dante,

I can only assume you have fallen out of love with me. With your absence from my life an empty ache possesses my heart that I cannot seem to fill, but I will try. For whatever your reasons Dante, I wish you well, and I wish you happiness.

Truly yours,

Juanita

Two weeks went by and Juanita had heard nothing from Dante. She sent him a few letters, but got no reply. She decided to go to the mansion. James answered the door. He told her the family was on an extended holiday and had no return date. Juanita was crushed. She could only assume Dante had changed his mind. Then she received his letter.

The last week of August Juanita left for New York to study at the Art Students League. She said a tearful good-bye to her parents. Her grandmother was too distraught to come to the station. The porters carried her trunk onto the San Francisco, Napa and Calistoga electric train. In San Francisco she would get a tourist sleeper car on the Santa Fe Railroad to

Chicago arriving three days later. In Chicago, the New York Central line would take her to New York City.

The electric train passed through the town of Napa and moved south. Juanita looked out of the window to see in the distance the Rivera mansion with hillsides full of grapevines. The Mighty Oak Winery whizzed by as the train picked up speed. With hardened emotion she thought, "How foolish I was to think a young man like Dante could love me?"

Magritte consoled her heartbroken son. He should go to South America for a long trip. There was a horse farm in Argentina he'd wanted to visit. Why not go there for the winter? When Dante came back, he could throw himself into the running of the family business, maybe consider getting into politics.

The next note James posted to Magritte arrived saying that he'd heard Juanita was gone. Magritte made a miraculous recovery. Her convalescence was over. She ripped the note in a thousand pieces and burned it in the fireplace. The weather was changing to fall and when the ferry left the next time, the Rivera family would be on it returning to Napa.

Magritte craved the narcotics that she had learned to love more with each injection. At night she felt empty, and her skin itched. She took more nerve pills, but they did less. Her body sweated profusely. She had accomplished what she set out to do in separating Dante and Juanita. She would pay a dear price for her actions, developing a new, profound lover in morphine.

***

Cranky old Samuel opened the door. He huffed up the five flights, complaining with each step. Juanita walked up behind him carrying her heavy bag while the empty-handed old landlord complained that if she took the room someone else would have to carry her trunk up.

The door pushed open and Juanita looked in.

The streetlight barely illuminated the small room through the dirty paned window with ragged curtains. The advertised scenic view was a pigeonhole-sized view of the East River. The tiny coal heater would pump out just enough heat to take the chill off. A cot-sized bed sat in the far corner with a rolled-up mattress. Bed springs hung down below the wooden frame, and a paint chipped gateleg table with two wooden ladder-backed chairs sat near the heater.

Juanita looked at the ad in the newspaper. The room, in her price range, was advertised as broom clean, furnished, with a view, and to date was the best she'd seen.

"Take it or leave it, I don't care. Toilet's two flights down, rent's due on the first. Two months in advance now. You buy your own coal, electricity included but shut off the light when you go."

Juanita reached into her handbag, counted out the money, and handed it to the old man who then handed her the key. He took a long look at her and noticed her dark skin.

"You ain't no gypsy, are you?"

"No, why?" said Juanita.

"Never mind, don't bother me unless you have to."

The old man gave her a halfhearted wave good-bye and shut the door. The dim light from the hallway disappeared. Only the streetlight shined in the window. Juanita fumbled around to find the pull string for the light above the table, the only source of light in the room. She looked out of the window through the cracked and dirty windowpane to the street below. An almost bare-leaved, half dead tree echoed back her inward sentiments. An old woman sold apples to a passerby. To the west sat a newsstand attended by a blind man. A gust of wind blew lifting up a woman's skirt to the amusement of some men standing on the corner drinking rotgut hooch they shared from a glass bottle in a brown paper bag. When a policeman rounded the corner, they scattered in different directions.

A blue mood fell over Juanita. She was homesick for the valley, and she'd only just gotten to New York. Her head felt like a pincushion with every thought of Dante pricking her brain. She wondered if anything was left up there. Juanita pulled out a sketchbook from her bag and began to draw in the dim light. She would use her art to take her mind away from any discomfort. Hours later a knock came at the door. Two men had carried up her trunk.

It took Juanita some getting used to having strangers up against her body as she rode the crowded Fifth Avenue street-car uptown to the Art Students League on 57th Street. Something about the elevated line frightened Juanita. Perhaps it was the loud squealing sounds that made her cover her ears or the spark spitting wheels that made her think of it as a beast. When she couldn't afford the streetcar, she walked.

She got a job at an art supply store in the Village on the weekends to afford enough coal to keep from freezing and just enough food to keep from starving. Young and talented Bohemian artists patronized the store. The burly Frenchman, Frankie Parnell, gave up his French citizenship when he moved to America but not his French ways. He opened late, closed for lunch, and stayed open past seven. In the evenings he frequented the coffee shops in the Village filled with the Bohemian underground. Frankie sensed Juanita's loneliness and invited her to join him for a coffee one Saturday night. She accepted, reassured his intentions were only platonic.

The small, smoky establishment filled with long-haired, scruffily dressed Bohemians was overwhelming. She stepped cautiously behind Frankie, using him as a human shield against the revelers who stayed as long as their money held out, or traveled from coffee shop to coffee shop in a nightly pilgrimage to converse the issues of the day, seek artistic recognition, and sex.

Two women kissed passionately in the corner. Juanita tried not to stare, but her curiosity got the best of her, making Frankie laugh.

"You never see that before, two women together. They are lovers. They call themselves lesbians. Those two men over there, they are lovers too." Juanita, to the amusement of Frankie, showed her embarrassment. He howled out an infectious belly laugh.

Juanita had firsthand exposure to artists like Georgia O'Keeffe, Edward Steichen, and Alfred Stieglitz, which changed her own work. Photography took on a new meaning. Conversations in coffee houses were of revolution and unconventional thoughts on religion. She met agnostics and Buddhists, pilgrims and outlaws. It was an intellectual's candy store. All provided a diversion from her past and a more prevalent fear that America might go to war. She became less homesick while buried under her activities.

In the late winter of 1916, her mother sent her a clipping about Dante's engagement to Cassandra from a San Francisco newspaper. Juanita took to her bed for two days before she forced herself out. She cried until there were no more tears. She'd pushed Dante far back into her thoughts, but a secret longing that they would get back together helped her cope with the sorrow.

***

Miserable, heartbroken, and apathetic, Juanita's rejection humbled and crippled Dante. He wanted to find out what happened and went over different scenarios in his head until he had to stop or go crazy. He returned from South America in the spring intending to confront her, only to find out she'd left town and gone to New York to study art. The few times he drove by the Bonnetia house, he never stopped. He was too broken and didn't want to bother her parents or really find out why she didn't love him anymore. Work was his salvation, but it didn't totally help. He began drinking heavily, and at his mother's request, he began to see Cassandra. He could barely tolerate her and unconsciously looked at their relationship as a punishment. He persevered despite his dislike of her, not to please his mother but out of self-deprivation. He finally gave in to his mother's wishes and let her arrange a marriage with Cassandra.

Cassandra Gillette flaunted the large pink diamond engagement ring in a pink gold setting that had belonged to Magritte's mother. Both women considered it a medal of achievement. A society wedding would take place in the early summer of 1917 when the flowers were in bloom and the weather in the valley was ideal.

Dante drank on the weekends until he passed out. He paid attention to Cassandra in public and avoided her in private. At parties the playful game was to find where Dante passed out at the end of the night. Cassandra would help him into the car and drive him home where James would then undress him and put him to bed. In the morning he'd wake with an intense headache, feeling terrible, and not remembering the night before. As painful as the hangovers were, it hurt less than thinking about Juanita. When he did think about her, his heart would ache and thoughts of suicide would enter his brain. He bought a new expensive car and a motorcycle that his father forbid him to ride for fear he would kill himself on it. His only joy in life was riding Starr. He'd ride Starr into the hills to spots where he and Juanita had spent time. His life was drudgery without her.

CHAPTER THIRTY-FIVE

Lita Nannie

Early 1917

Juanita crossed snowy 59th Street. Memories of kicking dried leaves in the fall warmed her feet in her thin leather shoes. She skipped around a snow bank and nearly fell slipping on a patch of ice she didn't see as she walked toward Central Park on her way home. She regretted that she'd agreed to get together at a bench in the park with a young man she knew from the village coffee houses. Both were financially strapped souls who didn't have streetcar fare. She pulled her muffler tighter around her neck to fend off the cold. The laughter of skaters echoed from the ice rink. The aromatic smell of hot chestnuts from pushcart vendors was enticing and reminded her that she'd skipped lunch, but some cheese and crackers waited for her in her room. She waved to the young man who was flapping his arms and jumping up and down to ward off the cold.

He took her art box and carried it for her as they walked over to Fifth Avenue on a journey downtown. Their vaporous breath turned into frosty clouds. They walked briskly, trying to warm up and reduce the chill in their bodies. Passing the homes of the city's social elite, this young Russian man, Igor, called out to them, "Nouveau riche scum."

They passed the Astor House. Mrs. Astor, whose husband John Jacob had been lost on the Titanic a few years earlier, had recently given up her fortune to marry her girlhood love. They passed the Bristol Hotel and forged through busy two-way traffic on 42nd Street to the other side where the Public Library stood with its regal lions sitting sentry in front. As they reached 23rd Street a gust of wind roared through the canyon of buildings. They walked east until they reached the tenement building where Juanita lived. Igor tried to kiss Juanita, but she pulled her face back and turned her cheek.

"I must return to Russia; a revolution is imminent."

Juanita held back a smirk. Igor had talked about a revolution every time she saw him for the past year and many times had said he'd have to leave soon. It was a come-on, she thought, to enlist her sympathy.

"Have a safe trip," she said as she'd said to him many times before.

When she walked inside, there was a note on Samuel's door for Juanita; he had something for her. A telegram had come. "Come home, grandmother sick, money gram at W.U. office."

Juanita looked out of the train window as it rambled over the hills of the Napa Valley, a different person than when she left sixteen months ago. She'd immersed herself in the culture of New York, the museums, galleries, and music from classical to the new jazz. She'd marched with suffragists for the women's right to vote, and despite being a good Catholic, she supported the idea of birth control.

She was filled with a new appreciation for the quiet serenity of the valley after crowded, fanatically stimulating New York. As tantalizing as New York had become, she missed the valley and her family. She stepped off the train, felt the sultry winds, and took a deep breath, her lungs filling with clean California air.

Joe Bonnetia vigorously waved to his daughter as he watched her walk toward him on the wooden platform alongside the train tracks. He grabbed her in a bear hug, his eyes watery. He pulled back to look at her face before kissing her forehead and embracing her again. He'd missed and worried about his only child and the feeling of relief at having her safe in his arms overwhelmed him. The porter placed her trunk in the back of the old Model T Ford.

It was a short trip to the house from the station. Not much had changed in the time Juanita was gone. There were more automobiles and fewer horses. The town looked more pristine than she remembered. The fragile smell of roses filled her nostrils even though there were none and then a vision of Dante confiscated her brain. She closed her eyes tight and pushed his image away.

They drove down Main Street, past Cook and McKenzie's General Store, Tompkins Movie Palace, Wong's Chinese Laundry, Cannon's Blacksmith, and Saint John's Church. The boarded-up Muller's Butcher Shop drew her attention.

"Dad, what happened to Muller's?"

Juanita went to school with Henry Muller. She knew he was sweet on her, but far too shy to ever act on it. They were a good family, who supported many charities in the valley and had been there longer than most, three or four generations.

Joe Bonnetia said nothing at first, only shook his head.

"Rumor got started they were German spies. Stupid people. First, they stopped going there for their meat. Then the name-calling started, and finally the store was vandalized. Stupid town forced Mr. Muller, a good man, out of business. Now the town has to travel miles for their meat."

Insanity, thought Juanita. The Muller family had lived in the valley since the gold rush days. One of Mr. Muller's grandfathers came in search of gold and never left. He fell in love with the valley and sent for his family. Ever since then they'd had the butcher shop in town. Young Henry would have been the next generation to operate it.

The car sputtered down Main Street, turning right at First Street to their home. Joe pulled the Model T into the driveway and cut the engine.

The back door creaked open. Dalila Bonnetia came down the steps to give her daughter a long, hard hug. Dalila looped her arm into her daughter's, and they walked into the house.

Juanita was used to seeing her grandmother in the kitchen. When she glanced into the room, she saw the reflection of her grandmother's favorite apron in the window. She called out, "Lita Nannie."

"Nannie is upstairs in her room, Juanita."

"Please, try not to let her see you disturbed by the way she looks. It upsets her," whispered Dalila.

Lita Nannie was a proud woman who had always taken care of herself. Juanita was shocked when she entered the room and could barely recognize her sleeping grandmother. The once vivacious woman had turned frail and old. She had broken her hip in a fall and could no longer get out of bed. Her pure white long hair that was usually tied back in a familiar bun hung loose and down. Her tawny skin had a milky white hue with dark purple splotches, and was draped loosely over the outline of her bones. It seemed like every ounce of muscle and fat was gone. A box of Lita Nannie's favorite peppermints sat on the table next to her bed. She would have one or two every night to help her digestion. Juanita sat down in a chair next to her grandmother's bed. The smell of lavender dusting powder and the peppermints were the only familiar reminder that her grandmother was still there.

After a few minutes Lita Nannie woke up. She stared into space for a moment before stretching her thin arms in the air. She turned to see her granddaughter.

"My baby!"

Juanita softly fell into her grandmother's arms. The old woman wrapped her granddaughter in a loving ethereal embrace.

Juanita lifted her head to study her grandmother. She pushed loose hair off Lita Nannie's face and stroked her cheek with the back of her hand.

"I missed you so, Lita Nannie. It's good to be home."

"They told me you were coming. I waited for you. Can you stay for awhile?"

"I won't leave. I promise."

Juanita took her grandmother's hand and squeezed it.

The old woman closed her eyes and went back into her other world.

***

Juanita Bonnetia enjoyed a new appreciation for the valley's beauty. Its open fields of golden grasses and rolling hillsides with scrub trees that became green near the rivers inspired her new work in photography. With what little money she had left, she set up a darkroom in the kitchen pantry and sent away for an enlarger and a used box camera from San Francisco. She darkened the only window in the pantry and used long shallow enamel pans for developing.

She was excited when the equipment arrived and couldn't wait to set up her tripod and box camera to begin. She set out to photograph a landscape that intrigued her. She looked through the viewfinder, fussed with the aperture, and focused the lens. Across the street was her subject. A heavy old rusted iron gate in front of an abandoned entrance to an old building set for demolition stood juxtaposed next to a field of golden grass. In the distance was a river. She adjusted the aperture again and waited for the sunlight to hit the gate where she wanted. She covered her head with black fabric and looked through the back of the camera at the upside-down image. A man was walking past. His head slumped forward, his face looking downward toward the ground. His feet scuffed along like an old man. She peeked around the side of the camera.

"Henry? Henry Muller?" she called out.

He turned toward her with a scowl on his face, but when he recognized Juanita, his expression softened. As she walked across the street, Henry wanted to run and hide. His feet moved from one side to the other in an uncontrollable shuffle. By the time she reached him, he stood perfectly still.

She heard him take a deep breath and stop breathing. Juanita touched his arm, and he gave off a slow, long exhale as his body straightened.

They talked for a while. When the light was just right, Juanita took her picture, and Henry helped pack up her camera and tripod. Afterwards they went for coffee.

Henry told Juanita he had a menial job at a lumberyard to support his parents. This was the only job he could find. His father Carl was very ill. He had never recovered from a stroke brought on by the loss of his business and the town's condemnation. His father had been a generous man who helped the poor and needy. When a customer with a large family had no money, he gave them meat so their children wouldn't go hungry. He started a fund-raiser to build the high school believing everyone deserved a good education and that a good education would help eliminate hatred and prejudice. This was not the case. Their name was German, and no German was any good in the eyes of the townspeople.

They reached the simple frame house at the edge of town. The yard was neat, but the house was in need of repairs that the Mullers could not afford. Henry offered to continue further into town to carry Juanita's equipment for her. When she declined, he slumped and his eyes fixed toward the ground as he opened the worn white picket gate and said good-bye.

"Wait, would you like to go to a picture show with me? Maybe this week?" she asked. Instantly Henry's pale cheeks turned a rosy pink, his face lit up like a child. They set a time and date.

Juanita walked home with the ghosts of all the anarchists and socialists she'd met in the coffee houses of Greenwich Village. She could more easily understand how their views might be right after seeing how narrow-minded gossip had such a terribly devastating effect on this decent family.

***

Dante rode Starr on the mornings when his hangovers weren't too bad. When he had bouts of sheer soberness, he worked hard at the winery developing new wines and more outlets for distribution. The winery thrived while Dante deteriorated. One morning he returned from his ride and received a notice that equipment and the new vines he ordered were in. He drove into town with two of his workers in a company truck. The truck's tires splashed through puddles that dotted the streets from last night's rain.

Dante headed over to the post office while the equipment and vines were being loaded into the truck. He peered out from inside the post office through a dirty window that filtered the outside world. A woman was walking toward the post office. Her hat was pulled down over her face, and her long coat was buttoned to her chin, protecting her from the cold and the onset of more rain. She reached the sidewalk in front of the post office and stood under the overhang, loosening the collar of her coat revealing her face. Dante was on the other side of the window only inches away. Deep-seated hope resurfaced. Unconsciously his hand reached up to touch her. He tapped on the window but a car horn muffled the tapping sound. He was about to run out to see her when Henry walked up. Dante watched Henry kiss Juanita on the cheek and they walked away. His heart sank. When the worker came to tell him the truck was loaded, Dante snapped.

He locked himself in his room, and did not come out for two days. He might have stayed in there longer had Grandfather Raul not knocked on his door to tell him Lita Nannie had died.

Father Pinca gave the graveside eulogy that was attended by Lita Nannie's children, grandchildren, Henry, his mother and a few friends. Juanita sobbed when the casket was lowered into the ground. Dalila hugged her daughter, and they cried together. Juanita turned to the other mourners. Her eyes settled on Grandfather Raul Cristoval Rivera, and she walked over to greet him. There was an older woman with him, his sister Angeles. She was a successful female doctor from the East whom Juanita had heard so much about. Grandfather Raul took Juanita's hands in his and noticed the ruby ring Juanita was wearing.

"Such a beautiful ring," he said.

"It was my grandmother's, she gave it to me before she died. It was one of the last things she had left from her former life. The only jewelry she kept."

"It's lovely and she loved you very much."

Grandfather Raul didn't elaborate on the ring's history. Others came up to her and her family to express their condolences. Juanita looked out in the distance to the cemetery's paved roadway. She noticed a long black limousine that had to belong to the Riveras. Dante stood leaning against the car. When he saw her looking his way, he stood up. Juanita's face went pale. Dante started walking toward her. He was halfway there when her father noticed and called out to Henry. The two men gathered around Juanita and walked her away. Dante stood in solace, dejected, waiting for his grandfather and great aunt.

***

The old vaudeville theater in town had been converted into a movie palace. There was a new Harold Lloyd movie, *Lonesome Luke*, playing. Henry thought it would be a good idea to take Juanita's mind off her sorrow by seeing a funny picture show.

When they arrived, there was a full house with few empty seats. They walked down the aisle looking for two seats together as the lights began to dim. Juanita didn't see Dante, but he saw her. The couple found two seats in the front. Dante waited until the lights were down and the audience was laughing before he left. His frustration had increased, his depression unbearable. She was so close but unattainable. He mulled over in his mind what must have happened to turn her away. He could barely stand being around Cassandra. When he looked at her, all he could see were her flaws: her square jaw, her big hands and feet, the way she cackled when she laughed, her yellow-red hair, and her pasty colored skin that she sometimes over rouged. The more he drank the worse his hangovers became. His body, mind, and heart ached until he couldn't take it any longer.

CHAPTER THIRTY-SIX

The Understanding

Napa, June 1917

Dante parked discreetly down the street from Juanita's house and waited, determined to confront her. She walked out of the house alone carrying her art box and walked up the street toward the hills. He waited until she was far enough away from her house. His car raced up the side road and pulled next to her. He got out of the car and stood in her way.

"Please, I want to talk to you, I need to talk to you. Will you get in?"

Juanita averted her gaze and tried to walk around him. He reached out and grabbed her arm.

"You at least owe me an explanation,"

"What?" she responded. "I owe you an explanation?"

"The letter you sent me. You didn't want to see me anymore," he said.

"What are you talking about. That was the letter you sent me."

Suddenly things were becoming clear to Dante.

"I think I can explain, if you'll listen."

They drove up into the hills to one of their old spots and Dante parked.

He opened the car door and Juanita slid out. At her feet was a maverick summer wild flower, too early for the season. He reached down and picked it, handing it to her. She looked out at the grasses waving with the wind and at the vista of purple-hued mountains as their color turned golden with the sunlight. She sniffed the flower.

"I love you, Juanita," he said.

He explained it must have been something his mother did. She never got the note from him explaining why he'd be gone. He told her of his mother's suicide attempt and the supposed note he received from her that she didn't love him anymore. Juanita softened but was still not totally convinced. Dante reached up to touch her face. He removed her hat and pulled some hair pins out to let her raven hair fall around her shoulders. He held a piece of hair to his nose to smell the fresh lavender scent and looked into her eyes. Tiny flecks of amber floated in the clear dark sea of her brown eyes like golden stars in a dark sky. Soon his arms were around her and their bodies melted together. There was an honest sincerity about him. Her body relaxed and they kissed.

"Marry me, marry me now, right away," he said.

Dante drove Juanita home and told her he would return in the evening. When he arrived home, he sat in his car and tried to calm down for fear that when he confronted his mother his anger toward her would be so intense he might hurt her. Magritte was upstairs in her room in the master suite doing needlepoint when he entered the room. His rage scared her.

"What did you do Mother? I just saw Juanita, and she knew nothing of my letter."

She cowered as he raised his hand and smashed the wooden frame that her needlepoint was on. "I will marry Juanita, and no one will stop me this time."

He left his mother and went to the Gillette mansion. Cassandra remained calm when Dante told her he never loved her, something she already knew. When he told her that he planned to marry Juanita, she took off the pink diamond ring and handed it to Dante.

It was late when Dante arrived back at Juanita's. She would be asleep, and he didn't want to disturb her parents. A light tapping sound came to Juanita's second-story bedroom window. Dante sat in a high branch of the oak tree in the back yard. She opened the window.

"Are you crazy?" she whispered laughingly to him.

He climbed in.

They sat on the edge of her bed, and he slipped the pink diamond ring onto her left index finger.

"Let's run off and get married right away," he whispered.

"I have to tell my parents first, but we can do it soon."

She had to break the news to Henry. He was a good man and had been through too much in his short life. They were only dating, but she knew how much he liked her. She wanted to tell him and not have him hear it from someone else.

In the weeks to come the lovers were inseparable. Juanita's parents accepted Dante back into their family with a cautious mind. Gabriel told Magritte to accept the inevitable and not to interfere again. She told Dante she was sorry and would give them the wedding they deserved if they waited. He declined.

She knew she had to do something soon.

Dalila heard a knock on the front door and went to answer it. On the other side of the door stood Magritte Smith Rivera. The two women had never met, but Magritte's image graced the Sunday society picture page of the newspaper often enough for Dalila to recognize her. Juanita had not elaborated to her parents the entire extent of Magritte's actions, only saying she had disapproved. Magritte knew the lovers would be gone until late and now was the time to strike.

Dalila invited Magritte in and called to Joe. Magritte told them tearfully how it hurt her to tell them that her son was no good. She would have come sooner to warn them but it pained her so to admit it. He'd broken many hearts in the past. He was a cad who would break their beautiful daughter's heart if they let her marry him. He drank in excess and used ladies of the night to satisfy his urges. She sold it beautifully and even broke down in tears of anguish over the thought of her handsome playboy son ruining another young, innocent girl's life. He would deny it. She knew this, but she was his mother and knew better the ways of her son.

When Juanita came home that night, her bags were packed, and she was told in the still dark morning hours that she would be returning to New York to finish her studies. Earlier in the day, Joe had wired the money from the Western Union office to the Art Students League and to her old landlord for a room. No questions asked. She could not marry Dante was all her father said.

Juanita couldn't sleep. Confused, she cried all night long, not knowing what to do. She wanted to run to Dante and disobey her parents, but they had always been good to her and always had her best interest at heart.

CHAPTER THIRTY-SEVEN

The Courtship

San Francisco, 1860

The first three months were the most difficult. Juanita Delgado was depressed and suicidal. Aunt Alicia or a private nurse never left her side. Juanita ran a high fever and refused to eat. She became dangerously thin. Aunt Alicia stayed up nights with her. She would place cold compresses on her forehead to bring down the fever and spoon-feed her soup. In the moments when Juanita had some clarity, Aunt Alicia would reassure her that someday her heart would not hurt so badly. In a few weeks, she would meet her intended and things would be different. If at first she didn't find him pleasing, she should give him time and maybe she would learn to love him.

Don Carlos Delgado delayed his trip back to Washington by a month to watch over Emanuel for as long as he could, but his return to Washington was pressing. The Democratic Party was divided. The Southern faction wanted slavery to continue while others in the party, like Don Carlos, didn't. The unrest in the country was becoming stronger. His promise to throw his support and campaign for his party member, Stephen A. Douglas, haunted him. Don Carlos was convinced Douglas was the only candidate who could prevent conflict over the slavery issue. Douglas was a strong believer in democracy and had in the past introduced legislation to appease the slavery issue. He would compromise with the South, unlike the Republican candidate, Abraham Lincoln, who wanted to totally abolish slavery.

Don Carlos sent for a doctor from the French Hospital in San Francisco to tend to Emanuel who was still weak from the surgery and fighting off infection. He was months away from recovery. They hoped he would be able to walk again with the aid of a cane and perhaps even ride. Don Carlos agreed to let Huan and the children stay on the ranch for the time being. They would live apart from Emanuel but could visit him daily to spirit on his recovery. When he was better and on his feet again, the courtship with Esmeralda Sims would begin. Emanuel was in no condition to argue. His plan was to bide his time until he was well enough to take his family to Montana.

Don Carlos stayed over in San Francisco for two days on his return to Washington, D.C. He had forgiven his son Emanuel for his folly, but Juanita was different. She was a female who in a silly bout of frivolity had tainted her virtue. There was no way for sure he would ever know if she was still a virgin, the shame of which he would hide from her future husband and his family for her good and the family name.

When he saw her, he told her she was keeping on with her foolishness by not eating and that she looked terrible. Fortunately, Franco Navarro's return from Spain had been delayed. Juanita had time to recover before meeting her intended. Don Carlos' attitude was cold and distant. She would start the courtship when Franco Navarro returned. In the meantime, he postponed her meeting with the future in-laws by telling them she was not feeling well, but was anxious for Franco Navarro's return to San Francisco.

Her close, loving father was gone. Her lover had abandoned her. She was being treated like a piece of cattle to trade, knowing she would live the rest of her life in a loveless marriage with a man she didn't know.

***

Franco Navarro was from a long lineage of Spanish and Bourbon French. Their wealth went back several generations in the shipping industry. His grandfather, Ferdinand Vaspucci Navarro, saw a new market for shipping in America and moved his family to California long before the gold rush, establishing the first shipping company on the West coast. When he died, he left a very profitable business to his son, Miguel, with the impression that his grandson Franco would eventually take it over, but by 1857 shipping was in a decline. The country was in a recession and gold rush fever was waning. The Navarro Shipping Company still turned a profit, just not as nice of one as a few years before.

Franco was sent to Salamanca, Spain to be educated and made into a gentleman. This was at his grandfather's request, and he set up a trust fund to cover his education.

From the day Franco was born until his grandfather's death, Franco was his favorite. Ferdinand Vaspucci Navarro spoiled his grandson, calling him the Prince and telling him a lie the child believed—that he was of royal blood and could do anything he wanted. The young, impressionable boy believed he could do no wrong. His parents continued spoiling him and granted his every whim creating his rapacious attitude. He took after his grandfather physically being of short stature with a thick middle and a pleasant but not handsome face. His demeanor gave the impression of slovenliness. Like his grandfather, Franco was smart in a cunning way, but unlike his grandfather, he was lazy and preferred the easy way out his entire life.

Instead of a university education, he was schooled in bad manners and cultivated a taste for decadence. Early on he learned how to pay other students to sign him in and take tests for him. He never went to class. He spent his days at the dog races or in casinos gambling and drinking, and his evenings were spent with prostitutes at private clubs. He then slept all day until it was time to party again. He developed an insatiable taste for drinking, gambling, and women.

Because the official and formal courtship began three months later than originally planned, the Navarros agreed to a nine-month courtship instead of the customary one year. The wedding would take place in December 1860.

Don Carlos Delgado gave his daughter a substantial dowry. It was to remain in trust until after the wedding and not to be used until after the birth of a son. The intended were to meet twice a week for nine months, always chaperoned by Aunt Alicia, and there was to be little or no physical contact. Miguel Navarro and Don Carlos Delgado signed the agreement in early December of 1859. The two men had been in contact with one another for many years through a marriage broker. Don Carlos feared that the Navarros might find out about her indiscretion and call off the wedding.

Franco returned to San Francisco from Spain in March. He would have stayed longer, but his trust fund was running low. He staggered off the Navarro ship when it docked in the San Francisco harbor, his mother's chagrin evident. Señora Simone Navarro had arranged for a reporter from the society page of the newspaper and her ladies club to come along for a greeting.

The drunken Franco grabbed hold of the railing on the exit ramp to prevent himself from falling, only to trip at the bottom of the ramp and fall face down onto the wooden dock in front of his mother. Laughing hysterically, he rolled over and faced her with his breath reeking of liquor and cigars. The front of his tie and shirt were stained with drool and red wine. The reporter helped him up. Money exchanged hands to insure a favorable article in the newspaper announcing Franco Navarro's return to San Francisco after studying abroad in Salamanca, Spain. The ladies of his mother's club all received cut crystal goblets. Even so, gossip prevailed.

**

The courtship, as planned, started immediately upon Franco Navarro's return. The first meeting was at the Navarros' home, a pretentious, ornate Gothic mansion with an irregularly pitched gable roof and pointed stained glass arched windows that offered a breathtaking view of the harbor.

Aunt Alicia and Uncle Ferdinand represented Don Carlos and accompanied Juanita to a dinner party. It became apparent early on that the engaged couple had very little in common. Juanita was immediately disappointed in the way Franco looked and handled himself. His gluttonous eating and drinking habits at dinner disgusted her. His clothes were expensive, gaudy, and ill-fitting. In the one private moment the engaged couple had together, Franco told Juanita to bulk up because she was too thin. He wanted a wife of substance who could bear him a son.

Franco excused himself early to the drawing room for cigars and brandy with the men. After that night, Juanita didn't see him again for several days until his mother insisted that he take Juanita and Aunt Alicia to dinner.

Franco searched for new haunts. His tastes for gambling and prostitutes led him to pool halls. The favorite place of his surly new friends was an underground club, the Peninsula, run by Ramon Salvatore and his courtesan wife, Anita. Every night Anita danced her sensual flamenco to entice men to pay for sex with her. Franco found what he was looking for in Anita, a dance with the devil. Franco's first encounter enthralled him. Once they had sex, he was in love. He became jealous of the other men, and whenever possible, he would buy out her night.

The nine months passed slowly for Juanita. She remained disgusted at the thought of what awaited her. Aunt Alicia felt for her and wrote Don Carlos about Franco's behavior. It did no good. The contract Don Carlos signed was binding.

The twice a week rendezvous with Franco turned into once a week, to twice a month, to when he made time in his decadent lifestyle. As December approached Juanita braced herself. For Franco, his love for Anita grew to be obsessive with a deep resentment for Ramon. Franco believed he had won Anita's affections.

CHAPTER THIRTY-EIGHT

The Wedding

December 1860

Boxwood and holly wreaths hung on the double front doors of the pristine white Greek Revival style Catholic church at the foot of Nob Hill. White gardenias lined the steps and the view through the opened doors to the inside of the church was of an all-white interior with gold trim, a large Christmas tree decorated with gold glass globes and hundreds of small lit candles. Ambient sounds from a choir accompanied by a small orchestra resonated through the opened doors, greeting wedding guests as they entered the church.

In a back room off to the side of the church, Aunt Alicia dabbed pink rouge on Juanita's gray-tinged cheeks and lips. Aunt Consuelo knelt at a small altar in the corner praying for her and secretly asking God for forgiveness, feeling guilty about what was about to happen. Juanita's hair had become thin, dull, and brittle from malnutrition. Aunt Alicia stood back and looked at her. The rouged cheeks and lips made her look like a corpse. The closer to her wedding the more weight she'd lost. Aunt Alicia wiped off the rouge on Juanita's catatonic face as a seamstress frantically sewed her handmade tulle and lace wedding dress to her.

The church was crowded, mostly with the friends of the Navarros. Eduardo and his new wife Palmira, who was glowing with pregnancy, were there as was Emanuel, still walking with the aid of a cane. His intended, Esmeralda, sat with him on the bride's side chaperoned by Uncle Ferdinand.

A few months earlier Emanuel agreed to meet Esmeralda to convince his father they were not suited to one another. Much to Emanuel's surprise he enjoyed Esmeralda's company. They began seeing one another on a regular basis through the prearranged courtship, and he had begun to love her.

Juanita felt her life was ending. The last twelve months had been a nightmare. She'd gone from ecstasy with Dr. Rivera to horror with Franco Navarro. After the seamstress finished sewing her into her wedding dress, Juanita knelt at the altar to pray that Franco would not touch her—that he would never touch her.

Don Carlos Delgado entered the room. He looped his arm around Juanita's and nodded his head toward Aunt Alicia and Aunt Consuelo for them to leave. The two women scurried out of the door to their seats. Don Carlos led the hesitant Juanita to the doorway. The wedding march music began, and she felt like her execution was imminent.

The blood drained out of Juanita's face and her knees buckled. Don Carlos slapped the back of Juanita's hand. Her eyes shot open.

"Pay attention, my daughter," he said.

She looked down the long aisle. Franco and his cousin stood in front of the altar with the priest. The next thing she remembered was saying, "To love, honor, and obey." As she uttered the words, it seemed to revive her. God, forgive me for lying, she thought. She turned and looked directly at her father who sat in the front row and gave him back the same steely, cold look he'd given her a year before when he told her she would not be with Dr. Rivera. A cold shiver ran down his spine. He tried to control a head tremor. Just for a split second he considered that perhaps he'd made a mistake.

Franco was drunk but in control of his faculties during the ceremony. By the time the couple reached their reception party, he was inebriated to a state where most would have passed out. He waddled more than walked into the hall, much to the amusement of his friends who applauded to encourage him. The guests toasted the newlyweds when they left to begin married life together.

Inside at the reception, Don Carlos Delgado took an easy breath knowing his daughter was married and no one had found out about the indiscretion between Juanita and Dr. Rivera. His daughter's well-being and virtue were now set in stone. She would be taken care of financially. His journey back to Washington would happen before the holidays. Congress was in session and there was trouble brewing. The newly elected President Lincoln would take office in March.

***

Four white horses with feather-plumed headdresses, tethered to a white wedding carriage covered in gardenia and rose garlands, waited to take the newlyweds to their new home. Gaslights burned in the windows of homes as they passed. Nothing was said between the newlyweds on the post wedding ride. Franco continued to drink from a champagne bottle as a horrified Juanita sat next to him. The white horses pulled the carriage through the streets until they reached the new house. Franco stepped out leaving Juanita in the carriage. The driver helped her down to the stepping stone.

The new house, a gift from the Navarros and built near their mansion, was pretentiously grandiose with a granite foundation and resembled an ornate, formal Italian city villa.

Franco staggered up the granite steps glancing over his shoulder toward Juanita as if she were a puppy he was curious to find if it was following. The double front door opened. On the other side stood a tall, elegant older black man in formal butler attire who Franco didn't acknowledge and walked past.

Juanita held out her hand to him and introduced herself as Juanita Delgado. Witnessing this, Franco snickered.

Simone Navarro spared no expense furnishing the flamboyantly decorated interior. Juanita, who was never consulted, was inwardly appalled. The gaudy colors and furniture hurt her eyes. She much preferred the simpler Spanish-Mexican ranch style she was used to. She tried not to compare it to Dr. Rivera's simple but elegant stone ranch house or the ranch hacienda she grew up in.

Franco started up the stairs and turned, looking toward Juanita who stood with the butler, Carter. He called out, "Stop talking to my darky and come!"

Franco held open the door to Juanita's set of rooms. The front room was a small salon with maroon velvet chairs and a matching couch. In front of a fireplace was an iron screen in the shape of a peacock with fake jewels outlining the pattern of feathers. A large vase sat in the corner filled with peacock feathers. The paisley wallpaper picked up the colors of the feathers. A large canopied bed in the next room was covered with a bright purple and gold brocaded bedspread that was pulled back to expose a lace-trimmed wedding sheet. Matching cut-glass kerosene lamps sat on either side of the bed on matching tables. Paintings of angels and cupids were frescoed on the walls. To Juanita it was all vulgar.

"These doors lead to my rooms," said Franco. He opened the pocket doors, stepped into his room, and abruptly closed the doors. Juanita was alone, perhaps her prayers were answered. Moments later a quiet knock came to her door. Cleo, a young black woman, entered.

"Welcome, missy, me name is Cleo. I be your maid."

Cleo helped Juanita out of her wedding dress and into a pretty nightgown.

"Mr. Navarro, he go out, Missy Navarro. He probably no come back until late."

Cleo lowered the gaslights.

"Good night, missy Navarro."

Hearing her called Navarro gave Juanita a shock. Exhausted she nestled under the brocade cover and fell asleep.

In the middle of a dream the brocade spread was pulled abruptly off her. Half asleep she clung to the wedding sheet. Franco stood next to the bed. She tried to focus. Early morning light filtered through the curtains. He grabbed onto the sheet and ripped it off, the lace edge still in Juanita's hands. He pushed her nightgown up exposing the bottom half of her body. When she modestly tried to cover herself, he ripped her nightgown off. She wanted to cry but was too scared. He undid his fly and pushed her legs apart, mounting her and thrusting his penis into her hard. His heavy boots bruised her legs. The smell of cheap perfume, cigars, and sex made her gag. Two or three thrusts and it was over. He looked down into her face; his breath was repulsive. When she turned her face away, he pushed it back toward his.

"Don't you ever turn away from me again. You understand?"

Juanita in shock, said nothing.

He slapped her face. "Say you understand."

Terrified she shook her head yes. He leaned down and kissed her with his slobbering mouth before he pulled his penis out of her and rolled off. He pushed his penis back into his pants, not bothering to close the fly, and began to leave.

"Expect more of the same until you give me a son."

The slam of his pocket doors followed. Juanita buried her face in her hands to muffle her crying.

This behavior was repeated every night for two and a half months until Juanita became pregnant; then it stopped. Nine months later she gave birth to a baby girl. She'd hoped for a boy only to appease Franco. She named her daughter Dalila and loved her. Franco had nothing to do with his baby daughter.

Their one-year anniversary came with Christmas. Juanita wrapped Dalila in swaddling to take her to her in-laws for Christmas Eve. Franco, who was rarely home, had agreed to meet her at his parents. She'd grown fond of Miguel and Sim-one Navarro who had been very kind to her. Her father had not seen her since the wedding and had only sent a few letters asking about his granddaughter.

Franco arrived long after dinner. Miguel Navarro had lost his patience. Money was disappearing from the ship-ping company's safe, and Miguel knew who was taking it and where it was going. Tonight he would confront Franco who had just strolled into his parents' home reeking of alcohol. Miguel called to his son, and the two men went into the den and shut the pocket doors. Loud voices and shouting were heard followed by a long silence.

Miguel was in the middle of shouting when he grabbed at his chest and gasped for air. The next moment he dropped to the floor. Franco calmly walked over to a chair, sat down, and smugly watched his father struggle for breath. After a few minutes of silence, the pocket door opened and Franco walked out smoking a cigar. Miguel was lying on the floor dead.

***

Within months of Franco taking over the shipping business, there was barely anything left. He spent money they didn't have and tried to get into Juanita's dowry. When Juanita became pregnant again, a new hope surfaced for him. When she gave birth to another girl, Lucy, he was furious.

He spent all his time and what money could be had at the Peninsula. Ramon tried to wean him off his addiction to Anita by letting him have sex gratis with a few of the fleshy, full-hipped women he liked, but Franco remained obsessed with Anita, and his resentment toward Ramon grew. Ramon laughed it off when Franco pulled a gun on him one day but knew that in time a real altercation would surface. As long as Franco's money held out, Anita would service him while Ramon kept a watchful eye. When all the financial resources from the business ran out, Franco mortgaged his house and his mother's house.

When Lucy was four months old, Franco insisted Juanita hire a wet nurse so they could try for another baby. By now he wanted the money more than a son. When Juanita objected, he threatened the baby. She barely had time to put the baby in the crib before he took Juanita by force and then beat her. When he was finished, he left her on the bedroom floor, where she laid for a while unable to get up. For several days she hid in the house with the babies, not wanting to go out in public with her bruised face and cut lip. She asked a servant to find a wet nurse for her baby. Franco came to her every night until she was pregnant again.

Simone Navarro was forced to sell her house and furniture when it went into foreclosure. She moved in with her sister. Juanita confessed to her priest about what her marriage was like. He told her that she needed to give back to society, and God would help her. Juanita and Simone helped organize food drives to feed hungry children. Simone's high society friends reached deep into their pockets and donated money to start a foundling home and nursery connected to the French Hospital where Juanita performed charity work. It kept her children safe and away from their father during the day.

CHAPTER THIRTY-NINE

French Hospital

San Francisco, 1865

The head nurse walked Dr. Rivera toward the nursery. He was in San Francisco to study the progressive French Hospital as a model for his recently opened Rushing River Hospital in Napa. Unconsciously, Juanita poised herself when she heard the deep baritone voice with the unmistakable Castilian accent in the hallway. Smoothing out her apron over her pregnant stomach, she wondered if it was him. Instinct made him turn when he entered the nursery.

He was astonished. His knees slightly buckled, and he leaned toward her.

"Juanita!" he gasped. "Juanita, I've hoped for this moment for so long."

They spent the afternoon together, both with unsaid feelings for the other—feelings that had never changed. Juanita was still hurt by what had happened. She did not tell Dr. Rivera how her life had turned out. Her father's words stuck in her head. This man had abandoned her, and Dr. Rivera sensed Juanita's hurt.

She showed him her two daughters and that she was expecting again. Dante told Juanita how much Angeles and Raul missed her, and how they loved Buttons. Hours passed. Dr. Rivera dreaded the moment he had to leave, so did Juanita, but she kept up an air of indifference. As they stood in the doorway of the nursery to say good-bye, it became difficult for the doctor to contain his feelings. He kissed the back of her hand.

"Juanita, I die every time I think about what happened. That our life together didn't happen haunts me. I am glad for your happiness." He backed away and looked at her in the doorway.

"You are even more beautiful now than the first time I saw you. I still love you Juanita and always will."

She wanted to crumble down the walls she'd built around herself. She wanted to jump into his arms, but her pride and stubbornness won out. He'd abandoned her. He'd caved in to her father's threats. How could he love me? she thought.

Seeing Dr. Rivera again only made her situation seem even more hopeless. She was wounded, more than she realized. What her father had done was horrible. What Dr. Rivera did was unforgivable.

Juanita was sleeping downstairs with her baby girls in the main salon, close to giving birth to her third child. She hadn't seen Franco in days and had no idea where he was. The rest of the house was empty. Long ago she'd closed off the upper floors and sold the furniture to pay off debts for food, heat, and other essentials. Except for what was in the main salon—beds, a table and a few chairs—the rest was gone. The house was in the process of being sold. Juanita hoped to pay off the mortgage that had not been paid in months before Franco got his hands on the money. A foreclosure notice had arrived. With the pocket doors closed, the coal heater in the front room gave off enough heat to keep the children warm. It was late that night when a knock came to the door. It was the police.

Franco was on a week-long bender and had been sleeping in the streets. He was disgustingly dirty when he arrived at the Peninsula. Ramon told him Anita was with a customer and to wait at the gambling tables. Franco became belligerent. Ramon, seeing his chance, told the bartender to give Franco a free bottle of whiskey knowing more alcohol would accelerate Franco's anger. He didn't have the money to see Anita. He sat at the blackjack table, impatient and insulted. The addict's voice inside him fueled his conviction that he would eventually win enough at the table to spend the entire evening with Anita. When that didn't happen, Franco accused the dealer of stealing his money. Staggering backwards, he drew his pistol from a vest pocket and threatened to shoot the dealer if he didn't give him back his money. Ramon stepped in with his Smith and Wesson.

"Franco," Ramon called out.

When Franco turned, Ramon fired aiming at Franco's heart. Franco crumpled to the floor. Ramon calmly walked over and smiled at him as he died.

"Die my friend and good riddance."

Franco's eyes rolled back. Ramon reached for a bar towel to wipe his hands.

"He was a nuisance and he smelled."

Juanita listened to what the police officer was saying.

"Your husband Franco Navarro was killed, shot to death."

The police escorted her as she dropped the children off at her mother-in-law's and went to identify Franco's body at the Peninsula. A white sheet covered him. Blood was splattered on the wall; his body lay in a pool of blood on the floor. Anita had to see what Franco's wife looked like. She wrapped her satin robe around her naked body and strolled out of the back room. She stood next to Ramon and snickered at Juanita, as the police uncovered Franco's face.

"Yes, that's him," said Juanita.

She turned and glanced at Anita, the woman who had so influenced her life and the lives of her children. She is beautiful, thought Juanita. There was no resentment or unkindness from Juanita, which caught Anita off guard and deflected any animosity toward her. Juanita walked home at sunrise filled with a sense of relief. Her foolish husband was dead, and the horror her life had become was over. A part of Juanita felt sorry for Franco who had thrown away a promising life.

Juanita gave birth to a baby boy she called Miguel. She collected her dowry and packed up what few possessions were left. Her wish was to move back to the valley she loved and to raise her children in peace.

CHAPTER FORTY

The War

June 1917

A day and a half had passed since Juanita left for New York. Dante was packed and prepared to leave to be with Juanita when a man in uniform knocked on the mansion's front door. Dante was being conscripted because of his skill in hot air ballooning and was to leave immediately for duty to serve his country. He had no choice. He had to serve or go to jail. He sent Juanita a telegram from the train station in San Francisco explaining what had happened and that surely the war would be over in a few weeks. The telegram got delayed at the Western Union office with the overwhelming demands on the wires as millions tried to get in touch with one another.

In New York things were getting more chaotic with each passing day and the fanatic energy around Juanita was infectious. Young men waited in line to enlist in the armed services to protect their country. Some were fraught with disappointment when they were turned down for being too young or for some physical ailment, like flat feet. Rumors and suspicions ran rampant. Juanita heard that Germans had landed in the States and were hiding among regular everyday people as they planned to blow up factories.

Juanita received Dante's telegram and stayed another month before she decided to return to Napa. It was foolish for her to try and study. She couldn't concentrate; all she could think about was Dante, hoping he was safe. The war would be over soon, and they would be together. She sent a telegram to her parents about her return in Napa.

On the long train ride from Chicago to San Francisco, Juanita felt tired and already seemed to know. She had missed her period and had noticed that her clothes were fitting tightly. She rubbed her belly and thought about her passionate time with Dante under the phantom moon. When Dante was back from the war in a few weeks and they were in each other's arms, she would tell him about their baby on the way.

Joe Bonnetia picked Juanita up at the station. There was a letter from Gabriel telling her they were waiting for word about Dante's whereabouts. A letter he'd sent to her from France was forwarded and arrived back in Napa two months later.

My Dearest Darling,

I miss you so. I should have gone with you that day and dealt with my finances later, but I didn't and am now suffering through the consequences of my actions. A service man came to my door telling me I had no choice. I guess they would have found me in New York as well. I am unsure of what will happen next. I know that with the United States in this war it will be over soon and then we can be together. The first thing we must do when I get back is to marry. I have time on the ship and am drawing plans on how to restore my great-grandfather's stone ranch house for us to live in if we decide to return to Napa. I miss you my darling and hope to see you soon. Be well. I will write you and let you know where I am.

My love to you.

Dante

Dante was shipped out in an ill-fitting new wool cavalry uniform. On his back was a bedroll, a small shovel and a bag for supplies. On his cartridge belt was a canteen and pockets for ammunition for his .30 caliber rifle.

With a few hours of training, he became part of John J. "Black Jack" Pershing's first American Expeditionary Force landing in Europe at the end of June 1917. Fourteen ships carrying 14,500 men crossed the ocean landing at the port Saint-Nazaire, France. Some were regular army, some raw recruits, a battalion of marines, an elite group gathered from around the country, and a handful of young men who were experts in different areas. For Dante it was ballooning. The balloonists would be used to observe the advancement of German troops.

Dante befriended another balloonist, Roddy MacLoud, who reminded him of his brother Raul. Roddy MacLoud was an innocent farm boy from North Carolina with a heavy drawl in his speech. He was born on a dirt farm where they grew cotton and tobacco and had witnessed one of the Wright brothers' first flights. From that moment, he became hooked on flying, especially ballooning, and had a natural understanding of how weather worked.

Dante stood on the deck of one of fourteen ships that landed the Americans at the French port of Port Saint-Nazaire where General Black Jack Pershing stood on the dock to greet the men. The heavy losses of life and the mutiny of the French soldiers had paralyzed the war effort, but Black Jack insisted his troops be trained first in France, except for a few. The balloonists were needed immediately to monitor the front.

While Dante was trained in hot air balloons, he'd never worked with highly explosive hydrogen balloons. A British army balloonist took Dante and Roddy up on what was supposed to be a training exercise in a safe area close to Alsace. It had been quiet for some time. They floated high above the open French farmlands. A gust of wind pulled the balloon up to the north east. White puffs of smoke and flashes of light from ammunitions became visible. Once beautiful farms

marked with tree-lined borders dissolved into muddy burned-
out fields with deep trenches carved in the earth where the
soldiers lived, fought, and died.

As the balloon rose higher a German presence became
apparent. The Germans had won a battle that moved the western front in their favor. The wind pushed the balloon farther
to the east. Bullets rang out from below but out of reach of the
balloon. Roddy looked through his binoculars to see three or
four German planes, far enough away to look like toys hover-
ing in the sky. The British balloonist swore and maneuvered
the balloon to the west, but it was too late. The German planes
swarmed the balloon. The Brit screamed for them to put on
their parachutes as he scrambled for his. Dante grabbed his
and put it on. The balloon lumbered.

"Jump!" the Brit screamed as he leapt over the side hoping he would land behind friendly lines. Bullets whizzed by
Dante and Roddy in the basket. One hit the balloon tearing
a hole in the fabric. Instantly the hydrogen caught fire. The
roar from the flames deafened their ears as a draft pushed the
flames down momentarily engulfing Roddy. His wool uniform burst into flames. Dante grabbed Roddy and slapped at
the flames as he ripped the jacket off and pulled Roddy over
the side of the basket with him. They were free-falling. Dante
fumbled to find the lever on the chute and pulled it, hoping
it would open and that the flaming balloon wouldn't engulf
them on its way down. All this within seconds. Roddy clung
to Dante. The force of the opening chute pulled them upward,
like a kick from a mule. Roddy screamed with excruciating
pain but held tightly onto Dante, his hands and body trembling from pain and fear. The remains of the flaming balloon
fell within inches of them as they floated downward. In the
distance gunfire from the trenches rang out at the returning German planes. The hissing sound of bullets whizzed by
Dante and Roddy.

They hit the ground splattering in deep mud, just missing a barbed-wire fence. Disoriented, Dante laid flat on the

ground with a sharp pain in his right arm. Rounds of ammunition from a machine gun flew over his head. There was a
silence, then the machine gun rattled again. Dante rolled over
onto his back figuring he'd been shot or hurt in the fall. He
didn't have time to think about it; they had to get out of there.
His thoughts cleared enough for him to see the Brit fifty feet
in front of them running hunched over and zigzagging toward
a trench with bullets and shells exploding around him. There
was no cover. They were in the middle of a battle.

The Brit disappeared into the trench. It seemed to be
the only answer for safety. Time didn't exist. Roddy's moan-
ing in pain grabbed Dante's attention. Dante, on his back,
fumbled in his pouch for his pocketknife to cut himself out
of the chute. Hearing movement coming toward them, Dante
crawled, dragging Roddy around a clump of dirt. They laid
as flat as humanly possible while a group of German soldiers
charged up the hillside. Roddy's body convulsed. Dante stifled
his moans until the Germans passed. When the German soldiers were a safe distance away and there was a lull in the
gunfire, Dante grabbed Roddy, and they crawled in the thick
mud toward the trench and tumbled into it.

The gagging smell of rotting bodies, excrement, and
blood hit them in the face. No one seemed alive. Dante spotted the Brit sitting still, leaning against the dirt wall of the
trench a short distance away. Dante motioned to Roddy to
stay still and headed down the narrow dirt trench. He scaled
sand bags that had caved in and landed calf-deep in stag-
nant water. Floating in the water was a dead rat the size of
a large cat. Dante looked back toward Roddy and saw a wall
of enormous rats running into the trench. They seemed to
have an uncanny way of knowing when a battle was over and
wasted no time in beginning to devour the dead soldiers. The
Brit looked wide-eyed straight toward Dante. When Dante
touched his shoulder, the Brit fell over. Dante held him up and
noticed a small trickle of blood on the side of his head where
a bullet had entered. His back was awash with blood below a

deep bayonet wound. Dante heard German being spoken in a dugout nearby. The German soldiers that had charged up the hill seemed to be preoccupied with eating the food rations left behind by the French soldiers. Dante pushed the dead Brit's body back toward the mud wall of the trench and silently moved back to Roddy.

Dante and Roddy climbed out of the trench. They crawled to a bank of trees over the bodies of dead and wounded British, French, and German soldiers. One dead German soldier lay on his stomach with a broken bayonet stuck in his back still quivering. Others had their faces blown off or chopped at. Arms and legs lay strewn about. Dante and Roddy reached the bank of hardwood trees, a boundary line between two farms, and walked until they reached what looked like a small deserted farm about a mile from the field where the battle had taken place. Things seemed quiet there. They went into the barn. Inside there were two horses. Roddy pulled the scorched shirt that had become attached to his body with blood and burnt flesh. He ripped it loose and screamed with pain. Blood seeped from his wounds and mixed with his scorched flesh. A part of Roddy wanted to put his gun to his head and pull the trigger, a part of him wanted to live.

They settled in the barn's hayloft. A short time later an old farmer with one arm followed by his simpleminded son entered the barn. The farmer took no notice of the men in the hayloft being consumed by his task of tending to the horses. Small bits of hay fell from the loft as Dante peaked over the edge. The simpleminded son saw the pieces of hay fall and looked up at Dante. He poked at his father's arm and pointed toward the loft. Dante pleaded with the farmer in French saying his friend was badly burned and needed help unaware the farmer was stone deaf. In the distance, Dante heard a truck's motor. The truck with a horse trailer approached on the dirt road to the farm. The old man ran out of the barn and toward the truck which stopped. Two German soldiers climbed out of the truck as the old man began talking and pointing at the barn. The simpleminded son who had remained in the barn looked up at Dante with a big smile and gave a childlike wave.

Bareback, Roddy and Dante rode the two horses out of the back of the barn. They followed the bank of the river they'd visually mapped from the balloon, looking in vain for a place to cross. They could hear the truck's motor advancing toward them. Dante motioned to Roddy to stop. They dismounted and slapped the two horses' hindquarters and took off along the riverbank. Dante and Roddy dodged behind poplar trees and waded into the reeds along the riverbank until their bodies were submerged in the cool water. The German truck motored by. When it was quiet except for the rustling leaves on the trees, Dante and Roddy floated out into the water. The wonderful quiet and fresh smell of water washed the rancid smells and sounds of war away momentarily. They swam to the other side of the river and scaled the bank. The truck stopped when the soldiers saw the riderless horses grazing on grasses up ahead. The Germans backed up their truck to the poplars and watched Dante and Roddy running on the other side of the riverbank. One of the soldiers took out his Luger and fired a few rounds in the air before they went back to their original mission to gather the horses.

Roddy stumbled with his head hung low. He wrapped his arm around Dante's shoulder as they walked in the pitch-black night with no place to stop and rest. Without warning, the sky opened up with shell fire from the German's Big Bertha, and the war blazed around them. Shell fire from both sides filled the air. Dante grabbed Roddy tightly and looked for cover when gunfire lit the sky. A grenade exploded near them throwing dirt into Dante's eyes and leaving a ringing in his ears. He lowered Roddy to the ground to clean his eyes as another grenade hit, not as close as the other. Then there was a lull in the battle and darkness returned. With compromised vision Dante reached around in the dark to find Roddy. He called out his name, but there was no response. As he stepped forward, he tripped and fell into a deep hole. The gun fire opened up again. His eyes stung from dirt and tears, all he could hear was a ringing in his head, and his body ached from the fall. The battle lit up the sky enough for him to realize he'd fallen into a defunct cistern. A ball of fire passed over head and a strong smell of burning filled Dante's nostrils. He tried to crawl out of the hole but the slippery wall made him fall back to the bottom. The rat-a-tat-tat of a machine gun was over head, and he heard German spoken. Dante sat back down inside the hole, his mind a blur. He covered his ears from the deafening sound of war. He was sure the earth had swallowed him.

Daylight found a still silence above Dante. His body convulsed in a spasm from the wet cold, hunger, and shell shock. He looked up at the top of the hole to the light as an eerie slow-moving mist traveled over the hole until it was completely covered. In daylight he saw the stone and brick-lined, abandoned cistern he had fallen into. He wedged his feet and hands between the stone and brick crevices and successfully climbed out of the twelve-foot deep well. His head popped out above the ground-hugging mist to a clear day. Next to the hole was a pile of rocks, all that was left of a farmhouse. In front of him a German soldier was leaning against an old plow, his helmet partially over his face as if he were asleep. There was no sign of Roddy. Dante reached for his pistol and moved toward the soldier. The smell of gunpowder and a foul scent of horseradish or mustard lingered in the air. Still blurry-eyed, Dante tried to focus on the soldier who didn't move. Dante pointed his gun at the soldier and got no response. He pushed the helmet off the soldier's head and let it fell to the ground. A young, angelic face with a euphoric look and pale blue eyes stared at Dante. Curly white, blond hair crowned the top of the stiff dead boy's head. He looked to be around sixteen, maybe younger. Dante's head was spinning. He needed water. He staggered away looking for Roddy. The smell of death was becoming all too familiar. Past the ruins of the farmhouse and its barn, he surveyed the field ahead of him. There a sea of dead French and German soldiers laid in perfect rows, their faces gray, green, and yellow, as if they were the field's crop. Delirious, he grabbed at a dead soldier's canteen and shook it. Water sloshed back and forth inside. He screwed off the top and poured the water into his mouth when something hit him on the back of the head.

"Time to wake up, darling." Juanita's face smiled down at him.

He woke up with the sun in his eyes. It was a nice, clear day. In the blue sky, white billowy clouds lumbered above. He was prone on his back and had a brutal headache. Dante tried to move but couldn't. Something was weighing down his legs. He turned his head slightly and saw the face of a dead French soldier staring blankly toward him. Large blisters covered the French soldier's face. Dante realized that he lay among a pile of dead soldiers who had been gassed. The cistern lid he tripped on saved him from the gas.

The soldier's blank eyes began to move away from Dante. The corpse was being dragged off Dante's legs. He looked down at his feet; his boots were gone. He reached down to his belt; it was gone too. Dante looked around, rolling on his side to see the soldier that was on top of him being placed in a row of dead French soldiers all arranged neatly and segregated from the Germans. One of the dead soldiers moved. Maybe he was alive. Maybe the dead body's swollen belly had let out air. He could be French or German, it didn't matter. The German soldier who had dragged the body off of Dante pulled out his Luger pistol and shot the moving body out of mercy. Seeing this, Dante laid back down and played dead. Moments later someone grabbed his bare feet. His eyes glanced ahead to the back of the German uniform in front of him. Dante stayed limp. The soldier dragged him, placing him in the tidy row next to the dead French soldier. Bugs crawled over Dante onto his face and into his ears, but he remained still. Another German soldier came along and reached into Dante's pockets, but there was nothing there. He grabbed the ID medallion hanging around Dante's neck and yanked it off, placing it in a bag he had strapped across his neck. He moved on to the next soldier doing the same.

Dante waited for the Germans to walk away and then stood up. Disoriented and barefoot, he crossed the field of fresh dead soldiers. Unsure if he was dead himself, he wondered what happened to Roddy, and if he would ever see him again.

He walked for some time until he noticed smoke floating up from a stone chimney of a farmhouse. Crickets jumped around preparing for night. Dante walked out of the tree line into the field of jumping crickets and up to the clothesline next to the farmhouse. Among the fresh, damp laundry were men's pants, underwear, and shirts. A tied-up dog barked at Dante but responded with a wagging tail when Dante got close enough to pat his head. No one came out to check. A box on the window ledge contained a bottle of milk and some cheese. Dante drank the milk and shared the cheese with the dog to keep him quiet. He stripped off his dirty uniform to rid himself of the smell of death and put on the clean, damp clothes. As he walked away, he raised his good arm to his nose to smell the clean shirt.

He walked all night. In the morning tall grasses waved with the wind, and a hazy purple horizon reminded him of home. The sun had fully risen when exhaustion caught up with him. Time was an illusion. There was no way for him to remember how long it had been since he'd slept. He fought it as long as he could until he found what he thought was a safe place to close his eyes. On the other side of a woods was an empty, stone-fenced pasture. He sat under a chestnut tree with his back against the trunk and could feel the texture of the tree bark. He moved his body back and forth to scratch an itch. The branches overhead swayed in the wind and whispered through the tree. He looked at the skeletal remains of large plumes where white blossoms had formed from buds, bloomed, and now wilted next to young leaves that had become a natural canopy. When he woke up he would continue his search for the Allies. He hoped he was in French territory. His eyes closed and he fell into a deep sleep.

Someone kicked his thigh hard. Dante looked up at a handful of renegade German soldiers.

"Rouse mitt do."

"Vas?"

Gunfire made the renegades turn and scatter in opposite directions. Dante didn't understand what they were saying, but they began to run away as fast as they appeared. Dante sat up. One of the running soldiers pulled out his Luger, turned, and fired at Dante. Dante's head flew backward. The bullet grazed the right side of his head by the temple above his ear. Dante looked up toward the sky. Such a beautiful day. The sights of a budding summer surrounded him. The green color of the leaves seemed more intense as they fluttered softly on the trees. Wildflowers dotted the field. A butterfly landed nearby. How lucky they were, he thought, not to be trampled by war. He studied a flower close to him. How strange something so delicate could force the hard earth apart and bloom, like the flower he gave to Juanita when they got back together. His beautiful Juanita.

Then everything went dark.

CHAPTER FORTY-ONE

Fiona

1865

The dark mood inside Dr. Rivera returned after his unexpected meeting with Juanita. He had to figure out in his own head why he had abandoned the woman he loved, and why Don Carlos' threats had intimidated him. The answer came in his sleep. He relived the time the Carlists came to his door searching for an Isabellian rebel. They were ready to burn down his house with his sleeping children inside. Even though Dr. Rivera convinced the Carlist soldiers that he had not helped the rebel, he knew eventually they would find out the truth and be back. It was the reason Dr. Rivera left Spain. He hadn't understood how much this incident and the war had affected him until now.

He resolved to stop punishing himself. He had the children, his practice with the new hospital, and the developing winery. The life he'd carved out would be enough for him to go on, and Juanita was happy.

Fiona O'Donnell's youngest child, Jamie, was born around the time Dr. Rivera left Juanita. Jamie was a difficult birth, and Dr. Rivera had been called in by the midwife to help. Fiona's husband James, whom she described as a scrappy Irishman who loved a good fight, had gone to fight the rebels during the Civil War and been killed. An intelligent woman who could read and write, Fiona opened a bakery and lived above it with her children. Now a widow, Fiona was back for Dr. Rivera to examine her. She was pregnant. Fiona broke down in tears. She was a decent woman. To Fiona it would be a sin to have a child out of wedlock. She told Dr. Rivera the story of how she met a man at a church social. He'd recently returned from the war and said he knew her dead husband, although she now thought that was probably a lie. She fell in love and began seeing him. His intentions to marry seemed sincere, so one night she slept with him. The next morning he and the cash box from the bakery were gone.

She worried about the shame this would bring on her children. She loved Napa and had no place to go with the rest of her family dead or in Ireland. She begged Dante to help her abort the baby. He refused.

Dr. Rivera couldn't sleep. His thoughts were with Fiona and her situation. He worried that the stigma of her condition would make her do something rash. His mind wandered to his own culpability, Juanita, his sin of loving her and abandoning her like this man had abandoned Fiona. The man stole Fiona's money and good name. In Dr. Rivera's mind, he had stolen Juanita's virtue and innocence. If Fiona stayed in Napa, she would soon be ostracized in town and suffer painful gossip while the man who duped her went free.

The next day Dr. Rivera went to see Fiona at the bakery and offered to marry her and give her and her child his name. She was stunned. He told her in confidence about Juanita, the woman he loved and who he had recently seen by coincidence on his last trip to San Francisco. He would always love her, but now she was married and expecting her third child. Fiona was a good woman, and it was time his own children had a mother. She accepted, and they married that afternoon at the justice of peace office in St. Helena.

***

Don Carlos Delgado sat in one of the suede high-back wing chairs in his den. He was wrapped in a blanket and wore a stocking cap on his head to keep him warm. The curtains were open, so he could look out onto the barns and see the cattle grazing in the distant fields. His post in Washington was now filled by Eduardo who would finish out his term. Esmeralda entered the den and served him a cup of broth. He could no longer use his right hand or arm, so she helped him lift the cup to his mouth with his left hand.

The stroke he suffered had hit the left-side of his brain and affected his right-side functions and speech. He cried easily. Emanuel told him they had received a letter from Juanita. She had given birth to a boy, and her husband had been killed in an accident. She wanted to come home. The patient and caring Esmeralda was the only one who could decipher what Don Carlos was trying to say. It was frustrating for Don Carlos to try to communicate with anyone else. He had been very quiet all day and did not try to talk at all. He sipped at his broth and looked in the distance. When Esmeralda got up to leave, he reached his left arm out and weakly held on to her, trying to tell her something. She sat down again and concentrated on what he was trying to say.

"You want to see Juanita? Is that it? You want her to come home?"

Don Carlos shook his head yes. He lowered his head and began to cry.

Emanuel wrote to Juanita that their father was ill and wanted her to come home.

Juanita and the children were staying with their mother-in-law in the cramped apartment of Simone's sister when she received the letter to come home. There was nothing left to keep her in San Francisco. Two small trunks, an oversized wicker baby buggy, and all three children boarded the ferry to Napa.

When the ferry passed the numerous olive, plum, and grape groves, her heart filled with a joy that only coming home could bring. Bright red blossoms from the pomegranate shrubs were in full display as were the last plumes of the horse chestnuts. Farther down the river signs of a drought were apparent. Her children could breathe fresh air and play with abandon in open fields. She hoped to finally have the stability of life the ranch offered. She would see her father and tend to him. She would talk to Emanuel about staying and what role she could play. She thought about Dante and the possibility that things might finally work out. If she could forgive her father, she could forgive Dante.

Juanita was deep in thought when Dalila grabbed her arm and clung to it. Her babies were hungry, and they needed their mother. She prayed that her resentment toward her father would be gone and only love would fill her heart.

Her father was lying helpless in his bed. His advanced age and the war years spent in Washington proved to be too much for him. Many had died and suffered in the war of brother against brother. Now his body was crippled and his mind wandered.

Esmeralda gently shook Don Carlos' shoulder to wake him. Juanita stood next to his bed in disbelief of how ill her father was. His face was sunken and thin; his body was wasting away. When he opened his eyes and saw Juanita, he began to cry. Esmeralda left to give them privacy. Juanita held his hand as he struggled to talk to her. His body tossed in frustration. He closed his eyes and laid his head back to calm down. A few minutes later Esmeralda returned with Dalila and Emanuel who carried Juanita's two babies in his arms. Don Carlos gave a crooked smile when Juanita showed him her son. When the little girls came into his sight, uncontrollable tears streamed down his face.

"Forgive me. Forgive me," came out of his mouth in a profound clarity.

Juanita fell gently onto her father's body in a hug.

Don Carlos Delgado died in his sleep that night having lived a life that spanned from the end of the eighteenth century into the latter part of the nineteenth. A man of means and prominence, he lived a life he commanded, a life for his time, and was never overshadowed by others for better or for worse.

Juanita and her children were welcomed to the ranch with open arms by Emanuel and Esmeralda. The childless Esmeralda's maternal desires would be satisfied as she helped Juanita care for the children.

Juanita waited an appropriate amount of time after her father's funeral to send a note to Dante. He returned the note asking her to meet him in town for dinner.

Juanita entered the restaurant. Her hope rapidly dwindled when he told her he had married. He explained why he married and now regretted it. She wanted to scream, to punish herself for not telling him in San Francisco how unhappy she was and for not writing him sooner. If she had only told him then that she still loved him. She hadn't and now both were heartbroken. Dr. Rivera took Juanita's hand in his and looked at the ruby ring he'd given to her years earlier.

CHAPTER FORTY-TWO

We Regret

Napa, 1917–1918

The chauffeur waited next to the limousine and worried about his boss. Grandfather Raul's usual vigorous stride had been replaced with a slight shuffle and stooped shoulders—the gleam in his eyes was gone. The old man knocked on the door of the white cottage with the periwinkle trim and waited. Juanita answered. He could barely get the words out. The Red Cross had notified them that Dante was dead. Juanita crumpled to the floor.

It was becoming evident Juanita was pregnant. People were beginning to talk. Her love was now gone, and she tried to remain strong. Days passed. The gossip mill churned.

Henry Muller carried a bouquet of flowers up the walk and opened the gate. He was determined. Juanita answered the door. In her sorrow she'd forgotten about Henry. Months had passed since she last saw him. Henry asked if he could come in.

A small wedding ceremony at the Saint of the Sacred Heart Catholic church was performed by Father Pinca. A few friends and family attended and a small party followed at the Bonnetia home.

The newlyweds moved into the Muller house to help Henry's mother care for his father, Carl. As sole provider for his family, Henry was exempt from the war. He wanted to serve to prove to the world he hated Germans as much as they did, but now he had a good reason to stay home.

Two months later, Carl Muller died. His funeral was followed by a graveside eulogy. Juanita's round belly filled out the skirt of her dress. She hadn't felt well that morning. Her face was pale. She put her hand on her stomach and sat motionless at the graveside until her body slid off the chair. She hit the ground in a pool of blood. The baby was dead.

Henry struggled to nurse Juanita back to health. She was unwilling to live. He loved her. She was in love with a dead man, and the one thing she had left from him had died also. Henry told her he would understand if she wanted to leave him. He cherished the months they spent together; they were enough to last a lifetime.

A few months later she was pregnant again. The growing life inside of her gave her a renewed desire to go on. When the baby was born the following June, they named him Henry James Muller, Hank for short.

CHAPTER FORTY-THREE

The Rescue

French/German Border, 1917

Two young German milkmaids meandered along the country road near where a battle had been fought the day before. They were going to an upper field with a small herd of milk cows and a donkey cart. Yesterday the lower fields on the farm where they worked were full of crops and a grassy meadow for the cows. Today there was nothing but mud. The milkmaids hurried their cows to the upper pasture as fast as they would go. There was a small cottage on the edge of the pasture where they would stay, milk the cows, and daily take the milk into town on the donkey cart to sell.

Frida saw the man's body first under the horse chestnut tree, laying on his side in a ditch half filled with water. The part of his face they saw showed a handsome profile.

Lena was the braver of the two.

"I wonder how he died. There might be something of value left on him."

She reached into the pocket of his pants and pulled out the empty lining.

"So handsome, too bad he died so young," said Frida. She peered down into his face. A small ripple passed over the water.

"Help me turn him over, so I can look in his shirt pockets."

The two girls rolled Dante over and a gasp of air expelled from his lips. The two young women jumped back.

"Is he alive?"

"No, it was only the death rattle."

Dante gasped for air again.

"My God, he is alive. What should we do?"

Lena thought for a moment, looking at his handsome face.

"We shall take him with us and try to nurse him back to health."

"We don't know who he is. What if he's a bad man, a spy, or a Frenchman?"

"Do you want to die a virgin, Frida? Or die possibly having experienced lovemaking with this handsome young man? We have prayed to our Lord for a miracle like this and here it is. Or maybe you want to marry fat old Gus the butcher or wait and see if any young men survive the war?"

They placed Dante in the donkey cart and covered him with a tarp. Frida slapped the donkey's behind hard to get it to move. The cows followed.

A week went by. Each day the milkmaids took turns delivering their milk to town while the other would stay behind tending the cows and nursing Dante back to health. The bullet had missed his brain but pierced his skull. They spoke no English and only a smidgen of French. When Dante came around enough to speak, they spoke French. The milkmaids had never met an American, and when he told them he was from California, they assumed with his good looks he was a movie star.

Months passed. Summer turned to fall. Dante improved slowly. He could walk only a few feet. The milkmaids encouraged him prodding him to do better each day. Thoughts of returning to Juanita helped.

Dante knew he must be close to the French border. The milkmaids tried to explain where they were, but their knowledge of geography was limited. He couldn't remember much of what had happened to him and wondered if he would ever fully recover. Even when he did feel stronger, it would be too dangerous for him to cross the German line over the trenches and the battlefields to find his way back to the Allies. Still weak, unarmed, and with no stomach for war, all he could do was work on his physical recovery.

Winter hit hard that year. When a storm front came in, Dante was well enough to help the milkmaids get the cows to the shed and help hunt for game. Dante was not used to cold weather, and with his weakened body, the cold penetrated to his bones. For warmth, the three slept together at night. Dante charmed the milkmaids with stories about America, Juanita, his family, the Napa Valley, and the winery.

Winter faded into spring, spring into summer, and soon warm summer breezes turned cool at night and the leaves of the hardwood trees started to change color. The upper pasture remained untouched by the war.

Both milkmaids had gone into town that day taking a few of the cows with them to return them to the farm. Dante sat down in the grasses to enjoy his daily meditation. He looked closely at a potato he'd just dug out of the earth. A beetle crawled along the potato vine and dropped off to the ground. Who knew how much longer the world would be torn apart. He wondered if he would ever see Juanita again, or his family, or the valley. He closed his eyes to visualize her face. Juanita's brown eyes came to him first, speckled with golden flakes, then her full lips. He concentrated, pretending he could feel them on his. In his meditation he heard a familiar humming sound coming closer. In seconds British planes were overhead. He wanted to wave his arms and tell them he was there. Pamphlets dropped from the sky. When another plane approached, this one lower, Dante ran into the woods thinking he might be shot. Once it was clear, he herded the remaining cows into a makeshift corral that he helped the milkmaids build in the woods. He looked at one of the pamphlets that was in German and tried to make it out. He decided to stay in the woods with the cows that night to protect them for the milkmaids.

In the morning Dante woke to the distant sound of dropping bombs and explosions coming from the direction of the village. He ran to a high point where there was a partial clearing with a view of the village. Smoke clouds billowed up into the air. Fear, concern, and curiosity propelled him through the woods on the forty-minute trek to the village. Dante stood in the edge of the woods. The entire village was either burned or on fire.

He looked at the small picturesque German village that was the victim of being too close to what the Allies thought was a German army supply depot. He had never been to the village, but the milkmaids had described it to him. Smoke and flames lapped at what remained of the homes and businesses. Some of the townspeople stood watching. There were still a few pamphlets on the ground that British planes dropped the day before warning of the bombing to come.

Worried about the milkmaids, Dante decided to take a chance and try to find them. He walked around the edge of the woods. One house on the far corner lay in ruins. Some villagers were frantically digging by hand trying to unearth people from the rubble. Somehow in the rush to gather up what they could, the townspeople had forgotten to warn the new young mother inside what was about to happen. The villagers, too busy to question where Dante came from, barely noticed him as he joined their digging. A muted baby's cry spirited him on and he unearthed the newborn infant alive. The crowd cheered, but their good mood ceased when the mother was found crushed to death.

With their attention on the baby, Dante backed away unnoticed and went in search of the farm. Frida appeared first, coming out of the woods. The few cows that they returned to the farm had been herded into the woods to protect them from the bombs and the scavenging villagers. She rejoiced at seeing Dante alive. Lena was back at the farm. It had been hit and only the barn survived. The old farmer they worked for was dead.

There was no time to mourn, only to bury the dead. No time to rest, only to keep alive. Some of the surviving villagers began to leave while others remained in the only home they had ever known. The ones who left on foot carried whatever valuables they had salvaged on their backs or in small carts.

The two milkmaids remained at the farm. Dante left with the refugees, hoping to find the Allies and perhaps a way home. Death and disease followed the displaced villagers leaving them desperate and disillusioned. There were more bombings. Many died while others wished they had. The tide of the war changed in favor of the Allies. The population of displaced villagers grew bigger every day. Dante avoided the German soldiers and had little contact with the refugees while pretending to be shell shocked. He fought off disease and starvation and was soon no more than skin over bones.

In October the survivors wondered how they would make it through the winter. In November, the war was over.

**

The news that Dante René Rivera was alive hadn't reached the Rivera mansion yet. The 1918 influenza had.

Magritte lingered in her bed. In the year and a half since Dante was reported dead, she'd succumbed to full-fledged drug addiction. To calm her nerves, her doctor had prescribed heavy doses of morphine. The doses increased with her body's insatiable desire. When it wasn't enough, she turned to opium. The pain of losing her favorite child and the guilt of what she'd done to him wouldn't go away. She raised herself out of her bed, dressed, and had the chauffeur drive her to San Francisco's Chinatown where he left her. Magritte's body urged her on to purchase her new love—opium. It was the only thing that entirely took away the pain of her loss and her guilt, at least for a time. Magritte wandered the streets until she found someone to help. She spent two days in an opium stupor before Gabriel found her crumpled in an alley and brought her home.

A few days after her visit to San Francisco, she died from the flu. Gabriel got a milder case of the flu too, but survived. Grandfather Raul never got it. Young Raul Paul was traveling from the east for the holidays. Still suffering from losing his brother, his father decided rather than to telegram Raul Paul, he would wait until his son reached the valley to tell him of his mother's death.

On the long train ride back to Napa, Raul Paul, still not knowing his brother was alive or his mother dead, contemplated his future and decided that even though he was almost finished with school he would not return to Harvard. He belonged in the valley where he was happiest. Eastern ways and weather were not for him. He tolerated school at best, but he could no longer do that. He ran through his mind several scenarios on how to break the news to his parents. When he arrived in Napa, his father was at the station waiting with the news that his mother was dead. The next day a letter came. Dante René Rivera was alive.

CHAPTER FORTY-FOUR

Family Life

Napa, 1918

Juanita laid in bed bottle nursing her four-month-old son, Hank. Her breasts seemed more sensitive than usual. She assumed it was still from her milk drying. She hadn't discovered yet that she was pregnant again with her second child with Henry. When Baby Hank fell asleep, she placed him in his cradle. The sleepy Juanita forced herself out of bed. She helped Henry finish the holiday decorations in the house and set the dining room table. Her parents would be arriving at six. Mother Muller was cooking the Christmas Eve meal; the smells of a traditional goose and red cabbage sweetened the air and nauseated Juanita.

In late November Dante reunited with the American and British troops. They marched into the German town that Dante and some of the other refugees had wandered into looking for food. The American soldiers told them the war was over. They fed the grateful Germans and questioned Dante about why he was in Germany. Dante was jailed. The military police contacted the milkmaids who confirmed that he'd accidentally wandered into German territory. They told the military police how Dante was wounded, how it took over a year to nurse him back to health, and how he wanted to get back to the Allies but it was too dangerous.

After the investigation, the United States Army returned Dante to the States in time for Christmas. He was unscathed by the flu that had flourished around him as he wandered through war-torn Germany. By the time he reunited with the Americans, the worst of the flu was over in Europe. Not wanting them to suffer a second time in case he didn't make it home, he waited to send a telegram to Juanita and his family that he was alive.

Returning unannounced and anxious to see the woman he loved, Dante walked up the sidewalk and opened the gate to the Bonnetia home and knocked on the front door. Dalila Bonnetia was dismayed when she opened the door and saw Dante. She told him things had changed. Dante still weak and now in shock, staggered backwards. Mr. Bonnetia grabbed him before he fell and drove him to the mansion.

Young Raul greeted his crestfallen brother with a long embrace. Raul lost his brother once; now he rejoiced that they were together again. Dante wondered why heavy black mourning curtains covered all the windows. The drawing room where Magritte's body was laid out was kept dark and cool to help preserve it. Hundreds of flowers surrounded the casket to ward off the smell of decomposing flesh.

Dante entered the room and pulled the pocket doors closed to be alone with his mother one last time. He looked at her corpse; his feelings vacillated from sorrow for his love for her to raw hatred for a woman who tried to control his life and had ruined it. A deep-seated resentment would remain.

He stayed in the room for half an hour. When he came out, he collapsed in tears.

***

That spring Henry's mother, Mrs. Muller, held her beautiful, chubby-cheeked grand-baby boy in her arms. He played with his favorite toy, a stuffed brown doggy that was a Christmas gift. One of the eyes was already missing, and he loved to suck on one of the floppy ears, de-fuzzing it.

"No, Hankie, no suck on the doggy's ear."

She took the toy away and placed Hank in his high chair, so she could concentrate on lunch. He began to whimper which turned into a full, hard cry until she gave him back his doggy.

Juanita walked up the sidewalk toward the back door. She'd been out photographing all morning to chase away her blues. Putting her camera equipment down to check the mailbox, she wondered how much longer she could carry the heavy equipment with her growing belly.

There was a single letter addressed to her in the mailbox. Juanita moved to the side of the house for privacy and opened the letter. Raul was asking her if she would come and visit Dante for closure. Anger hidden inside her surfaced. Closure? How could life be so cruel to take him away from her twice and then return him again when it was impossible for them to be together.

She folded the letter up and placed it in her jacket pocket.

A week later with her baby boy by her side, she drove up the long path to the Rivera mansion.

James answered the door. He looked different. He'd grown old in the past few years. He tried to hide the tremor in his right hand and arm as he escorted Juanita to the library where she would wait—her heart was pounding. Juanita was determined not to let Dante know how much she still loved him. She held Hank in her arms for comfort. As he played with her necklace, she silently repeated the speech she would say to Dante.

"Juanita." His familiar voice shattered her thoughts and mind. His red-rimmed eyes, sallow skin, and war-ravaged body shocked her. Losing Juanita was life's final insult. He didn't want to live. They stood close. He looked deep into her eyes searching for what he'd lost. He gently placed his arm around her waist and held her close. Hank reached up and grabbed the collar of his shirt, breaking their moment.

"He's beautiful."

"I'm having another one. In four months."

Dante reached in and kissed her on the cheek.

"I'll always love you, Juanita."

"Oh, Dante, I love you too. I have to tell you about what happened and why I..."

"You thought I was dead, I understand."

"But there's more, I want you to understand."

She told him about the baby she'd lost, their baby, and how Henry had married her to save her from the gossip mill when she thought Dante was dead. Henry had been so kind to her. When she lost their baby, Henry told her she could leave if she wanted because he knew she only loved Dante. She got pregnant with Hank, and now with another one on the way, this was her life. There was a pain in Dante's heart when he stroked little Hank's hair and thought about how this little boy was almost his.

Juanita endured an early, painful labor until they decided to take the baby by Caesarian section. The preterm baby girl had dark exotic eyes like her mother. Juanita named her Anne. A sudden change in hormones caused her to fall into a deeper depression. Since her meeting with Dante, her emotions had become erratic and unpredictable. She stayed in the Rushing River Hospital to recover with the baby, who grew stronger every day.

Henry's mother had taken sick after the beginning of the year. She willed herself to stay alive until she could hold her new grandchild in her arms.

Henry quit his job to look after his ill mother and son while Juanita was in the hospital. Mr. and Mrs. Bonnetia helped. When Juanita and the baby came home from the hospital, Mrs. Muller held her granddaughter and cherished the moment as she looked down on her beautiful, little face. The baby's tiny lips puckered with a sweet, faint hunger cry. Mrs. Muller handed the baby back to Juanita who sat in a rocker in the room and nursed the baby until she went to sleep. The next morning Henry found his mother in a coma. She died a few days later.

It was not an easy time for Juanita. She mourned for Dante and their lost child. Suffering from postpartum blues, she fed and changed her baby but could barely hold her or even look at her. Henry cared for Juanita and the two children. In the mornings he encouraged Juanita to get out of bed and welcome a new day. She would roll over and refuse to even acknowledge him. If he tried to touch her, she would cringe. She could not bear even the kindest touch by him.

In her will, Henry's mother left him the house and a small life insurance policy, enough for him to start his own business.

The town of Napa spilled over its boundaries. The small house that Henry's parents purchased at the edge of town was now in its center and surrounded by businesses. With the money from the life insurance policy, Henry broke ground. By spring of 1920 his butcher shop was open. With the war over, the anti-German sentiment was fading. It would be convenient to live behind the butcher shop and cheaper than renting a store. What had been a front porch became part of the store; a meat cooler built on the side of the house had a door opening into the store. What expenses the life insurance policy didn't cover were covered by a business loan from the bank.

Henry carried baby Anne in a basket. He turned on the lights. The early morning darkness would be gone soon. He placed the baby on the counter and prepared the store for its grand opening. At seven a knock came at the door. It was Dalila Bonnetia to pick up the children. At eight he flipped over the sign to read "Open." The butcher shop was busy all morning. When it slacked off around noon, a big limousine pulled up and the Rivera cook got out. The wealthiest family in town would buy meat daily. Henry knew his future was secure. His only concern now was for his wife.

Juanita improved slowly. It was guilt that finally got her out of bed. Henry worked hard with the business during the day and then cared for the children at night. Her conscience could no longer allow her to remain so self-indulgent. With some extra money, Henry surprised his wife and bought her a used car for her photography. It was the ultimate guilt catalyst to get her out of bed.

Juanita's photography business started in the pantry darkroom off her parents' kitchen and then grew into the living room which became her studio. Joe turned the upstairs into an apartment for Dalila and himself and gave Juanita the downstairs for her business. With the country's new post-war affluence money grew, and both Juanita's and Henry's businesses flourished.

She put her sorrow about Dante away in the old cardboard box she'd started after the time they spent at the Panama-Pacific International Exposition. Hidden high on top of her closet shelf, the memorabilia from their relationship lived: the two engagement rings, a diamond brooch, the tin ring from the expo, photographs, love letters and Valentines, two telegrams, ticket stubs from picture shows, and the remains of the flower Dante gave her when they were reunited.

At times when she thought it was safe, when the children were taking their naps and Henry was busy in the butcher shop, she would take the box down and look inside it. When it became too painful to handle, she would put the box away for another day.

CHAPTER FORTY-FIVE

Prohibition

1919

A new problem threatened the Rivera family—Prohibition. On January 29, 1919, the United States Congress passed the Eighteenth Amendment prohibiting the sale of liquor. Three generations of the Rivera wine business were threatened.

This new crisis forced Dante to put aside his personal problems and concentrate on business. He went in and out of emotional rawness and tried not to indulge himself in drink. He made a deal with the Catholic Church, which was exempt because it was a religion, to provide communion wine for their services, a small step to save the Mighty Oak Winery.

Gabriel's nerves were shot. Despite years of an unhappy marriage, he missed Magritte—maybe out of guilt, or perhaps out of love, or his being used to her big presence. Something always stood in the way. Mostly it was the business he had to run after his grandfather's death, and then the war happened. Gabriel had never been to Europe. He wanted to go to Spain and relive the stories his grandfather told him as a child. He also wanted to see Paris, Rome, and London. The business-minded part of Gabriel would scout for places in post-war, cash-strapped Europe where they could invest their money while his father Raul Cristoval worked on expanding the hospital to accommodate the growing population of the valley. This would compensate for the loss of revenue from the Mighty Oak Winery that Young Raul and Dante were left to run.

Grandfather Raul's alert mind kept him young. He was almost seventy, but mentally, he was years younger. His newfound happiness that Dante was alive fought off the depression he'd possessed in recent years. Dante was alive and Raul Paul was home for good where he belonged. He felt for Gabriel's anguish, but what went unsaid was his relief that Magritte was gone. Her controlling nature and volatile mood swings never sat well with him. There was a new tranquility in the mansion and in their lives. No matter what, he somehow knew they would persevere.

***

Early morning light streamed into the glass breakfast room. Gabriel opened the gilded birdcage and took out the body of his favorite bird. The bird's limp head flopped into his other hand. He slowly scanned the tiny corpse trying to find the answer to its death. The female bird was covered with perfect buttery yellow feathers with a beautiful peach-colored face. He stroked her cool, velvety smooth feathers and wondered why—his heart sank into a longing for his favorite bird.

Dante's gaunt appearance and depressed demeanor when he entered the breakfast room didn't help. His sunken eyes disappeared into a vacant face. His hoarse voice managed to speak a "Morning."

"Not a good one." Gabriel held out the bird's tiny body to show Dante before he brought it close to his heart and stroked the dead bird tenderly. "My favorite. She should have lived a long life. Every morning she greeted me with singing even before the others."

Two of the other birds began to fuss and fight. Gabriel scolded them to make them stop. His attention went back to his dead bird.

"They are both males and both loved her as I did. I'll miss her sweet singing in the morning. When I first saw her I knew, I had to have her. She was so beautiful. I can't blame them for fighting or mourning for her."

Gabriel looked toward his son.

"They mourn much the way you do. I can buy them each a new mate to love. For you it's different. I hope you can find someone new to love someday, but for now please eat, son, to regain your strength."

Dante threw himself into his work. He heard from a friend that, with a little financial persuasion, the authorities in San Francisco turned a blind eye toward the illegal sale of liquor. He made a contact in Canada for liquor, and Dante traveled to San Francisco to talk to restaurants and the speakeasies that sprang up around town. One private club quickly turned into ten. He would provide them with good quality wines and liquor. He paid off the right authorities, and all agreements were made with an easy handshake. Prohibition issued in the Roaring Twenties and the development of the flapper.

Money poured into the Rivera boys' pockets as fast as liquor poured into a glass. Raul Paul suggested they invest heavily in the deregulated stock market, a legal way to launder the money from their product. As long as they paid taxes on the profits, the government didn't seem to care.

***

Raul fell in love at a September picnic. He was delivering some product to Police Chief Sullivan when he saw Sullivan's daughter, Heather, a feisty, zaftig, freckle-faced, redheaded beauty with long legs and emerald green eyes. Heather's laugh caught his attention, and when he turned and saw her, the usually shy Raul didn't hesitate. It might have started on its own at the picnic but it was fate that brought them together again, an irony when they first met and he saved her life.

A storm hit with rains that swelled the riverbank and made them spill over and flood the low-lying areas of town. Sand bag barriers were put in place, but that morning's torrential downpour caused the water to breach part of the barricade. Heather Sullivan, who was late for work, came to an underpass where the water didn't seem very deep and surmised she could make it. She stepped on the gas of her model T and zoomed into the water but the car stopped. She pressed the starter button again and again, to no avail. The engine was flooded and the water was rising faster than she could have ever imagined. A wall of water rushed down the hillside and began to move the stalled car into the floodwaters toward the river. The current was too strong and the water was too high by now for her to chance wading out in it. She had never learned to swim and would have surely drowned had Raul not come along.

Raul was rambling along in his truck when he came upon the flooded underpass and saw Heather's car. He quickly stopped his truck, grabbed a rope from the back, and tied himself to one end and the other to the truck's bumper. He swam out as far as he could in the rushing current and reached her just in time. As he grabbed her, Raul quickly tethered her to him and pulled them both to safety. They sat in his truck and watched her car wash away into the river. Raul, already smitten with the redheaded beauty, was too shy to ask her name.

After they met again at the picnic, they started dating and within weeks were engaged. The impetuous Raul wanted to marry right away. To be closer to her parents, Raul bought a piece of property nearer to town and built a large Mediterranean-style house. They settled into a happy marriage. When their first child was born, a boy, they named him Robert after Heather's father.

CHAPTER FORTY-SIX

Hollywood

1919

Dante traveled to San Francisco and northern California while Raul stayed home running the winery and distribution in Napa. In order to be more hands-on with their lucrative San Francisco clients, Dante rented an apartment in the city and began frequenting the clubs and speakeasies. Handsome, dark, rich, and brooding, he was irresistible to women. The rise of the flapper introduced an era of uninhibited love making. World War I left a depletion of young men and made a profusion of women at Dante's disposal—neither could get enough.

Little did Magritte know when she told the Bonnetias that Dante was a womanizing playboy that one day it would become true. His looks and charisma lured all sorts of women in an effortless way, and each gave him a temporary fix for his heartache.

Booze gave Dante a hangover that only went away with a drink for breakfast. He'd tell himself a fantasy about his life while he shaved, so he could get through his day. He was charming to everyone. To fill the dark void in his heart, he indulged in liquor and women. In the morning he'd wake up with a strange woman next to him in bed, and his dark moody blues would resurface. Dante dated indiscriminately, always remaining a gentleman and usually never seeing the same woman twice.

Business increased. They had a good, safe product. Bootleggers sprang up peddling bad hooch that made people sick or killed them. The Riveras had a reputation for providing the real thing and the word spread. When the word about their product spread to Los Angeles, club owners there wanted to buy the Rivera product. San Francisco and northern California were lucrative, but with Los Angeles in their war chest, the brothers could become bootleg barons.

***

Dante boarded a train with a case of their finest wares. He was greeted at La Grande Station in Los Angeles by movie producer Francis Foreman's assistant, Merrill. After loading Dante and his product into Foreman's Packard car, Merrill drove to the Alexandria Hotel on Spring Street in downtown Los Angeles.

Francis Foreman had a permanent suite at the Alexandria for business. A small, impish man with a full mustache grown to hide a thin lip, he kept his coarse wiry hair greased and combed over a bald spot and, despite the California sun, his pockmarked skin always looked pasty. All his clothes were tailor-made because of his small, slender physique and big ego. With little formal education, he was one of the smartest men around. He was the product of a one-night stand between a housemaid and married hotel night clerk. Because he grew up in hotels, he felt comfortable in them. He'd recently built a house in Holmby Hills, part of the Golden Triangle of Beverly Hills, where his wife lived and he sometimes stayed.

A small group of men and one woman waited in the Alexandria Hotel suite. Along with Francis was the mayor, the chief of police, a high-ranking member of the FBI, some club owners, Mafia boss Vito DiGiorgio, and Lucille Devine—a movie star, diva, and Francis' biggest moneymaker. She was a slim-chested, pale blonde with little talent and tons of sex appeal. She'd had an affair with Francis when she was an extra.

He liked her feistiness and on a lark gave her a small lead in a money-laundering movie. She took the part, juiced it up with sex, and the movie made money.

Francis languished on the balcony and looked at the view of the city as the lights seemed to magically come on with evening approaching. Lucille was handing Francis a drink when the front door of the penthouse swung open. The porter wheeled in the Rivera product; Dante and Merrill followed. After handshakes, the group tasted Dante's product. Francis saw something besides booze in Dante. His charm and looks would make him a good companion for the Hollywood scene. With the product approved, the chief of police, the FBI special agent, and mob boss DiGiorgio all agreed that for a part of the action the Rivera product would do well.

The group lingered until well after dark. When it began to break up, Lucille invited Dante to a party. Never wanting to turn down a beautiful woman, he accepted. Her white Pierce-Arrow limousine waited downstairs. When they walked out of the lobby of the Alexandria, her black driver, who stood like a soldier in a white uniform trimmed in gold, opened the car door. Lucille lowered the curtain between the front and back seat and flipped open a small door to a mini bar. She lit a cigarette.

"Help yourself, pretty man."

As Dante poured himself a Scotch, Lucille undid the top of her dress and let it fall to her waist, exposing her small perfect round breasts and lithe body. She took Dante's hand and placed it on one of her breasts, and they began to make love.

The car pulled up to the Hollywood Hills estate of Tubby Bryson. His career as a director was on the skids since a scandal broke about his touching an underage boy. This was his final party before the trial. The place was dripping with Hollywood celebrities and their entourages. Heads turned when Dante entered, all eager to find out who the handsome man was with Lucille. That night Lucille claimed Dante as her own and made sure they were photographed together and put in print. The next month the story hit *Motion Picture Classic*,

Photoplay, and *Hollywood Studio* magazines, knocking Constance Talmadge, one of the biggest stars in Tinseltown, off the covers.

CHAPTER FORTY-SEVEN

The Reunion

Los Angeles / Napa, 1922–1929

ante languished poolside at Lucille's Hollywood Hills home. His trips to Los Angeles were becoming more frequent. He enjoyed the balmy southern California weather and being far enough away from his family, so they couldn't interfere with his decadent lifestyle. Even with his eyes closed and wearing sunglasses, he sensed a shadow come over him. Lucille's bathing suit clad body covered the sun from his face. She held a fluted glass and poured champagne into it.

"Here's your poison, pretty boy."

He was hung over and in pain from the night before. They'd gone to the premiere of her latest movie. His blue eyes were still sensitive from the flashbulbs and lights for the newsreels. His head hurt from his morning after hangover. She leaned down and kissed him. He squeezed her behind and downed the champagne before standing up. He dove into the pool and swam underwater. His head surfaced at the other end. With one sweeping motion of his hand, he flicked his jet-black hair into place and jumped out of the pool.

***

A week later, Henry and Juanita managed a night out to themselves. They were seeing the new Rudolf Valentino movie, *Moran of the Lady Letty*. The audience was full of women anxious to see their matinee idol. A newsreel came on first showing President Harding and his wife in the garden of the White House, and the Bolshevik's defeating the Basmachi Troops, which made Juanita cringe thinking about the young Russian she'd known in New York. A civil war was starting in Ireland. Music played as the newsreel changed from the news to Hollywood. The image of Dante's face filled the screen. The women in the audience swooned uncontrollably. It cut to a wider shot with Lucille on his arm as they entered the new Grauman's Egyptian Theatre for the premiere of her new movie *Since You Left Me*. It cut back to Dante's matinee idol face again. The women in the audience went wild. Henry sat stoically and wondered what Juanita was thinking. She said nothing.

***

Dante's life spiraled with one party night melting into another. Money came so easily to the Rivera enterprise that it seemed like play money with the stock market thriving and their investments growing from bootlegging.

Francis encouraged Dante to socialize and date young starlets and to see less of Lucille. Dante was growing tired of Lucille's insistence that he do everything with her. He took Francis' advice and began dating several actresses. Lucille had slept with many men from grips to studio heads and never wanted to sustain a long-term relationship with any of them, but Dante was different. For once she could see herself in a relationship and maybe even married.

It was early Thursday morning, and Lucille had already done her morning run and was sitting down for breakfast. Monday Lucille would begin prep on the most important film of her career. A serious part, something she'd worked hard to get, a part that could give her the critical acclaim she longed for.

She opened the newspaper and drank her orange juice. A picture of Dante was in the paper with a beautiful starlet. Lucille had been moody lately. She lit a cigarette and made up her mind. She called to her maid, Conchetta.

Conchetta brought in the toast and set it on the table.

"Not that, Conchetta, I need to visit your cousin this weekend."

Conchetta knew what she meant. This wasn't the first time.

Lucille picked up her white Bakelite phone and dialed the studio.

"I'm going to a spa for the weekend and won't be back until Monday morning, so change the photo session and make-up and hair tests to Monday afternoon."

Lucille's driver, dressed in casual clothes, picked her up early the next morning in his own car and drove her to the Mexican border. She crossed over the border on foot to a car with Mexican license plates.

The next morning her driver waited for her at the spot where he dropped her off, but she never came. On Monday morning the studio called to see where Lucille was. An hour later the studio detective knocked on her front door. He spoke to Conchetta and the driver before he headed to Mexico. There he questioned the clinic where she'd gone in a persuasive way until the head of the clinic confessed. Lucille died on the operating table. She was farther along with a pregnancy than she admitted to and bled to death because of the clinic's limited facilities. She was buried in a shallow grave in the town's graveyard with her baby.

Tuesday morning the newspapers reported Lucille missing. The next day the papers read: "Lucille Devine, famous star of the silver screen, set sail in her sailboat off the coast of southern California for Santa Catalina Island and failed to arrive. She was assumed drowned when her boat was discovered capsized."

The studio left her body in Mexico and buried her fabricated life and career in a Hollywood cemetery. They recast her part with one of the dozens of actresses waiting in the wings.

Dante was upset but believed the story about the sailboat and soon his sex life became as diverse as his Wall Street portfolio.

***

The phone rang several times in Juanita's studio before anyone answered it. Her father was walking down the back staircase when he heard it. He still wasn't used to having a telephone in the house, but it was a necessary part of Juanita's business.

"Who?" he said. "Wait, let me get my daughter."

Mr. Bonnetia knocked on the door of what used to be the kitchen that Juanita had turned into her darkroom.

"Juanita, there's a call for you. It sounds important."

"Get a number Dad, I can't come out now."

She had been in there all morning and forgot about the call until she saw the note. Francis Forman wanted her to come to Los Angeles and photograph the stars. She had become well-known for her photography and had shows in major galleries and museums around the country. In the spring of 1929 there was a major retrospective of her work as a portrait photographer at the Morris Gallery of Photography in Los Angeles. Francis Forman saw it and was impressed. The money was too good to pass up, so she accepted the project.

The studio car picked up Juanita at the Pasadena station and drove her to the studio. She set up a black backdrop, lights, and her camera in a small room near the stars' dressing rooms. The studio's A list stars and a few B listers would have their portraits taken by Juanita, known professionally as J.B. Muller, over a two-day period.

The first was Buzz Benton, a freckled-faced kid that had been one of the studio's biggest moneymakers starring as a young, sharp-shooting orphan in a series of westerns for kids. A parade of stars dropped in and out of the little room over the next two days: Anita Page, John Gilbert, Norma Shearer and more. Merrill gave Francis positive reports three times a day until Francis decided to come himself and have his portrait done. While he was sitting and having it done, he had a brainstorm.

Cyprus trees surrounded the pool of a small, deco ranch-style house off of Doheny that Dante had purchased and sparsely furnished with modern style furniture. Gemmy, his current girlfriend, carried a tray with drinks out onto the patio. She handed Dante a drink and sat next to him. He took a few sips and put down the book Francis had asked him to read, *All Quiet on the Western Front*, because of his experience during the war.

Gemmy got up and dove into the pool. Dante followed, diving deep into the water and coasting toward the bottom. When he came up to the surface, he began his daily laps. Gemmy stretched her arms out onto the side of the pool and watched him go back and forth. The repetition of the laps calmed him down. He had become agitated. His life was hollow, unfulfilling. The cascade of women, liquor, drugs, and parties weren't enough for him anymore. He was trying to figure out a way to wean Gemmy gradually off from him, so she wouldn't be too upset.

Gemmy got out of the pool, stripped off her one-piece bathing suit, and loosely wrapped a towel around her dripping wet body. The phone rang and she answered it. Dante never liked to be disturbed when he did his laps, but it was Francis and he said it was urgent.

"It's for you. It's Francis."

She purposely called out to Dante, so Francis would know he was there. Dante had no excuse; he had to answer. She held the phone receiver out over the pool's edge and squatted down onto her heels, the California sun to her back. Dante swam over to the edge of the pool as she held the receiver near his wet ear. Streams of bright light shot into Dante's eyes. It annoyed him.

"What Francis? When? But...okay. Good-bye."

Gemmy hung up the phone.

"Go get dressed, we're having lunch with Francis."

She stood up and the towel fell off her, and the sun silhouetted her naked body. For a minute he had to stare at her. It was the frame of her body's silhouette that reminded him of Juanita. His mind drifted back to the magical summer they'd spent together.

"Sure, Sweets." The high pitch of her voice broke his mood. She wasn't Juanita, but Juanita was in his thoughts.

Tall stucco walls fortified the studio in the center of Hollywood which took up over one hundred acres of prime California real estate. A monumental iron gate at the entrance and a small sentry style guard house with a guard kept the unwanted out.

Driving his 1928 Bugatti convertible with the top down, Dante pulled in front of the studio gates. He gave a mock wave salute to the guard who was used to seeing Dante several times a week. The guard saluted back and pressed the button to open the gate. Gemmy's flimsy silk dress fell down off her shoulder and exposed her left breast as the sports car's powerful engine roared into the studio's main lot. She held onto her oversized picture hat with one hand and pulled the shoulder of her dress up with the other. Dante pulled in front of Francis' office bungalow and parked. He took off his sunglasses, threw them on the dashboard, and pulled down the visor to look at himself in the attached mirror. The white suit he wore complemented his tan. He pushed back into place the few stray hairs of his patent-leather-looking hairstyle. Strands of gray were beginning to show in the sideburns. He got out and moved to the other side of the car to open Gemmy's door. Taking his hand, she coyly looked up at him and smiled. She tripped forward on her high heels that were not meant for walking and attached herself to his arm. Her sheer dress only slightly camouflaged her body underneath and the outline of lacy briefs filtered through. A couple of young men walking by couldn't help but look. One whistled.

The ladies that worked in Francis Forman's office loved Dante. He knew how to make each one feel special. Ethel was older and sat in the outer office. She had been with Francis longer than anyone. She was brilliant at gossip gathering and reported it to Francis daily.

"Mr. Forman is waiting for you in studio B. I'll call and tell Merrill you're here."

Gemmy sat in a chair in the waiting room. Dante grabbed hold of her hand and pulled her up off the chair. She was this month's accessory to have on his arm. Merrill waited at the entrance of studio B for them. They walked down the long hall of glamour. Each door had a star on it, and behind the star was the dressing room of the biggest names in Hollywood.

"What's going on?" asked Dante

"You'll see soon. It's a surprise," said Merrill.

At the end of the hall Merrill opened the door.

"Mr. Forman is waiting for you inside."

Dante purposefully grabbed Gemmy in his arms for his entrance to tease Francis. Standing in the doorway as it opened, he gave her a passionate, long kiss that ended with a victorious smile. Dante looked into the semi-dark room expecting to see Francis. There stood Juanita, more beautiful than ever. Not in the Hollywood way of an emaciated, excessively made-up actress. She was beautiful in an earthy way with rounder hips and a fuller body than when they first met. Her long jet-black hair with silver running through it was tied back in a braid almost to her waist. Her dark eyes sparkled a joyful greeting when she saw Dante, her tawny skin tinted to a natural pink on her cheeks and lips. She was genuinely happy. He was flabbergasted until he remembered Gemmy and felt like a fool for what he'd just done. His knees weakened. Francis' voice came out of the dark.

"Surprise, Dante, you're going to have your portrait done by the best photographer I've ever seen, J.B. Muller. It's my gift to you. I wanted to capture those handsome good looks before your beauty floated away in booze. Here stands the playboy prince of the Western world."

Francis came out of the shadows and gave a mock bow. Dante, speechless, looked toward Juanita. He moved away from Gemmy, embarrassed by her presence. She sensed a change in him and grabbed hold of him like he was her prize. He gently unwrapped her arm from his.

"Go wait in the car," said Dante.

"What? I want to stay here," said Gemmy.

"Do what I tell you! Wait. Merrill, take her home."

Gemmy slunk away with hurt feelings. The door slammed shut leaving Francis, Dante, and Juanita alone in the room.

Francis strutted around Dante observing him and noticing his reaction.

"Good to see you again," said Juanita.

Then it all made sense to Francis.

"Is that what it is? You two know one another already, don't you?"

Dante said nothing. His feelings for Juanita were too precious to expose to someone like Francis. Dante was meek, awash with shame for the useless life he was living. The shallowness and decadence of his everyday existence had caught up with him.

"That's right! You're both from the Napa Valley. You must have known one another there," said Francis.

"Yes, we did. We're old friends," said Juanita.

"Well, in that case no need for introductions. I need to get back to work. You can thank me later, dapper daddy." Francis left and they were alone together for the first time in twelve years, not since that night under the phantom moon in 1917 when they made love and promised one another they would love each other forever.

Dante moved closer to Juanita.

"I had no idea it was you I was waiting for. Francis only said he had a friend coming. How are you, Dante?"

He reached out and touched her face.

"Are you real or a figment of my imagination?" asked Dante.

He moved his hand from her face to her hair, stroking it the way he used to. He moved closer until their bodies touched slightly.

"All the times I've imagined what it would be like to see you again, alone…no one else, no babies, just the two of us. I never thought it would happen."

He waited for her response. She looked down in thought, and then reached out and took hold of his hand.

"I love you, Dante. I love you."

Dante fell to his knees and melted into her body. Juanita stroked the top of his head. Her body collapsed down into his arms. They kissed. After all the life experiences they had in their years apart, their love for one another was still strong.

After making love, they lay on the floor wrapped in each other's arms. There was a knock on the door. Juanita was about to answer, but Dante put his fingers to his lips and motioned for her to be quiet. He kissed her lips. "I'm not going to share you. It's not fair. It's cruel not being with you."

"We're together now until I have to leave. Yes, it's a punishment not having you in my life, but that's the way our lives are. There's nothing we can do about it."

"Promise me when I die, the last thing I see is your beautiful face," said Dante.

"And if I die first, I want to see yours."

Juanita took one last picture that day, the photograph of Dante.

***

The old Victrola pumped out Christmas music. Outside, a cool overcast morning fog blanketed the town. Inside the warm house, Hank and Annie, still in their pajamas, tore open their presents in a frenzy. Juanita and Henry watched the children, happy they could give them a nice Christmas. After they opened the last gift, Juanita made coffee. The children were too excited to eat breakfast preferring to play with their toys. Later in the day, after Christmas dinner, Juanita, Henry, Joe, Dalila and the children cranked up the Victrola again and sang along to carols.

On October 29, 1929, Black Tuesday, the stock market crashed. Henry had been smart and saved his money, investing it sparingly in the market and only in safe stocks. He remembered the hard times during World War I when there wasn't always enough food to eat. He never wanted Juanita or the children to go through that.

Most of his money was tied up in his business, but Juanita was a rare woman of her time, successful as an artist and making good money on her own. Henry was proud of his wife and happy she was doing the work she loved. The butcher shop had risen from the ashes of discrimination and became a viable business in Napa. They would survive and do well regardless of the economy.

High rollers and fat cats who were rich one day, were poor the next. Henry made sure the families in need with children had a goose, ham, or turkey on their table for their holiday—even the ones who'd soiled his family's name during the war. He was a charitable man, with a wife he loved and two beautiful children. His family would never go hungry. He was the luckiest man in the world.

Christmas morning in the house Raul Paul Rivera built was different. He and Heather watched their children play with toys under their Christmas tree. Tomorrow he would have to tell Heather the extent to which the crash had affected them. Soon there would be nothing left. They would have to sell the house and move into the mansion. The Rivera men had already tried to mortgage the mansion only to find out it was worthless. It was a big, archaic, drafty house that no one wanted. They still had the vines. They might have to sell some of the land if they could. Everything else was gone. The trucking company, the barrel-making factory, and all the stocks were worthless. They hoped the Rushing River Hospital would survive because it was losing money. It had become a charity hospital for the unfortunate people affected by the Crash and had lost their money, businesses, and jobs. They would have to fight to save the winery.

That evening Grandfather Raul and Gabriel Rivera arrived for dinner at Raul Paul's house. Dante remained in Los Angeles trying to raise money to save the winery. When the phone rang, it was Dante to wish everyone a Merry Christmas. He seemed upbeat.

"Things are looking up," he said. "We'll have it better next year."

The phone rang again in the middle of the night. Raul woke up in a start, his nerves jangled. When he realized what it was, he jumped out of bed and worked his way downstairs. The phone continued to ring. Francis Forman was calling. Dante tried to kill himself. He had taken pills and turned on the gas to his stove. He was in the hospital. Gemmy found him just in time. Raul would have to come get him.

The charity ward of the City Hospital of Los Angeles overflowed with patients. Beds lined the hallways. Twenty men were in a room that usually served twelve. There was just enough space in between the beds for a nurse to stand and care for the patients. A sheet covered the stiff corpse of a man who had died during the night. It had not been discovered for hours and waited to be taken to the morgue. An emaciated man coughed up blood. When Raul arrived, some orderlies

rushed to restrain a psychotic man who had become dangerous. He'd been quiet all night and unnoticed until he went
into a rage. The orderlies subdued him and took him to the
psychiatric ward.

Raul looked down the row of beds not recognizing his
brother until Dante turned his face and Raul could see his
unmistakable profile. A chill ran down Raul's spine. He was
the one who originally thought to invest all their money in
the market to cover up the bootlegging. He was the one who
chose the investments. Dante opened his eyes to see Raul.

"Hello Raul."

Overwhelmed, Raul began to cry.

"Get me out of here," said Dante.

Dante had gone to all his rich friends in Hollywood
looking for money to save the winery. Everyone turned him
down. Even Francis wanted nothing more to do with him.
Dante became despondent when he realized how desperate
and needy he must have appeared. In the months since his
reunion with Juanita, he'd stopped partying and only wanted
Juanita.

CHAPTER FORTY-EIGHT

The Crash

1930

Spring came early, ushering in long breadlines for hungry people.

Raul's house sold for a fraction of what it was worth. Dante's house in Hollywood was lost to foreclosure. Whatever possessions could be sold were sold. That money was just enough to keep the creditors at bay and bought enough time to hope for a miracle. The entire Rivera family would live under the same roof. Most of the workers were let go. Gabriel, Raul, Dante, Heather and the children did the physical work of running the winery, tying up the tender new vines, cutting back the old vines, and planting new ones. In the fall they would all help with the harvest. Grandfather Raul did what he could.

The hard work agreed with Dante who grew stronger and developed callused hands. His years of a decadent lifestyle were behind him. He enjoyed working at the winery again. He would only have an occasional glass of wine and the necessary wine tasting of the vats. Early to bed became the rule.

Starr was very old, and her coat was now dappled with gray. Dante loved his lifelong companion and would ride her easy to check the vineyards. Sometimes he would ride her up into the hills to the old cemetery to his great-grandfather's grave. He would look out at the view of the vines and valley below.

The Mighty Oak Winery waited, hoping for the repeal of Prohibition and for a reversal of fortune. They continued doing business with the church and some underground restaurants in San Francisco, which kept the winery barely alive. Unable to earn enough money to pay their debts, the interest piled up. As the day of reckoning came closer, Gabriel went to the bank again to see if they would reconsider and mortgage the mansion.

***

Henry was cutting up a chicken when the bell on the front door jangled and Mrs. Williams, the wife of the bank president and a regular paying customer, made her daily call. Henry wiped his hands with a towel and gave her the usual warm, welcoming smile. He cut a few extra strips of bacon for her at no charge and then wrapped up half a chicken while she rambled on with the town's gossip.

"Too bad about the Riveras. They tried to mortgage that old drafty place again. Looks like they might lose the winery this time. My husband would like to help them but, you know, times are tough and the bank can't afford to lose any more money. He has to save the hospital and that will cost a lot. How are the pork chops today?"

"Good," replied Henry.

Most of the time Henry only half listened to her. He would just smile and shake his head pretending to listen. This time he listened to every word.

The day passed into night. The smells of dinner were wafting from the kitchen into the shop when Henry flipped over the open sign to closed. He pulled down the shade and locked the door before taking off his apron and hanging it on the hook next to the door leading into the house.

Juanita was placing the last of the dishes on the table when Henry walked in. She called to the children. Henry's thoughts drifted to the sweet kiss he would be giving his wife in a few minutes. A kiss that, but for a bit of ironic fate, would belong to another man. In his heart, he said a little prayer for the Rivera family. In the pre-war years when the name slinging began, they stood by his father and tried to help. They remained loyal and bought meat until the butcher shop closed.

Juanita called to the children again. They raced to the table with their dog Uno, an English Bulldog, running after them. Henry was in a particularly good mood as he lathered up to wash. He covered the bottom part of his face in a lather beard and turned, playfully growling at the kids. Uno growled back before cowering and hiding under the table. Henry gave out one of his giant infectious belly laughs and finished washing his face.

Juanita said grace and they began to eat. Juanita asked Henry and the children about their day. At first Henry hesitated, not wanting to sound pompous.

"Mrs. Williams was in today. Told me the Riveras might lose the winery this time." Henry looked toward Juanita out of the corner of his eyes. She sat placid, not reacting. Maybe she wasn't really listening, he thought.

"She said they tried to mortgage the mansion." He looked again, but there was still no reaction from her.

"How was your day, Hank?" she asked to change the subject.

The next morning after the children left for school, with a stream of light coming through the eastern window into the bedroom, Juanita opened up the bottom drawer of her dresser and took out a cloth bag. She reached for a valise in the back of the closet and then for a shoebox on top of the shelf next to the fraying tattered cardboard box where she kept her memorabilia from Dante. She placed the shoebox and the cloth bag in the valise and went back to the dresser. In a top small drawer where she kept her jewelry, she took out a small key and placed it in her pocket. Juanita looked around the room. She patted her pocket with the key, a reassurance to know it was there, and shut the door to her bedroom. She grabbed her camera bag downstairs and leaned through the door to the butcher shop.

"I'm going out for the day to take pictures. I'll be back in time for supper."

"Have a good day," said Henry.

Dante and Raul were both up early that morning; neither one had slept well the night before. Too much was at stake. They went to work at the winery as usual. Work always helped them forget about their problems and what the day might bring.

They turned bottles and skimmed the particles from the young wine that had surfaced in the mixing vats. They wrote in the ledgers and checked the supplies for what materials they needed to replenish. Periodically when one would sink into a mini-depression, the other would try to pick up their spirits. They talked about the upcoming harvest—at the very least they could sell the grapes. All the hard work the four generations of Riveras had put into the winery might soon be over.

The cellar was long and deep with a high vaulted ceiling. It was lined on both sides with huge wooden aging barrels, and in the middle sat the mixing vats. Dante and Raul were at the far end of the cellar near the door leading into the room where the bottled wine was stored and aged. They sat at a table with a special bottle of unopened wine, originally bottled by their great-grandfather from his finest reserve. Dante swirled red wine from the current batch around in a glass to open up the aroma and smelled it to see how it was aging. The vapors filled his nostrils with a pungent, young fragrance. He took a sip and wrinkled up his face from the taste when the door on the other end opened and a flash of light entered the cellar. Both men looked toward the far end of the cellar and wondered if this was it. The overhead lights made it difficult to see who was walking down the stairs. Dante and Raul could only make out that it was a woman. She walked under the bare glare of lights that lined the cellar ceiling. It became clear it was Juanita.

Dante stood up.

"Dante? Raul?" called out Juanita.

"We're down here," said Dante.

Dante unconsciously brushed back his hair. He felt his unshaven face and wished he had shaved that morning. She was the last person he expected to see and the one he most wanted to. He looked down at his rough and callused hands, no longer soft and manicured like she might remember. He put his hands behind his back as she came closer. When she stood before him, he couldn't help but reach out and touch her. They looked into each other's eyes. Raul backed away.

"Oh, well. I have something to do, I…"

"Please, don't go Raul. I have something for both of you."

Juanita put the valise on the table and opened it. She took out the box and bag, and dumped thousands of dollars onto the table. Then she turned the valise over and dumped out the rest of the money she'd taken out of her safe deposit box at the bank.

"I hope this is enough to get you out of trouble. If need be, I have a bit more saved."

Both Dante and Raul were speechless. Dante looked deep into Juanita's eyes.

"I can't take this from you. It's not right. But thank you."

"Why not?" said Juanita. "Take it as a gift. I always wondered why the universe gave me the gift of art and the ability to make money at it. Now I know why. To give back to the one I love, the one who inspires me. Without you I never would have been able to do it. Please, you must take it, to make me happy, to make me complete," said Juanita.

Dante reached down and kissed Juanita on the cheek. There was a sudden popping sound. Raul had uncorked the special bottle of wine. He poured three glasses and they drank it.

Later, Dante walked Juanita toward the cellar door. Before they reached it, he took her hand in his and guided her to a dark spot and wrapped his arms around her.

"I love you, Dante. I always will. I'm sorry we didn't spend our lives together."

"Somewhere we'll be together," said Dante.

They kissed one last passionate kiss before they parted.

Juanita's money saved the Mighty Oak Winery and in 1933 Prohibition was repealed. The winery began to thrive again. With hard work and perseverance, it soon was the top winery in northern California. They offered to pay Juanita back many times with interest, but she always refused. A gift was a gift.

CHAPTER FORTY-NINE

Berkeley

Berkeley, September 28, 1964

A clean-cut young man in a white buttoned-down collar shirt, tan corduroy coat, brown cord slacks, and short brown buck boots stood in front of the glass-enclosed bulletin board at the library looking at a list of grades. Unconsciously he ran his finger down the glass looking at the names. His short, sandy-colored Princeton style haircut needed its two-week trim. He pushed his horned-rimmed glasses back up his nose. He'd taken the law school admission test a week ago and was scanning the list for his name. At the end of the term, he'd have his undergraduate degree from Berkeley.

His finger moved impatiently down the glass: Perkins, Richards, Rivera. There it was. He was in the top percentile of his class and from one of the richest and most influential families in California, the Rivera dynasty. He had nothing to worry about. He could go to law school anywhere, but Berkeley is where he would go so he could stay close to his family.

A cool, willowy, blonde with a Dutch-boy flip bouffant hairstyle walked up to him, gently took his free hand in hers and leaned her head on his shoulder.

"I did okay."

"Of course, you did," she replied.

They were members of an elite crowd graduating from Berkeley in 1965. They belonged to the right clubs and had all the right friends. He was breaking family tradition by going to Berkeley. His father Robert, great-grandfather Gabriel, and great-uncle Dante René, whom he was named after, had graduated from Harvard, plus his grandfather Raul Paul Rivera had an honorary degree from Harvard as well. Dante Gregory Rivera, was a Californian, and Berkeley was as good as any Eastern school for him.

Dante grabbed his girlfriend's hands and swung her around. She gave out a little squeal, not expecting her conservative boyfriend to do anything like that. The full skirt of her pink, gray, and white striped dress swung as her many petticoats crinkled. She spun gracefully on four-inch-high, pointed toe, spike heels. Her gold charm bracelet jingled on her wrist.

The normally reserved young man dragged his girlfriend down the hallway to the building's exit for their next class. A moment of euphoria took over, and he pushed the door forcefully open and made a sweeping gesture for his girlfriend to exit. The door stopped abruptly. There was a whooshing sound of papers flying in the air followed by a thud on the other side of the door. A tiny, dark-haired girl now lay prone on the ground surrounded by dozens of pamphlets.

She reached up and pushed her long, teased hair out of her face, revealing her pretty, almost exotic, looks. Mod style heavy black eyeliner and mascara ran down her face from her tear-stained brown eyes making her look like a Pierrot clown. Her short mini-skirt was hiked up dangerously high exposing the top of her pink tights and a hint of frilly red underwear. A pink crocheted top bunched up under her breasts showing her flat, tawny-skinned stomach.

"I'm so sorry," came a bit frantic from Dante's lips as he reached down to help her up. She leaned forward for a bit, but then her arms and body fell back onto the sidewalk, and she stayed flat staring into space. The concerned Dante leaned down to see if she was breathing. With his face directly over hers, she focused and looked into his eyes. She pulled her top down to the waistband of her mini-skirt and reached up, lightly slapping his face with the back of her hand, before sitting up.

"Watch where you're going, buddy!" spurted from her pale pink lipstick-covered lips.

He reached down and lifted her up. Her slight frame dangled in the air like she was a rag doll, and one of her mule styled shoes fell off her foot.

"Let me down," she yelled.

Dante placed her down on her feet. She tried to hobble off on her left leg. He grabbed her to steady her and placed her on a bench. Looking down at her leg, she began to moan as if in pain. He picked up her shoe that had fallen off and knelt down on one knee to place it back on her foot. Blood trickled from a large tear in her pink tights. She looked at the blood and whimpered. Dante's girlfriend, Beverly, came over and stood next to her kneeling boyfriend for support.

"Do you want to go to the infirmary? I'll take you."

The girl began to cry. "It's my tights; they were brand new, and I paid a lot for them."

Dante reached into his pocket and pulled out a ten-dollar bill and his card.

"I'm sorry. Will this cover it?"

The girl looked at the money in shock. She could live on ten dollars for two weeks.

"Are you sure you don't want to go to the infirmary?"

She shook her head no.

"Well, keep my card if you need to reach me. I'll pay for whatever damage I caused."

Beverly wrapped her arm around Dante's to pull him away.

"Come on," she said, "or we'll be too late for class."

They walked away.

The girl's scruffy, long-haired boyfriend, who wore torn jeans and a T-shirt along with Jesus sandals, walked toward her. He parked himself next to her and gave Dante a "this girl is my property, don't mess with me" look.

"What's going on, Nita?" he asked.

"Look!" She showed him the ten-dollar bill.

The young man's card fell to the ground and Paulie picked it up.

"Jesus, look who he is…Dante Rivera. This is bitchin'. I heard he was at school here. Money, baby. Big money, baby. Sue!"

"Forget it, Paulie, he gave me ten dollars! Dante Rivera? His family lives in my valley and way back one of my great-grandmothers was the nanny for his family or something. Come on and help me pick up the pamphlets."

Dante stopped to brush off his pants. Beverly studied one of the pamphlets.

"I never got her name," said Dante.

"Look at this." She handed him the pamphlet. "Who cares? What do you expect from an anarchist like that?!"

Twenty-one-year-old Dante Rivera and eighteen-year-old Nita Lezeta couldn't have been more different from one another. He was rich, conservative, and from a privileged family. He had his entire life planned out for himself by the time he was a teenager. Nita, was a free-spirited only child of middle-class, liberal-minded teachers. She had socialistic ideas and unconventional values for the time and was eager to experiment with life. She was studying art on a scholarship having been exposed to the arts at a young age by her grandmother, the world-renowned artist and photographer J.B. Muller.

Paulie pulled the door open for Nita to an empty hall. The long table directly next to the door was covered with hundreds of different pamphlets, flyers, and small books on a variety of different subjects. Nita casually looked around again to make sure no one was watching. When she was confident that she and Paulie were alone, she pushed aside the most prominent pamphlets on the table and replaced them with the ones in her hands.

"Okay, let's go," she said to Paulie.

CHAPTER FIFTY

Christmas Break

Napa, December 1964

When Christmas break came, Nita was ready to go home. She'd worked hard and was terribly homesick. She packed her bags and, not wanting a confrontation with Paulie, wrote him a note saying she wanted to break it off and wished him good luck and a happy holiday. She left it in his dorm mailbox and headed for the bus station. Nothing seemed better than her own bed in Napa right now.

Nita got off the bus in the commercial center of town and walked several blocks up a street past the family butcher shop and waved to her Uncle Hank inside. Years ago her grandparents had lived behind the original family butcher store, but it was now long gone. Now the shop was in a new building. Her grandfather had retired last year and turned the multigenerational business over to his son. A few streets over a small sign in front of the white and blue trimmed Victorian cottage said J.B. Muller Studio.

"Grammie," she called out. There was no answer.

There was a note. *Gone out photographing—See you later…*

A half-filled cup of coffee was sitting on her desk. Nita touched it and felt some warmth still coming from it. She couldn't be far. Several 35 mm slides sat on a turned-off light box. Nita picked up one of the slides and held it up to the light coming through the window. The images were from a recent trip her grandmother had taken to the Midwest. The photos of farm families that had worked the same land for a century and were threatened with a future of being swallowed up by big conglomerate farm companies. Next to the slides were negatives of photographs her grandmother had taken of victims of the dust bowl in the 1930s from the same area. Next to that were photographs of local farmers whose ancestors had migrated to northern California in the 1930s looking for a better life and had found it. The pictures would accompany a story for *Life* magazine. Nita put the slide down and looked for a piece of paper and a pen.

> J.B.
> I came by to see you. I'm back. love you.
> Nita.

She placed the note on a long wooden worktable with a framed picture of herself so her grandmother would find it.

Nita walked half an hour to her home. She knew she'd be walking into an empty house since both her parents worked at this time of day. She threw her bag on the bottom step of the stairs, went into the kitchen, and dove into the refrigerator. A letter from her father's family in Pennsylvania with pictures of her cousins was on the kitchen table. She sat down to eat her sandwich and looked at the pictures before tossing them aside to finish eating.

The town of Napa had a growth spurt after World War II when GIs pushed west to California looking for opportunity and discovered the ideal climate. Nita's father was one of those GIs.

Lou Lezeta, a mixture of German and Basque, was a dark nutty-complexioned, ebony-eyed man who was drafted into World War II in 1941. He grew up in steel country. All his family worked in the mills. He played football in high school and hunted deer in the fall. While on leave in San Francisco during WWII, he fell in love with Annie Muller at first sight. He was walking the streets of San Francisco with his buddies when he saw an angelic face in the window of a trolley car as it passed by. He abandoned his buddies without saying a word. He took off running and jumped onto the trolley. He worked his way through the crowd to Annie and ended up asking her out.

They corresponded by letter for two years until he was wounded in the South Pacific and honorably discharged. He hitchhiked across country from his hometown south of Pittsburgh to Napa and to Annie. When the GI bill passed in 1944, he went back to school and became a teacher like Annie.

The town of Napa pushed out even more. One town began to flow into the next with ribbon-like roads anchored by small strip malls tucked in between housing developments. In the valley miles of grapevines covered the terrain. A number of wineries opened with the repeal of Prohibition, but by the 1960s only a few remained.

Nita soaked in the tub, thinking. No one was home. Her mother's car was parked in the driveway. As she languished in the tub, the thought that it would be a good time to start her Christmas shopping came to her.

She found one small spot where her mother's 1958 Chevy would fit in the full parking lot of the shopping center. Inside hordes of shoppers mingled under Christmas decorations, going from store to store. A chubby Santa with a synthetic beard and a polyester suit sat on his plastic throne in the middle of Wilson's department store under a cardboard North Pole. Nita found a fishing hat for her newly retired grandpa, a tie and aftershave for her father, and perfume for her mother. There was a toy mounted deer head she thought would tickle her Uncle Hank. It was easy to shop for the kids and the rest of her family.

She wanted something unique for her grandmother. She staggered in a shoppers' frenzy loaded down with packages and shopping bags as she combed through several stores when the Nature Boutique came into view. In the window display sat the perfect gift for her grandmother. The clerk said it was a one of a kind. The cut-glass crystal prism reflected light and made hundreds of rainbows around the room. It would bring back a special memory she and her grandmother shared. Her grandmother had taken her to see the movie *Pollyanna* when she was younger. Afterwards, they went back to her Grammie's studio and strung together several small cut crystal prisms, like in the movie, from an old kerosene lamp her grandmother had gotten from her grandmother. They hung the string of prisms in the window and watched rainbows dance on the walls, floor, and ceiling—a memory they still talked about.

Satisfied with her choices, Nita worked her way back to the parking lot. She carried three shopping bags and balanced two boxes. When the shopping bag with the toy deer head ripped open, she put it on top of the two boxes creating a pile she could barely see over. Her grandmother's gift was held by the string on her right index finger. Her mother's Chevy was parked further away than she remembered. She cautiously moved her way down the rows of cars peeking around the side of the packages to see where she was going. Almost to the car, she became relieved that she would successfully make it to the car without dropping one present.

Thinking about the next step, she reached for her keys in her pocket when it happened. He was bent down to tie his shoelace on his brown desert boots. He noticed dirt on the tip of his shoe, brushed it off, and rose up too quickly. He staggered backward into Nita. Her gifts flew up into the air and scattered on the ground. She could hear the shattering sound of the glass prism breaking in its box. Nita fell against the side of the car and landed on the pavement next to her gifts. It took her a minute to focus. She heard a man's voice saying something. He was sorry.

"Oh my God, are you okay? I'm so sorry."

She looked up into the face of the voice. He was leaning over her. He pushed up his horn-rimmed glasses and reached out a hand. He was kind of cute in a very conservative way, and there was something familiar about him. He helped her back up onto her feet and began retrieving her packages. She watched him curiously wondering why he looked so familiar. Everything was okay except...she looked down to see her grandmother's present on the ground. She picked it up to hear broken glass rattle around inside.

"This was a one-of-a-kind gift. It was the perfect gift for my grandmother and look at it now. Better yet, listen."

She jangled it in the air.

"I'll pay you for it and for anything else that's broken. Are you okay? Can I take you to a doctor or emergency room?"

"Wait a minute. Wait a minute. I know who you are... Berkeley," she said.

"Yes, I go to Berkeley."

"Yes, I know, so do I. You knocked me down there too!"

"Oh, Jesus, no."

"Yes," said Nita.

Nita gave Dante a scolding look. She had to look away for fear of laughing when she saw the expression on his face. He offered to buy her anything she wanted for her grandmother and to take her to dinner.

Nita wiped off the little hand mirror she'd taken out of her purse and looked into it. Black eyeliner smudged down from her eyes. She licked her index finger and wiped at it, smoothing it over the best she could. When the waitress came over, Dante knew what he wanted. Nita hadn't looked at the menu yet.

"I'll have a glass of red wine. How about you?"

"If you want to go to jail. I'm only eighteen. I'll have a cola."

There were long silences between the two. The staggering differences in personality and lifestyle gave them little to talk about. Dante tried to broach different subjects like school. He'd be starting law school when they returned in January after the holidays, but it did little to interest Nita.

When he asked about her grandmother, things changed. J.B. Muller was one of his favorite photographers. There was a portrait of his great Uncle Dante, his namesake, hanging in the Rivera mansion where his uncle and grandparents lived that J.B. Muller had taken in 1929. His great uncle had been a famous playboy in Hollywood at that time. This photograph had first introduced him to J.B. Muller's work. Dante had seen many of her shows. He believed his great uncle had been a friend of hers at one time. Dante's enthusiasm hit a soft spot in Nita's heart and she opened up.

Nita ended up helping Dante pick out some of his Christmas presents, and they searched for a new gift for her grandmother. It was getting late and she hadn't found anything yet, which made Dante feel guilty. They walked to the far end of the shopping center where there was a tiny specialty shop Nita hadn't seen before.

"Look, those are interesting." He pointed into the shop.

On a display table sat six of the very same cut-glass prisms the other store said was one of a kind. They could only laugh. Dante bought them all for Nita.

"Maybe now they are one of a kind," he said. They loaded the six prisms into the back of her mother's Chevy next to the rest of her gifts.

"Merry Christmas. I hope Santa is good to you," said Dante.

"Wait."

Nita grabbed one of the prisms and gave it to Dante.

"Merry Christmas. I had a good time."

"Thank you. Yeah, we did have fun, didn't we? Maybe I'll see you back at school sometime."

"Sure, maybe. Have a nice holiday, and thanks again for everything."

"When I see you again, I'm calling you Juanita. That's your name, right?"

"Sure, right, it's my real name."

"It's a pretty name."

Nita got into her mother's Chevy and started it up. A pinging sound sputtered from the engine.

They were both feeling a bit uneasy about saying goodbye. Nita sat thinking while she watched Dante walk away in her rearview mirror. They were so different. How could she be attracted to a guy like that? Conservative, straight, probably a Republican. "Maybe someday he'll grow his hair out," she said out loud to herself.

Dante started humming Roy Orbison's "Pretty Woman" and thought about the afternoon. "What a funny little thing she is. Cute, no pretty, and smart. Jesus, those clothes though, her hair, and that make-up. Maybe she'll clean up her act someday." He got into his Aston Martin sports car and drove off.

***

School was all-consuming. Nita immersed herself in her artwork and in the underground free speech movement. Nita did not run into Dante that next term. By June of 1965 Dante had completed his first semester of law school. He'd worked hard and decided to take a break over the summer. He and Beverly traveled through Europe viewing art and tasting wine. In the fall Dante started his most difficult year of law school, and Beverly got a job in advertising as a copywriter at a San Francisco agency. She took an apartment in town close to work while Dante stayed on campus to concentrate on his studies. They saw each other on weekends.

Beverly wanted to marry Dante by the time she was twenty-four when he was finished with law school and be pregnant by twenty-six. They still weren't engaged, and he hadn't even broached the subject of marriage. There was no shortage of men interested in the Beverly, but she wanted Dante—none of the others would do.

CHAPTER FIFTY-ONE

The Peace Rally

Haight-Ashbury, 1966

Friday night Grant, Nita's new boyfriend, sat in his idling VW bug. Nita ran out of her dorm wrapped in her two-dollar vintage '50s cashmere coat she'd gotten at the thrift shop and a small overnight bag. She bounced more than walked down the sidewalk in her tiny satin slippers. Nita slid into the front seat. Grant drove to Nita's favorite burger joint, the Burger Roust, and parked. He placed his hand on Nita's knee and pushed the button on the speaker to order.

"Name it, baby."

"A Filthy burger with barbecue sauce and a cola."

They drove downtown to the Avalon Ballroom to listen to Big Brother and the Holding Company. Nita stripped off her coat and carefully placed it on a chair. Under her coat she wore another thrift store find. This one cost a dollar, a 1940s bias cut clinging satin nightgown showing off her every curve. They danced and listened to music until early morning.

They got to the commune where Grant lived in Haight-Ashbury in the early morning hours of Saturday. Nita had never been there before. One of the residents, a thirty-year-old black man with a haunting face, walked down the dark staircase as they walked up. He and Grant slapped hands as they passed.

"What's happening," slid out of Grant's mouth like it had been greased with butter.

"Peace rally Sunday, noon," said the man.

"That right," said Grant.

Grant and Nita traveled up the four flights of stairs to his room on the top floor of the old Victorian. Grant locked the door behind them. The old Victorian house was in bad shape. The house had settled leaving a two-inch gap between the wall and the floor. Nita took off her coat. Grant flopped his six-foot-five frame into a chair and took hold of Nita's hand pretending to nibble on it before pulling her down onto his lap. He kissed her hard and slid his hand inside the top of her nightgown.

Grant woke up first, around noon. He rolled over and stroked Nita's naked body until she woke up. They made love again. Grant finished first and jumped out of bed. Nita was perturbed— selfish bastard, what about me she thought.

"Get dressed and I'll take you to breakfast. I got things to do today."

Nita looked around the room and noticed several of Grant's nice clothes, a new stereo system, and albums that were neatly placed on a table.

"The peace rally tomorrow, where is it? I want to go," she said.

"No can do, baby. It's not going to be peaceful. You might get hurt."

Nita opened her bag and pulled out a peasant blouse and jeans.

After breakfast Nita waited outside of the local greasy spoon in Grant's VW while he talked to a friend. They chatted for a few minutes before Grant got into the car. Nita sipped coffee from a paper cup. She flipped off her sandals to scrunch her legs up onto the seat of the VW, sitting cross-legged.

They headed for the bridge to Berkeley and passed a group of stores in a ritzy neighborhood when Grant stopped the car abruptly in front of a jewelry store. He stared at it for a minute and said, "Opportunity."

He backed the VW up about half a block and turned it around the corner.

"Wait here, baby. I'll be right back."

He reached into the back seat and grabbed a paper bag.

"I'm leaving the car running. Don't turn it off, okay?"

"Okay," replied Nita.

It all seemed too strange to the innocent young girl. She sipped her coffee and looked out at the neighborhood, thinking she should get back and do homework. A few minutes went by and she heard gunshots. Nita's body jerked. Her body stiffened as Grant came running around the corner with a ski mask in his hand. He jumped into the car and threw the ski mask over the back seat. He jammed his foot to the floor making the tires spin and U-turned the car, and they raced up the hilly street into a residential neighborhood.

Nita smelled the hot, caustic odor of metal and gunpowder and noticed a bulge in Grant's pocket. He opened his window and took a small handgun from his pocket and threw it out the window into some bushes.

"What did you do!?" cried out Nita.

"It's okay, baby. Don't worry, nobody got hurt."

Nita was in shock. When they reached a corner and had to stop, Nita jumped out of the car. She tried to grab for her shoes and bag but Grant took off with the passenger side door still open. She saw Grant's long arm reach over and close the door.

Nita stood on the street in her bare feet shaking and holding her almost empty paper cup of lukewarm coffee. A police car sped up the hilly street. Nita nervously began walking down the hill trying to look nonchalant.

She walked for a long time, still holding the paper cup. She thought about calling her father collect from a pay phone, but he had scolded her when she got arrested during a protest and didn't want to face his wrath again. She knew her grandmother was out of town on an assignment. She walked in the direction of the ferry, but it was still miles away. Perhaps someone would take mercy on her. She tried to stay away from the bad neighborhoods and lost track of time. Her feet hurt. She looked up toward the sky. The sun was over the ocean, and it was getting late. She could see the water beyond the large apartment buildings that sat in rows up and down the posh street. A police car drove by slowly; the cop looked at her. After it passed she crossed over and went down a side street. She was worried they might stop her. She could be considered an accessory to a crime and jeopardize her scholarship.

Nita began to cry. She had given up hope and was sure the police would pick her up on their next pass. She closed her eyes and said a prayer. When she opened her eyes, Dante was crossing the street to get into his sports car.

"Dante, Dante Rivera, is that you?" She screamed out.

He turned in shock as Nita ran up and grabbed him.

"Thank God I found you," said Nita.

She told Dante about what had happened. How could Grant do anything this bad? She was pissed off about losing her beautiful vintage coat and her purse. Dante calmed her down.

"It'll be all right. Get in. I'll take you back to school," he said. "In the future, stay away from guys like that."

Nita shivered in the open car. Dante reached back and handed her his suede jacket to wear. They drove to Berkeley, and Dante dropped her off at her dorm.

"Keep the jacket for now. When you can, drop it off at my frat house. Until the next time I see you, remember, stay away from guys like that."

Nita watched Dante pull away.

Grant came to Nita's dorm room later that night. Nita grabbed her two-dollar coat, sandals, and bag and tried to close the door on him, but he put his foot in it and pushed the door open.

"I don't want to see you anymore," said Nita.

"Come on, baby. I went back and tried to find you. No one got hurt. I promise I won't do it again."

"Now I see how you can afford the nice clothes you wear," said Nita.

Dante's jacket hung on the back of her closet door.

"Speaking of nice threads, are you seeing someone I don't know about?"

Nita went over to her dresser and applied a fresh layer of black eyeliner to give herself time to figure out how to get rid of Grant. He walked over to her and began to rub her back. She shrugged her shoulders and pushed his hands away. He leaned down and kissed her cheek.

"Don't do that! Please leave. It took me an hour to scrub my feet clean. Yes, I am seeing someone else, and he's a big football player. Now go!" said Nita.

"Okay, I'm sorry you feel that way," said Grant.

To get away, she walked past him and down the hall to the bathroom shutting the door. He stood in the open doorway to her room. He grabbed Dante's suede jacket from the closet door and bounced down the hall.

When Nita came out of the bathroom, she was happy to see Grant gone. She locked her room door and promised herself to cut Grant and radical causes out of her life. She fell into bed to read, happy to be alone.

It wasn't until the next morning she realized Dante's jacket was gone. It had to be Grant. Incensed, she got dressed, determined to get the jacket back and went over to the commune in Haight-Ashbury.

It was late morning when Nita arrived at the Haight. The streets were filled with neighborhood people who'd lived there all their lives, dressed in their Sunday clothes coming from church and young hippies from around the country. Some of the hippies were throwaways and others were from middle-class and privileged backgrounds seeking the answers to life.

Many waited near a soup kitchen for lunch or at the Diggers free shop to get a fresh set of clothes.

A dilated eyed, Afro-American girl of about seventeen, with beads in her hair, torn chartreuse hip-hugger bell-bottom jeans, and a thin tie-dyed tee shirt that barely covered her chest answered the door. In her hand she held a bejeweled roach clip that clasped the remains of a joint. Her fingernails had been chewed down past the quick and some were bloody. Unconsciously she began to chew on her right ring finger nail and looked blankly at Nita. Music blared in the background so loud the young woman had to ask a few times before she understood that Nita was asking for Grant. "Yeah, he's here."

She left the door open and Nita walked in. A single bare 40-watt bulb screwed into an old light fixture in the ceiling lit the hallway of the old Victorian.

A black man walked down the once elegant staircase that led up to the other three stories. Ancient wallpapers lifted away from the walls revealing the crumbling plaster underneath. The young girl stumbled away from the door and walked through one room into another. Nita assumed she should follow, but the man stopped her.

"Who are you?" he asked defiantly.

"I need to see Grant right away. She told me he was here."

They went into the next room where the music was coming from. The music was so loud it left a ringing noise in Nita's ears. She covered her ears and looked around the room. Several young people, all stoned, lounged around the room, but not Grant. The young Afro-American girl slunk down next to a bare-chested Afro-American man who looked so much like her he could be her twin. Nita looked toward her for guidance, but the spaced-out girl had already forgotten about her. Nita felt someone push at her back, not hard but with authority. It was the defiant black man from the front door. He gave Nita an angry "what are you doing" look and pointed his finger to the next room.

Nita followed him through the pocket door. A small group of black men were congregated, deep in conversation. One man stood up giving Nita a threatening look as she entered. Nita backed away.

With an inflection of sarcasm in his voice, the black man said, "She said she had to see Grant right away,"

Grant jumped to his feet and came to her rescue.

"She's okay. She came to help us."

"Welcome to the peace rally."

Sensing she'd walked into a dangerous situation, Nita sat quietly with Grant and said nothing. They were talking about bombing Berkeley. They were planning to set fire to some of the buildings and bomb the library. Nita was scared. She wanted to get out of there.

When the group broke up, Nita thought she heard one of the men under his breath call her a stupid white bitch. She could feel them watching her every movement. Grant took her upstairs to his room. The jacket was on the bed. She grabbed it, and was about to leave.

"You can't leave now. Not until I tell you. You're in it too deep now. You have to do what I say."

There was a loud racket downstairs and the music stopped. Several San Francisco police officers ran up the stairs.

Nita had on Dante's jacket. She peered out of a detention cell with several women, prostitutes, transients, drunks and a few hippies strung out on acid who paced around the cell, some with mean looks that frightened Nita. The young Afro-American girl was there too. Grant was on the opposite side in a detention cell overflowing with the black men from the so-called "peace rally." She could see the front desk of the police station. A white man in a suit came in and talked to the desk sergeant. He signed some papers and a few minutes later Grant was released. Grant smiled at Nita as he passed by, and the man in the suit handed her his card. He was a lawyer.

About an hour later the lawyer appeared again and the charges against Nita were dropped.

The next day a small crowd of people stood around looking at the display television models in the window of an appliance store when Nita happened by. She glanced toward the screens. A full screen picture of the Victorian house in the Haight flashed on every set.

"What's going on?" asked Nita.

"Cops busted a group of black militants yesterday. They were planning to bomb Berkeley; one of their guys turned them in."

Nita watched the footage closely. The police marched the men who'd been taken into custody out to a police bus when they were being transferred to the county jail. She never saw Grant again. He was on his way to Canada. He had made a deal with the authorities and setup the meeting with the Black Panthers in exchange for a bus ticket to Canada. He was going to be thrown out of Berkeley anyway and would be drafted immediately or gone to jail. Grant told the lawyer Nita was innocent. The lawyer told the authorities and she was exonerated.

CHAPTER FIFTY-TWO

Summer of Love

Berkeley, 1967

Nita's style of dress changed from Mod to pure hippie. She started parting her long hair down the middle and wearing it in two braids. Long granny-style dresses replaced her short skirts, a beaded headband crowned her head, and a small ransom in turquoise jewelry complimented her wrists, ears, and neck. She smoked pot while others dropped acid, participated in love-ins, and met a new boyfriend, Hugh a hippie art student from England.

Word spread that there was going to be a three-day pop concert in Monterey from June 16–18 at the county fairgrounds, and word traveled from coast to coast. By mid-June a pilgrimage of flower children crossed the country crammed in psychedelic painted buses and VW vans making their way to Monterey for "the summer of love" and rock-and-roll music.

Nita was meeting Hugh at a local coffee shop called The Hip Bean. She was somewhat annoyed by the way Hugh liked to clown around, but he always had good pot and wasn't political—a breath of fresh air after dishonest Grant.

Hugh got there first and found some friends in a booth toward the back. On a small stage in a dark corner, a long-haired hippie played a moody guitar. Five small tables overflowing with students sat in a row down the center of the

coffee shop with booths of planked pine lining the walls.
Low-hanging plastic Tiffany-inspired lamps hung over each
booth, and two long poolroom style lights hung over the tables. Thick cigarette smoke with a tinge of pot clouded the air.
There was a constant low drone from the crowd that made it
almost impossible to hear.

Nita worked her way through the crowd looking for
Hugh. She heard his distinct accent before she saw him. He
was doing his Jerry Lewis imitation of "Hey Lady" in a booth
with six people when Nita arrived. Hugh pushed over as far
as he could which left just enough room for Nita to fit one
butt cheek. She hovered on the edge of the booth's bench
and spread her right leg out into the aisle for balance. Hugh
wrapped his arm around her shoulder to hold her in and to
give her more room. An overworked waitress gave Nita a dirty
look and asked her to put her leg in further or move as only
six people were supposed to be in a booth. Nita was already
in a foul mood. She didn't like smoky crowds and the intense
sounds were giving her a headache. Hugh continued his Jerry
Lewis imitation. He waved his free arm in the air and hit the
pendant light, sending it swinging. The light swung over Nita's
head briefly lighting her face.

"Hello, Juanita."

Nita looked up. Dante's green eyes smiled down on her.
She smiled back sweetly and stood up.

"It's been a long time," said Dante.

"I like your jacket," said Nita. Dante had on the infamous
suede jacket. He looked down at his jacket, working his mind
to figure out what she meant. Then he remembered the rescue.

"Oh, right," he said. He looked over at Hugh. "Did you
take my advice?"

Nita turned her head slightly in Hugh's direction.

"Kind of," she said.

They both laughed. Someone called to Dante from the
very back booth.

"Nice to see you again. Maybe someday we'll run into each other in the valley," he said and moved on to his friends in the back. Nita stood watching Dante join his friends until Hugh, who had stopped talking and noted Nita's behavior, grabbed hold of her hand.

"Hey, who was that?"

"A friend from the valley," said Nita. She sat down again in a much better mood.

CHAPTER FIFTY-THREE

Monterey

June 16–18, 1967

On Friday, Hugh, high on acid, picked up Nita and the rest of their friends in his old VW bus and traveled south to Monterey. They smoked pot and sang songs from their favorite groups. They arrived in Monterey to find a sea of hippies already there and had no choice but to set up camp at the far end of a makeshift campground. They roasted weenies, cooked beans, drank beer and cheap Chianti while listening to Johnny Rivers in the distance.

Hugh and Nita wanted to get closer to the stage and traveled through the sea of people, at one point getting separated. Eric Burdon and the Animals began to play and some enthusiastic non-ticket-holding fans formed a human chain and parted the crowd to storm closer to the stage. Hugh was on one side, Nita on the other. He looked for Nita but didn't find her and decided to drop more acid. He placed a tab in his mouth and waited for it to melt. Hugh was mingling with the hippies around him, stamping his feet, and dancing to the music when a barely-clad girl, who witnessed him taking the tab of acid, asked him if she could have some too. Hugh gave her a tab. Both high, they began to make out to the amusement of several people who formed a circle around them and cheered them on. Nita was wandering around looking for Hugh when

she heard the loud cheers and saw a circle of hippies witnessing something that amused them. She went to investigate
what all the cheering was about. At first she only saw bare
legs. The female's legs were wrapped around the male whose
pants were down around his ankles. She had to jump up to see
their faces. She was on her tiptoes and still couldn't see them.
Then Hugh began to sing.

Nita and Hugh fought all night. At sunrise the swollen-
eyed Nita grabbed her knapsack and forged off on her own.
The morning saw a crowd that had grown to even more gigantic proportions. Drugs were given out freely and erratic
behavior was becoming the norm. Nita maneuvered through
a forest of campsites determined not to spend another miserable night with Hugh. Suddenly a young man with a crazed
look on his face swept her off her feet and began to carry her
away. She looked into his hazy eyes and instinctively knew he
was trouble. She screamed and kicked until he let her down.
The crazy guy grabbed her again saying she was his girlfriend.
Nita screamed for help and kicked her feet, finally punching
the crazy in the face before a few hippies came to her rescue
and tackled him. He dropped Nita, and she took off thanking
the hippies on the run.

Maybe she'd been hasty and should go back to Hugh
and her group. She tried to navigate her way back, but it was
an impossible task. She was on her own. Her stomach was
growling, so she changed direction and forged toward the
concession.

Dante and Beverly traveled to Monterey in his Aston
Martin. He'd booked them into a bed-and-breakfast in nearby
Carmel. Beverly wasn't keen on being among a profusion of
dirty hippies and preferred classical and folk music, but Dante
wanted to go, and she had a fantasy that this would be the
weekend he would propose to her.

Dante's plans were different. It was his duty to serve his
country in the army. His mother's father was a retired admiral

from the United States Navy. On his grandmother Heather's side of the family, the Sullivans were in law enforcement for several generations. His Grandfather Raul had been 4-F from World War I because of his hearing, and his father Robert was also a 4-F in World War II because he had flat feet. Only his great uncle Dante told his nephew about the hellishness of war and tried to discourage him. If he hadn't been saved by two milkmaids, he most likely would have been killed or gassed. Still the young Dante was determined to go into the army when he was drafted and serve alongside his fellow Americans. As far as marriage, he told Beverly until he'd served his country and returned safe he couldn't commit. He left unsaid that after seven years in a relationship with Beverly, he wasn't sure if he could commit at all. She was beautiful, smart, and loyal—only something was missing.

Dante and Beverly got into an argument that night about something minor that escalated into a full-fledged fight when marriage came up. In the morning, still upset, they had breakfast and went to the festival for the afternoon concert. Dante's friend had arranged with the promoters for backstage passes. On the drive over to Monterey, Beverly continued to badger Dante and finally came out and told him she wanted a commitment from him or else. When he wouldn't commit, she was heartbroken.

Dante and Beverly dodged the groupies and were escorted backstage. A number of the musicians and their entourages mingled as they waited to go on. Beverly, with emotions already on edge, was repulsed by the close proximity and physical jostling she was experiencing by the unkempt people she was now surrounded by backstage.

The sounds of Big Brother and the Holding Company on stage playing "Ball and Chain" pounded in her ears. Every pore of her body seemed to ache. They finished and the crowd gave a thunderous applause. Time ticked by slowly for her. She looked toward Dante who was applauding and mixing with his friends as Janis Joplin begged to go on again. By the time Country Joe and the Fish went on, she was in the middle of a panic attack. The floor beneath her feet bounced with the vibrations of the music on stage. Dante seemed a great distance away even though it was only a few feet. She grabbed onto his arm tightly.

"I want you to take me home right now! Not to the room but to San Francisco!" she yelled to him.

Dante didn't understand what she was going through, only that she was demanding he respond to her command. He was still holding tangled emotions from their fight the night before. He told her to calm down and turned back to his friend.

Beverly ran out the back of the stage and fought her way through the groupies who waited for the performers to arrive or come off stage. Beverly got into a cab that was dropping someone off.

The loud music and crazy sounds of the fanatic crowd resonated in the air, but inside Dante there was the quiet peace of freedom. Beverly was gone. An overwhelming, enjoyable feeling of life without Beverly filled him. She was beautiful, they'd rarely fought, and they seemed homogeneous to many, but in that moment, he realized he didn't love her. Life without her never occurred to him before— he felt emancipated.

Late the next morning the newly single Dante cruised up Highway One to a little breakfast place he knew about. The balmy weather produced a fine mist over the water. A pictorial vista of water gently crashing on the rocks and the distinct sound of a seagull diving into the shallows for fish entranced Dante for a little too long. When he turned his attention back to the road, the tiny figure of a hitchhiking girl with her arm swinging out high and wide, her thumb pointing toward the heavens, flashed by his eyes. His sports car sped by. Was that a mirage? He looked in the rearview mirror. The gust of wind from his car rustled her braided hair and granny dress. The car behind him slowed up, and she quickly sent them on their way. Dante pulled over to the side and let the car pass. He turned back toward the tiny figure and stopped on the opposite side of the road from her.

"What are you doing hitching alone out here? Don't you know you could get into trouble?" he said.

Nita screamed with joy. She looked both ways and ran across the street. Tears swarmed in her eyes as she jumped into Dante's car.

"Not again!" he said.

Dante softened up when she told him her story. When she went to get a hot dog, she discovered her money was gone. She'd either dropped it or was pickpocketed. That was enough to make her decide to leave the festival. She hadn't slept in more hours than she could remember. She'd been on the road walking from Monterey since before sunup and she was hungry.

Dante's car zoomed up the highway toward the breakfast joint. Nita finally calmed down and put her head against the leather seat to rest. She noticed a box of partially eaten Jack's Corn Pops in the back of the sports car. Without asking she grabbed the box and downed what remained. Her hand fumbled in the bottom of the box and found the prize which she handed to Dante.

"For gallantry above and beyond the call."

"No, it's yours, my pleasure. For suffering through the trials of concerthood."

Nita ripped open the small envelope. Inside was a red plastic decoder ring. Nita put it on.

"Look, I can decode the whereabouts of the Smoky Mines treasure. I'll give you half."

"You keep it. I won't need it where I'm going," said Dante.

Nita gave him a puzzled look.

"The army," he said.

"I told you not to get drafted, didn't I?"

At the greasy spoon off Highway One, they ordered breakfast from a partially balding hippie waiter who wore feathers and beads in his long thin hair.

Nita wolfed down half her food before she took a breath. Dante sipped at his hot coffee and laughed at how much she could eat.

"Why don't you go to Canada?" she asked.

"I believe in the war. We need to fight Communism."

"You're crazy. What if you go to Vietnam and get shot?"

"Don't worry about me. What are you going to do after school?"

"Teach art. I have one more year. Already have the promise of a job in the valley. Look at you. Vanilla man. My white knight."

Nita's eyes were closing. With food in her stomach and not having slept for so long, she couldn't help it. Dante looked down at his clothes. He was dressed all in white.

"I'll drive you home tomorrow. I want to go to the concert tonight. The Who are scheduled and some guy named Jimi Hendrix that everyone is raving about. You can come with me if you like."

Okay, was all Nita could say. As Dante paid the bill, she laid her head down on the table and fell into a deep sleep.

Dante slung her over his shoulder and carried Nita to his car. She came out of her stupor long enough to hold out the red plastic decoder ring in front of Dante's face.

"I'll give you this ring in exchange for the ride home."

Dante only laughed and slung her into the passenger seat.

"You know what? You have the heart of a butterfly," said Nita.

"A butterfly, what does that mean?"

"A butterfly's heart runs almost the length of its body. It has a big heart, just like you."

When they reached the bed-and-breakfast, Nita was in a deep sleep. He carried her up the stairs to his room and placed her on the couch. She rolled over into a fetal position and didn't move again for hours. Dante wrote a note saying he would be back in the early evening and covered her with a blanket.

She woke up on the couch feeling disoriented, not knowing where she was only that she was thirsty. Dante's face came into her head. She saw a note on the glass-top dining table.

Dear Juanita,

I'll be back in the afternoon to see if you want to go to the concert with me tonight. There's food and wine in the fridge.

Regards,

Dante

She relaxed and walked over to the small fridge, opening it. Two wrapped deli sandwiches, potato salad, and a bottle of white wine from the Mighty Oak Winery cooled inside. She opened the bottle of wine and poured herself a glass. There were two open suitcases, both very expensive. Curious, she looked inside. A pair of woman's sandals, a frilly silk nightgown, shorts, and fancy underwear were in one. The other had initials D.G.R. in gold. Inside were boxer shorts, golf shorts, button-down shirts, and white undershirts. She wondered what the G stood for as she grabbed one of Dante's clean white tee shirts and her backpack and went into the bathroom.

Nita soaked in luxury. Thank God, she thought, a real bathroom. It felt nice to get clean after the last few days. No more dirty VW bus jammed with six other people or cheap Chianti. When she finished, she put on the clean tee shirt, a pair of her clean panties and grabbed one of the sandwiches. Turkey, pastrami, and Swiss cheese with mustard, how heavenly she thought. She had another glass of wine, turned on the TV, and crawled under the covers on the couch.

She woke up in a start. She looked around the room and over toward the bed. Dante was asleep in it. Not wanting to wake him, she quietly got up and passed by him to go to the bathroom. She glanced over toward him again. He was laying on his side bare-chested, his muscular right arm poking out from the covers. She never realized how buff he was. She tiptoed into the bathroom, and when she came out, Dante was awake and sitting up in bed.

"Morning, sunshine, you finally woke up," he said.

"Good morning," replied Nita. She jumped onto the bed and demurely sat cross-legged in front of him.

"Want some coffee? I can make it," she said.

The domestic sound of her own voice humiliated her.

"Not yet. Help yourself," he said.

"No thanks."

He looked like such a kid without his glasses. She leapt on top of him and began tickling him. Hitting one of his more vulnerable spots, he made a high-pitched, funny laugh. The more he laughed the funnier Nita found it. When he couldn't take it anymore, he softly pushed her off and pinned her to the bed.

"Stop that," he said.

She looked up into his face. He was really handsome. The serious turn in their play was awkward for both. Dante rolled off of her and checked the time.

"We still have a few hours before we have to check out," he said.

"Yeah, what does that mean? Nita replied.

"Nothing, only that we have a few hours."

Nita studied his green eyes and strong face. She reached over and grabbed his hair.

"Why don't you let your hair grow out?" she said.

Dante pretended to be in pain.

"Ouch! That hurts."

Nita let go. He was laughing. As if another being possessed her, on impulse she jumped on him and began kissing him passionately. He pushed her off.

"What got into you?" he said, slightly shocked.

"I don't know," she said. She cast her eyes downward ashamed of herself.

He stared at her for a moment before grabbing her and tossing her back down on the bed and kissing her back.

"You asked for it. Now you're going to get it."

They stayed in bed all day, never leaving the room. They made love until both had nothing left. Dante booked the room for one more night and ordered food from a local restaurant to be delivered. They ate, drank wine, took a bath together, and made love.

The next morning, they drove north taking the scenic route up Highway One toward San Francisco. They didn't talk. They listened to music, enjoyed the ocean breeze, and occasionally held hands. When they reached San Francisco, Dante dropped off Beverly's suitcase at her apartment leaving it with her doorman. Nita never asked what happened, and he never told her. They crossed over toward Berkeley and arrived at Nita's dorm. Dante cut the engine, and they sat in silence. He was deep in thought about the past few days. To break the serious mood, Nita darted her hand under his nose with the red decoder ring on her finger.

"Thanks for the ring and thanks for saving me. Again."

He reached over and kissed her. They stayed lip-locked for several minutes. Nita started to ask him when they'd see each other again but stopped. She was the one who initiated their lovemaking—to ask that question would be too pushy.

He was confused. He'd been in a relationship with Beverly for so long he'd forgotten how to react and what to say, and the freedom felt good. This girl was a quirky little thing who always seemed to be in trouble and dated a certain kind of guy. His conservative side took over and he had doubts. Dante didn't say anything for a long time.

Nita waited for a response. She was used to rough and tumble guys. She took the long silence in a negative way and realized this was just a fling to him. She jumped out of the sports car and grabbed her backpack.

"Thanks, it's been real."

Nita walked toward her dorm as Dante watched. He was confused, lovesick, contemplative. He wanted to call out to her, but he didn't. He waited until she disappeared inside before driving off with a thousand thoughts running through his brain.

Nita waited until she got inside before bursting into tears. She'd made a fool of herself. Why would he want to see a girl who threw herself at him…why had she done that? She pulled her top up to her nose to smell him on her clothes. In her room she picked up the prism from three Christmases ago and wondered if he still had his.

CHAPTER FIFTY-FOUR

Napa

August 1967

Aweek after Dante returned to Napa, he received his draft notice and reported for six weeks of basic training. At the end of his training, he received bad news. His beloved great uncle Dante René Rivera was dying and had asked to see him. Young Dante got leave and returned home immediately to see his uncle and namesake for the last time. The senior Dante was fragile. His suffering heart was so compromised that even standing was too much exertion. He could only spend a short time with his nephew. Someone else was coming, someone he hadn't seen in a long time. It took a minute for the old man to compose himself after seeing his nephew with his buzzed haircut and uniform. The old man's eyes were thick with cataracts.

They hugged, and Dante kissed his great uncle's forehead.

"Take care of yourself. I don't want to see you too soon where I'm going. Do you feel that strongly about going to war?"

"Yes, Uncle, I do," said Dante.

"Fifty years ago, almost to the day, I went to war. Not my choice. It changed my life, forever. I was bitter for a long time.

Now I'm thankful for the wonderful things I've had in life. Even what I had for a short time."

Young Dante squeezed the old man's hand.

"Only family and one or two others matter. I love this valley, and to me this is heaven."

Dante's grandfather Raul had just returned. He opened the door and motioned for young Dante to come out.

"I have to go now. I love you, Uncle."

"I love you, son."

He stood up, reached over, and kissed his uncle's forehead. His uncle looked into his nephew's eyes and grabbed at his arm.

"When you fall in love, don't let her go."

Dante's eyes welled up.

Dante pulled his car around the circular driveway as another car pulled in. Through the rearview mirror, he watched an older woman get out. She walked up the stairs carrying an old tattered box and a photo album.

CHAPTER FIFTY-FIVE

Among My Letters in Black and White

Rivera Mansion, August 1967

J.B. pulled out a lock of dark hair tied in a pink ribbon from the old cardboard box.

"Remember this?" she asked.

"You kept it. My hair you cut under the tree in your backyard. Look at the color. Now I'm all white. Funny, isn't it, how cut hair never loses its color?"

J.B. leaned over and ran fingers through his hair.

"You're still the handsomest man I ever saw."

Dante leaned over and rummaged through the box and picked out a picture.

"A picture of Lita Nannie. Every time I drink a glass of lemonade I think about you and the day we met," said Dante.

J.B. smiled. She took the picture and looked at Lita Nannie's image.

"When I see a sunrise or a sunset, I wish I was with you. My every breath has been yours since the day we met. Since then, you've been locked in my heart," said Dante.

"Oh, Dante, we could have had a wonderful life."

"Hush, darling. Don't think about what might have been. I have you now. For the rest of my time. Promise me you'll never leave me again."

"I promise," said J.B.

"Open the top drawer of my desk. There's a stack of letters I've written to you over the years but never sent. One for each anniversary on the day we met."

J.B. walked over to the desk and opened the drawer. Lifting the stack of letters from the drawer, she held them next to her heart.

"The letters are for you to do with as you wish. They're the black and white of how I feel about you. Of how I will always love you."

J.B. placed the letters on the bed and a ticket from the Panama-Pacific Expo fell out from them. Her bottom lip quivered. On top was the dance card from the Pavilion Dance, gray with age and dog-eared. She opened the dance card with Dante's name on every line.

"I saved it. You put it in the pocket of my tux jacket, remember?"

Dante pushed the cover back. His frail body was exposed beneath his open pajama top. He patted the bed and J.B. lied back down next to him. She put her arm around his chest and placed her face in the curve of his neck. They fell asleep in each other's arms and lay like that all night.

When the morning light came through the windows, Dante opened his eyes. She was still there. His beautiful Juanita. Her dancing brown eyes with specks of gold and her warm, broad smile. He stroked her skin until her eyes opened.

They relived their summer together throughout the morning and into the early afternoon as they held each other in their arms. Dante began to hum softly.

"Do you remember the song they played the night at the country club when we danced off the floor toward the lake?"

"Oh! you beautiful doll, you great, big, beautiful doll! Let me put my arms about you, I could never live without you; Oh! you beautiful doll, my beautiful Juanita, if you ever leave me how my heart would ache…"

J.B. was afraid to look up. She touched his chest. A big exhale came from his lungs. J.B. pulled herself up to Dante's face. His eyes were still open. She looked through the milky coating at his cobalt blue eyes and remembered the first time she looked into them and could see into his soul. Now they were vacant—his soul gone. She kissed his cheek, the side of his mouth, and reached up to close his eyes and kissed his eyelids.

"Good bye, my love, my darling. You'll always have my heart. You are my heart."

Grief rippled from her scalp down to her feet. She gathered up the memorabilia, the stack of letters, and ticket stubs and placed them back in the tattered box. Her eyes filled with tears when she looked at the dance card. She looked at Dante through a wall of tears one last time and walked out of the door. Raul sat sentry outside of the door, so no one would enter and disturb them. He gave J.B. a hollow stare.

"Is he?" asked Raul.

"Raul, I'm so sorry. I know how much you loved one another."

CHAPTER FIFTY-SIX

The Lake

August 1967

The oppressive August heat wave and his life were getting to Dante. Losing his uncle devastated him. Having never lost anyone close before, the pain was profound.

His mind traversed from grief to reality. He was going to war. In the last few weeks in basic training he'd heard so many horror stories about what was happening in Vietnam that his fears were getting the best of him. He couldn't get Nita off his mind either. Being back in the valley after finishing basic training didn't help. He felt depleted, vulnerable.

The phone rang. It was one of his buddies asking if he wanted to go swimming at the country club. It hadn't changed much. The old gazebo had been replaced ten years ago and a new path led down to the lake.

Dante dove deep into the cool, pristine lake at the country club. The water rushed over his body until he was completely submerged and his mind relaxed. There was only this moment. Nothing else was real.

He stayed under the deep, dark water until his lungs felt like they would burst. His head broke through the water and out into the air. He took a long, deep breath of air. Without his glasses things were a blur. In front of him, a female figure stood with her hands on her hips. She might have looked menacing to others, but to Dante, she was soft around the edges. He shook his head to get rid of the excess water and jumped out. The woman wore dark glasses and the smallest bathing suit possible with a pose to stand her ground.

"Nita," said Dante.

"Hey, you."

Dante was smiling ear to ear.

"I didn't think I'd see you again," said Nita.

"I wasn't sure you wanted to see me again," replied Dante.

Nita's body slumped and she lost her toughness.

Dante noticed the red plastic ring hanging on a chain around her neck. He reached out and touched it.

"It makes me feel safe. It protects me," said Nita.

"If I have a butterfly's heart, you must have a velvet one," replied Dante.

"I read about your uncle in the paper. I'm sorry."

They drove up into the hills to a secluded spot and made love. The rest of Dante's time home was spent with her. By the end of his leave, Dante knew what his uncle meant when he said when you fall in love don't let her go. Dante was ready to commit. So was Nita.

***

An old, rotting wooden gate hung precariously on rusty hinges, half attached to a stone wall. Overgrown weeds camouflaged the path. Dante pushed the wooden gate open and took Juanita's hand to guide her to the ranch house. There was a fairy tale quality to the quaint-looking old stone ranch house covered with rambling overgrown rosebushes and vines.

"My great-great grandfather, Dr. Dante Rivera, built this home when he came from Spain. No one's used it in years. My uncle always wanted to restore it and live here, but never did. He said it was unique."

When Nita walked through the front door, an intense cold shiver ran down her spine that was so disarming she had to grab onto Dante's arm for support.

"What's the matter?" asked Dante.

"Déjà vu," said Nita.

She closed her eyes and described the next room to Dante as if she'd been there before. "There's a large stone fireplace with Mexican tiles. The staircase has an ornate iron railing."

"That's crazy," said Dante. "You're right."

Nita's whole body tingled. They walked through the empty house and up the stairs to the second floor. Dante opened the door to the master bedroom and walked over to the bank of windows.

Dante's words reverberated in the large empty room.

"Come over here so you…"

"Can see the view of the vines," Nita finished his sentence.

"How did you know I was going to say that?" asked Dante.

"I don't know how. I just did."

Nita walked over to Dante and stood next to him. He wrapped his arm around her and pulled her close. They looked out onto the vineyards.

"It's like I've been here before. Like this happened yesterday, only it was a long time ago," whispered Nita.

"This is our moment," said Dante. He opened one of the French windows and then wrapped his arms tightly around Nita. An oak leaf carried on the wind floated into the room.

CHAPTER FIFTY-SEVEN

J.B.'s Studio

August 1967

J.B. dried her hair with a towel and looked in the bathroom mirror at her aging face. Her lover was gone, and so was the young girl Dante fell in love with all those years ago. In the mirror, the face of an old woman stared back at her.

She hadn't noticed some of the lines on her face before. Henry must be worried, she thought. She'd been gone a long time. He never questioned where she was when she was gone for long stretches. She couldn't have faced him yesterday, anyway. It would have been impossible to hide her feelings after she left the mansion, so she stayed away, locked in her studio. The promise was fulfilled. She thought about the night in Los Angeles so many years ago, the night they made the promise to one another. How strange life was to have them meet up again in that way. She was sent there to take photographs of movie stars. The trip resulted in an unexpected reunion with her lover.

Over the years she thought of Henry as her best friend. He was in love with her, she knew that, and she loved him in her way. His love was unconditional; her love was out of kindness. He'd nurtured her back to health, physically and emotionally. He always put her first and never questioned her actions. They shared their lives and family together, both in good and bad times. He encouraged her work, and in later years often accompanied her on her photography trips as her assistant. He never expected more from her than she could give. He worshipped her. She could tell him almost anything, but she couldn't tell him about the last forty-eight hours. She would never intentionally hurt him. When she returned to her studio, she read Dante's letters and one by one burned them so no one would ever see them. They were too personal. They were his expressions of love for her that only she needed to know.

She'd stayed with Dante until he took his last breath, and now her heart was breaking—something she couldn't let show. She wished now that she would have been the first to die. Only Raul knew about their last moments together, and only he would remember their love for one another. She dressed and came out of the bathroom. It was early evening. The old back screen door creaked open.

"J.B.," Nita called out. "Where are you? Grandpa said you'd be here working."

J.B. pulled herself together and put on a happy face. Nita came in.

Nita's face was one big grin. "Guess what, I'm in love."

Nita's grandmother hugged her.

"Congratulations, honey. Where did you meet this guy?"

"At school. Oh, it's too crazy. We met three years ago. Remember the glass prisms?"

"Yes, I have them here." J.B. walked over to her bookshelves. She hadn't put the old, tattered cardboard box and scrapbook away yet. She tried to discreetly push them out of sight.

"What's that?" asked Nita.

"Oh nothing. Look, there they are, all four." She pointed to the prisms as she stepped up onto the ladder to put the box and scrapbook away.

"I never told you the whole story, remember? It was Dante Rivera who ended up buying them. He said he loved your work."

J.B. froze on the top rung of the ladder.

"Well, it's him."

"What?" said J.B.

"I'm in love with Dante Rivera," said Nita.

***

The old shack near the graveyard had been replaced with new workers' quarters. A machine now did the backbreaking work of digging a six-foot-deep grave. The cars drove up the gravel road behind the Cadillac hearse to the family grave site. Here great-Grandfather Raul Cristoval Rivera was buried next to his wife and the baby she lost in childbirth, his sister Angeles and her husband. His son Gabriel and Gabriel's wife Magritte were further up the hill. The family patriarch, Dr. Dante Rivera, was buried under a large oak tree with his second wife Fiona, her son James and their daughter Violet, who had never married. There was a marker with the name Buttons on it. No one was quite sure who or what Buttons was until Grandfather Raul Paul said it was his grandfather's pet dog when he was little. Grandfather Raul Paul held his head low. His wife, Heather, of almost fifty years put her arm around him. Next to them were their sons Robert and Kent and their granddaughters. Dante and his cousins were pallbearers. The service was short, and at noon they lowered Dante René Rivera into the ground in a sunny spot near his namesake and great-grandfather Dr. Dante Rivera.

***

J.B. hadn't slept much in the last few days and was emotionally exhausted. She returned home late in the day from her studio. Henry had made dinner, and they ate together in the dining room. After, Henry went into the living room to watch TV, and she cleared the dishes. The day's newspaper sat on top of a stack of papers. The photograph of Dante René Rivera she had taken years ago stared up at her from the front page. J.B. told Henry she was tired and went to bed early. Extremely fatigued, she fell asleep quickly. In her dreams she heard humming in the distance, then laughter and singing. Dante danced toward her, singing.

"Oh! you beautiful doll, you great, big beautiful doll!"

Dante was young and beautiful again and dressed in his tuxedo.

"Come on baby, grab your dance card and dance with me," Dante said.

J.B. swung her legs over the side of the bed and looked at her old face in the mirror hanging over the dresser.

"But I'm old and you're young again," she said.

He held his hand out toward her.

"Oh, come on and take my hand."

"What about Henry? He's downstairs. He'll miss me. I'm putting a show of my photography together."

"The show will happen. Your family will see to that and much more. Henry's had you for over fifty years. Now you're mine."

Dante pretended she was in his arms and danced closer.

"Let me put my arms around you, I can never live without you."

J.B. smiled and reached out her old hand to Dante. When they touched, her hand became young again. She looked in the mirror. She had on the pink dress her grandmother made for her. She touched her smooth young skin. Her dark hair was in a soft roll with flowers in it, just as she wore it to the dance. Dante gently pulled at her hand.

"Come on baby, I've waited forever."

He spun her around, and they danced around the floor. The band played "Oh, You Beautiful Doll." They danced into the darkness and kissed. The darkness faded, and they were in the stone house Dr. Rivera built. They danced into the great room and heard laughter. On the couch sat a young Dr. Dante Rivera and eighteen-year-old Juanita Delgado in her fancy Christmas party dress.

J.B. stared at the young woman who looked so much like her.

"Are you my Lita Nannie?" she asked.

"Yes," said the young woman, "and welcome."

J.B. never woke up. A few days after Dante René Rivera's funeral, there was a funeral for Juanita Bonnetia Muller. She was buried near her grandmother in the church graveyard. The show of her work went on as scheduled as a memorial to her life.

Acknowledgments

Oh, You Beautiful Doll, lyrics by Seymour Brown, music by Nat D. Ayer.

Special thanks to San Francisco Public Library, Napa Library, Napa Valley Museum, Napa Historical Society, St. Helena Historical Society, California Historical Society, Sharpsteen Museum, California State Library, United States Air Force Library, United States Army, Eric Villard, Dale Andrede, Kenneth Meissner, Berry Spink, to my niece Rebecca, Lauren Wood-Radcliffe, Cathy Shuman Miller, Mary Garripoli and to my little Buttons who made my friend José so happy.

KB 2/24/18

About the Author

My Scot-Irish mother loved to tell stories. Usually they were about family and always with elaborately stretched truths woven into their fabric which changed with each telling. I inherited her love for storytelling.